T0365074

The Devil Incarnate

A Novel

by

Becky Roach

Order this book online at www.trafford.com
or email orders@trafford.com

Most Trafford titles are also available at major online book retailers.

Printed in the United States of America.

ISBN: 978-1-4269-9306-0 (sc)
ISBN: 978-1-4269-9307-7 (hc)
ISBN: 978-1-4269-9308-4 (e)

Library of Congress Control Number: 2011914975

Trafford rev. 08/26/2011

 www.trafford.com

North America & international
toll-free: 1 888 232 4444 (USA & Canada)
phone: 250 383 6864 ♦ fax: 812 355 4082

To my husband with love, who gave me the most wonderful two children ever.

Also As Niki Jordan:

Loving Daddy: 2004
Open Wounds: 2007

Introduction

Lamont Hallmen had been the perfect child, his parents would tell anyone who asked. Smart and witty, he'd been an adorable child, with deep-set dimples, and a quiet way of taking everything in. Obedient and respectful, he'd never given his parents any worries.

As he grew older, he seemed to get along with just about anyone. His teachers were impressed with his intelligence, and he'd seemed to have the respect of his peers. Girls could only dream of being his date, and a smile from him could set any girl's heart on fire.

But although he seemed to have it all, it seemed that no one REALLY knew Lamont "Monty" Hallmen. Because deep inside of him, there seemed to be a fire building, and as time went on, it grew stronger, until it became all-consuming. And although he seemed the same on the outside, a battle waged inside of him: a battle between good and evil.

With his charm and good looks, no one ever suspected what Lamont was really capable of, until it was too late.

As Monty grew up, he seemed to play by his own rules, and would change them whenever he saw fit. He rarely made a move that wasn't calculated, and no one ever boxed him into a corner and got away with it.

His mother's heart would shatter into a million pieces one day, as she faced the horrible fact that the beautiful baby with the cherubic face, that boy she'd always thought was her angel, was really The Devil Incarnate.

1998

The wind howled with an unrelenting force outside the musty walls of the prison. Winter had come overnight, bringing high gales and a blustery, cold wind, and the weather forecast promised an ominous storm before the weekend was over.

Inside his cell, Lamont "Monty" Hallman sat quietly, listening to the wind howl, and working on one of his sketches. Although he'd already done 50 or more of the same sketch, he inevitably always ended up sketching the same thing, whenever his mind wandered too much. Inside these four walls, Monty's mind was always wandering, since there wasn't much else to do.

The chaplain had visited him earlier in the day; had gotten out his Bible and prayed for Monty's soul. Monty feigned the same interest in religion with the chaplain, Father McClure, as he did with the prison ministry team that stopped by the prison one Sunday a month, trying their best to save the lost, one soul at a time.

He chuckled to himself now, thinking of the first time he'd laid eyes on her. He'd never met a woman quite like Sheila Hardesty. She reminded him of a quiet church mouse, afraid of her own shadow. He remembered how her hands had shook, as she tried to find the page in the Bible that she was looking for.

"Relax, I don't bite," Monty had softly whispered to her. Well, not TOO often, he thought to himself, quelling the hysterical laughter that began to build up in his throat. The total timidity and lack of self-confidence that this gal radiated filled Monty with almost giddy excitement.

Oh yes, he'd thought to himself from the moment he'd laid eyes on her; this one is MINE, he thought gleefully; she will definitely serve my purpose he thought to himself, as he folded his hands in prayer.

Sheila Hardesty fanned herself as she sat at the busy intersection, waiting for the light to turn green. Although it was quite a chilly day, she felt warm inside, and one of the nuns that had gone inside of the prison with her had teased her about the looks that Lamont Hallman had given her.

"You better watch him; he's quite the lady's man; a real charmer," Sister Katrina chuckled, obviously amused with herself.

"At least you never have to wonder where HE is every night," she'd added, a fit of laughter overtaking her.

Struggling with the annoyance that she'd felt with her comments, Sheila had laughed in spite of herself at Sister Katrina's last comment, of not having to wonder where he was at night. She was annoyed though, because she felt something for this man that she'd not felt for anyone in years. Frankly, she really didn't want to feel it at all, especially not for a man that was in prison, serving a 40 year sentence for murder.

Although Sheila didn't know all the details, she found herself repulsed and excited by Hallman at the same time. Before today, she didn't know that it was possible to feel both of those emotions at the same time.

Hallman had reached over to take her hand in his, when she'd suggested they pray the Lord's Prayer, and she'd looked up at him in surprise.

"I'm sorry; I was used to holding hands during this prayer my whole life; you don't mind too terribly, do you?" Monty had asked, his face earnestly searching hers.

"No, no, that's quite alright," Sheila had assured him, rather hastily.

His smile that he'd given her then, lit up the whole room, Sheila had thought at the time. His teeth were so white and straight, and his smile was beautiful. Sheila felt her heart race whenever he smiled at her.

The disappointment she'd felt then, was tremendous, when the warden had stopped in front of the doorway and told them that it was time for Sheila to go. She'd hoped she hadn't looked too obvious about it. When Monty suggested that Sheila stop by again for a visit, she found herself happily agreeing.

Now, stuck in traffic, Sheila kept thinking about Monty, wondering why she found this guy so attractive and exciting.

"It's gotta be the super dull life I lead," she said to herself out loud, as though saying it out loud would give her the true explanation that she'd needed.

Sheila found herself excitedly counting the days until she could go back over to the prison again. She wondered what Monty thought of her and if he would be excited to see her. In her mind, she daydreamed about him all the time. At work, she would find herself thinking about him, wondering what it would be like to feel his lips on hers. She even went so far as to imagine herself as the heroine of the story; prison ministry team member frees innocent man wrongly accused. She saves his life and he sweeps her up into his arms. His handsome, radiant smile melts her heart, as he takes his bride back home.

Sheila snapped her head back, annoyed with herself that she'd been daydreaming. Looking around quickly, she was relieved to see that no one had seemed to really notice that she'd been lusting after a man sitting in Vesting County's minimum security prison. Sheila shook her head, wondering what in the world was wrong with her.

She knew that the clock was ticking. Already pushing forty, Sheila was totally running out of time, in many ways. She'd always wanted a child, but lately, she'd begun to wonder if she was ever supposed to have one. Her own childhood had been one of torment and negligence, so Sheila wondered if she'd even have it in her to take care of a baby. She liked to think that she would be a great parent, but she'd never really known what a good parent was, either. She knew that a couple of her childhood friends had had worse parents than she did, but growing up with a mother with a lot of mental problems sure was no walk in the park, Sheila thought to herself.

Most days, Sheila didn't much care anymore whether or not she had a baby. It WOULD be nice, she thought, but it would also be asking for too much. No, it would be better to just have a man, and not be alone.

Stuck in traffic now, she pulled out her compact and checked her appearance. She was surprised to see that her cheeks were so flushed. Deep down, Sheila knew she was nothing to really look at; how many men had told her that, she mused. While she certainly wasn't ugly, she knew that as the days and weeks rolled on, she wasn't getting any younger OR better looking, either.

She thought now again of Monty, and his perfectly straight white teeth, the dimples at the corners of his mouth, and the deepest, darkest green eyes she had ever seen in her life. His hair was raven black, and just a bit wavy, and aside from a couple crinkles at the corners of his eyes, he was still quite young looking and devilishly handsome, and oh so hot, Sheila thought to herself and smiled.

Pulling up to her mailbox, she was pulling out mostly junk mail, when she caught sight of a long, white envelope that fell in her lap. Turning the envelope over, a surge of heat flowed through her when she noticed that the letter was from Monty. The back of the envelope had two hearts, side by side, and a big smiley face. A long arrow shot through the first heart, and Sheila dared to think that that was supposed to be Monty's heart. Practically gasping for air, she plunked herself down on her couch, and, ignoring the plaintive cries of her cat, she tore open the envelope with an eagerness that she was quite unaccustomed to.

With shaking hands, Sheila began to read the short, but sweet note:

Dear Sheila:
I can't begin to tell you how much your visit brightened my day. Your words that you read to me from the Bible were so comforting, and your voice was so gentle and soothing, just

like an angel. I have to tell you, Sheila, I just can't stop thinking about you. I have tried to, but I just can't. I sure would like to see you again, and I need to tell you what really happened to put me in this place. I need to see you again, my sweet, beautiful angel. Until then,
Monty

    Sheila reread the letter a couple of times, excitement building up inside of her. Pulling out her stationary, Sheila wrote a letter back to Monty:

Dear Monty:
It was good of you to write. I too enjoyed your company, and I must admit that I have thought of you often, as well. I will plan on a visit this coming weekend, more than likely. Thank you for your kind words, Monty; you have no idea how much they mean to me.
Your friend,
Sheila Hardesty

1974

"What are ya, a chicken? BAAAAWWWKKKKK, BAWWWWKKKKK, chicken, chicken, look at the baby chicken, " Dwight taunted, giving Monty a hard shove.

" I am NOT a chicken; I just don't want to do it; I don't feel like it, " Monty stammered, finding it hard to speak right now.

"What a wimp," Dwight sneered. "I've seen old women with more guts than you got," Dwight added, giving Monty another shove.

Monty sighed to himself. Dwight could be such a bully, and the older the two boys got, the more Dwight dared Monty to do things, and the harder he made it for Monty to refuse him.

Monty could never tell his mother the truth about his cousin Dwight. Dwight's parents were filthy rich, and could never begin to fathom their precious son doing anything remotely wrong.

When the cousins were younger, Monty tried a couple times to talk to his parents about Dwight, but his father was always doing chores around the farm, mostly in silence even when Monty would try to help him, and his mother only wanted to hear good things about everything and everyone. Monty knew that he could never talk to his mother about anything; she was fragile, and she just couldn't seem to begin to deal with any of the evils in the world whatsoever. She ran off to town every chance she got, for one church function or another, and seemed to thrive in that environment. She was decent and took care of Monty and his dad, but yet there always seemed to be a part of her that was a bit disconnected to them as well, and to most of the rest of the world, for that matter.

Monty was 13 and Dwight, 15. There was a part of Monty that couldn't help but admire Dwight. He was so cool and so tough; he was never afraid of anything or anyone. Monty thought that was pretty cool, and Dwight always seemed to have good advice for him too, where girls were concerned.

"You can't let em' win," Dwight would tell Monty. "You gotta keep an upper hand with chicks," he added, clapping Monty on the back.

"Ever been with a girl yet?" Dwight asked Monty one day. " You mean like on a date?" Monty asked.

"No, stupid, I mean like have you ever done it before? What do I gotta do, draw you a picture or something?" Dwight asked, his voice starting to rise in his usual taunting fashion.

"Well…..," Monty began, unable to finish. "Yeah, that's just what I thought," Dwight sneered. "Well, we're gonna have to fix that problem for you, " Dwight offered. "I know just the woman for your first time," Dwight added, howling with an almost manic, hyena-like voice. "Yep, I know JUST the lady for you," Dwight roared, doubling over with laughter, clapping his thigh with his hand.

"She'll just lay there and let you do what you want to her; she'll be PERFECT," Dwight gasped, a tear rolling down his cheek, as he willed himself to stop laughing long enough to tell his cousin who he had in mind.

"Who? Who are you talking about? I really don't want a woman right now," Monty said, fear beginning to creep inside of him.

"What are you, some kinda queer?" Dwight demanded, the hilarity on his lips now forming a sneer.

"Nnno, no, I just don't want to do it right now; I want to find someone I like a lot first," Monty told Dwight, sure that this would let him off of the hook, but no, Dwight would not be easily dissuaded.

Dwight jumped up off of the log he was sitting on, and grabbed Monty by the front of his shirt. One handed, he was doing a pretty good job of scaring Monty into thinking that he would choke to death soon, at this rate.

"Listen, you little scaredy-cat freak, I got the perfect first lay for you all picked out, and this is what we're gonna do; we're gonna slip her a sleeping pill in her nice cold ice tea while we do a couple chores for her, and when we're finished, she'll be fast asleep, and you'll be driving it home," Dwight whispered, his voice taking on a dangerous edge to it.

Monty felt fear course through his body now; there was only one person that the boys did chores for once in awhile, and that was old Mrs. Crason that lived on the corner of the next block. Surely Dwight wasn't talking about him and her.........

"Didja figure it out yet, dumbass? Mrs. Crason probably hasn't gotten
lucky in quite a long time; you'll be doing her a favor. Too bad she won't be awake to enjoy it," Dwight laughed, his voice rising yet another pitch.

"No, no, I don't want to do that; I WON'T do that," Monty said, his voice rising as the anger inside of him began to build.

His cousin was such a royal pain in the ass; always bossing him around, and bullying him into doing things he didn't want to do. Now, the anger that Dwight had triggered inside of him was beginning to build at a dangerous clip.

"Awwww, whatsa matter, you big baby, are you afraid of big bad ol' Mrs. Crason? Whatcha think she's gonna do, smack you with one of her big ol' bloomers?" Dwight demanded, now roaring with hysterical laughter.

Monty was walking away now, repulsed beyond reason at Dwight's so-called bright idea. He just couldn't begin to fathom doing what Dwight suggested.

"Hey, I said let's go; I mean NOW," Dwight taunted and yelled, not used to not getting his way.

Monty turned around to look at his cousin one last time, and then shoved his hands in his pockets and kept walking. He heard Dwight making more comments, and then saw him run off in the opposite direction. Relieved that he no longer had to deal with Dwight and his sick taunts, Monty sat down for a moment, until it dawned on him, right out of the blue, where his sick cousin was more than likely heading….

"Oh God," Monty moaned out loud. He looked around frantically now, hoping beyond hope to see a glimpse of Dwight, but no, he knew deep in his heart where Dwight was, and it sure as hell wasn't in this empty old beat up schoolyard.

Fear seized his heart now, and he began to run, slowly at first, but then with a speed that he never even knew he possessed, as though he was running for his life. For several minutes he ran, his chest on fire and his lungs feeling as though they might just burst. Racing up the huge hill, Monty could now see Mrs. Crason's house from here, but he knew it would take him at least three more minutes, running as fast as he was right now. Deep in his heart, he hoped that his cousin was just kidding; he wouldn't really do that, would he, Monty asked himself as the sun was beginning to slowly fade. Try as he might, though, he just couldn't say no and mean it.

Monty knocked on the door, but no one answered. There was no sound at all, and the house seemed strangely quiet. The only noise that Monty could hear at all, was old Mrs. Crason's black forest cuckoo clock that was about to announce the new hour. Startled and almost jumping out of his skin, Monty could feel his heart race now, as the cuckoo clock began its six o'clock ritual.

Monty let himself in the back door, still hearing nothing but the clock. He called out then, hoping that Mrs. Crason was down in her cellar picking out fresh vegetables for the evening meal, or that perhaps she was out walking her little ankle-biting Pomeranian, Dooley. But just as that thought popped into his head, Dooley suddenly charged out of the kitchen and ran straight to Monty, barking his fool head off, like always. Monty was about to yell at that little mutt, when suddenly he thought he heard a sound that he couldn't really place. It sounded like it was coming from the kitchen. Rounding the corner of the living room into the kitchen, Monty stopped short at the dining room table, staring in disbelief. He practically gasped for air, then, sure that he would vomit everywhere.

Lying on the floor with her bloomers hugging her ankles was Mrs. Crason, looking as though she were out cold. Her smock that she liked to wear around the house was ripped off as well, along with the old brassiere that did nothing to support her more than ample figure. Splayed out on the floor like a broken doll, Monty thought. He walked over closer to Mrs. Crason and noticed that she was laying almost TOO still. He bent down and put his fingers up by her neck, like they'd taught him a few years ago in Cub Scouts. After several seconds, Monty still couldn't find a pulse. He never saw the rise and fall of her chest either; didn't feel her breath on his face when he put his cheek down by her mouth. My God, Monty thought to himself, I think she's dead.

Just then, Dwight came sauntering into the living room, grinning from ear to ear. "Hey cos, you missed a helluva good time, man; Crason's a really cheap date. Drank a couple sips of her tea, and went out like a light. Too bad she wasn't awake to enjoy it all," Dwight laughed.

Monty said nothing at first, staring at the scene lying in front of him. He could never have imagined his cousin doing something quite this terrible, this absolutely VILE, but here was poor Mrs. Crason; a victim of Dwight's sick mind.

"I guess we'll let you off the hook this time, but next time I tell you I'm up for a good time, and I make us some plans, you better follow through," Dwight said, a menacing tone already creeping back into his voice.

"I am never going to join in with something like that, man; I can't believe you did that to her; that is SO sick," Monty said, watching the rage build up inside of Dwight's eyes.

"And do you know I can't find a pulse anywhere? I think she's dead, man," Monty added, shaking his head, and running a hand through his hair.

"SICK???? Gimme a break, you little freak. Maybe you'll be the one next time knocked out cold on the floor with your pants down around your ankles. When you wake up, you'll wonder what the hell happened to you," Dwight added, as he sidled up to Monty. Standing nose to nose now, Dwight glared at Monty as though almost daring him to do anything at all. Monty had never done anything ever to really challenge his cousin before, so Dwight never saw the powerful punch coming; right smack in his most prized possession, too.

As Dwight doubled over in agony, Monty stood over him now, a feeling of hatred brimming from his eyes. Dwight finally stopped crying and looked into those eyes. He was so shocked at what he saw in those eyes, that he could do nothing more than stare. Monty stared back at him, his eyes cold, unfeeling, and empty. For the first time in his whole life, Dwight felt very afraid. Monty grabbed him by the neck of his t-shirt and threw him against the large curio cabinet, and now, Dwight was beginning to panic. Luckily, nothing got broke, Dwight thought to himself, a feeling of unreality beginning to wash over him.

He wondered what Monty was doing over there by the fireplace, and then he assumed he was building Mrs. Crason a fire, as the boys sometimes did when they came over, because Mrs. Crason didn't do well going up and down the stairs. Indeed, if her rheumatoid arthritis was hurting her too badly, some days she just didn't go up and down the stairs at all. On those days, if the boys came over and asked to do chores for her, she would send them down for wood to build a fire, and bring up anything else that she might need. But then, Dwight thought to himself, if Mrs. Crason is really dead, why is he building a fire, anyways?

Watching more closely, Dwight could see that Monty had gotten a fire going, and it was already going full tilt. Dwight was afraid that the fire was too much, though, and he began to admonish Monty about it, telling him that the fire was too strong, too tall, too much. Now, he could see that the fire really wasn't totally contained in the fireplace, either.

In no time at all, Dwight thought to himself, that raging fire will begin to spread out here in the living room. Dwight shook his head, not understanding at all what was going on.

What the hell was that asshole cousin of his doing, anyways, Dwight wondered. His jaw hurt from where Monty had walloped him the second time, and now he bent over for a minute, massaging his aching jaw. He never knew the little pipsqueak had it in him, actually. Raising his head back up now, he looked up just in time to see Monty swing the fireplace poker right in Dwight's direction, and before he could move, everything went black.

Rage still coursing inside of him, Monty was just now starting to settle down. He dragged Dwight's body across the carpeting, and with all the strength he could muster, lifted him up and threw him close to the fireplace. Every time that Monty looked at his cousin, all he could ever hear was his taunts and schemes. Just as he was about to push his good-for-shit cousin into the fireplace, Dwight opened his eyes. It took him a minute to adjust his eyes to everything around him and he had one major headache now. He was frightened of Monty, and wasn't quite sure why his cousin had flipped out the way that he had. He'd never seen that side of Monty before.

"You're awake, huh? Good, you can watch the fireworks, then, " Monty added, a wicked laugh starting in this throat.

"Fireworks," Dwight croaked, with a very dry throat. "What are you talking about, cos? It's like the middle of winter, man."

"Yeah, it is, but for you, I'm gonna make an exception, buddy. In about two minutes, this whole damned place is gonna be one huge fire pit. If nothing else, I guess it's good that you got laid one last time before you burn in hell," Monty sneered, standing over his cousin, his eyes void of anything at all.

Fear struck at Dwight's heart now, and he began to wildly think of what he could do, but now he discovered that his head hurt so badly, he couldn't even think about trying to get up. It looked as though he wouldn't be going anywhere.

Monty went out the back door now, and Dwight knew he was heading out to the garage. What the hell is he doing out there, Dwight wondered.

Whistling as he came back in with the old gas can, Monty smiled brightly at Dwight as he cheerfully set the gas can down next to him. "What luck, man, this can is almost completely full. Who would have ever guessed," he chuckled, slapping Dwight playfully on the knee, the brightly colored camouflaged gloves he was wearing giving off an odd glow.

He looked around the room then, almost as if he were surveying it all one last time, then strode over to the gas can, and began to pour gas all over. Dwight lay there watching, trying in vain to talk sense into Monty, but it was no use.

Begging him to stop, Dwight began to cry like a little child. Monty stopped pouring for a moment and looked at his cousin. He listened to his pleas, watched the tears roll down his face, and listened as he apologized profusely for doing what he did to Mrs. Crason, and for anything else he may have done to offend Monty. Dwight thought that Monty was really listening; maybe he would really get through to him after all.

But then, Monty just nodded his head, stood back up, and picked up the gas can.

"It's good that you got all that shit off of your chest," he told his cousin. "They say that confession is good for the soul," Monty added, beginning to pour the gasoline all over Dwight's body now.

"No, please, Oh God, no, please stop," Dwight begged, his voice breaking, his throat started to close up on him from the heavy fumes of the gasoline.

"You know, cos, I am willing to bet you that Mrs. Crason begged for her life too, right before she breathed her last breath," Monty said, talking in a matter-of-fact tone.

Reaching into the flap of his jacket pocket, Monty pulled out his lighter, and played with it for a moment, watching the flames, before turning away from Dwight.

Monty began to walk away, and Dwight suddenly began to relax. He closed his eyes for a second, trying to concentrate on his breathing.

"Maybe he changed his mind, he can't really burn me alive; he just can't do it," Dwight told himself.

Dwight was still convincing himself that his cousin could never light him on fire, as he watched large flames licking at his body, felt the searing heat blister his skin, then finally knew nothing at all.

1998

Sheila Hardesty sat stiffly waiting for the warden to bring Monty in. She chewed at her fingernails, and then sighed disgustedly, seeing their ragged, bloody stumps.

Sister Katrina had fallen ill yesterday with the flu, so she was unable to accompany Sheila today, and now she sat nervously on the hard chair, straightening her skirt several times, and stealing furtive glances across the hall.

She couldn't say that she felt real comfortable being here, but so far at least, she hadn't broken out into a cold sweat, so at least there was that, she told herself. The Valium that she'd taken on the ride out here had long since kicked in, and it helped in calming her frayed nerves. Why was she so nervous, Sheila had asked herself on the trip out here. She knew the answer to that; his name was Lamont, and Sheila had a huge crush on him, to say the least.

She was also nervous, because she'd found out why he was locked up. He'd murdered his girlfriend, in cold blood. Premeditated, obsessive rage had coursed through his veins as he'd followed her out of the bar that night. The irritation he'd felt when she'd told him in no uncertain terms that it was over had turned to rage, and when she'd gone to use the restroom and then walked outside to her car, he could feel himself seething inside, and he followed her out. First he'd had his fun with her, and then he killed her.

Married at 18, Cathy Grenaldi Hammond was a real looker. Her naturally platinum blonde hair was down past her shoulders, and she wore it long and loose. Her reckless, quick smile showed her perfect white teeth that her parents had paid a lot of money to fix when she was 14.

Cathy had been a friendly, brilliant girl, and made all A's in school, but her older sister had always been a thorn in her side. Her parents compared the two girls constantly, and Cathy had grown weary of it all by the time she was 13 or so. She never tried to compete with her sister by then, because she no longer cared which girl her parents liked the best and found the smartest. Cathy had a strong personality, and a heart the size of Texas, but her choices in men weren't always the best. Her husband was 20 when they'd married, and already had had quite a long juvenile record from ages 11-17 for shoplifting and burglary. He'd never used a weapon, and he seemingly didn't have a violent bone in his body; he just wanted to score big once, and retire at a young age, and be done with it. It took him a few years to understand the way the world seemed to work, and now finally, Roger had gotten the message, or so it seemed. But the reckless, happy-go-lucky, devil-may-care Roger was gone. He was replaced by a serious, no nonsense, I just found religion and now everyone else needs to too, attitude, and Cathy was tired of it all. Roger's latest complaint was that married couples should only resort to intercourse when they wanted to make babies. Since the couple had had their first baby 6 months after they'd married, and then the second one, 13 months after that, Cathy wanted no part of baby making, but she enjoyed the sensual part of life tremendously.

Meantime, heads always turned and men gave Cathy all the attention she could ever possibly want. Regardless of their ages, men flocked around her like lovestruck puppies, and they'd do anything at all for her, it seemed.

Monty had known all this, but it didn't make it any easier. To this day, just thinking about that last day, made him seethe inside with rage. He'd seen a psychologist for a long time here inside the prison to get his rage under control and to find out what indeed had caused so much of it.

As always, Monty did everything right. Nodded his head when spoken to, looked sad and apologetic, even downright remorseful when the situation called for it, as it did when interviewed about the night he'd killed Cathy.

Hell, once in a blue moon, he'd even muster up a few crocodile tears, whenever he'd talk about Cathy, while telling the shrink that he'd been regretting it ever since it had happened.

It's all under control though now, he'd remind the shrink. The meds they'd given him seemed to keep him happy and relaxed, and he didn't have any thoughts anymore when it came to killing someone, and looking into their eyes as they died. He could still remember his cousin's eyes as he'd thrown him into the fire pit. Fear and terror were mirrored in Dwight's eyes, and he'd looked like he'd wanted to scream in terror, but hadn't made a lot of noise, really. That had suited Monty just fine; he hadn't needed a big audience, and as the house started to really burn, he'd looked at old Mrs. Crason one last time, said a prayer for her, and turned on his heel and walked home.

The next day, his parents had found out about poor Mrs. Crason and the terrible fire that burned down her house, but it had been another day before anyone had identified his cousin, although he had been reported missing.

The shock was too much for Monty's mother, who had never seemed emotionally able to handle much of anything. She practically began to live in town, and spent every evening at church, praying, knitting, baking, whatever anyone needed, she was there doing it. She never seemed to want to be home anymore, so after awhile, Monty and his dad just quit asking her to stay home with them.

Monty was good at fooling the world, with his charming smile and his repentant attitude. His shrink thought that just maybe, his forty- year sentence had a good chance of being greatly reduced, for good behavior.

Sheila sat in the uncomfortable chair now, waiting for Monty to come out and mulled all of this over in her mind. Perhaps he'd had a psychotic break, that had caused him to behave so violently, she'd told herself. He seemed so gentle and lovable, so that girl must have really made Monty angry, Sheila thought to herself.

Sheila was still convincing herself that this girl probably got what she'd deserved, when she looked up and saw Monty standing by the visitation room, getting ready to be let in for their visit. She smiled a bit too enthusiastically, and almost tripped over the chair leg, in her haste to grab her things and get in there with him.

He pretended not to notice the near accident, and his handsome smile made Sheila oblivious to the rest of the world.

Not even the rage that had consumed Monty that night, and its horrible outcome, seemed to strike much of a chord with Sheila, as she sat down happily and opened the Bible.

"I've lived with this regret for the past several years," Lamont was telling Sheila sadly, shaking his head and bowing it now, looking up at her with puppy dog eyes.

Sheila's heart went out to him; he did seem to feel bad about what he had done, and that girl had just been awful, Sheila had thought to herself. She'd researched the story from old newspaper archives, and Monty had told her quite a bit in his last letter to her, so Sheila was inclined to believe that Monty was just at the wrong place at the wrong time.

She was also convinced that he would never hurt anyone ever again. At the end of their Bible reading session, they would chat a bit, and Monty would take her hand into his and kiss it, gently, while he looked purposely in her eyes. Sheila felt herself growing warm under his gaze, and by the time she'd walked out of the prison that day, her whole body was on fire.

"I'm telling you, that girl was the town slut," Sheila was telling her sister Debbie on the telephone that night. "Maybe if she hadn't been such a ...."

"WHAT???? You are NOT going to justify what he did to that poor girl, are you? Because I am going to tell you what I think, now that you asked me a few minutes ago. I really don't care if she was the town slut; hell, I don't care if she blew everyone in that entire town, it still gave him no right to take her life, especially the way he did," Debbie roared, disbelief at her sister's ridiculous comments irritating her beyond belief.

"Well, I'm just saying," Sheila started, before Debbie cut her off.

"There is nothing you can say, okay? Prison ministry is a great thing, mind you, but you surely don't have to go in there and get involved with someone like him. Hell, how do you know he won't do the same thing to you or someone else when he gets out?" Debbie asked, daring her sister to use her brain, just a little bit.

"Furthermore, I think you have done more than enough ministering to this guy; you need to tell Sister Katrina that you don't want to go out there anymore; I am sure she will understand," Debbie admonished, shaking her head in disgust on the other end of the line.

"Oh heavens no; I can't do that," Sheila practically cried out. "Do you know how it would devastate him if I just suddenly quit showing up there? He really looks forward to our visits, and he says that it is the only thing that he looks forward to, because that place is just awful," Sheila explained, as more and more sympathy crept into her voice.

"Oh my God, it's a prison, Sheila, not a damned country club; it's not supposed to be fun and exciting in prison," Debbie told her sister, who was now sighing loudly into the phone.

"I thought you were a good Christian girl, " Sheila intoned sadly, trying to lay a guilt trip on her sister.

"I am, Sheila, but this guy is playing you like a fiddle, and you are letting him. End it now, before it all goes any further,"

Debbie told her, before wishing her a good night and hanging up.

Sorry sis, I just can't do that, Sheila thought to herself, as she got ready to climb into bed for the night. Her toy poodle climbed in bed with her, and Sheila fell asleep almost immediately, as she began to dream about the life she and Monty would have someday.

1974

As everyone began to file out of the church, Monty strode over to the back of the church where there were lots of trees, and lit a cigarette. Damn, that was a helluva long service, he thought to himself. Long and totally boring. During the sermon, Monty's mom had poked him twice, and Monty would jerk himself awake for a few minutes, then fall back to sleep.

And what the hell was all that damned incense about, Monty thought angrily. Monty still couldn't get that smell out of his nostrils. That was some nasty shit, Monty said to himself. He watched the procession now, and saw his parents darting furtive glances around the place, obviously wondering where in the world he was. Monty didn't really care though; he hadn't wanted to come to his cousin's funeral, but his parents wouldn't take no for an answer. Usually his dad was really cool about stuff, but this morning, he had flat out demanded that Monty attend his cousins' funeral. His mother had gotten to that gutless wonder again, Monty had thought to himself, with disgust.

Now he watched his aunt, Miss High and Mighty, dab delicately at her eyes with her fancy, lace handkerchief. God, she is so fake, Monty thought to himself. She can't even act real at her own kid's funeral, Monty thought, shaking his head.

Not one hair was out of place, even though the wind was blowing with a brutal force, bringing a cold north wind along with it. His aunt seemed to act like she was from another planet, and when she'd looked at Monty a couple of times, it was like looking at a zombie. Tossing his cigarette behind the bushes, Monty walked quickly back to the church, before anyone could really miss him and wonder where he was. He stood over by his parents as Dwight's coffin was lifted up into the hearse. He found that he neither missed his cousin, nor did he remotely care that he was gone.

1979

Monty walked down the long county road that led up to his family's farm, but he was in no hurry to get there.

He'd had a horrible day today at school, and was glad that it had finally come to an end, thanks to that white trash whore, Connie Watkins.

She'd asked Monty out last Friday, to some stupid juvenile party, and he'd told her he couldn't come; he'd had other plans. That was on Friday. By the following Monday, Connie Watkins had spread every type of malicious lie known to man about Monty across Thomas Jefferson High School, to all 179 students in their little hick town. How she even managed to dream up some of it, was a mystery still to Monty.

In Biology class, she'd managed to sidle up to him in the lab, and when he'd tried to get out of her way, she'd shoved her more than ample chest in his face, since she was a good five inches taller than him. His friends used to call her the Amazon woman but it would seem now, that they were too busy having sex with her, to mind how much she towered over them.

In front of the entire class, Connie started spewing venom like a volcano, ready to erupt. Seeming to forget where they were, she accused Monty of everything except being a white boy. All because he'd turned her down for some lame party, Monty thought to himself. All the little country bumpkins just stood around, watching. A couple of the guys snickered, and one of Monty's friends, Jeremy, was still in shock that Monty had turned Connie down.

Heading down the path from the school yard, Monty was already several minutes later than his usual time, and was surprised and repulsed, all at the same time, to see Connie standing there at the end of the path, waiting for him.

"Hey Monty, what's your problem?" Don't you like pretty girls"? Connie asked, a sneer already forming on her usually pretty face.

Monty sighed audibly, and attempted to walk around her, although she was blocking his path. He tried to go the other way, but just as he was about to get away from her, she yanked him to her, and held him up against her heaving breasts.

"NOBODY ignores me and gets away with it," Connie hissed in his ear, making him angry at her all over again.

"Look Connie, I don't know what the hell your problem is, but just get over it, will you?" Monty said, brushing her off, and pushing her away from him.

"I still think you just don't like girls; maybe you're just a queer or something," Connie said, her voice edgy, and dangerously close to a whine.

"I like girls, I just don't like you, you trashy slut," Monty shouted at her quite suddenly, surprising himself with the depth of annoyance he was feeling.

Rage was escalating at quite a steady pace, Monty noticed, as his heart rate went way up and he found himself clenching and unclenching his fists.

Shoving her out of his way one last time, Monty began to walk away from Connie, but she grabbed the back of his coat sleeve and began shouting at him, almost hysterically.

"You know, I still wonder to this day what really happened to your cousin Dwight. He was quite a jerk all right, but he was magic in the sack. I never believed that shit about some accidental fire. Maybe you can tell me what REALLY happened, Monty," Connie added, her voice taking on a new menacing quality that Monty just didn't like.

"Whatever, Connie, believe whatever the hell you want to believe, because that's what you will do no matter what, anyways. I sure as hell don't owe you any explanations, now do I? Besides, if you thought Dwight was so great, it just goes to show how bad your taste in guys really is," Monty added, seeing the fire in her eyes as he spoke.

"There's nothing wrong with me; you would be able to see that if you just gave me a chance, Monty Hallmen. Why don't you meet me a bit later, and I'll show you a really good time, I promise, " she began to whine and beg all at the same time.

"Will you finally just leave me alone then, if I meet you this one time?" Monty asked.

"Whatever you want, sugar," Connie crooned into his ear, suddenly all smiles and sweetness.

"BUT, you just might not ever want me to leave you alone again after today, Monty Hallmen." Connie added, a smile playing at her lips.

"Alright, fine, where do you want me to meet you then?" Monty asked, feeling resolve just drain right out of him.

"You know the place; there's an old empty shack at the edge of Sheldon's Creek, and that's where we all meet," Connie added, giving Monty a playful squeeze.

"Don't be shy; just me and you, sugar. I know I can show you a GOOD time," Connie purred, planting a kiss on his cheek as she turned and walked away.

"Hey, don't forget to bring me a Coke, Monty," Connie yelled over her shoulder.

Monty sighed out loud as he watched Connie walk away, wondering why in the world she insisted that he meet her. Wondering why he said that he WOULD meet her, when Connie was definitely someone he despised.

Shoving his hands in his pocket, the million dollar question he asked himself now, was why in the world he was so turned on by her, when he knew that he found her to be irritating and quite despicable. He'd known Connie for years, and in the fifth grade, she started blossoming, and then started her sexual explorations and adventures as she headed into 7th grade. By high school, Connie remained popular with all the boys, although the girls rarely invited her to do anything with them.

Monty thought now back to the moment in the lab class when Connie had shoved her well endowed breasts into his face. He thought of the cologne that she always wore, and how exciting he found it all when he was around her, and he found that he was quite aroused.

You'll be showing me a VERY good time, Connie, Monty chuckled to himself as he headed up his driveway.

Monty sighed irritably to himself, as he slammed the front door shut. For someone who was never around to even finish the laundry for them, his mom sure as hell liked bossing him around, he thought to himself.

He had a plan and a schedule to keep and now his mother had thrown a damned monkey wrench into it all. Instead of dropping off the bottle of Xanax to her sister on her way out to town, Monty's mom insisted that he take the pills over to his aunt's house, even after he'd calmly told her he had to be somewhere else in less than an hour.

"There's nothing so important that you can't take a few minutes to help out your aunt," Monty's mother droned on, in her usual monotone.

"MOM, I do have a life, you know," Monty began shouting at her, and then noticed that his mother was already at the other end of the house and wasn't listening to a single word he said, anyways.

What the hell else was new, Monty now mumbled to himself as he practically ran the six blocks to his aunt's house.

His thoughts again turned to Connie, and her voluptuous, curvy body. There was just no way he was going to make it to the old shack on time, now, unless he ran as fast as he could, the entire way. It could work, he thought to himself, but the last thing he wanted, was to show up drenched in sweat and stinking to high heaven from it.

The way Connie's big mouth flapped constantly, it would be all over the school the next day that Monty showed up sweaty and smelling rank. When he thought about it, that was really all

Connie was good for, was talking trash and letting all the guys have their way with her. He still wasn't sure what he would do, either, when he showed up at the shack.

He felt almost sick, as he thought about the fact that he'd never been with a girl yet, and he was pretty sure what all Connie had in mind with their get together. What if she laughed at him, or he didn't do something right? That was another thing he didn't want to have discussed all over the school. His indecision was making him crazy, Monty decided, as he jogged the final block to his aunt's house.

"Bout time you showed up, sugar," Connie complained to Monty, having been ready to just get up and leave.

"I thought you was gonna just stand me up, and I would have had to tell everyone at school what a big pussy you are," Connie added, a sneer forming across her lips.

"Why would I do that? Oh, here's your coke," Monty added, handing the bottle to her.

"Oh, I don't know; you just seemed like maybe you weren't really into this little party of ours, but I could be wrong," Connie purred in his ear now, her breasts rubbing up against him, making Monty think thoughts that he never usually had.

"And I would really like to be wrong about that, Lamont," Connie added, her lips just a couple inches away from his now.

"Let's sit down for a few minutes; drink some of your coke," Monty said, pretending a calm air that he didn't remotely feel.

"We aren't in a hurry, are we? I mean, do you got somewhere you gotta be soon, like you carved out a whole 20 minutes for me or something like that?", Monty asked in a gentle, teasing sort of voice.

"Well, okay, I got an hour or so before I gotta be home for dinner," Connie said, glancing at her watch. "What do you want to do, just sit here and talk?" Connie asked, a look of surprise on her face. She definitely wasn't used to a lot of small talk, Monty thought to himself with a smirk.

"Yeah, sure, let's talk," Monty told her, starting to enjoy this little game they were playing. It was like a dance, he told himself, but better, because finally, he was in control of the situation, and he was determined to pull Connie's strings himself, instead of having her throw her weight around like she did with everyone else. It was not something that she was at all accustomed to, though, and as Monty stared into her eyes, he had to fight the hysterical laughter that was threatening to make its way out of his throat.

Connie took another long pull at her Coke, savoring its sweetness, and reveling in the sheer joy of being able to have a whole coke to herself. Her parents were total health food junkies, and sodas of any kind at all were forbidden in their home. Which was a real shame, Connie thought to herself, since she seemed to have become a Coca-Cola addict overnight. Connie was also forbidden to drink them, but since almost all her friends drank sodas, she could usually get her daily fix from someone. Besides the ice cold Coke, Connie was also reveling in having Monty sitting right next to her. She had waited for this day for so long, had wanted Monty for so long, as well, since he was definitely the most gorgeous guy at school, even if he didn't seem to notice or care.

But that's part of what makes him so hot, Connie thought now to herself, taking another long pull of her coke, before replacing the cap on the bottle. She looked at him now, a smile tugging on the sides of his mouth, and those adorable dimples of his threatening to actually break out into a huge smile.

"It's nice being with you this way," Connie told him, snuggling up against him, and allowing her hand to trail its way down to find his hardness.

She could feel Monty's reaction, although he didn't show it in his eyes, that he was enjoying this. Getting more brave, she began to slowly kiss him, first on the mouth, then letting her tongue trail down to his chest.

Suddenly she stopped and took her hand away, swaying a bit in her seat.

"What's wrong; why did you stop?" Monty asked, his face looking innocent and his voice thickening with passion.

"Oh, I don't know, I feel really weird right now, like I can barely keep my eyes opened at all," Connie mumbled, her eyes now looking like slits on her face.

Shifting a bit in his seat, Monty put his arm around her, and allowed her to lay her head down in his lap. A few moments later, Connie was totally out, her snores deep and gentle. The serene look on her face gave nothing away to the state she would find herself in when she awoke. Her nude body lay in a heap when he was finished, with the slightest trace of blood tinging her insides, as to the violence with which he rode her.

"Was it good for you, dear?" Monty laughed to himself as he zipped up his coat and left the shack. The sun was beginning to set, as he began to jog his way home.

Connie woke up to total darkness, and fear immediately clutched her chest. Her fear turned to panic when she realized that she was completely naked, as she groped around in the darkness for her clothes. Her head ached and throbbed, and her mouth was completely dry. Thankfully, she found her bottle of coke while she lay in the still darkness, and practically finished the bottle in one long pull. As she began to put her clothes on, she tried to remember why she'd come to the shack in the first place, wincing as she stood up to tug her jeans on. She wondered why she felt cramps coming on and tried to remember if it was time for her period. She would have to look into that when she got back home, she decided. As she tugged her jacket on, she opened the door to the shack and looked outside, noticing how dark the sky looked and wondering what time it was. Whatever the hour was, she was in big trouble, Connie thought to herself, hoping that her parents wouldn't get on her case too badly. Stumbling out of the shack and closing the door behind her, she felt like she'd been riding a horse for days, the way her private area felt, and once again, as she ran down the dirt road towards home, she wondered what the hell had really happened.

1998

Monty sat in the prison infirmary, waiting for the nurse to come back from her lunch break. All he wanted was some of his special migraine medicine, and the longer he sat there and waited for the dumb bitch, the angrier he got. Like the warden couldn't just come in here and get the damned pills, Monty mumbled to himself, cursing softly in the dingy, tiny room. This place is smaller than my cell, Monty mused. No wonder that nurse is in no big hurry to come back from lunch, he thought to himself. Finally he heard her slow, plodding footsteps coming down the hall, coming closer and moving as though she had all the time in the world. Probably hard work carting that huge ass of hers around, Monty thought, suppressing a wicked laugh.

"Hey Monty, what can I do you for," Reva cackled, obviously quite pleased with her play on words.

"You got another migraine, sweetie?" she asked, putting a sweaty, clammy, hand on his brow.

"Yeah, you know it, Reva," Monty said gently, allowing a small smile to play at his lips, knowing just how much it delighted this big ox every time he came in here.

"That's just terrible, honey; let me get you some of those pills, and maybe you'll get to feeling better real soon," Reva said, all business now, bustling around the tiny room, and digging out her thermometer.

"Do ya feel like maybe you're coming down with something, or ya got a fever or something?" Reva asked, trying to make this stretch out as long as possible. "Let me see here...." she mumbled to herself, rustling through the cabinets for his file.

After she busied herself taking his temperature, Reva announced that he did not have a fever, and finally got to getting his medicine. Monty felt like his head was going to explode and this cow was not helping at all, he thought irritably. Nevertheless, he put a charming smile on his face and was just as nice and polite as can be.

"Well, I DO hope that nasty ol' headache goes away real quick," Reva soothed, almost purring like the big ol' cheshire cat that she was.

"Seeing your pretty face already made me start feelin' better, darling," Monty lied, the words sliding off of his tongue so naturally.

Swallowing the pills, Monty forced one last sweet smile on his face for Reva's benefit, since he knew she was still watching him as he began to make his way back to his cell.

Sheila Hardesty was having a really bad morning. First, she'd spent ten minutes sweeping all the snow and ice off of her car, the wind whipping around her face. Drawing her scarf tighter around her neck, Sheila slid thankfully into the Accord, finally out of the cold, biting wind. As she'd made her way around the apartment complex, she'd almost slid right into another car. Her heart beating wildly from the narrow miss, she'd finally pulled out onto the highway, and turned on the radio to keep herself company on the twenty minute drive to work.

Her thoughts turned once again to Monty, like they almost always did. She wondered if she was going to make it to the prison this weekend, the way this snow was coming down. Monty will be so disappointed if I can't make it out there, Sheila thought to herself, then admitted that SHE would be the more disappointed out of the two of them, if she was unable to make it.

As they spent more and more time together, Sheila's fantasies about her and Monty sharing a life together became more intense. She purposely didn't talk about him to anyone now, since her last conversation she'd had with her sister, Debbie.

Sheila began to replay that conversation now in her mind, lost in her thoughts. She'd called Debbie to tell her the good news that Monty was talking about the two of them having a future together when he got out. He'd explained to Sheila that the word out there was that he was getting his sentence reduced to half of the original sentence, and probably less than that for good behavior. His original sentence had been for 40 years, since he'd been convicted of premeditated murder, in the first degree, but thanks to his penitent spirit, and because he always kept his nose clean, he may only have to serve half of that.

A couple of times, Monty had had to get really nasty with that stupid girl, because she just really didn't seem to have a brain in her head, which played right into his hand most of the time, Monty smirked. Twice now, she'd missed the appointed time set aside for phone calls. Once, she was talking to her damned sister, when she should have hung up and taken HIS call. Monty had raged and fumed, and then he'd refused to call her at all for well over a week, until he knew that Sheila would be completely beside herself with fear and worry. She slunk back to the prison the following weekend, her eyes puffy and her nose swollen and bulbous looking. Monty had to fight off fits of hysterical laughter when she'd first gotten there, between her appearance and the unbelievably long apology and ass-kissing session she'd had with him.

Thankfully, he kept his mind occupied on other thoughts while the lame cow chewed on her cud, over and over again. From time to time, she would dab at her eyes, then her nose, with her crumpled up tissue, then work her hands nervously, when he would explain to her what he needed from her. And when he obviously had needed to lay the law down, Monty chuckled to himself, he'd finally offered the tiniest of smiles, and the little church mouse perked right up in a hurry. No one should have this much fun at someone else's expense, Monty had thought, careful to not break into hysterical laughter.

Thank goodness he forgave me, Sheila thought to herself now, as she began to slow down for the traffic light. I just couldn't forgive myself if he ended things with me, Sheila thought, fear stabbing at her heart at just the thought of it. No, her and Monty were going to get married someday, and have a life together, she reminded herself, vowing to only let positive thoughts in.

Damned snow, Sheila thought to herself, as she came to a stop at the next intersection. Pulling out her compact, she checked her appearance, then snapped it shut again. She sure did have lots of gray hairs coming in, she thought to herself.

Glancing up at the traffic light, she looked into her rear view mirror, just in time to see the box truck slam into the back of her car.

1988

Cathy Grenaldi Hammond quickly hung up the phone as she heard her husband's old pickup truck making its way up their graveled driveway. She'd begged Roger for years to get some of his buddies together and pave their driveway; she was tired of all the rocks and rubble, but Roger seemed to not really care whether they improved the condition of their property or not.

Cathy had to admit, though, that once in awhile it came in handy to have all that gravel, because she always heard his vehicle coming, and sometimes, like today, she'd had just enough time to get off of the phone and finish getting dinner ready. Roger hated to wait very long for his dinner, and he would whine petulantly if he came home from work and had to wait another hour while it finished cooking.

Cathy'd been busy chatting with Monty for well over an hour, and had forgotten to get dinner started until a few minutes ago. Luckily, it was just burgers and fries tonight, so it wouldn't take very long to make, and hopefully, she wouldn't have to listen to Roger complain. They seemed to just exist these days, and at times, their conversations only seemed to center around their two children, 14 year old Jason and 13 year old Jessie. For whatever else Cathy felt was empty in her life, she was always thankful for her son and daughter and shuddered to think of life without them. Her affair with Monty was not her first; she'd been involved with two other men before he'd come along. For Cathy, the thrill of a new romance was unlike anything in this world, and she could no more pass up the chance to be happy and loved in another man's arms, than she could throw her children in a river and drowned them.

The romance was often more exciting than the sex, but Cathy knew it was still a lot more than she ever got at home. The rare times Roger touched her, it was like being mauled by a stranger, she thought to herself. Because their lives had become so dysfunctional, they didn't do a whole lot together, and seemingly didn't mind the fact that they hadn't been in love with each other for well over a decade.

Cathy had often times begged Roger to get counseling with her, or by himself, in the first few years of their marriage, when they started having so many problems, and a couple times Roger did go. But that was so long ago, and because he wouldn't stick with it, it never did help them. Cathy had wanted to continue to go herself, but they'd really never had the money for that sort of thing, and Roger was embarrassed that he'd ever gone at all. His family didn't believe in counseling; they didn't believe in airing one's dirty laundry to perfect strangers, and thought people that did that sort of thing must be Hollywood wannabes of some kind because normal people just didn't do those sorts of things, they reasoned with each other. Roger's mother was strong-willed, with a tongue as sharp and deadly as a knife. Cathy had discovered what kind of person Roger's mother really was when she'd turned up pregnant with their first grandchild, and was called every horrible name in the book. Roger's father was quiet; he reasoned that there was no cause for him to speak, because his wife talked enough for the both of them, and he'd turned a deaf ear to her many moons ago. Still, she managed to get in the last word and make everyone around them stand up and take notice of her and what she believed in and wanted. Roger's father told his son on his wedding day, that he'd always liked the Grenaldis and found them to be decent folk, and was secretly glad that Roger was in love with such a wonderful, pretty girl. He'd admonished his son to never repeat his words, knowing that such an admission could only make his life more miserable, although there were days when he couldn't see how.

Cathy's mind snapped back to her cooking, and she hurried things along, because she had plans to meet Monty in a couple hours. Every Friday night, Cathy usually went out and stayed out until the wee hours of the morning. Since she worked outside of the home at the local small woodworking factory during the day and kept their home running smoothly all week long, Roger had never cared that Cathy went out. At times, he had secretly wondered if she was seeing another man behind his back, but he found that while he did still care, he obviously didn't care enough. As long as she never does anything stupid to embarrass me or my family, Roger had always told himself. If she is sleeping with someone else, Roger thought to himself, she better not get herself pregnant and she had better be real discreet. Roger studied her face now, as she flipped the burgers one last time, and poured milk in three glasses at the table.

"So don't you ever get tired of going out every Friday night?" Roger asked her, watching her eyes and waiting for her response.

"No, not really,"Cathy said, flashing a smile at Roger, and just for a moment, Roger saw the carefree gorgeous teenager he fell in love with.

"Why do you ask, honey?" Cathy said, looking his way, her face serene and innocent.

"Just curious, I guess; me, I don't much miss that bar scene, " Roger added, throwing enough onions on his burger to kill a vampire.

"I hope you don't be dancin' with any of those guys you see at them bars," Roger said, stuffing a wad of the burger in his mouth, and chewing thoughtfully.

"No, I rarely dance, Roger; you know that," Cathy told him, as she fixed her own burger. "Now you know you needn't worry about me; I can take good care of myself and I always do," Cathy told him, heaping his plate with salad and fries.

Jessie sat down at the table and piled her plate with fries and salad. Cathy just shook her head at her and laughed. Her daughter, the vegetarian. Just the thought of eating meat seemed to be too much for Jessie, and at some point, Cathy gave up on begging the girl to eat meat. For awhile, Jessie ate chicken and fish, but now she rarely ate those, either.

Jason plopped down across from Jessie and eyed her plate with a smirk. "What a freaky freak," he teased, assuming his nightly ritual of conversation with his sister.

"Shove it, dipshit," Jessie replied, calmly stuffing a forkful of salad in her mouth. Meantime, Jason's burger was so thick with condiments and fixings, he could barely open his mouth wide enough to eat it. Jessie watched in contained amusement as Jason opened up his mouth so wide it hurt, and attempted to get that burger in his mouth.

"What a maroon," Jess laughed, throwing a french fry at her brother. Jason tossed the french fry back and it stuck on her hair. Before Jess could toss it back again, Cathy stepped in with her protests.

"Okay, guys, enough," she laughed, never really tiring of the comedy routine with these two. She began to clear plates away, cleaning them off and putting them in the dishwasher. Roger was chatting with the kids about school and the classes that they took. He told Jessie that she was doing a good job in school and got on Jason for only making B's and C's last trimester. Cathy was absently listening to the gentle flow of their banter when the telephone rang, and Roger began to get out of his seat.

"No, sit; I'll get it," Cathy told him, quickly wiping her hands on the dish towel and walking into the next room to grab the phone.

"Hello? What? Dammit, I told you never to call here," Cathy hissed into the phone, annoyed at Monty's stupidity.

Monty feigned hurt feelings, and Cathy could almost hear him sigh into the other end of the phone. "Oh, now darlin' that is so uncalled for," Monty drawled, apparently oblivious to the anxiety he was causing in her life.

"I just wondered if you were gonna be late, that's all," Monty said.

"I don't know, probably...I will see you later...and don't call here any more," Cathy whispered into the phone, quickly hanging up when she saw Roger heading her way, out of the corner of her eye.

"Who was that?" Roger asked, concern furrowing his brow. "Oh, just a sales call," Cathy said, her face already composed and free of worry.

"You know those darn people always call during dinner time," Cathy complained, as she went back to loading the dishwasher.

Roger glanced at her again, and then at the phone, as though it could tell him what he wanted to know. No matter, he thought, I got me some chores to do outside while it's still light.

Cathy was changing her clothes when Roger came in the bedroom after he'd finished the chores he'd wanted to do outside. He watched her brush her long, blond, hair and slide the headband through it.

"You be careful now," Roger said, giving her a peck on the cheek, as he left the room.

Cathy gave him a buoyant smile that she didn't feel; part of her really wasn't into going out tonight, especially with Monty, after the stunt he just pulled. She felt like he was becoming too pushy, too bossy, and too big of a drag, in general. The whole idea of the affair for Cathy was just supposed to be fun times, along with some great sex. But more and more lately, Cathy was feeling like the sex was so-so, and Monty's demands were becoming tiresome.

I may just have to break it off with him tonight, Cathy told herself. With a sigh, she picked up her purse and her keys and walked out the door.

Monty sat at the bar, one eye on the big screen TV and one eye on the door. He was getting angrier by the minute. Cathy knew how he felt about being kept waiting, and still, here it was almost 8 o'clock and she was already nearly a half hour late. He could barely stay seated in his stool when she finally breezed in at five minutes after eight. She seemed conpletely unconcerned that she was late, which only made Monty even angrier. He stewed a bit longer; a slow burn that threatened to get out of control.

"Hey, you....Sorry I'm late," Cathy told him, planting a kiss on his cheek. "I had to drop the kids off at their friends' houses on the way out, and then I got stuck waiting on a train at Byron's Crossing," she added, making sure to LOOK sorry for his benefit, as well as hers. She knew that if he got angry enough, the evening would not go well, and there was nothing worse for her than to look forward to going out on Friday night, only to find that her boyfriend was having anger management issues.

Monty looked up at her then, seeming to size her up. His eyes almost seemed to silently ask her if he was being played. Monty seemed to have no faith or trust in women, and he'd never had a relationship last as long as this one had. Yet he was feeling more and more lately, like he was being played for a fool, and he'd be damned if THAT was going to happen. Still, she DID look sorry...

"Okay, then, what'll ya have?" Monty asked her, his dimples lighting up his entire face, making Cathy feel relieved and excited, all at the same time.

Grabbing their beers from the bar, they made their way to the last table in the back of the bar. It was dark back there, and the music was soft. No one hardly ever came back that way, which made it the perfect little hideaway.

1998

Monty sat in the holding room for what seemed like 5 minutes, doodling on his pad, and getting angrier by the minute. Where the hell is that stupid cow, anyways, he thought to himself. How damned long does it take to walk down a couple hallways, he muttered to himself, his irritation with Sheila seeming to grow by leaps and bounds.

For a moment, he closed his eyes and imagined the look on Sheila Hardesty's face as his wide hands closed in around her worthless chicken neck. Her dumb, brown cow eyes would practically bulge out of their sockets, as the look of shock and terror registered on her face. She would silently beg for mercy; her eyes would fill with tears, and those dumb cow eyes of hers would eventually glaze over as she wordlessly begged him for her life. Like he really cared, anyways, Monty thought with a ruthless chuckle, the visions of watching Sheila struggle to live, filling him with an excitement that had become almost foreign to him.

Suddenly the door buzzed, and, speak of the devil, it was the old cow. Monty almost laughed out loud, but stopped himself in the nick of time.

Her eyelashes batted at him, and she smiled nervously at him, standing at attention, as though she were in the military and was awaiting further instructions. She stood ramrod straight, her hands folded, carefully hiding the bloody stumps that her fingers usually displayed.

"Well, hey there, beautiful, sit down," Monty said benevolently, trying his best to quell the hysterical laughter that threatened to escape his throat at any moment.

Sheila nodded for an instant, and then, very gingerly, pulled out the chair and sat down.

Hmmmm, Monty thought to himself, no bible today. "Did you forget the bible, Sheila dear?," Monty asked her, pretending to really care one way or another.

"Uh, um, yes, actually I was halfway here before I even noticed I'd forgotten it. I am so sorry, Monty, really I am," Sheila babbled , like a river that never stopped, Monty thought to himself.

"Hey, it's alright. I reckon you probably know almost all those Bible verses by heart, so maybe you can just pick out a few from memory," Monty told Sheila, in a quiet, soothing voice.

Sheila's head bobbed up and down in response, and she took Monty's hand into her own. Her hands were damp and clammy, almost to the point of being gross, Monty thought to himself, doing his very best to pretend that he didn't notice that little problem at all. Inwardly, he felt like hurling all over the old cow, but he knew that if ever he needed his fine acting abilities the most, it was going to be now, with Sheila.

He pretty much already had her eating out of his hand, and he wanted that to continue, until at some point, Sheila would never really know what had hit her. Perhaps literally, Monty thought to himself with a chuckle. Bowing his head contritely, he closed his eyes and began to pray.

For almost a half hour, Monty chatted freely with Sheila, listening to her babble once again about nothing at all, and fighting all the annoyance that conversations with her always brought him. But she would never ever know that, at least not while he was still locked up inside, he thought to himself.

Now Monty pulled out all the stops on seduction. "Hey, beautiful, before I forget to tell you, my parole hearing will be coming up in another few months. I really hope you can be there," Monty told Sheila, allowing the faintest of whines to permeate his voice.

"Oh , of course," Sheila soothed, immediately getting out her date book and looking to see what day the hearing was on. Now she was busying herself trying to find a pen in that suitcase she called a purse, Monty thought to himself, once again feeling the hysterical laughter welling up in his throat. This ol' girl just makes it all too easy, Monty thought to himself, a beatific smile beaming down on the clueless Sheila Hardesty.

Thinking of course that Monty was just growing fonder and fonder of her, she gave him her best smile right back. "There's nowhere else I'd rather be," Sheila breathed in his ear. "You can count on me, Monty," Sheila added, apparently making sure there would be no mistaking how she felt. Monty took all this in stride, always amazed how Sheila treated every conversation like it was just one huge, secretive conspiracy. Her words were very soft-spoken and she always spoke in the kind of hushed, whispered tones that reminded Monty of how a person would speak to a small child, if you were attempting to quiet them in church or in the library.

Chuckling to himself, he just kept laying it on even thicker. "Okay, well, I guess time will tell," Monty alluded, letting his words just hang in the air for the fool to devour.

"I mean, people always make promises and they hardly ever DO seem to keep them," Monty added, watching Sheila's expression out of the corner of his eye.

"I mean, I know it's a whole lot to ask, and maybe it's just not fair at all for me to ask this of you," Monty told her, keeping his eyes averted just right, and waiting to see how long he'd have to wait for Sheila to grab the bait, hook, line, and sinker. He fought the terrific impulse to laugh out loud, and gave Sheila his best puppy dog face he could possibly muster.

"Sheila, I can't begin to tell you how much these past few months have meant to me; I don't know now how I ever got along without you in my life. I mean, you are my world.

Going in for the kill now, Monty took Sheila's hand and held it tenderly, kissing it gently.

"I am so nervous," Monty said, reveling in his outstanding acting abilities. "What I am trying to say, Sheila dear, is, will you please marry me? I have lots of money in the bank, you know, and it will all be yours," Monty finished, looking into Sheila's eyes so earnestly. Damn, he thought to himself, I should be in fuckin' Hollywood; I'd be winning an Emmy for best actor. My God, the performances I have had to give, he thought to himself, fighting off the temptation to laugh like a hyena.

"Of course I'll marry you," Sheila gasped, her face lit up like a Christmas tree. She dug now for the tissues she kept just for these types of occasions, Monty told himself. With tears brimming in her eyes, Sheila was now prattling on happily about something, but Monty was no longer listening. He watched now as Sheila finally shut up, gathering her things and making swipes at her eyes with the balled up tissue she'd managed to find at the bottom of her suitcase.

Still playing his role to a "T", Monty nodded solemnly, and took Sheila's damp, clammy hand into his own, once again, kissing the top of her hand, and then allowed himself to be led back to his cell.

Debbie squeezed her eyes shut for a few minutes, massaging her temples, as she listened to her sister rattle on. Barely able to catch her own breath, Sheila had been at it for well over 40 minutes now, Debbie thought to herself as she glanced up at the clock in the living room. She shook her head in disgust, unable to even begin to fathom what the hell was wrong with her sister. Was she just flat-out stupid, Debbie asked herself. Was she that desperate? As Sheila prattled on, the answer soon presented itself.

Seizing her chance once Sheila had managed to pause for a deep breath, Debbie cut her off mid-sentence.

"What the hell is wrong with you, Sheila?" Debbie asked, her mind reeling around, trying desperately to make sense of a situation that didn't even begin to make sense.

"Oh, what do you mean? You sound angry, sis, what's wrong? You know this is probably my last chance to get married, anyways," Sheila added, now, as Debbie sat on the other end of the phone making gestures to her husband as though she was going to shoot herself.

"Are you serious? You drop this king-sized bomb in my lap and you seriously have to ask me what's wrong? Honestly, Sheila, why the hell do you feel the need to marry this man? Of all the men in this world, you have to marry a man in prison for killing his girlfriend? And if this was my only damned choice for a husband, I would gladly die a spinster! Unfreakin' believable," Debbie finished, having a hard time finding words to express her mounting frustration.

"Well, now that's not very Christian-like, sis," Sheila told her sister, in that patronizing, hushed, whisper of a voice she had. "He's a born again Christian, and he'll never again do anything like that, I assure you. Besides, that girl was the town tramp, from everything I've heard. You'd never know that she was married and had children," Sheila added, in that hushed, whiny voice she had.

With the knowledge now that children had been left behind, Debbie was fit to be tied. There wasn't words in the English language, she thought to herself, that began to show how she was feeling. My God, Debbie thought to herself. Two beautiful children were robbed of their mother because of this man that my sister calls "reborn" and "a changed man".

"I seriously hope to God that you are not even thinking about justifying what this man did, Sheila, because I can assure you that there is absolutely no justification in this," Debbie spat out.

"Oh, um, no, I didn't mean that he had a right to kill her; I was just saying that I can understand what led him to make that mistake," Sheila answered, sounding like this man had just bought the wrong kind of detergent by mistake. Debbie was trying really hard to keep it together, but Sheila was making it difficult. Debbie couldn't understand her sister at all.

"Look, you have to really pray about this and give this a lot of thought," Debbie finally told Sheila. "Please....there are so many ramifications if you marry him. If he ever gets out of prison, do you know what kind of life you are going to have with him?" Debbie asked.

"I don't know, I haven't thought that far ahead, " Sheila explained, getting ready to launch into yet another conversation about her man.

"Sheila, you don't understand. Do you really think he is going to get a job anywhere? Do you really think you are going to have friends? And how do you know for sure that he won't do that to you, someday?" Debbie finished, hoping that SOMETHING she said was getting through to her sister.

Sadly, though, Debbie could tell that her pleas were falling on deaf ears, as her sister immediately explained to her why she felt that Monty could never hurt her.

"Plus, he said he's got thirty five thousand dollars in the bank, that will be mine if I marry him, because we are in love and it will be helping him out as well," Sheila told Debbie. "There aren't a lot of options for him after he does finally get out of prison; he either lives with me, or he goes to some kind of halfway house somewhere," Sheila babbled.

"And this is your problem because.....", Debbie began, but Sheila once again cut her off with an endless barrage of explanations.

"Don't you remember how it feels to be in love, sis; I mean, it's bad enough that he's still in prison, and we only get to see each other once a week; that's just absolutely terrible," Sheila lamented, as Debbie could feel her last nerve beginning to fray.

"Besides, this is my chance to finally have a house, not just a stupid small, cramped apartment. I have always wanted a nice house," Sheila commented, pausing for a breath.

Finally, after almost an hour of talking, pleading, and listening, Debbie hung up the phone. She found the whole business completely unsettling. What she did not tell her sister, was that if she did indeed marry Monty, and he ever did get out of prison, he would never be welcome at their house. Debbie's children were young and she was adamant about protecting them and wanting to keep them safe. Nothing about this sounded safe, Debbie decided. She'd even told Sheila that she never wanted to get a call to come to the morgue and identify her sister's body, and that she was very afraid that she might have to do that if she went ahead and married this man. But in the end, Sheila left everything and everyone behind for Monty, without hardly a backward glance.

1988

Cathy sat nervously sipping her beer, rehearsing over and over in her mind what she would say to Monty when he returned from the bathroom. Her heart was racing, and now her hands were starting to shake, she noticed with disgust. Deep down, she was very worried that Monty would get extremely angry when she told him that she thought maybe they needed to take a break from each other for awhile.

Cathy needed time to think, that was true, but more and more lately, she was uneasy about Monty. If anyone asked her why, she really couldn't give them a firm answer; she just knew that there was something about him that she couldn't put her finger on, that seemed to frighten her. And now that he was calling her house, she felt even more uneasy, almost like he was just hoping that their little affair would be made known to Roger. Cathy had never walked away from a fight, and while she picked her battles fairly well, she knew deep inside her gut that it was time for her and Monty to go their separate ways.

Lost in her own thoughts, Cathy was startled when Monty slipped into the booth next to her. He stared into her eyes intently, and, after waiting a few seconds, raised an eyebrow as well.

"What gives, princess? What has you so deep in thought that you didn't even see me come back to the table?' he prodded, his paranoid mind already working overtime.

It was bad enough that Cathy's old flame, Jared Winston had been eyeing Cathy up and down earlier, soon after they walked in. He'd given her an appreciative smile, and she'd had the nerve to stand there at the jukebox for a good five minutes talking to him, when she'd gone over there to select some music to listen to. Winston had walked up to her, with that swagger of his, Monty noted, and had given Cathy a hug. They stood close to each other, smiling and chatting, while Monty sat alone, seething inside. How dare she stand there jabbering with Winston that way, Monty kept thinking to himself. Didn't she have any respect for him at all?

Monty was like a pot that was about to boil over, but he couldn't help it. He wouldn't share her with anyone, and if she didn't know how to treat him, then maybe it was time that he taught it to her, he thought to himself, as he waved the bartender over to his table.

Now as they sat sipping their beers, Cathy felt like her nerves were about to collapse. She had the feeling that Monty was angry with her for catching up with Jared, although that whole scenario was irritating in its own right. Cathy had never done well with having anyone tell her what she could and couldn't do. Roger had learned very early on, that Cathy was a free spirit, and that attempting to change her, boss her around, or control her in any way, wouldn't go over well with her at all.

Monty had already made it very clear that he would not tolerate her spending any time at all with Jared, or any other man that she'd dated in the past, and as he scolded and eventually threatened her, Cathy grew more and more uneasy.

She wondered why she'd never really noticed what a controlling bastard Monty was before.

Had she been that swept away with his charm and good looks, Cathy asked herself now. She knew that she had, and he'd seemed the perfect gentleman when she'd first met him. He always knew just the perfect things to say, and always said the things back then that Cathy had so wanted to hear from Roger, but never did. She felt special and it was exciting the first time they'd made love. Monty was so tender and gentle; his movements were slow and deliberate, as though he wanted the hours they'd spent together to last forever.

Now, Cathy didn't even want Monty to touch her. She made up excuses lately, telling him that it was either that time of the month, or that Roger was getting suspicious, or that she had to leave early to go pick up one of the kids.

"So what's the problem, Cathy? You look like you have something on your mind," Monty stated, his tone surly, as he sullenly looked at her from across the table.

"Er, well, I think we need to have a talk, Monty," Cathy began, feeling her heart about to beat out of her chest. Monty was looking at her so oddly, and it was making her even more uncomfortable.

Taking a deep breath, she told Monty that she thought that they should stop seeing each other, at least for awhile. Cathy watched his face, waiting for a reaction that she knew was going to come. She felt like she was waiting for a volcano that was about to explode.

"Hmmm, I don't think I much like this conversation at all, missy," Monty said, his voice becoming dull and monotonous.

"What brought all of this about? You never said anything about being unhappy with me before. Now all of a sudden you think you can just up and dump me? You wanting to leave me so you can go back to Winston again; is that it?" Monty asked, his voice starting to rise.

Cathy noticed his nostrils flared when he was really angry, and his eyes, which Cathy had always thought were so beautiful, and one of his very best features, now looked hollow, dark, and empty.

"No, Monty, please, you have to believe me, this is not at all about Jared. I haven't thought about him at all since you and I have been together, and just because we ran into each other, doesn't mean that I am breaking up with you to go be with him," Cathy said, her voice warm and gentle, hoping to get Monty to understand and calm down a bit. She was getting the feeling that this whole evening was going to be a bust. Cathy wasn't a big fan of fighting in public, but she also knew that she wouldn't back down if Monty started something, because she just wasn't that kind of person. She had never been a man's doormat, and wasn't about to start now.

"Really; well, if you say so. You still haven't told me why you suddenly think it's so necessary for us to break up. Am I starting to cramp your style, or what?" Monty challenged, a bit of a sneer forming at the corners of his mouth.

"Look, I told you Roger is acting kinda suspicious; the last thing I want or need is for him to find out about this. My kids are teenagers, too, and I don't want them finding out, either. Monty, please, I just need to take some time to think things through, and see what direction I want to take with my life.

Can't you understand that? Isn't it worth it, for both of our sakes, for me to be absolutely sure of what I want and need?" Cathy implored, her voice taking on a firm kind of gentleness.

Monty just sat there for a few seconds after she finished talking, just staring at her, as though he were trying to decide if she was telling him the truth or not. He chugged the rest of his beer down, and reached for the bill. Still not saying a word, he made a show of looking at the cash in his wallet, and digging a couple bills out.

Plunking them down on the table, he stood up, and grabbed his coat. Cathy was really getting nervous now; Monty was always so talkative, and he still hadn't said a single word to her.

"Monty, please don't be angry with me," Cathy pleaded with him. "This really is for the best right now. I haven't stopped caring for you; really, I haven't. I just want us both to be sure, before I make the huge changes in my life I'd need to make so that we could be together. I have two kids to think about as well; it's not about just me; I have to consider other people's feelings, too. Please tell me that you understand, Monty," Cathy finished, her fingers gently tracing his cheek.

Monty stared down at her; gazed into her eyes long and hard, not quite able to decide if he really believed her or not. At this point, though, Monty guessed it didn't matter if he believed her or not. She was dumping him.

"Okay, princess. I can't tell you how sad this has made me, but I will give you what you want, and I won't bother you. If you want me, you know how to find me, right?" Monty asked, searching her eyes.

"Yes, of course. And I will be talking to you again soon; I just need some time to figure things out," Cathy promised, brushing her lips up against his, then against his cheek, as she gave him one last glance, before she walked out the door into the night.

1998

Sheila Hardesty opened her eyes, feeling like her mouth was so dry that her throat hurt. She tried to speak, but barely a croak came out of her mouth. She was alarmed; where in the world was she?

She searched her memories for some type of clue, but found that her head hurt really bad. She picked her arm up and saw that there were tubes running in and out of her. Now it was all finally starting to come back to her. She was in a hospital, hooked up to an IV, and God knows whatever else they'd hooked up to her. She remembered stopping for a red light, looking into her rear view mirror just in time to see the old, rusty, white van come crashing into the back of her car. Sheila remembered the incredible force she felt as she'd gotten pushed into the steering wheel. She remembered the paramedic telling her that it was a damned good thing she'd been wearing her seatbelt, because if she hadn't, she probably wouldn't still be here.

Slowly, painfully, Sheila tried to grab the call button. On her first attempt, she accidentally dropped it into her bed railings. Mumbling a curse to herself, she felt around for it, then had to gingerly try to pull it through again, fighting other wires and tubes as she did. Sheila felt irritation, as she pushed the call button and waited to hear a voice. Finally, someone said hello, and Sheila croaked out a greeting; her voice nothing more than a loud, scratchy nusiance that could barely be understood.

"Wonderful, you're awake. Welcome back," the nurse told Sheila in a chipper, lighthearted voice that Sheila didn't remotely feel.

Sheila was startled to see her, since she had just tried to call a nurse into the room, but doubted that anyone could even hear her at all. As if she could read her mind, the nurse, whose name tag read "SHONDRA" told Sheila that she was walking past her room when she thought she heard something, then poked her head in the room for a moment to find that Sheila was awake.

"Let me fluff these pillows for you, and I'll give you a sponge bath a bit later tonight, after dinner. You should be real hungry; it's been a good coupla days since you ate anything," Shondra continued, busying herself. "I'll be sure to let the doctor know you woke up. Would you like some water, hon?" Shondra asked sweetly.

"Yes, please," Sheila croaked, her lips feeling cracked and dry, and her head pounding like crazy.

"How's your head doing; does it hurt?" Shondra asked, and Sheila nodded her head, miserably.

After Shondra had finished taking her blood pressure and elevating her bed so that she could more easily sit up, she turned on the television for Sheila and made sure that the switches for everything were easily accessible for her.

"I'll be right back with some medicine for that headache, hon," Shondra told her, bustling out of the room, with an almost dizzying speed.

The news was on, and Sheila was about to change the channel, when suddenly something caught her attention, and she hurriedly turned the volume up.

"Police are still searching for two inmates, still at large, who escaped from Vesting County Prison, earlier today," intoned the curvy brunette, who looked like she should have been a model, instead of standing outside in the cold wintry air, probably freezing her ass off.

"More on the eleven o'clock news tonight," the brunette informed anyone who cared, as Sheila sighed deeply, praying to God that Monty was not dumb enough to try to escape prison.

At the thought of Monty, Sheila suddenly remembered that she was on her way to work and the roads had been bad, when she'd gotten rear-ended at that intersection. She searched her memory further, and remembered that that had been last Friday, and that she'd had plans to go visit Monty the next day. Suddenly, she began to freak out, not sure at all what the date was, or how long she'd been here. Did she miss the hearing?

"Now WHAT is going on, missy?" Shondra was saying, suddenly reappearing at the side of Sheila's bed. "What on earth has gotten you so excited, young lady; now you know the doctor is not gonna be a happy man if he comes in here and sees you like this, so whatever has gotten you so agitated, you need to just relax; just let me help you," Shondra soothed.

"What day is it? What day is it, please?" Sheila croaked, her voice still not revived from the water that she'd just drank.

"It's Monday, the 22nd of February, girl, do you need the year too?" Shondra asked her, chuckling out loud.

"Now don't you worry at all, you only been out for a coupla days, not a couple months or years," Shondra laughed, noticing the look of relief wash over Sheila's face.

"Oh, yes, okay, very good," Sheila mumbled, glad for just this once that her voice was too scratchy and sore to be of much use. She felt the heat in her face move through her cheeks, and now she really just wanted nurse Cratchit to leave her alone to lick her own wounds of stupidity in peace.

Shondra bustled right out of the room, then, promising Sheila she'd be back with a nice cold glass of orange juice to soothe her throat. Sheila closed her eyes again, seeing Monty's face in her mind. Suddenly she thought of her mother, who had no idea what had happened to her, and now Sheila dreaded having to make a phone call to her, to explain God knows what.

Conversations with her mother could be downright trying on one's nerves, Sheila lamented to herself. But considering the fact that she barely had a voice at all, Sheila told herself that that phone call would probably have to wait another day, and God knows what kind of hell she would catch for this latest "stunt" as her mother would call it.

As Shonda bustled back in and put some stronger medication into her IV, Sheila drank some of the orange juice. It was refreshing but also quite sour and tarty. But beggars can't be choosers, she told herself as she finished up the juice and pulled the covers up as high as they would go. She wished she could just pull the covers up over her head and when she woke up, this would all be a foolish nightmare. Or click her heels a few times, and wake up to find herself back home in her tiny, cramped apartment. As she allowed herself to dream, Sheila moved from her pathetic reality into a world she found so much more exciting; a world with only her and Monty and no one else.

1979

The high school gymnasium buzzed with so much noise, that it was impossible to pick out any one given sound. Sixty two high school seniors were about to get their diplomas and walk out of Thomas Jefferson High School one last time. Girls laughed and smoothed their hair, while the guys laughed and watched the girls, basically.

One girl, though, seemed to be oblivious to everything going on around her, and the girls next to her were whispering among themselves about her.

"Do you think she's stoned or something?" Amy Jason asked her best friend, Cindy Ann Parkens.

"Oh, I dunno, Ames, but she is like totally creeping me out; hey you didn't invite her to the party at my house tomorrow night, did you?" Cindy asked, suddenly concerned that a zombie might be attending her main event of the summer.

The girls had all been noticing Connie Watkins' strange behavior this past week, and they'd all put in their two cents when it came to voicing their opinions on what they thought was wrong with her. The Connie Watkins they'd always known, was, of course, the hoe of the high school, but yet, Connie had always been likable in her own right. In truth, some of the girls freely admitted some longstanding jealousy, too, when it came to Connie, because with her body and sexual expertise, they couldn't even begin to compete with that, when it came to their boyfriends.

There were only a small handful of guys in their graduating class that Connie hadn't slept with, mostly the nerds and a few of the jocks. A few of the guys too, that ended up getting kicked out of school early on, because they couldn't stop fighting or getting into some type of serious trouble. Most of the kids had done their share of grass, the most popular drug of choice, and lots of parties were scheduled at someone's house that had lots of property and very few, if any neighbors, so that the music could be cranked without any visits from Remy or one of his deputies.

Now Amy was still watching Connie, her face a stony mask. "She's freaking me out," Amy complained to Cindy Ann. "And of COURSE I didn't invite her to your party; do you think I want to lose yet another boyfriend to her?" Amy pouted.

Gasping for air, Cindy Ann had burst out laughing. Amy had had the worst luck this past year with boyfriends. The two she'd had, decided to sleep with Connie while they were still dating Amy. And then after awhile, they just quit calling Amy altogether, because it was easier to be with Connie, anyways. Go cruising with a six pack, maybe head for the lake, and be Connie's sex slave for the night. She was a cheap date and a great time, plus she never asked a bunch of stupid questions or talked your ear off. The sex was too delicious to pass up, and Connie was unbelievably sexy.

There was some gossip getting around that no one had gotten confirmed, that Monty Hallmen had slept with Connie the other day. Connie's best friend, Jackie Howle, had accidentally let that one slip out at lunch, the other day. Upon her accidental faux pas though, no one had been able to get anything else out of her, until, quite by accident, Jackie's other friend, Madison Hurley, had overheard Jackie and Connie in the girl's locker room after gym class, when they'd thought they were alone.

Madison heard Jackie ask Connie point blank if Monty had raped her, and then she'd heard Connie's very quiet "yes, I think so." Jackie had sworn Madison to secrecy, wanting to protect Connie, and wanting to make sure that this news didn't somehow find its way back to Connie or her parents.

Everyone knew that that was part of the problem of living in a small town like they did. Everyone knew everyone else's business, whether you wanted anyone to know or not. People had often gone to great lengths to try to keep things quiet in this sleepy little hick town, but eventually word always seem to get out, anyways.

In the meantime, though, Connie had clearly not been herself, and made little, if any, attempts at conversation. Even her sexual overtones had come to a screeching halt, and the normally gorgeous, outrageously sexy girl, now seemed to have become a wallflower overnight, while Monty Hallmen seemed to act the same as he'd always been.

And then after all the preparations and fanfare, the ceremony was over, and Connie Watkins seemed to have taken her diploma and vanished into thin air.

Monty hated doing stuff around the farm. Clearly, he'd always felt like much more a city boy, and someday, he vowed to leave this dump of a town, once and for all. As far as Monty was concerned, college couldn't start soon enough for him. He'd be counting the days until it was time to go. While he would only be attending community college, Monty reasoned that it was the first big step in the right direction to getting the fuck outta dodge. Having to look at the same old scenery and the same old people had been a major drag, by the time he'd gotten into high school. And now that graduation was over, he could concentrate on having some fun this summer, and with any luck, he'd have to spend less and less time at the family farm. It was a win-win for Monty, who rarely did anything unless it was going to be to his advantage.

As he was finishing up cleaning Thunder's stall, the beautiful palomino nuzzled him, in hopes that Monty had brought an apple or a carrot or two with him. Monty let Thunder search his pockets, and the horse managed to find the apple that Monty had hidden from him. Monty's thoughts turned to that afternoon in the shack, when, for all intents and purposes, he had raped the shit out of Connie Watkins. He'd felt nothing but ecstasy when it was over, and still, days later, watching Connie's erratic, zombie-like behavior, illicited only a fleeting glance here and there from Monty. One of his friends had asked him if he'd heard the rumor that had started circulating about him raping Connie in the shack, and Monty grew instantly angry.

"What? What the fuck is that? How can you even ask me that?" Monty raged, as his friend David took a step back and stammered an apology.

"Um, no, I am not saying you did that; hell, I know you wouldn't do that, but I just thought maybe you'd like to know what I had heard yesterday," David tried to explain, hoping to calm Monty down in a hurry. He knew that Monty was short-tempered at times, and he just chalked it up to life in the tiny town that they lived in. He knew how bad Monty wanted out of "shitland USA" as he called it. Hell, he'd been over once last fall, when Monty had gotten into an argument with his mother over where he would be attending college. Monty had wanted to go all the way out to California, and his mother wouldn't hear of it.

David's father owned a car dealership, and David had already been working there on weekends, sometimes, learning how to detail cars. He really wanted to become a salesman; it seemed like easy work, but David's dad didn't seem to think he was a good fit for that line of work.

"The old man is always bustin' my balls," David had complained on a few occasions. Monty nodded, understanding the complete lunacy of it all.

But when a Saturday sales position opened, Monty had applied, just for the hell of it, and the two friends had laughed until their sides split. David never thought of Monty as sales material, but as far as his dad was concerned, he was perfect for it, David soon learned.

So every Saturday, Monty got to leave the farm, and go into town, dressed up in his Sunday suit and tie, to go work from 9am to 4pm. The second Saturday he worked, he managed to sell his first car, and David's dad had wasted no time letting David know what an asset his friend was to the company. The buyer was a pretty 20 year old girl, who needed a reliable car for work and school. She worked at the textile factory in town during the day, and went to school four nights a week at the local college. David's dad had watched Monty in action and had been completely blown away by how smooth and glib Monty had been.

He'd gone home for dinner that evening, telling his wife that that kid could sell a plate of shit, and get top dollar for it, more than likely.

David remembered being surprised, to a degree, but after he'd really thought about it, he knew he shouldn't be, just because Monty almost seemed to have two sides to his personality. The super nice guy, with the adorable dimples and handsome, good looks, or the explosive guy that no one usually messed with who had been known to have a really bad temper.

Now David glanced back over at Monty, who seemed to be calming down some, anyways. Deep down, David was concerned that maybe Monty really DID rape Connie. He knew that Monty's disdain for Connie went above and beyond the normal realms, and he also knew how Monty could be if someone pushed him too far, which he knew Connie seemed to do, with maddening regularity. In the end, though, David decided it was best to just leave it alone.

1998

Sheila Hardesty finally got off the phone, a look of irritation still on her face.

"I surely don't know who made you mad, missy, but they surely did," Shondra told Sheila, shaking her head in dismay at the scowl on Sheila's face.

"Who make you so mad like that?," Shondra demanded to know, watching Sheila rub her temples with shaking fingers.

"Oh, it's just my mother," Sheila told her, shrugging her shoulders and trying to look completely disinterested.

"Hmph," Shondra tutted, as she scurried about, fluffing pillows and checking Sheila's temperature and blood pressure.

"Now look, she got your blood pressure all high again," Shondra stated, and as Sheila opened her mouth to protest, she just closed it again and faced the fact that Shondra was now on a roll.

"You need to just relax and calm down and for God's sake, stay off that phone with your mama, or I am going to come back in here and unplug it and take it out of here with me," Shondra said, already on her way out the door. "You hear what I'm sayin' to you; I'm not playin'," she added

Sheila managed a smile at Shondra and sank back against the pillows, willing her body and her mind to relax. She closed her eyes and thought of Monty, wondering if he was thinking of her and missing her, as much as she missed him.

1988

Cathy just about jumped out of her skin, whenever the phone rang at home. After draining most of the pot of coffee, she'd regretted drinking so much of the stuff, finding that now her nerves were even more jangled and on edge than usual.

She went over the events of last night in her mind, trying to decide if she'd handled things with Monty well enough. She resented the fact that he seemed to make her so nervous; she was normally not the sort of gal that gave in to other people's demands, but there was still that nagging feeling of something not being quite right, when it came to Monty. She'd looked into his eyes last night, and had felt a shiver of fear course through her body, that was an unknown feeling to her. She'd never really reacted to anyone else that way, and even when she'd tried to reason with herself over Monty's attitude, she found that she just couldn't lose that fearful feeling.

Now it was almost noon, and she'd really not done much at all today, besides drink coffee and empty the dishwasher. The phone had already rang twice this morning; once was her mother, asking if they were still on for their shopping spree tomorrow, and the next was some sales call, begging for a donation.

Cathy knew that just because she'd asked Monty for time and space, it didn't mean that she would get it, even when he promised to let her be. Monty always acted like promises and rules applied only to the rest of the world, and got real angry when others didn't keep their end of the bargain, but when it came to him, he just seemed content to do whatever the hell he wanted.

Roger had looked at Cathy funny, too, this morning, when they'd sat at the kitchen table looking over the paper. Cathy hadn't realized that she'd been looking at the same article for several minutes, without really even seeing it. Roger HAD noticed though, and asked Cathy if she was okay this morning, to which she smiled brilliantly, giving him one of her famous Miss America smiles, as she called it, and set out to make him believe that she was just fine.

A few minutes later, Roger announced that he was going into town to pick up some lumber for the new part of the barn that he was adding on to. Cathy felt sheer relief flood through her then, relieved that finally this charade could end, at least for the time being. Maybe she would feel better if she went out for a run, she told herself.

Arming herself with her headphones, and sliding her ankle weights on, she threw a sweatshirt on at the last minute, taking into account the dampness of the day. Her motto had always been that, when working out, she would much rather sweat a lot, than be too cold. Actually, she felt that way always, now that she thought about it. She dreamed every winter of finally getting out of this dump, and moving somewhere tropical, but she knew that Roger would never go for it. He absolutely hated heat, and preferred winter to summer. The snowmobile he'd purchased two years ago from a good friend of his that had moved to Florida, got caressed and taken care of, in some ways, better than Cathy ever had. She liked to tease Roger about it once in awhile, that that was his true love, that beautiful, big snowmobile. Unfortunately, this winter had been extremely mild, and now that February was nearing to a close, it was doubtful that the snowmobile would ever get used this winter.

Now Cathy was beginning to round the corner, and, seeing Roger out of the corner of her eye, she waved and smiled brightly at him. He'd waved back, pointing to the snowmobile. it's black, sleek armor looked so shiny that Cathy bet she could see herself in it. Cathy began to pant as she started up the big hill past their place, trying to pace herself and concentrate on her breathing. She'd always had mild, manageable asthma, but last winter she'd gotten pneumonia, and it seemed that it was taking her lungs awhile to fully get back to normal.

Leaving the hill behind, Cathy fell into an easy trot, feeling her body starting to relax and unwind. Nothing like a good run and a good sweat to make a girl feel better, Cathy told herself. She noticed some robins fluttering about, and hoped it was a good sign that spring was just around the corner. Losing her worries, she sang along to the song that was playing, not really paying attention to anything else, as she turned up the volume.

It was a big shock, then, when a car suddenly came out of nowhere, careening dangerously close to Cathy, and just missing her by an inch or so. It all happened so fast, that Cathy found that she didn't even get a good look at the car, because at the last second, she'd jumped off the road, and stumbled into some brush that lay in front of the ravine that she almost rolled into. Cathy felt shock waves course through her body, and then anger soon followed. What the hell was that, she asked herself. It was like someone was purposely trying to hit her, or at least run her off the road.

Picking herself back up, she brushed the twigs and leaves off of herself, and suddenly decided that she didn't much care about the run anymore. She turned around and started walking towards home, her thoughts turning to Monty.

She began to wonder now if that had been him in that car. Would he really do something like that, Cathy asked herself. And if not, then who would do something like that? Cathy found that the first question was much harder than the second; no one else in this town would even THINK about doing something like that, Cathy knew. She'd been here in this town her whole life and knew everyone well. These were good people here, Cathy reasoned. If not anyone else, then could it really have been Monty? Cathy tried to tell herself that he would never do such a thing, but found that a part of her honestly wasn't sure.

1998

Now that she was finally getting out of here today, Sheila Hardesty felt the weight of the world starting to come off of her shoulders. It's not that she wasn't treated well, she'd decided; it was just that she really had always hated hospitals, from the time she was a small child. She really believed that that fear and massive discomfort still came from the fact that she'd only been 7 years old, the first time she'd had to come to the hospital and saw her mother, lying quite still, with tubes running in and out of her. All these years later, she found that she still had recurring nightmares about it, when her mother had accidentally overdosed on sleeping pills all those years ago.

Doris, Sheila's mom, had always insisted that she'd not been suicidal; she'd been exhausted from not sleeping well, and had asked the doctor if there was anything he could prescribe for her insomnia. Worry over finances and trying to take care of Sheila, and having just relinquished her parental rights to the courts for her youngest child, Doris was having a rough time of it, and the fact that she'd gotten little or no sleep for almost a week wasn't helping anything. She'd been delighted when her doctor had given her some mild sleeping pills. The only problem had been that Doris should have asked him more questions about the correct dosage. Instead, she'd assumed that it would be okay to take an extra pill or two.

She'd been doing the bills, and had already taken one sleeping pill an hour before, but she still didn't feel sleepy, so she took two more, as she was closing her checkbook and trying to get Sheila to bed.

Suddenly, though, she found that her vision was blurry, and that everything around her seemed to be spinning around. As Doris, standing at the kitchen table, felt the world begin to spin around her, faster and faster, she'd groped for the chair, but didn't find it. What she DID find, was that she'd fallen to the ground, and had almost taken Sheila with her, but thankfully, the child was able to move out of Doris' clutches, and she stood, horrified and almost catatonic, as her mother lay in a coma-like heap on the floor. Reason had finally made its way into Sheila's brain, and she was galvanized into action, finally, picking up the phone and calling the operator.

At first, Sheila was able to tell the nice lady on the other end of the phone what had happened, as far as she knew. Unfortunately, she didn't know what kind of pills her mom took, or why. She just knew that she saw her take pills and then fall to the floor. When Sheila was asked where she lived, she stupidly stared at the phone, willing it to give her the correct answer. She didn't know her address, she finally told the lady on the other end. How old was she? Why, she was seven, Sheila proudly announced. The lady on the other end was biting her tongue. She couldn't believe a 7 year old didn't know her address or her phone number. Could Sheila describe her house and what her apartment looked like? She could only tell the lady that it was a brownish orange building that had lots of apartments in it, and finally the nice lady had been able to trace the call.

The paramedics had gotten there the same time that the policeman had and after answering his questions as best as she could, Sheila was told that she had to go to the police station with him. She was excited to ride in the police car, of course. Wait till she told the kids at school about that, Sheila thought to herself. They will finally like me, after I tell them that; they will all wish that they could've done that, Sheila told herself.

It was all good until they'd actually gotten to the police station and Sheila was given a stale donut to eat and a glass of water. While she munched on the tasteless thing, she heard the policeman talking about where she was going to live. What was he talking about, Sheila wondered, setting the donut down and drinking her water. Why can't I just go back to my own house, Sheila asked herself.

"Come along, child," the policeman, whose name tag said "Bill" told her. "We gotta go for another ride. We're gonna swing by your house and get some clothes for you, then we're gonna take you to your new home," he informed her, opening the door so she could slide in.

"No, I already have a home; I don't need a new home," Sheila had retorted back to the policeman. "I want to go see my mommy at the hospital," she added, looking up at the great big policeman.

For a moment or two, the policeman had looked like he was about to protest, but then he finally agreed to take Sheila to the hospital.

Sheila had happily climbed into the squad car, listening to the siren with excitement. She would go see her mother, and then her mother would be able to take her back home. Sheila would go to school tomorrow and tell all the kids about getting to ride in the squad car not once, but twice.

Parking in the front, the policeman held Sheila's hand as they checked in at the front desk. Hearing that Doris was on the 5th floor, Sheila ran to the elevator and hit the button. She was practically busting with excitement now; this just keeps getting better, she told herself, as the door closed and the elevator began to move.

As Sheila tiptoed to her mother's bed, she was startled to see that her mother lay so still, sleeping a deep sleep. The policeman was talking to the nurse that seemed to be in charge and once in awhile, they would glance at Doris and then at Sheila.

Sheila wished she could hear what they were talking about. She'd tried several times to wake her mother up; first, by calling her name, over and over again, and then later, she tried unsuccessfully to shake her awake, but Doris slept the sleep of the dead and never even moved.

"Okay, time to go now," the policeman suddenly announced. A tired, haggard looking woman stood with the policeman, nodding her head when he would speak to her.

"Come along, Sheila. I will take you to your new house for a few days," the woman told her.

Sheila stayed at her mother's bedside, fear breaking out over her entire body. She shook her mother again and again, silently willing her to wake up so they could go home to their own house. But Doris continued to sleep, and Sheila tried to fight the panic that was getting worse inside of her by the minute. How could she do this to me, Sheila asked herself. I don't want to go live with some stranger. What is happening to me, Sheila asked herself, as she allowed the strange woman to escort her out of the hospital.

Sheila played with the oatmeal that resembled concrete, as far as she was concerned. She couldn't believe she'd already been here for two weeks, and now she began to fear that she would never see her mother again, and never be able to go back home. She had a few dolls, a couple of trucks, and a few crayons and coloring books back at home, but only had a book and a doll here at this house. While she couldn't say that this woman was mean, she definitely didn't much like her. Sheila found that the strange woman was always staring at her, and Sheila wished she could shrink down to the size of a gnat and just disappear. There were six other kids in this house, too, and only one of those kids were biologically hers. The strange woman had asked Sheila to call her Mama Cat, which she explained was her nickname.

"It's short for Catherine," she'd explained. "Everyone has always called me "Cat" since I was a little girl, and I don't really much like Catherine," the strange lady explained further.

But Sheila found that she couldn't really care less about this woman, or what her name or her nicknames were. She rarely ever spoke to the woman at all.

To make things even worse for Sheila, word had somehow gotten out that Sheila's mother Doris had tried to kill herself by taking a whole bottle of pills. Everyone at school in the 2nd grade was talking about it, and now the rich kids were taunting her, calling her names and telling her that her trashy mom was a crazy person. For the millionth time already in her life, Sheila wished that she could just disappear. It never seemed to matter whether she stuck up for her mother to the other kids or if she just clammed up and said nothing. It was going to be bad no matter what, Sheila thought sadly.

As the final bell rang, Sheila felt relieved that another day of hell was over. The policeman that had driven her around before was out at the curb with his car, motioning for her to come over to him. He leaned up against his car and waited patiently. He smiled and gave her the best news ever.

"You're going home, kiddo," he said. "Let's get going."

1998

"Finally," Monty Hallmen mumbled under his breath, as the guard announced that he had a visitor.

Monty had been fighting a serious rage off and on for the past week, brooding over where he'd gone wrong, when he hadn't seen or heard from Sheila in over a week. He'd planned to really lay into her and let her have it. Who the hell did she think she was anyways, playing these little head games of hers, he had asked himself several times a day.

Now Monty drummed his fingers on the table, boredom already setting in, as he amused himself by trying to guess what that stupid cow's excuse was going to be.

Monty's head came up at the sound of his name. His first thought was that Sheila really looked like shit. Not that he was expecting a movie star; far from it, but even for Sheila, this was bad. Big, dark circles appeared underneath her eyes, and Sheila's nose was still bandaged from where it had gotten badly bruised and cut. She walked with a bit of a limp, now, and Monty watched her shuffle over to the table where he sat, waiting to hear the latest.

Putting on the face of serious concern, Monty reached across the table and took Sheila's hand in his. For once, her hand was not sweaty and damp. Today, it was downright cold. He looked at her again, and wondered what in the world had happened to her.

"Oh, Monty, I am SO SORRY I couldn't come out these past two weeks," Sheila began, hoping against hope that Monty would take pity on her and not be angry with her.

"Sorry for what, Sheila? What happened to you?," he asked her, giving her a gentle smile that melted her heart immediately.

"Ugh, you won't believe this. I got rear-ended at a stoplight, almost two weeks ago," Sheila explained, trying to fight the urge to babble and talk way more than she needed to.

"Oh no, baby girl," Monty moaned. "Are you okay? Did you have to go to the hospital? Tell me what happened, and don't leave anything out," Monty admonished, laying it on thick, even for him.

"Oh, honey, you have no idea how good it is to be out of that hospital," Sheila told Monty. As she sat with him and relayed the story to him, Monty couldn't have seemed more loving and attentive. His eyes were mirrors of concern and outrage of all that Sheila had had to go through. Now he would be able to pull this big, dumb fish in, he thought with an almost giddy sense of excitement.

His parole hearing was scheduled for the following month, and when Sheila paused to take a breath, Monty jumped in to remind her of it.

"Oh, hey, darlin', before I forget, I got my hearing next month; you ARE plannin' on being there, right?" Monty asked, a look of tremendous need coming over his face.

"Of course I'll be there, of course," Sheila assured him, bobbing her head up and down like one of those dime store dogs that people put in the back window of their cars.

Monty allowed a look of pure relief to cross his face, then, making sure that Sheila would notice just how much he needed her to be there with him.

Now he smiled easily at her, and kissed her hand, before he stood up, to head back to his cell. He blew kisses Sheila's way, murmuring all kinds of endearing words.

Monty could hardly get away fast enough, before the hysterical laughter threatened to echo, quite loudly, down the corridor. He thought of Sheila's puppy dog eyes and began to laugh. He was still laughing as the door of his cell clanged shut.

1988

Cathy climbed out of her old 79 Monte Carlo and felt a distinct feeling of unease. At first, she couldn't begin to understand why she was feeling this way, but standing in her driveway, it suddenly occurred to her that it was way too quiet. Normally, her Great Dane Duncan, even at 9 years old, was barking up a storm the moment he saw her pull into the driveway. Cathy felt the hairs on her arms stand up straight now, and silently chided herself for being so silly. Maybe Duncan was crashed inside the house, and just didn't hear her, she thought to herself, even while doubting that that would be the case.

Moving quickly, Cathy found herself bolting to the back of their house, where a huge fenced in dog run normally contained the mellow Duncan, always standing on his hind legs with his front paws folded on the top of the fence, just so happy to see Cathy.

Duncan had been a 7 week old puppy when Roger had brought him home to her as an early birthday present. She'd been thrilled and shocked by the thoughtful gift, just because Roger had never been overly keen on dogs. He'd gotten bit as a child by the neighbor's dog, and had gotten 12 stitches in his arm from where the Doberman had grabbed him. Roger had known the Doberman for years, and while he'd never been the friendliest dog, he'd been shocked that the animal was capable of such violence. He'd always taken snacks for the dog whenever he'd see him outside. No longer trusting the dog, Roger had kept his distance, and had felt a twinge of fear whenever the dog got loose, which thankfully, was not often.

Having Duncan had been healing for Roger, too, because he'd gotten over his apprehension of dogs, slowly but surely, as the lazy, mellow great dane grew and seemingly didn't have a mean bone in his body. Duncan would only growl at Cathy's sister Kellie, for some reason, whenever she'd stop by.

The sisters had gotten closer after school was over and Cathy had married Roger and had the children. While Kellie was currently single, she'd never had a problem getting dates, but after being married for 6 years and having her husband come home and surprise her with divorce papers, she was distrustful of men, and only too happy to get a nice meal or a night out on the town from them, and then cast them aside later. Deep down, Kellie knew it was wrong, but she had her four year old son to think of as well, and life as a real estate agent and broker was busy enough, without having to think about a relationship right now. She had her career and her son, and Cathy always volunteered to watch Dylan, Kellie's son, whenever she needed a break.

Kellie was very turned off by Monty Hallmen. She'd only met the man once, but he really had rubbed her the wrong way, and she wished sometimes, that Cathy and Roger would either just split up and be done with it, or be a married couple the way they should be. Kellie knew she was very old fashioned, and, while she didn't judge her sister, and totally understood where

Cathy was coming from, she didn't approve of the way Cathy was looking for love from other people, especially Monty.

Kellie had gone so far as to tell her sister that Monty Hallmen was Satan's child. Cathy had laughed until the tears ran down her face at that comment, but Kellie hadn't been joking around. Upon seeing the dead serious look on Kellie's face, Cathy had felt a wave of fear and apprehension. She knew her sister's heart had been badly broken by her husband's act of pure selfishness with the divorce and all, but this was different. Kellie had never given Cathy any indication at all that she felt like someone was just pure evil, so this was something new.

Cathy was glad that her sister was so protective, but she thought that maybe Kellie was being a bit TOO overprotective and way over the top on this one. Cathy knew that Monty was a charmer, gorgeously handsome, and a bit full of himself, but she'd honestly never noticed pure evil about him, as her sister had.

Now Cathy had finally gotten to Duncan's run, and at first, she didn't see Duncan at all. She was about to turn away, though, when she heard one of the most sorrowful, pathetic whimpers she'd ever heard in her life. Turning back around and opening the gate of the run, she almost tripped over Duncan, lying on the grass, blood trailing out of his mouth, his nose, and his chest, and as Cathy turned him ever so slightly, she saw the hunting knife, still stuck in the poor animal's chest.

Shock was reverberating through her whole body, and at first, Cathy couldn't move, couldn't cry, couldn't scream. She stood stock still, unable to do anything, but stare at her beloved dog. She desperately wanted to pull the knife out of Duncan, and almost did, but then stopped herself. What if that made him bleed to death, she asked herself.

Suddenly, from somewhere almost primal and deep within herself, a scream escaped Cathy's lips. The sound seemed to shock Cathy into action, and she raced to the house to call Roger and the vet. Holding her keys in her hands, she was about to unlock the back door, when it just pushed open. Fear unlike anything she'd ever known so far in her life, grabbed a hold of her. Why was the door unlocked, she'd asked herself. Mentally, she knew that she was the last person out of the house that morning, and remembered locking the door, but she didn't have time for this now. Grabbing the phone, she began to dial Dr. Herck's number when she happened to turn towards the refrigerator and saw the door wide open.

Stammering into the phone momentarily, Cathy quickly told the technician on the phone what had happened, and asked if she could bring Duncan in. The tech told Cathy she could, but gently warned her that Duncan would probably not make it long enough to get him to the clinic, the way Cathy had described him to her.

Cathy felt physically ill looking at Duncan; she knew that he was dying and that there was no way to save him. With tears rolling down her face, she spoke softly to her longtime friend, until the sorrow overtook her and she lay down next to him, with her arms around him, her cheek next to his, listening to his labored breathing. A moment, or maybe it was several; Cathy didn't know, but she looked into Duncan's eyes and said goodbye to the purest love she'd ever known, as Duncan gasped one last time, and then he was gone.

The next few minutes all seemed to run together, as Cathy began to slowly emerge from the fog that her brain had become. She almost jumped out of her skin when quite suddenly, Jason and Jessie called out to her, and she heard the front door open and shut, with the usual bang.

Oh, God, Cathy thought to herself, I can't let these poor kids see the dog this way, as she pulled the knife out of Duncan's body. She threw her coat over Duncan as though he might catch a chill, and Cathy knew it was ridiculous, but more importantly, she knew she didn't want the kids to know how poor Duncan had met his end.

Before the kids could come out to the run and look for her, Cathy quickly came into the house, attempting a feeble smile.

"Hey you guys," she said brightly. "How was your day, today?," Cathy asked them, setting a plate of cookies she'd baked the night before in front of them.

"Mom, where's Duncan at?," Jessie asked, her eyes darting around the kitchen, looking for him.

"Yeah, really, he wasn't barking his fool head off when we got off the bus like he does every other day of his life," Jason pointed out. "Is he sick or something, or is he in a doggie coma?" Jason asked with a laugh, not having a clue that Duncan was in a permanent coma.

"Hmmm, yes, well about that...Ummmm, look guys, you know how Duncan was getting really old, especially for a really big dog, right? You remember we actually just talked about this last weekend, right, about how real big dogs like Duncan don't live much past 7 or 8 years old?" Cathy asked the kids, never wanting to lie to them, but unable to bring herself to tell them that some sick bastard gutted their lovable dog as though he were a slippery fish being prepared for dinner.

Cathy just hated this; already, she could see tears forming in Jessie's eyes, and Jason had stopped stuffing cookies in his mouth, and now both kids were staring at Cathy, their eyes, worried, their hearts, unable to deal with the pain of their loss. Good old lovable Duncan; a mellow, sweet soul that never had hurt anyone got stabbed today, kids, Cathy thought, her mind racing ahead like a locomotive out of control.

"I am so sorry, you guys," Cathy said, gently, wrapping an arm around each child. "I never wanted to lose Duncan, either. He was really getting old, though, and we should be grateful that we had him for as long as we did," Cathy explained, her mind logically plowing ahead and saying what her heart clearly was not at all feeling.

How could she tell her kids what she'd really found when she'd gotten home? That the doors were unlocked, that the refrigerator was wide open, and that poor Duncan lay bleeding to death with a big hunting knife still stuck in his chest? How could she tell them all of that? No, Cathy thought to herself, there was no way that she tell the kids any of that. For that matter, she wouldn't tell Roger what had really happened, either.

She'd gotten the dog cleaned up right before the kids had gotten off the bus, and hid the bloody towels, to be tossed out later. With Duncan gently wrapped up in an old ratty bathrobe of hers, Cathy began the arduous job of dragging him across the lawn, and over to the old pickup truck. Since Roger had had the day off, he had gone fishing for the day with his friend Allen, who lived in the next county. Roger had told Cathy that he probably would be home before dark, and that he'd heat up his dinner when he got home. Cathy felt guilty not letting Roger see Duncan one last time, but she couldn't afford to let Roger see all that blood and he would see the knife wound, and he would ask SO MANY questions. Cathy didn't blame Roger; she knew she wanted answers, but she was terrified to ask the all-important question; who the hell did this to her dog? And why?

Cathy shook all over, a horrible chill taking over her whole body, making it impossible for her to stop shaking. She went in the house and told the kids to come say goodbye to Duncan one last time if they wanted to; Cathy also needed help getting Duncan into the back of the truck. They both came out then; Jessie's eyes already red from all the crying she'd done just in the past ten minutes or so. Jason stood next to her, unsure of what to say or do, but clearly, looking miserable, as he stared down one last time at Duncan after they'd gotten him onto the truck.

Cathy kissed them goodbye, and started down the road to the clinic, where they would have Duncan's body cremated. Cathy's mind seemed to be working on overdrive; one minute she was thinking of one thing, and then suddenly her mind seemed to go to a big dark hole of nothingness.

Cathy couldn't stop thinking about what kind of person would do something so horrible to a helpless animal. She kept coming back to the same scenario, over and over again, namely last week's breakup scene with Monty.

Cathy had started to relax a bit, when almost a week had gone by and there had been no phone calls, no letters, no messages, nothing at all from Monty. She'd stupidly dared to think she'd gotten away from him and now she could relax and quit worrying about what Monty would or wouldn't do. Clearly, she thought to herself, she'd totally underestimated the kind of person she thought him to be.

Pulling off the road onto the shoulder, Cathy gave herself up to the wracking sobs that came. Her shoulders shuddered and her mind felt fragile and in too much pain to think of anything at all. Duncan's adorable face appeared in her mind, and that only made her sob even harder. Why oh why did she have to hook up with the likes of Monty Hallmen, Cathy asked herself once again, for probably the tenth time this week. Was he really capable of such a heinous deed, she asked herself. But even as her sobs finally began to abate, deep down she knew better than to ask questions that she didn't really want the answers to.

Roger had come home just before dark, to a house that was unlike anything he'd dealt with, so far.

His children were camped out in the living room, each of them sprawled on the love seats, without the TV on, and with no lights on, either.

Roger didn't really know what to make of it, but he also wasn't a man prone to hysterics, either. Nor was he the kind of man to really sit down and talk to the kids about what they were feeling. He did, however, want to know where his wife was, and that seemed to be the final straw. The kids began to sob again, both of them talking together, and then Roger held up a hand, asking them to talk, one at a time.

"Duncan's dead, and mom took him to the clinic to be cremated," Jessie told her father, while Jason, who seldom cried, swiped at a lone tear that had managed to escape his eye, and had begun to trail down his face.

"What? She could have left him here till I got home," Roger began, but then noticed the time, and decided that maybe Cathy just wanted to get out to the clinic before they closed for the day.

"Does anyone know what happened? Did you guys come home to find him dead in his sleep?" Roger asked, not getting the information he thought he should have.

Just then, they all heard the pickup truck, slowly making its way up the drive. Roger thought that Cathy was definitely upset, because she never drove that slowly.

As she walked in the house, he gave her a hug, and asked her if she was okay, and Cathy nodded her head. She'd stopped to get fried chicken at one of the take-out restaurants next to the clinic, and now, she busied herself laying all the food out on the table for everyone.

Roger thought that this meal was the quietest he'd ever had with his family, feeling the sadness that seemed to cling to the air. He felt sad himself, even though he'd not been as close to the dog as Cathy and the kids were, but he'd liked Duncan and once in awhile, he'd toss a frisbee with him, or play a game of tug-of-war.

Cathy had managed to choke down a drumstick and a bite of slaw, but the food seemed to stick into her throat.

To say that she felt responsible, wounded, betrayed, and just plain sick, seemed to be the understatement of the year. Excusing herself, she told Roger that she had a terrible migraine starting now, and that she'd like to lay down for a bit.

Slipping under the cool sheets of their bed, Cathy dialed Kellie's number, hoping that her sister was home for the night now, and not out showing a house. As the blinding tears began to course down Cathy's cheeks, Kellie picked up on the second ring, and was shocked, then outraged, by Cathy's news on Duncan.

"How could anyone do something so terrible to a poor, innocent animal?" Kellie demanded, obviously completely shaken by the news.

"Do you have any idea who did this, Cathy?," Kellie demanded, her voice taking on an edge that Cathy rarely ever heard.

"Well...I have my suspicions," Cathy mumbled into the phone. "I just don't know who else would have done such a terrible thing," Cathy added, dabbing at her eyes with a new tissue.

"I told you that you were playing with fire with that creep," Kellie immediately pounced. "I told you that man was pure evil," Kellie continued, practically willing Cathy to debate the issue with her.

But Cathy was exhausted; emotionally, physically, and mentally. When she came out into the kitchen an hour later, she looked like hell and Roger just stared at her, looking as though he had something to say. Cathy poured herself a glass of water and reached for her bottle of sleeping pills.

As Cathy began to walk out of the kitchen, suddenly Roger loomed in front of her, his eyes wounded and betrayed.

"Cathy, if you know who did this to Duncan, you need to tell me right now," Roger demanded, folding his arms across his chest and staring at Cathy with pure disdain.

"What? What are you talking about, Roger? I told you; I have a giant migraine and I am going to bed for the night," Cathy told him quietly, trying to slip past him and head down the hall.

But Roger would not be put off, like some temperamental child. He needed, no, DEMANDED answers from Cathy, and he knew she was the only person who could give him the answers he searched for.

"Cathy," Roger said, his voice taking on a tired quality, as well. "Cathy, I know you are seeing someone. You need to tell me who it is; who you were talking about that is pure evil," Roger finished, his hands gently on her shoulders, a tear threatening to escape his left eye.

As Cathy stared at him in shock, she really didn't want to deal with this right now, but she realized she didn't have a choice. Roger did deserve answers, she told herself.

Suddenly, the full impact of what he'd just said hit her and hit her hard.

"You listened to my phone call with my sister, didn't you," Cathy accused, her voice starting to rise in anger and outrage.

"You gave me no choice, because I would never learn anything any other way," Roger told her, his voice taking on a new quality, an almost smug air that Cathy was not accustomed to, when it came to Roger.

Sighing loudly, Cathy walked into the living room and sat down on the couch. Pulling her robe more tightly around her waist, she took a deep breath and began the story.

After she finished telling Roger about Monty, she figured she might as well tell him the truth about how Duncan had died, as well. Roger's eyes got as big as saucers, and his hands began to shake. His shoulders finally began to shake as well, as he sat there, his tears coursing madly down his face, his body wracked with sobs, and his life forever changed.

Cathy's tears flowed freely as well. She never wanted to hurt Roger; they'd had an "understanding", at least to some degree, but she knew that she had really destroyed something precious and special, deep inside of Roger.

Neither one of them would ever be the same after this fateful day.

Cathy kissed the top of Roger's head and began to walk away, not wanting to hear him sob anymore. As she walked out of the living room, Roger suddenly began to talk again.

"Did he do it, Cathy?" Roger asked, his eyes searching her face for some kind of clue.

"No, I don't think so; I mean, I hope not," Cathy stammered, suddenly not sure of anything anymore.

Roger gave Cathy a look of distaste, as though he'd just bitten into something rancid. He walked over to his gun case, and pulled out his favorite rifle. In the course of ten whole seconds, Roger grabbed his keys, yanked open the door, and headed out into the night. Cathy felt a cold, clammy sweat take over her body, and she reached for the phone to call her sister again.

After reassuring her that Roger would never do anything stupid, Kellie decided to just throw a few things for her and Dylan in a bag and head over to Cathy's for the night. She wasn't going to sleep well, anyways; not after all of this, Kellie thought to herself.

Driving down the long, lonely county road, Kellie noticed how dark it seemed. She played with the radio to find something decent to listen to, and finally just turned it off again.

So lost in thought, Kellie had to slam on the brakes, as she almost passed up Cathy's driveway. She noticed that Roger's truck was still gone; she wondered if she should drive into town and look for him. She really didn't like the fact that Roger had taken his rifle with him, now that he knew who Cathy was having an affair with.

It's not that Monty Hallmen getting whacked would be a bad thing, Kellie mused to herself, getting out of her car, and grabbing her bag. It's just that he certainly wasn't worth going to prison for, Kellie thought with a sigh, hugging Dylan close to her as she climbed the old porch and headed into her sister's house.

1979

Connie Watkins sighed as she pulled her car up to the old Hallmen place. She wished she could just disappear into thin air and never have to think about Monty Hallmen, ever again. Just thinking about him made her skin crawl, she thought to herself.

Connie had managed to get away for a month after graduation, which she was eternally grateful for, since she felt like she was going to have a nervous breakdown if she stayed in this little shit town just one more day. She'd had to practically beg her folks to let her go visit her cousins who lived 6 hours away. They had a huge swimming pool and what seemed like, an unlimited supply of money. Two out of three kids were out of school, but only one of the two had actually graduated high school. Trey WAS the oldest, but certainly not the brightest, when it came to behaving himself long enough to get himself a high school diploma. He really didn't seem to care though, because he'd gotten his GED and the drug business never seemed to slow down at all. Trey always seemed to have wads of cash in his pockets, and endless energy.

Lincoln or "Linc" as he liked to be called, was bright and extremely handsome. He always had plenty of girls fawning over him, but he made no bones about wanting to get away and go to Harvard Law school, someday. Connie truly believed that

Linc could be an awesome lawyer, or whatever else he wanted to be in this life, because he seemed to have it all, and yet, he was completely oblivious to the charms and effects he had on the opposite sex. Connie thought that Linc was truly one of those rare people that was gorgeous, but totally without any conceit.

Two years behind Linc was Lorna. She could have been Linc's twin; they couldn't have looked more alike if they'd tried. While Linc seemed to be totally unencumbered by anyone, in general, Lorna was very intense, and while Linc seemed to love people and be very trusting, Lorna loved and trusted animals much more than people. She had big plans to own her own veterinary clinic someday, but for now, she could hardly wait for high

school to be over, so that she could get started studying animal science and anatomy in college.

Connie could always count on Linc and Lorna, no matter what she was going through, to make her laugh and be there for her. While Lorna was actually a year younger than Connie, she'd always been wise beyond her years, it seemed, and it never ceased to amaze Connie how much Lorna knew about life in general. Although she'd had many opportunities to date, Lorna rarely ever bothered with it; instead, she was only too happy to curl up on her bed and read.

Lorna was envious of Linc and Connie, because she was more than ready to get done with high school and move on to the "real stuff" as she liked to tell them. Very little that Lorna had learned through the years in high school seemed to whet her appetite for the real world. In Lorna's mind, the real world was all the animals in the world, who had beautiful souls that humans could only dream about. Lorna was convinced that animals loved you just the way you were, and she was anxious to begin her training to learn how to make them well and keep them that way.

Lorna knew that her cousin Connie was no virgin; they'd spent many nights holed up in Lorna's room talking and laughing until the wee hours of the morning. While Lorna didn't know the full extent of her cousin's

exploits, she knew that Connie knew more about the male anatomy than Lorna probably would by the time she was 30.

This visit with Connie was different, though. Connie was normally the life of any party, and could be counted on to make her cousins double over with hysterical laughter, until they begged her to finally stop. Lorna noticed this time, though, that Connie was just as nice as ever, but unusually quiet. The late, late nights of staying up playing games, telling stories, and watching horror movies were replaced this summer by hanging out by the pool during the day, and watching mindless sitcoms all evening. While there was nothing wrong with that, Lorna knew that something was really wrong, after a whole week had gone by and Connie had only said maybe 50 words all total.

Unable to wait any longer, Lorna had suggested a late night stroll through their huge neighborhood, knowing how much Connie had always enjoyed the lights and the fountains that most of their neighbors had. She was determined to find out what was going on with her cousin.

It had been a very warm day, with the temperature hovering around 90, until around 9pm, when it finally started to cool off some. Glancing at the kitchen clock on their way out, Connie was concerned at the late hour.

"Are you sure we should be out walking around? It seems rather dangerous and risky," she added, her eyes darting about, before they were even out of Lorna's driveway.

Lorna looked at Connie now, the shock she was feeling all over her face.

"What?" Connie demanded. "Why are you looking at me that way?" she added, as though she'd always been a little wallflower who'd been afraid to walk around their neighborhood at night.

"Really? Like you really have to ask?" Lorna demanded, stopping suddenly and gazing into Connie's eyes.

"I KNOW there is something going on, or something that's really wrong, Connie, and I want you to talk to me and tell me what's made you so different. And don't even waste my time by telling me that it's all my imagination, because we all know it's not. Besides, my imagination really isn't that good, anyways," Lorna teased, her eyes gently probing Connie's.

Connie stopped walking then. They were only two houses away from Lorna's, and they flopped on the ground watching the huge fountain at the end of the cul-de-sac. Lorna knew that this fountain had always been Connie's favorite, and she hoped that it would give her the strength to open up about whatever was bothering her.

Connie took a swig of the ice cold coke that they'd brought with them, and then sealed the cap back on, with a sigh. Lorna sat patiently, waiting for Connie to begin, and then, she finally did.

She told her cousin about the many nights she'd lain awake in bed, dreaming of Monty Hallmen, and of the many desires she'd had to keep under wrap for so long. While Lorna had no sexual experience, she knew that Connie did, as did most of her friends, as well. Lorna didn't begrudge any of them their sexual adventures; she just wasn't ready to have any herself, just yet.

Apparently, Connie must have had it bad for this guy, Lorna mused, listening to her cousin chat. At first, Lorna didn't understand what the problem could possibly be, but then it hit her. She wanted to be wrong, but the fear she felt deep down told her she wasn't.

1988

Roger's trip into town had proven useless and worthless, for two reasons. The first, and most important, was that, try though he might, he never did find that son of a bitch Monty Hallmen. He'd thought it would be real easy on a Friday night to find the slimeball. He'd gone into the two bars, and even drove out into the next county, where the bigger nightclub was. He'd paid a ridiculous cover charge of $5.00, just to get in the door of "Boogie Baby".

Roger thought it was one of the stupidest names for a club he'd ever heard of, and he looked and felt like a real fool when he walked in there. He'd probably never felt so out of place in his life, not even when he'd met Cathy's folks for the very first time, soon after he and Cathy began tearing each other's clothes off. Roger remembered the way that Cathy's dad,

especially, had looked at Roger, and in his mind, he felt like he was being sized up. He'd felt judged for not being a doctor, a lawyer, or a dentist, or even someone that owned their own store. But Roger was none of these; he was a simple boy that grew up in a simple home and had simple pleasures, and most of those pleasures were with Cathy Grenaldi. They'd had so much sex the first few years of their courtship and their marriage, and now, Roger stood in line at the Boogie Baby, thinking about how different everything was now between Cathy and him, and wondering if it was just too late for them. The strobe lights were twirling around, faster and faster, and Roger could feel the heat coming off the dance floor.

He began to tap his foot with impatience, as he waited for the idiot in front of him to find his driver's license. The kid didn't look like he could possibly be out of high school, let alone 21, Roger thought to himself.

Finally, Roger was up there, begging the bouncer to just let him scan the dance floor. He told him that he was just looking for his girlfriend, and that if he saw her on the dance floor, he would come back and pay the cover charge.

"The hell you will," the bouncer snarled, his body huge and muscular, and obviously pumped up with steroids, Roger thought to himself.

"You take two steps from here, you're gonna pay the cover charge, man," the hulking gorilla was saying.

Roger grabbed a $5 from his wallet and let the gorilla stamp his hand. He walked all around the dance floor, bumping into the crowd, and mumbling apologies as he went. He'd seen several people that he knew, of course, and got caught up in conversations with them, too, so it was no surprise when Roger looked at his watch and found that he'd already been at this place for over an hour. He finally had had enough, all the way around, and stepped over to the bar.

"Hey Roger, ol' buddy, how the hell are ya?" his old grade school chum Billy was saying to him.

Roger felt like he needed to sit down anyway, so he thanked the bartender for the drink, and threw a dollar bill in the tip jar.

"Whatcha drinkin', bud?" Billy was asking, peering into Roger's glass. "Looks like scotch. Need a refill?" Billy asked, already handing the empty glass to the bartender.

The next thing that Roger knew, there was a whole bottle of scotch on the table, and while he tried his damndest to listen to what Billy was saying, he found that concentrating was pretty useless. It was becoming increasingly apparent to Roger that his mind was shot for today, and unless he just happened to see that piece of shit Hallmen, he wasn't going to be getting anything else done tonight.

Two hours later, a massive headache coming on, Roger begged off another drink and began to look for the exit. He knew he was plowed, but he didn't really care. He knew the county roads like the back of his hand, and decided that as long as he kept the window open and didn't speed, he'd be alright.

Roger threw a couple singles on the bar, thanked Billy for the scotch, and made his way through the thinning dance floor. He'd wondered what the hell time it was, but he'd had trouble seeing the clock from across the room. Finally, he decided it really didn't much matter, anyways, and he continued to stagger out the door, grateful for the cold, fresh air.

As Roger continued his walk out to the gravel pit of a parking lot, he noticed how dark it was tonight. The moon was barely a slit in the sky, he thought to himself. His head still pounding, he stopped at his truck, digging his keys out of his pocket, and then dropped them on the ground. As he bent down to pick them up, he was suddenly grabbed around the neck, and found that some sort of sack or something had been thrown over his head. Roger could feel the hard, cold steel of his truck, as he kept getting punched in the stomach, over and over again. He tried, to no avail, to strike back, but it was like being at a birthday party where there was a colorful pinata, and you had the scarf over your eyes, and you just kept swinging at the air, hitting nothing.

Roger was now getting kicked in the groin, and as he doubled over from the severe pain, he felt like one of his ribs was cracked, as well. He'd taken a few punches to the face, and as he licked his lips under the ratty sack, he thought he tasted blood.

When it all got suddenly quiet, Roger thought that maybe, he could just climb into his truck and go home. Just as he'd almost gotten the sack off of his head, he got kicked in the face, along with the hand that was struggling with the sack.

As Roger tried to stand up, he found that it seemed to be too much of an effort for his wobbly legs. After his third attempt at standing, Roger felt his legs go limp, as he landed on the cold, hard gravel. The roaring in his ears was deafening, and his head hurt terribly. Roger could taste his own blood when he licked his lips. As everything began to spin around him, Roger felt almost grateful when the darkness came, and he closed his eyes, with a sigh.

Cathy wanted desperately to take a Valium, to quiet the rising anxiety that was making it difficult to breathe. She'd almost had to breathe into a paper bag at one point, but through a concentrated effort, she'd managed to stave off a full blown panic attack. Glancing at the clock yet again wasn't helping her cause, as she now noticed that it was after 2am.

With her sister Kellie sleeping soundly in her bed with her son Dylan, their soft, even snores told Cathy that they were completely zonked out. Cathy wished with all her might that it were that simple of a feat for her; wished that she could just forget about everything and go to sleep.

Her mind wasn't going to do her any such favors, though. In the still of the night, she kept seeing images of her beloved Duncan, the hunting knife deep inside his chest, his beautiful eyes staring at her. Cathy kept going over the whole day's events in her mind, even as she kept willing herself to stop. Glancing over at Kellie and Dylan, Cathy had been so thankful when her sister had shown up at her doorstep, soon after Roger had taken off.

Thinking about Roger was inducing a panic attack, because she couldn't seem to quell the fear she had inside of her, that something awful had happened to him. It wasn't like him to ever be out this late. They'd had fights before, of course, nothing this severe, but he had never come remotely close to being gone for this long, nor out for this late of an hour.

When Cathy dared to be honest with herself, she realized that most of her fear stemmed on the fact that deep down, she really did think that Monty had come over to their home, slipped into the backyard, and killed poor, sweet, Duncan, in his effort to maintain control over her. The fact that he could even fathom doing something so awful to a poor, helpless, animal gave way to severe waves of nausea and Cathy quickly ran into the bathroom.

Feeling chilled, Cathy threw an old robe around her, and padded out into the kitchen. As she splashed the cool water over her face, she stood up then, and gazed out into the backyard, that now seemed somewhat ominous. Hot tears began to stream down her face again, and Cathy began to wonder if she would ever stop crying. Hell, she couldn't even look out into the backyard now, without seeing poor Duncan, and thinking about how she found him, held him and kissed him, before he'd breathed his last breath.

Cathy chided herself for being so melodramatic, then stopped herself, as she realized that no amount of psycho babble was going to fix this mess, or take away all the pain she was feeling, or mend the obvious broken heart that Roger had had when he walked out of their house hours ago.

Unable to be alone with the millions of thoughts that kept swirling around her brain, Cathy got dressed and grabbed her heavy winter coat. She scribbled a note for her sister, in case Kellie woke up looking for her, grabbed her keys, and then, although she'd quit years ago, she grabbed one of her sister's cigarettes and ran out into the night.

1979

Lorna's worst fears were now coming to light, as Connie's words kept playing over and over again, like a broken record.

"I'm pregnant, Lorna," Connie had told her, as tears streamed down her face. "I'm pregnant, and I'm carrying Satan's child," she added, a nervous laugh tacked on for Lorna's benefit.

After Connie had told her the story of that evening in the shack, and how she'd woken up alone in the dark, with her insides feeling bruised, Lorna had been outraged.

Connie told Lorna how she had stumbled home and thanked her lucky stars that her parents were out for the evening, since she'd had no good excuse for the fact that she was over two hours late. She'd turned on the shower and had scrubbed and washed under the almost scalding water, trying to wash away the fragmented memories she was having.

She'd had time to think as she walked home, and slowly she began to remember things, here and there. Monty Hallmen was meeting her at the shack. He'd brought her a coke, and they'd been sitting in the shack; Connie taking happy swigs of the coke, and Monty suggesting that they just "talk".

As she turned the water off, Connie recalled how she'd felt Monty's hardness with her free hand, and how she'd brushed her lips against his. With a violent spasm, Connie's empty stomach convulsed over and over again, leaving Connie to lay her head on the cool tile.

When she'd awoken a few minutes later, Connie quickly put her pajamas on and slid into bed, as she heard her parents' car come up the drive.

The last thing she needed right now, was to have to deal with her parents and all of their endless questions.

Then the brutal realization came crashing down on Connie at the moment that she realized she'd been drugged and raped. But why?

Lorna was silent for quite some time after Connie had spilled her guts to her cousin. Finally, Lorna just wrapped her arms around Connie and pulled her close, as the bottled up dam finally burst, and Connie's tears poured freely down her face. She held her close to her for a long time, until finally exhausted, Connie fell asleep.

On her last night with her cousins, everyone went out for dinner at Connie's favorite pizza parlor, and for the next couple hours, she forgot her troubles, and could almost fool herself into thinking it was all just like old times.

Back at the house, though, all of Connie's old fears and worries crept up, when her and Lorna were packing up all of Connie's things. As they folded clean clothes and laid them in Connie's suitcase, Lorna looked up at Connie, and asked her how she was doing.

"Have you told your parents yet?" Lorna asked, as they folded the last of the clothes and pushed Connie's suitcase shut.

"God, no; you are the only person that knows, so far," Connie admitted, as a lone tear trickled down her face.

"You're going to HAVE to tell them, though, and maybe the sooner, the better," Lorna said gently, giving Connie a hug.

"I know, and I will make sure that I sit them down together later this week, after they've come back from the Bahamas," Connie said, worry etching her pretty face.

"What about Monty?," Lorna asked, glancing back up at Connie.

"Ugh, no, I haven't told him yet either, and I can't tell you how much I am dreading that," Connie admitted, shaking her head.

"I mean, I am waiting for him to either yell, or get mad and punch out a wall, or something. Or, he'll tell me that there's no way it's his kid, and that I should just go away and leave him alone," Connie added.

"Maybe he will want to marry you?" Lorna asked hopefully.

"No, I doubt it; I just don't think he'll be the marrying kind, kiddo," Connie told Lorna.

"But I will keep you posted on what happens, and let you know all the juicy details," Connie said, with a laugh.

"Unfortunately, I have to take my car over to his place and have it serviced. I need the brakes checked out, and some other stuff, too," Connie explained.

"And I am not looking forward to having to tell him about the baby, either," Connie added.

With one last look around the room, the girls walked down the stairs together and climbed into the car that Lorna always drove. Connie had to laugh sometimes, because everyone in the house had their own car. Lorna's dad had an old corvette from the late 60's that he drove around once in awhile, besides the Lexus he drove everyday for work. His short, stocky body and large bald head had been the source of jokes for a long time, but even more so, when he would take off down the road with his old corvette.

Linc and Lorna would laugh themselves into a stomachache every single time, as Zach would complain that anyone could spot their dad a mile away, just by the reflection bouncing off of his shiny, bald head.

Stanley, the kids' dad, took it all in stride though, and usually joined into the good-natured ribbing about his bald head himself. At times, he argued with everyone that he was actually in style now, since many men were now shaving their heads.

Mindy, the kids' mom, always looked like a model, and the kids always joked around about how opposite their parents looked. Mindy, tall and willowy, was a good four inches taller than Stanley, who just barely stood 5 foot 6 inches, and always looked like she was ready to pose for Vogue or something, according to Lorna.

Linc and Lorna seemed to be clones of their mom, while Trey worried that he would end up being bald someday, like his dad, since he seemed to share many physical characteristics with Stanley.

As Connie hugged everyone one last time, she wished with all her might that she could just stay here forever, where she felt loved and safe.

She wished that none of the events of a few weeks ago had ever happened, and that she could enroll in the beauty college here.

She'd tried to talk her folks into letting her do just that before she left on this trip, but they didn't want to hear it.

It was bad enough that neither of her parents were happy about her going to beauty college, even though that was all that Connie had really wanted to do for years. Hair and makeup fascinated and delighted her, and she'd always looked forward to helping women look their best. It just seemed next to impossible to get her parents to understand that though, because they wanted her to go to medical school, or at the very least, become a nurse.

Now, though, it all seemed like a moot point anyways, Connie thought to herself. There was no point in talking them into letting her stay with her cousins and go to school out here, when she was going to have a baby and become a mom. How would she ever be able to support her and her baby alone, Connie asked herself.

As she continued to be deep in thought, Lorna glanced at Connie a few times, feeling very sorry for her cousin, and wishing that somehow she could just wave a magic wand over the whole thing and make it disappear.

"What are you thinking about?," Lorna asked Connie, as they pulled out onto the interstate to head for the airport.

Sighing, Connie looked at Lorna and shrugged her shoulders. "Seriously, I just can't seem to turn my mind off at all, lately. At night, I just toss and turn half of the night, and then I am so tired all the next day," Connie lamented.

With a laugh, Lorna said,"Yeah, I HAVE noticed that you aren't keeping me awake half of the night with your snoring at all this visit, like you usually do."

Looking more serious, Lorna asked,"So, are you going to keep this baby? I mean, have you thought at all about just giving it up for adoption?"

"Because you know there's always someone out there that would be delighted to have a little baby to love and raise...just think about it."

Connie nodded, glancing out the window again. "I just wish …".her voice dropping to an almost inaudible pitch.

"What, Connie? What do you wish? You can tell me," Lorna prodded, wondering what in the world was so awful that Connie couldn't say it out loud.

Tears welled up in Connie's eyes, and in their blurry state, Connie could only shake her head slowly, as she wiped the tears from her eyes. For Connie knew what she wanted to say out loud, but could hardly wrap her brain around it herself.

I just wish he was in love with me, Connie thought to herself, as she closed her eyes and feigned a short nap for the rest of the drive to the airport.

"So, what's on your mind? What's so important that we gotta have a talk?" Monty asked, wiping his hands on an old cloth. "You said it was really important on the phone," Monty added, his eyes piercing through hers, making Connie feel like he could look into her soul if he so desired.

Connie looked around, casting furtive glances here and there, acting as though she wanted to make sure they were all alone.

"No one is here, if that's what you wanna know," Monty said, an eerie feeling passing through his stomach that he couldn't really put into words.

"Oh, and hey, so you just want me to replace the brake pads, change the oil, and basically just give it a tuneup?" Monty asked her, his eyes roaming all over her body.

"Um, yes, that's right," Connie nodded, feeling as though she was about to break into a cold sweat even though it was almost 90 degrees outside.

"So....how was your visit with your cousins? When did you get back?" Monty asked, making pleasant conversation and wondering when the hell Connie was going to just get to whatever the hell it was that she wanted to talk about.

"Oh, it was a lot of fun, just like always. I got back last week, actually," Connie felt herself starting to babble, as she desperately tried to get a grip on herself.

"Um, listen, Monty, besides setting up an appointment with you to work on my car, I need to talk to you about something," Connie told him, watching his eyes, and feeling like they were burning a hole in her skin.

"Okay, well, just talk Connie; not trying to be an asshole, but I ain't got all day to stand around and chat, you know?" Monty told her, standing dangerously close to her. She could smell his scent; a musky smell mixed with some of his perspiration from the heat. She imagined him holding her

close and kissing her...

"Connie? Earth to Connie," Monty teased, a small smile playing at the corners of his mouth.

"Oh, I'm sorry. It's just that this is so hard, Monty. I just don't know what you are going to say, or how you are going to react, or...

"Just say what you came to say, Connie; really, you're dancin' and swayin' around like you're a small child about to pee your pants," Monty told her, his voice laced with exasperation.

"It's just...I'm pregnant, Monty; I'm pregnant with your baby," Connie finished in a somewhat hushed tone.

Monty dropped the tools he was holding and stared hard at Connie. She couldn't even begin to imagine what was going through his mind, and the longer he stayed silent, the more nervous she was getting.

"Mine? How can it be mine? What kind of game are you trying to play here, Connie?" Monty asked, taking a couple steps closer to her.

"Dammit, Monty, don't act like it's all a big mystery to you," Connie told him, her voice starting to rise.

"Keep your voice down; we don't need everyone to know what's going on here," Monty muttered, looking around to make sure no one was close by.

"Monty, let's not dance around this, okay? I haven't slept with anyone since you, ...since you raped me," Connie finally spat out, surprising herself at how angry and assertive she was being.

"RAPED you? What the hell are you talking about? I never raped you, Connie; never," Monty told her, his voice shaking a little.

"Well, that night...in the shack....I fell asleep, and then I woke up a few hours later, and it was dark...and...there was a little bit of blood inside of me...and....I hurt...like I had been riding a horse all day," Connie finished, a huge part of her now totally relieved that all of this was finally out in the open, instead of locked up inside of her, the way it had been for the past two months.

"MAYBE you fell asleep because you were tired after all that good lovin' I gave ya," Monty said softly, standing right in front of her now, his warm breath on her face, his beautiful eyes, like green emeralds, boring into hers.

"I didn't rape you, Connie. You asked me to meet you there. Do you remember that?" Monty asked.

"Yeah, I remember. You brought me a coke; you're sure that you didn't put anything inside of it, or anything?" Connie asked him.

The look on Monty's face was almost impossible for her to read. He looked like he might be getting angry but yet...

"Seriously, Connie, are you stoned? You wanted me to meet you at the shack and you were very explicit about what you wanted. I showed up with your cold coke, we had some very hot sex, you fell asleep, and I went home," Monty told her, sounding like he was describing directions to an easy task.

"Really? All this time I just thought.....I mean, you have never liked me at all....like, I have always thought you totally hated me," Connie babbled.

"Like I really thought that you drugged me and then raped me because you hated me and wanted to get back at me for talking shit about you at school, so it just made sense to me that that's what happened," Connie said, her voice getting quieter as humiliation settled into her bones.

"No, Connie, that is NOT what happened. You asked me to meet you; you wanted us to have sex, Connie, and that's what we did. You were a very awake and willing partner, I assure you," Monty added, a small smile playing at his lips.

"So... now that I have answered your questions, perhaps you'll answer mine," Monty quipped, standing literally right on top of Connie now.

"Wha.. what do you want to know?" Connie stammered, starting to feel frightened and nervous all at the same time.

"Well, I guess I am wondering why you got pregnant anyways, I mean, I know that I surely was not your first by far," Monty smiled, enjoying the embarrassment that Connie was feeling at the moment.

"Um, yes, well, usually I have been on the pill and I have always made my...my....friends...wear condoms," Connie struggled, her face feeling hot and red with embarrassment.

"So....how do you know it's mine, then? Cuz, it could be a couple other people's too, right? Not tryin' to be heartless here, darlin', really, but I can't understand how you know it's mine," Monty said, speaking in a calm voice that he definitely wasn't feeling.

Connie stared at him for a moment, then seemed to snap out of her reverie, and began to dig in her purse. Pulling out what looked like a snapshot, she handed it to Monty, now.

Monty stared at the picture, then wordlessly handed it back to Connie.

He turned his back on her, and picked up the old rag he'd been wiping his hands with, although Connie noticed that one of his hands was shaking just a little.

"So ….this ultrasound was done yesterday? And they think you are about 7 weeks along, is that right?," Monty asked.

"Yes, that's right. Next time I go to the doctor, I will be able to hear the baby's heartbeat," Connie added, a bit of excitement in her voice.

Then Monty did something that totally blew Connie away. He walked over to her and drew her close to him, and hugged her. Connie reciprocated his hug, as Monty began to nuzzle her, and then he began to kiss her, slowly, at first, then with a kind of wild abandon that made Connie ache for him. Still kissing, they made their way to the office where there was a desk, a chair, and a small couch. Monty's dad had spent a few nights out here on this couch, working late and drinking even later. Now Monty eased Connie down on it, as they began to undress each other.

Moments later, they were getting dressed again, and Monty walked Connie out to her car. She couldn't get over this side of Monty; the tenderness and the passion that he'd just finished showing her. Surely, she thought to herself, I must have been very wrong about him. They chatted for a few minutes before Connie climbed into her car to leave.

"So you're not mad at me, then?" Connie asked Monty, searching his eyes worriedly, trying to make sure that she hadn't just imagined the last half hour or so.

"No, why would I be? It's not what I expected right now, but it's okay; we'll make it work," Monty told her, a gentle smile on his face.

"Well, I know you were going to Waylend Community College, in another month or so, and I don't want to disrupt your plans," Connie told him.

"Oh, don't worry, you won't disrupt any of my plans," Monty assured her, as he hugged her goodbye.

1988

Cathy lit the cigarette with shaking hands, as she slid into her car. At first puff, she almost threw the cigarette out the window; the taste of it made her feel almost sick to her stomach, all over again.

As she started down the dark county road, her thoughts turned once again to Roger, as she wondered where the hell he was, and why he had never come home. She just couldn't believe that he would leave that way, and not even bother to call or anything. As she drew on the cigarette, her cell phone began to ring impatiently, and Cathy struggled to locate it in her purse.

"Hello? Cathy? Is that you?" Remy Dodson asked, his voice almost crackling with electricity.

"Remy? Yeah, it's Cathy. What's going on, Remy? Is Roger with you?" Cathy rambled, her mind unable to stop its incessant whirling around.

"Cathy, yes, it's Remy here. Look, honey, I hate to have to be the one to tell you this...but I just wanted to let you know that we just took your husband to Jaxon Medical Center, over there on Jasper Ave. Now, don't worry, honey, I think that your man will be just fine, but it looks to me like he got himself beat up tonight," Remy finished, finally coming up for air.

"Oh my God," Cathy moaned into the phone, her fear starting to go into overdrive.

"Now, Cathy, why don't you see if you can't just get your sister, Kellie, to come on out here with you. I don't expect that you should be driving, the way you're feeling right now," Remy told Cathy, with his usual grandfatherly way.

Remy had known Cathy since she was in diapers, and he always had felt fiercely protective of the Grenaldi girls. He hated like hell having to tell Cathy that her husband was in the hospital, but he definitely wasn't going to tell her much more than that. No, he thought to himself, she should just get down here and then she would find out soon enough, he thought to himself with a sigh.

"No, Remy, I am almost into town. I decided to come look for Roger when he didn't come home tonight. Is he hurt badly? Is he going to be okay? Is he...

"Now, Cathy", the gentle giant Remy interrupted, "now, please, young lady, I need for you to be calm now. Roger's going to be just fine, now don't you worry yourself none," Remy told her.

"Okay, I should be there in about ten minutes," Cathy told him, then snapped her phone shut, and pressed down harder on the gas pedal. Speed limits be damned tonight, she thought to herself, as she raced into the night.

Cathy pulled into the first vacant spot that she could find, barely throwing the car in park, as she jumped out of the car and ran for the entrance. A paramedic stood outside smoking, killing time more than likely, and he gave her an appreciative smile. On any other night, Cathy would have taken notice of the attention, and given him her winning Miss America smile, as Roger used to always call it.

Roger. Poor, sweet, Roger, Cathy thought to herself, who the hell would beat Roger up? Roger wasn't exactly a small man, standing around 6'3" tall and weighing in right around 200 pounds. Aside from poker night, when he binged on cigars and beer, Roger was in top shape, and he'd always prided himself on weighing the same now as he had in high school. Cathy mentally went through a list of people in her mind, trying to figure out if any of them would have even a remote reason to beat up Roger, and she just couldn't think of anyone. No one at all, Cathy thought to herself, as she flew down the hallway towards the ER.

Remy saw her first, and stopped her from going right into the room, where they were just now finishing up with Roger. She'd only gotten a glance at his face, and that alone was enough to scare her half to death. One side of Roger's handsome, chiseled face, looked battered and bruised, and before she could give in to the hysteria that she was feeling, Dr. Steven Grant appeared right before her eyes.

"Hello, Cathy," Dr. Grant was saying. "It's good to see you; I wish I could have seen you under other circumstances, of course," he added.

Cathy was trying to force her mind to just focus, and she was having a hell of a time. She felt dizzy, and completely not herself right now, but more than anything, she felt so incredibly angry.

"Dr. Grant, do you think you would mind terribly if I took Cathy over to the cafeteria and got her some tea? I have to say, I am terribly worried about the poor girl," Remy was explaining to Dr. Grant.

"Of course, that's no problem at all. I will be here at least another hour or so. Tell you what; I will talk to you both after I finish my rounds for the shift," Dr. Grant said, already heading down to the elevators.

Gently but firmly, Remy tucked his arm under Cathy's elbow, and gently guided her down the hallway to the cafeteria. He ordered her to sit down and relax and he got her a cup of tea. He noticed Cathy's hands were shaking terribly. He wondered if she was just that shook up over what happened to Roger, or if something else was going on, as well.

"Cathy, are you alright, hon? Now, if there is anything at all bothering you, you know you can just sit here and talk to me about it, right? Anything at all, you know," Remy was saying.

And then suddenly Cathy was telling Remy all about Duncan; coming home and finding her beloved Duncan, gutted like game, bleeding out in his kennel run. She began to cry again as she told him about trying to keep how Duncan died quiet, but how she'd had to tell Roger, eventually. Very reluctantly, sure she'd incur some kind of loathing from Remy, she timidly told him about Monty Hallmen, about seeing him socially, and about breaking things off with him a week ago.

Remy was quiet for awhile. His eyes widened in surprise when she'd told him about Duncan, then narrowed again before they teared up a bit. Remy had always been an old softy, for as long as Cathy had known him. He was old school, but yet, he was probably one of the least judgmental people in this entire town, Cathy thought to herself. He didn't even look at me with disappointment or disgust, she thought to herself.

Finally, Remy began to speak. "Look, Cathy, I can't really go pick up Hallmen. I make an arrest like this just based on intuition or feeling, and it could all blow up in my face. But I am with you on this; like you, I can't for the life of me, figure out who else would possibly do this, first to Duncan, and then beat Roger to a pulp tonight. You and Roger have always been a part of this town, and everyone knows everyone, pretty much, and I can't figure anyone would have any kind of grudge against either one of you kids, quite frankly," Remy told Cathy, as he raked a hand through his thick, wavy hair.

Cathy sighed deeply; the sigh of a woman that is exhausted beyond her limits. She said nothing for a time, then spoke to Remy again.

"I appreciate you staying here tonight, waiting for me to get here," Cathy told Remy. "You have always been such a wonderful friend,"Cathy added.

"It's no trouble at all, Cathy; I wanted to make sure that you found Roger right away. They are probably done with him now, if you want to go see him," Remy added.

"Yes, I want to find Dr. Grant before he goes home to see exactly what Roger's condition is," Cathy told Remy, while her cell phone started to ring impatiently.

Walking over to the side of the hall, Cathy recognized her sister's number.

"Cathy? What the hell? Where are you? I wake up to use the bathroom, and you're gone. Are you okay? Where are you?," Kellie assaulted Cathy with constant questions.

Cathy sighed into the phone and told Kellie where she was and why. She asked Kellie if she could just stay at the house this morning, until the kids woke up, and after reassuring her that she would, Cathy thanked her and hung up.

Remy and Cathy walked into Roger's room, and Cathy had to suppress the gasp that almost flew right out of her mouth. Roger was sitting up in his bed, his face bruised badly on one side, his nose bandaged, and Cathy noticed that Roger must have broken some ribs, as well.

Dr. Grant was in there with Roger, writing things down on his chart, and asking Roger if he needed more pain medication.

His lips swollen as well, Roger didn't sound like himself when he spoke. Wincing as he turned his head slightly, Roger tried to give Cathy a smile.

"Hi, beautiful," Roger said softly, his eyes never leaving hers. "Sorry about all this," he added, turning his head away.

Carefully, taking Roger's good hand, she brought it to her mouth and kissed it. Though she'd tried so hard to be brave, tears now spilled down her face, and Cathy shook her head vehemently, as though willing the tears to just stop. She gazed into Roger's eyes, and saw a range of emotion that she'd not seen in a long time.

"Oh honey, you have nothing at all to feel sorry about, you poor baby. I am so sorry, Roger," Cathy whispered to him, her lips brushing his ever so lightly.

Roger was about to say something, and Cathy shook her head. "No, honey, don't try to talk right now. Dr. Grant gave you some heavy duty pain medication to help you sleep," Cathy told Roger, a fresh batch of tears now trailing down her face. Cathy tried in vain, to swipe at the tears and will them to stop, once again, but it seemed as though she was going to cry tonight whether she wanted to or not. This day had been an absolutely, horrible day. Looking back, Cathy decided it had been the absolute worst day in her life, and in her and Roger's married life, as well. How many people come home to find their precious pet gutted, basically, and then only a few hours later, their husband gets beaten to a pulp?

Dr. Grant came back into Roger's room, and after nodding to Cathy, asked her what questions she had that he could answer for her.

Her voice shaking a bit, Cathy asked Dr. Grant what the damages were. Dr. Grant looked at the bandaging on Roger's face, and told Cathy that it was a miracle that none of the bones in Roger's face had broken, besides his nose.

"Roger may need surgery down the line, but maybe not. Time will tell, as it always does," Dr. Grant told Cathy.

"He has two broken ribs, and one rib that is badly bruised, but managed not to break. How it stayed intact is nothing short of a miracle," Dr. Grant commented.

"Also, the fact that he isn't even more beat up than this, is a miracle. The police found a baseball bat right there at the scene by Roger's truck. They took the bat with them for evidence, but I have heard that they didn't find any prints on the bat," he added with a sigh.

"They DID say that there seemed to be some definite rage involved with this attack," Dr. Grant said.

Standing in the doorway of Roger's room, Dr. Grant asked Cathy if she had any other questions.

"I'd like Roger to stay all through the night tonight, if you don't mind too much, Cathy. He's been through a helluva ordeal, and I want to make sure he's okay before I send him home. Also, he's going to be having an MRI in a few minutes here, because I want to make sure there's nothing else going on that we are perhaps unaware of," Dr. Grant told her.

"Of course, I will keep you posted should anything new come up, and I will let you know what we find with the MRI, as well," Dr. Grant added, touching Cathy's arm in a gentle, reassuring way.

"Why don't you try to get some rest, Cathy? I won't ask you to go home, because I know you won't, anyways, so how about I have someone bring a cot in for you?," Dr. Grant asked.

"That would be so kind; yes, thank you so much, Doc," Cathy told him, and with a quick smile, Dr. Grant headed back down the hallway, and Cathy sank down on the chair that sat next to Roger's bed.

Just as Cathy was sinking into the overstuffed chair, Remy knocked politely at the door, and Cathy waved him in. Roger tried to smile, but that only seemed to cause a lot of pain, and Remy immediately waved it aside.

"Now don't try to be all hospitable, Roger; I know you got to be hurtin' pretty bad, there," Remy told Roger, who had finally just brought up the arm that didn't hurt too much.

"Thanks, Remy," Roger croaked, his voice raspy and his throat dry and raw.

" Did you find the guy who did this to me?" Roger managed, while Cathy poured some ice water into a glass for him. Putting the straw in, Cathy raised the glass up to Roger's lips, and he managed a couple of grateful sips.

"Well, now, Roger, that is the million dollar problem, I reckon," Remy said, shaking his head and looking over at Cathy.

"We got no witnesses, we got nothing. I dispatched an officer over to the Hallmen place, to ask Monty his whereabouts, so we'll see what comes outta that, but of course, we're going to do all we can," Remy explained slowly, as though he were talking to a small child.

"As it is, I gotta be real careful how I handle this investigation, as far as the way I question Hallmen, you know," Remy went on to explain. "I can't just barge over there like I own the place, and start hurling accusations around. These people been part of this town for quite some time, just like ya'll have, and well, they've been respected members of the community all these years too, so I gotta handle all this just right," Remy finished, his eyes darting from Cathy to Roger and back again.

"Sheriff," Cathy said slowly, emphasizing the word, "I seriously hope that you will remember the horrible events that have taken place the past several hours to both Roger and my whole family. I really feel that we are being harassed, and good upstanding citizens or not, re-election of the sheriff's seat or not, we need to know who is responsible for this," Cathy explained to Remy, as always, not pulling any punches whatsoever.

The sheriff smiled, and then his face broke out into a big grin, for the first time in the past few hours. He knew Cathy well, and she knew him just as well, too. He was never surprised to hear her speak her mind; she'd been doing just that since she was a little girl, for just as long as ol' Remy could remember.

He could remember her as a little girl, and she couldn't have been more than three years old. Like all the children in the county, her folks had brought her, as well as her sister Kellie, to the pavilion in town, where there was a children's Christmas party taking place. Each child got a chance to sit on Santa's lap and tell him what he or she would like for Christmas, as well as a dime store toy, a candy cane, and all the Christmas cookies and hot chocolate a kid could consume. The police department, as small as it was, always got together with the local firemen, and a lot of the business people in town. There was always a fantastic turnout for this yearly event, and most years, since as long as he could remember, Remy had been Santa Claus, mostly because he had the ideal body shape for the part, and Remy's laugh, when at all instigated, was a hearty bellow, more than anything else.

Some years, Remy's wife Janene, would dress up as Mrs. Claus, and she was more than happy to bustle around the place, handing out hot chocolate and cookies, as well as piping hot coffee for all the grownups. Those years that she'd played Mrs. Claus, Janene baked some absolutely heavenly pies for the grownups to kick back and enjoy, so they could visit with each other, while the kids played games and spent their time with Santa.

Remy and Janene had never been blessed with the patter of little feet, but it wasn't for lack of trying, Remy always had told everyone. But the years rolled by, and finally it became obvious that Remy and Janene would only be able to spoil other people's children, and not their own. Still, they both seemed to accept their lot in life, and were always more than happy to help out when it came to babysitting.

Janene and Remy had been together since they were both 15 years old. They'd been each other's first and only love. They married a week after they had graduated from Thomas Jefferson

High School, and they'd traveled all the way to Niagra Falls for their honeymoon.

A few weeks after Remy and Janene had celebrated their 19th anniversary, she'd complained of her joints aching terribly. Despite Remy begging her to make a doctor's appointment, Janene just kept putting it off, since she'd rarely ever go see the doctor. She had probably only gone to the doctor twice in her whole adult life.

One day, Remy had come home to find Janene curled up in a fetal position. Her face was wet from where the tears of anguish had fallen down her cheeks, and her whole body shook from the violent chills she was having. Remy piled her in the car and took her to the emergency room, where he learned his beloved wife's fate; she had cancer in her bones, and from what the doctors could see from all the tests that they'd ran, it had already gone up to her brain, too.

Remy could still remember crying in that waiting room, long after the doctor patted his hand and walked away. Finally, he stood up, and blew his nose loudly, trying to get himself together. Mentally, he knew this was tougher than anything he'd ever been up against, but he would spend every spare moment he had with Janene, since they'd given her a month to live, at the very most. The nurse had just adjusted her IV drip, and gave Remy a small smile on her way out.

Remy remembered sitting with Janene that afternoon, watching her sleep, watching her breathe, and being unable to wrap his brain around the agonizing twists and turns his life had taken.

Two and a half weeks later, Janene lost her fight. She'd just given up, basically, as far as Remy had been able to tell. She'd sat up straighter in her bed that morning, and they'd had a nice lunch together. Afterwards, they'd played several games of cards, and then Janene had gotten tired, and told Remy it was time for her nap. She'd gazed into Remy's eyes for a much longer time than usual, and after giving Remy a big hug and an extra kiss, she told him she'd always love him and asked if he would hold her hand, until she fell asleep.

Remy had done just that, but it had not taken Janene long at all to fall asleep, so Remy had tiptoed out of their bedroom, and had gone to the market to pick up a few things for dinner. Not a half hour later, he was back home, putting stuff away, and he decided to check on his wife. Bending over to kiss her soft lips, Remy thought they seemed a bit cold. He watched for the rise and fall of her chest and never saw it, and then he checked for a pulse, and there was none. Frantically, Remy called 911, even as he'd already started CPR, but it was too late. Moments later, Jack Edmunds, Remy's best friend, and one of the paramedics on the scene, gently took Remy away from Janene, telling him that she was gone.

That following Christmas, unable to sit home and feel the emptiness in his bones, Remy couldn't even bring himself to put up the Christmas tree. His friend Jack had suggested that Remy keep up with his usual Christmas traditions. Remy had instantly rejected that idea, until Jack had reminded him that that was what Janene would have wanted him to do. Thinking about it later, while he was at home that evening, watching a mindless sitcom, Remy had to admit that Jack was right. He'd be Santa Claus this year, after all, he thought to himself.

After he'd made that decision, Remy almost felt lighter, and sometimes he swore that he smelled the perfume that Janene loved to wear. After he got off the phone with Jack, making plans for the annual Christmas party, he definitely caught a whiff of Chanel No. 5, and he had to smile.

At the Christmas party that year, Cathy Grenaldi had climbed up on Remy's lap, and Remy asked her what her name was. Cathy told him, and then she asked him what his name was. Remy had laughed out loud, and had told Cathy that he was Santa Claus, of course, to which Cathy shook her head firmly and said, " No, you're not Santa; you're Remy," and Remy had laughed out loud again.

The memories had taken him back, as he looked into Cathy's eyes now, and for just a moment, he saw that headstrong, toe-headed girl with the big grin, beaming up at him.

"Don't you worry, none, Cathy, I will make sure I ask Hallmen all the right questions," Remy said, patting her on the shoulder as he walked out of Roger's room.

1979

Connie Watkins fanned herself, as she waited for Monty to finish up. He had a couple of impatient farmers coming over to drop off their tractors for his dad to repair, so Monty had wanted Connie to pick up her car as soon as possible.

"Okay, you're all set," Monty announced, slamming the hood of her car shut..."I didn't run into anything major, so I will just charge you for parts," Monty added, wiping his hands on an old rag.

He sauntered over to the wash basin, as Connie rummaged through her purse, looking for her wallet.

"So how much do you need?" Connie asked, a mixed wad of bills in her hands.

"What you have in your hands should cover it," Monty said, looking at her, a serious look on his face. The fright on her face was hilarious, and Monty began to laugh.

"Oh my gosh, were you just kidding?" Connie asked, a nervous laugh coming out of her mouth.

"Yeah, Connie, I was just kidding," Monty told her, shaking his head, and rinsing the soap off of his hands. He grabbed a fresh towel, and wiped his hands off, then threw the towel at Connie playfully.

"Seriously, I think $50 dollars will cover it all," Monty told her, wiping a stray hair out of his eyes.

"Are you sure?" Connie asked him incredulously. "That doesn't seem fair to you after all the work you just did," Connie added.

"It's fine. Besides, you are going to have to save your money for other things now, like our baby," Monty told her, putting his hand on her stomach. While it was still flat, Connie knew that soon she was going to start to show, and she'd still not told her parents yet.

"You still haven't told your folks, have you, Connie?" Monty asked her, his face now serious.

"Yeah, I know, I know. It's just so hard. For one thing, they are rarely home, and when they are, they aren't usually home together at the same time. And I really don't want to have to go through the speech twice, so I have been trying to time it when they are both at home. They are supposed to be home, both of them, this coming weekend, believe it or not," Connie informed Monty.

"Well, it looks like you have five days to get your speech ready, then," Monty told her. "Maybe it won't be as bad as you think it will be," he added.

"Oh no, it will probably be worse. My parents are total snobs, and very self-righteous in their own right. They still don't even know I have this tattoo," Connie laughed, pointing to the butterfly encircling her belly button.

"Well, it's not like it's a spot that they would always see anyways, since you manage to keep that covered up so well," Monty teased.

"You know; I was thinking....maybe we should get married," Monty told Connie, drawing her into his arms now. "What do you think of that; your self-righteous parents won't be able to complain nearly as much then," Monty told her, a smile crossing his face.

Connie looked up at Monty, a happy but shocked look on her face.

"Are you serious? Or are you just teasing me, Monty Hallmen?" Connie demanded.

Monty gave Connie a tender smile. "Of course I'm serious," he told her. "Do you really think I would joke around about that?" he added.

"No, I guess not, but what about college? What about all the plans you had to go to college and move out of here?" Connie asked him softly, her head down, her eyes averted away from him.

Taking her gently by the shoulders, Monty lifted her chin up until their eyes met.

"There's nothing saying that those plans can't still happen; it will just take me a little more time to get that degree, that's all," Monty assured her.

"Oh, Monty; you've made me so happy," Connie gushed, throwing her arms around Monty's neck, as a smile spread across Monty's face.

Connie smiled happily as she waved one last time to Monty. Driving into town, she decided that a double chocolate shake was in order. She felt like celebrating, and nothing could burst her bubble now, she thought with a smile.

Slowing down at the next intersection, she silently cursed her luck to hit all the red lights. The heat index was almost 100 degrees today, the weatherman gleefully informed anyone who cared.

Pumping the brakes, Connie was a bit concerned that they didn't catch as quickly as she thought that they should. Normally when she'd get the brakes worked on, you could hardly step on them, before you just about threw yourself through the windshield. Now it seemed that Connie had to pump them a bit. She'd have to call Monty about it when she got back home, she decided to herself.

After devouring the sinfully delicious treat, Connie felt bloated. I'm just about ready for a nap, she thought ruefully. Good thing I am not home right now, or I'd be crashed on the couch, she thought with a smile.

While an afternoon nap sounded perfect, she knew that she'd promised Mrs. Gordon that she'd head over to her house this afternoon.

Connie always had a few odd jobs in the summer, for the past three years. She cleaned houses, babysat, and took dogs for walks or checked in on them at various times of the day, usually because their owners were either working long hours, or on vacation for a few days.

Last summer, Connie had ended up house sitting for Mrs. Gordon, since the lively 65 year old woman enjoyed traveling immensely in the summer.

Mrs. Gordon had had a list of people that she'd wanted to see last summer, and while she'd spend a few days here and there with friends that had moved to warmer climates, she would spend two weeks every summer with her grandchildren.

Widowed at 56, Mrs. Gordon had a lot of spunk and life left in her, and she wasn't one to sit still for very long, Connie mused, smiling as she thought of the older woman.

Her twin sons, Eric and Josh, had just graduated from college with business degrees when their father had suddenly passed away. While Josh stayed in the area, Eric had always wanted to live somewhere else.

His girlfriend of almost two years, Maria Garvelli, was from the New England area, and she'd been overjoyed when Eric decided to accompany her to Cape Cod for two weeks, where her family had vacationed for the past several years every summer.

Eric enjoyed his time in the Cape immensely, and knew from almost the first couple days he was out there, that he could be happy living there. So it was a huge godsend when Maria's father Joseph, immediately took a strong liking to Eric and invited him to join him at the marketing firm that he was Vice President of. Eric had happily accepted, and a month later, after receiving a blessing from Joseph, Eric asked Maria to marry him, and she'd happily accepted.

Eric had flown his mother out to the Cape for a long weekend, for his and Maria's engagement party, and the families had a wonderful time together. Josh had accompanied his mother as well, and Eric couldn't have been happier to have his whole family together.

Soon after they'd been married for a little over a year, Maria gave birth to a baby boy, Sherman Joseph, after both grandfathers, and two years after that, Amanda Victoria was born.

Mrs. Gordon was only too happy to spend time with all of them, and relished her role as a grandma.

Connie loved hearing Mrs. Gordon talk about her children and their families. They all struck Connie as really nice people, and Connie always felt a little pang of jealousy when she would think about the fun they seemed to all have with each other, since she could never picture that happening with her parents.

It wasn't that Connie's parents were dumb, mean, or hateful; far from it, since they'd both gone to college and then medical school. They spent many hours a month donating their time to charities that they felt were very important. They were very well versed in so many areas of life, but it always had seemed to Connie, that maybe she'd been an accident, since she'd never had any siblings.

She remembered asking her mother that very question once, when she was about eight or nine years old. Her mother had gone practically ashen, and had demanded to know why in the world Connie would ask such a question.

Connie had heard one of her friends at school talking about how her mom and dad were going to have a baby. Her friend was not too happy about it, either, considering that she'd always been the baby herself, and she'd always heard her parents refer to her that way. Her mother had been on the telephone with a friend, and had referred to the coming baby as an accident.

When Connie heard that, she was certain that she'd been an accident, too. While her parents had always been good to her, and she'd never lacked for anything in her whole life, Connie hadn't fallen into that only child/ spoiled child syndrome whatsoever, because her parents had been adamant that they would not have a child who acted boorish and spoiled.

For Connie, all she knew was that she had never felt especially close to her parents, because for some reason, she always felt as though she was an inconvenience for them, more than anything, especially when she was little. They'd never said anything to Connie, of course; her parents were not the sort of people that would openly admit that to anyone, even if their lives depended on it. Still, Connie knew deep down that her parents loved her, and she loved them as well. They'd always told her they were proud of her, too, but now Connie worried that they would never be proud of her again.

Determined not to let anything get her down, today, Connie wiped away the one lone tear that had trickled down her face. She was almost to Mrs. Gordon's house, where she would spend the next couple days cleaning her home and getting it in tip top shape for her return this coming weekend.

Connie just about passed up the driveway, and had had to pump on the brakes a few times to get the car to stop.

I have GOT to call Monty and ask him about these darn brakes, she thought, as she climbed out of her car, and let herself into the house.

1988

Monty was just finishing his breakfast, when he heard the car coming. Wiping his hands on a towel, he peered out the window, just in time to see Remy getting out of his cruiser.

Before he could knock on the door, Monty was already there, holding it open for him.

Hey, Remy," Monty said. "What brings you out so early in the morning? Can I get you a cup of coffee or something," he added, glancing at Remy as he sat down at the kitchen table.

"Thanks, but no, I am flyin' on caffeine today. Been up since about 2:30 this morning, and haven't been back to bed since," Remy said with yawn.

"What happened to get you up so early?" Monty wanted to know.

"Well, now, that's part of why I came over here so early in the morning," Remy told him. " I hate to do this, but I need to know where you were last night and in the wee hours of this morning," Remy said, his gaze steady.

"Me? Well, I was out with Jack Higgins till about midnight, I suppose," Monty said thoughtfully, stroking the stubbles on his chin as he considered the question. "Why do you ask; did something happen last night? What's all this about?" Monty asked, sitting down across from Remy.

"Well, now can Jack verify that time line if I go ask him about this?" Remy asked.

"Sure, that's no problem at all," Monty told him. "I know I wasn't out too awfully late, because I needed to get an early start today," Monty added.

"Did your folks hear you come in, by chance?" Remy wanted to know.

"I doubt it; I sure didn't hear or see either one of them," Monty replied. "Besides, they are in bed by ten every night, like clock work, especially ever since my mom got sick last year," Monty told Remy. "She don't hear nothing' after she takes her medicine and goes to sleep every night. My dad snores so damned loud, that I don't think he hears much of anything over all that noise, either, " Monty laughed

"Hmmm, okay. I really hated to have to come over here and ask you all these things, but I had to check it out," Remy said thoughtfully. "Of course, I'll still have to talk to Jack," he added, almost apologetically. "Well, how about yesterday afternoon; where were you then?" Remy asked

"That's cool; I understand you're just doing your job, but what exactly happened?" Monty asked patiently, his eyes boring into Remy's.

"Oh, well, I guess I never did tell you about it, now did I?" Remy said with a rueful smile. You know Roger and Cathy Hammond, right? Well, some really bad stuff has happened to them in the past several hours, and I just have to check it all out," Remy said, squirming in his seat.

Monty didn't answer him but just continued to stare at at Remy, until finally, the older man said," Look, I know you and Cathy are involved."

"Involved with what?" Monty asked. "You know very well what I mean, Monty Hallmen," Remy retorted, his voice bristling.

"You and Cathy are having an affair; everybody in town knows it," Remy told him. "You gonna deny it?" Remy asked, leaning forward in his chair.

"Technically, we WERE having an affair, but that is no longer the case; it's been over for over a week, " Monty informed Remy.
"She told me to give her some space, cuz she needed to figure out what she wanted to do with her life, and she's got the kids too, and she didn't want them finding out about us, either," Monty added, looking Remy squarely in the eyes.

"Yes, she DID mention that ya'll had broken things off," Remy admitted. "Are you good with that, or are ya angry with her at all?" Remy asked, his eyes never leaving Monty's.

Monty leaned into the table and took a big swig of his coffee. "Look, I never seen it comin', but she explained why she needed some time, and I gave it to her. I'm not mad or nothin'; a little hurt, maybe, but that's it," Monty insisted.

"So what happened, anyways?" Monty asked. "Well, it seems as though someone went over to their home yesterday afternoon and pretty much gutted their great dane. He died soon after Cathy got home and found him," Remy said, shaking his head sadly.

Before Monty could say anything, Remy began to talk again. "Also, someone beat the hell out of Roger last night. Or I should say this morning, around 2am," Remy added, his eyes narrowing.

They both just looked at each other for a few seconds, and then Monty got up from the table and rinsed out his cup. Turning back around and facing Remy, he said," So ….you come over here to see if I killed their dog? Or beat up Roger? I don't even know Roger, except I know who he is, and that's it," Monty told Remy. "But is that why you're here? You think I did either one of those things? Or, wait, maybe you think I did both of them? Is that what all of this is about?" Monty asked, his eyes narrowing a bit as he stared into Remy's eyes.

Remy sighed deeply, and then pushed the chair in as he rose to go. "You know, sometimes I gotta ask people questions that I don't wanna have to ask, but that IS my job," Remy told Monty, another tired sigh escaping.

Monty shook his head sadly. "Yeah, I know, Remy, you're just doin' your job. But I don't even know where they live. And I would never hurt an innocent animal, and I would have absolutely no reason at all to hurt her husband either. Like I said, I don't even really know that guy," Monty said.

"Okay, Monty, well, again, I apologize for having to come out here and disrupt your morning, but I just wanted to check it all out," Remy assured Monty.

"Oh, hey, how is Roger doing, anyway; you never mentioned that?" Monty asked.

"Well, he's pretty banged up, that's for sure, but he'll be alright; he's just gonna be sore for awhile," Remy told him.

Monty walked Remy to the door, and said," Well, I'm glad he's going to be okay. That sounds crazy what's been happening to them," he added, shaking his head in disgust. "I really don't even know who would do something like that, either," Monty said, looking completely mystified.

"Yeah, it's the damnedest thing, for sure," Remy agreed. Bidding Monty a good day, and thanking him again for his trouble, Remy piled back into the cruiser, and took off.

1979

Connie glanced around, making sure that everything looked perfect. She wanted the place to look exactly like Mrs. Gordon had left it, but better. The house smelled fresh and clean, and with a satisfied smile, Connie locked the door, and pulled it shut behind her.

Unlocking her car, she looked up at the dark rain clouds that seemed to loom directly above her. They looked ominous, as though at any moment, rain would start gushing out of them.

Connie sighed as she climbed into her car. She was beat; she normally didn't do as much heavy house cleaning as she'd done here for the past couple of days, but Mrs. Gordon always paid Connie very generously, and Connie knew that she wasn't supposed to be doing those kinds of things anymore, anyways.

Her back was a bit of a mess, but that never seemed to stop her, Connie thought with a laugh. Her boys had finally gotten it through her head that she didn't EVER need to go on top of the roof again. She laughed as she remembered Mrs. Gordon telling her the story of her son Josh dropping over unannounced, seeing Mrs. Gordon on top of the roof, trying to get all of the leaves off, and completely oblivious to everyone's shouts of concerns.

To keep the peace, Mrs. Gordon promised her sons that she would never get on top of the roof again, but, she told Connie with a wink, I never promised I wouldn't climb the ladder to clean out the eaves.

Connie had laughed and told Mrs. Gordon that she really shouldn't be doing that either, and Mrs. Gordon had asked her if she would tell on her. No, I wouldn't do that, Connie had assured her, giving her a big hug.

With a big yawn, Connie began the long trip back home. Not five minutes into her journey, it began to pour, and Connie was tempted a few times, to pull off to the side of the road until the rain either passed, or slowed down immensely. Many cars were already pulled off to the side of the road, and the people that were still driving, were only doing about 30 miles an hour.

Feeling beyond tired, Connie wished she didn't have so far to drive. I COULD just turn around and go back to Mrs. Gordon's and then leave later this afternoon, Connie thought to herself. But no, she thought, I promised my parents I would polish the furniture in the living room before they came back home, so I really need to get going.

Finally, after almost 20 minutes of white knuckles on the steering wheel, the rain seemed as though it were slowing down. Connie could see up ahead that it almost looked as though it would be clearing up soon. She decided that she was too exhausted to keep driving this turtle's pace, and made a split second decision to turn off onto the highway, where she could go faster.

A policeman sat at the first exit, apparently waiting for someone he could pull over for speeding. Connie kept it to only 5 miles over the speed limit; she was in a hurry to get back home, but she didn't need to spend her very hard earned cash on a ticket.

Driving along, she turned on the radio to try to keep herself alert. This was one thing about the pregnancy that Connie didn't really like; she was so tired all the time, but she knew that it was very normal.

She'd forgotten to call Monty about the brakes, she chided herself, after she'd stepped on them a few times, and was reminded that they didn't seem to be grabbing well at all. I've GOT to remember to do it as soon as I get home, Connie told herself.

Singing along to the radio, the time went by quickly, and Connie was happy to see Cougar's Crossing coming up. She remembered that she'd always been frightened whenever she'd rode with her parents as a child, whenever they'd had to go up the tall mountain.

Her dad had decided to try to make a game of it, and told her to think of it as a fun roller coaster at the amusement park. Although Connie was scared of heights, she'd never been able to say no to a roller coaster. Her father had decided to use her love for roller coasters to their advantage, and showed her that there was nothing at all to be afraid of. Because the hill was so high, looking down could be frightening as well, but for whatever reason, Connie wasn't too afraid of being all the way up at the top of that hill.

Connie was feeling nostalgic, thinking about how simple everything seemed when she was a child, and how nothing seemed that simple now. She suddenly rolled her eyes at herself, thinking of how she almost sounded like her parents. I better not start saying "in my day," Connie thought to herself.

When she'd began learning to drive, she usually went out with her dad, instead of her mom. Her mom always begged off, and said that her nerves were bad, and that she didn't think she would be an easy person to learn from. The list went on and on when it came to the excuses, but Connie didn't care. She preferred riding with her dad anyways, since she'd only rode with her mother once, and they both had come back a nervous wreck. Her dad had also showed her how to handle the car when it was time to go down the huge hill.

Lost in thought now, Connie prepared to head down the hill, and noticed that the pavement was really wet. They must have gotten a lot more rain here, Connie mused.

She began lightly tapping the brakes as she started descending the hill, but again, it seemed that the brakes just didn't want to grab. Feeling irritated, but not at all frightened, Connie pumped the brakes again and again, thinking it would just take a few tries to get things going. She chided herself for not remembering to call Monty when she'd gotten to Mrs. Gordon's.

Tapping again and again, Connie began to feel panic well up inside her, as she began to stomp on the brakes now. Faster and faster the car went, and to her alarm, Connie noted that she was now going about 50 miles an hour. Since there was roadwork being done a bit past the end of the bridge, Connie was frantically trying to stop, because the road got real narrow, and there was a big drop-off to the side. Connie's heart was beating so fast now, that she could hardly breathe. No matter how she stomped on the brakes, she wasn't slowing down; rather, she was picking up more and more speed. At the last minute, she tried to use the emergency brake, hoping against hope that she would be able to stop, but instead, her car's tires hit a large oil slick on the ground, and before Connie knew it, the car slid off the road, and bounced down the embankment, rolling three times before it finally came to a stop.

1998

Sheila Hardesty sat primly in the front row, shifting her weight every now and then, and silently cursing herself for her ridiculous, lifelong habit of showing up everywhere a half hour early.

As more people began to file in the small room, Sheila fought off the urge to leap out of her seat and run out the door.

Having suffered most of her life from claustrophobia, this small, dank room that smelled like an NFL locker room after a game was giving Sheila the creeps. If any of her family members had cared at all about her, Sheila sniffed, she would have had some support, and wouldn't be sitting here all alone, contemplating getting out the brown paper sack that was stuffed in her purse, in the event that she'd start to hyperventilate.

Her bitch of a sister Debbie had the audacity to laugh hysterically into the telephone when Sheila had meekly called her last week and asked her if she would make a ten hour drive down here to be with her big sister, and hold her hand during this long and traumatic ordeal. It took a good two minutes,if not more, for that nasty girl to stop laughing, and, Sheila mused to herself, if THAT wasn't bad enough, then she had to listen to her explain to her that if she really was that nervous about being there at the hearing, and thought she needed someone that badly, that should send off some warning bells in that head of hers. That girl is entirely too smug, Sheila thought to herself. Just because she has a husband and a family, and..

Sheila snapped her head in the direction of the other door, when Monty was led in, shackled and handcuffed. Sheila thought how terribly inhumane and rude that was to treat someone like Monty so badly. Her thoughts turned back to her sister, Debbie, again briefly, as she could almost predict the incredulous reply that the little loud, know-it-all would make. She'd say something like,"Sheila, it's not a damned country club" or "My

God, Sheila, what the hell is wrong with you; he's in prison, not a five star hotel" and other shitty, smartypants comments, Sheila sighed to herself.

All the good it had done for me to listen to Doris, Sheila thought to herself.

"Please, please, fill out the paperwork, and send it in, Sheila, I need to find Debbie," Sheila silently mimicked her idiot mother. So being the good and dutiful daughter that she'd always been all her life, Sheila filled out the information and got the adoption search process under way.

Doris questioned Sheila at least three times a week, asking her if she was absolutely sure that she'd filled out the forms properly, or asking if she'd heard anything just yet.

Debbie was the baby in the family that Doris had given up for adoption when Debbie was 15 months old. Debbie had been happy to find Doris and Sheila at first, calling Doris regularly and the two had become fast friends. Sheila however, seemed to have trouble with relationships in general. She'd had maybe two friends her whole life, and her and her mother Doris had always had a rocky relationship. Sheila remembered telling Debbie once that at least once a week, her and Doris would have a huge fight.

A big part of the reason that Sheila could never make and keep friends, was because she had absolutely no concept of how it was to share your life with anyone. She was a compulsive liar, and only seemed to be remotely fond of people that she could manipulate. Having found out early on that Debbie was not going to allow herself to be manipulated or used as a pawn in the calculating, devious mind of Sheila Hardesty, Debbie was talking to Sheila less and less all the time.

Sheila thought about the fight she had with her mother last night. She had gone over there to ask Doris if she had some money that she could borrow, and Doris had sighed loudly.

"Sheila, why do you always need to take the little bit of money I get every month? I have only twenty two dollars for the next three weeks," Doris explained to Sheila.

"You must learn to be wiser with your money, Sheila," Doris added, shaking her head sadly.

"That has nothing to do with anything," Sheila snapped, taking the $20 out of her mother's wallet, then flinging it back to her.

"Besides, you don't need anything, anyway," Sheila told her, beginning to relax a little and simmer down.

"How do you know what I need?" Doris had demanded. "Are you some kind of a psychic now, with special powers to look inside my head and see what I am thinking?" Doris added, trying to lift herself up off of her chair.

Sheila sighed loudly. "What are you doing now, mother?" Sheila wanted to know. "Why are you getting up now?" Sheila sighed again.

Doris gave Sheila a look, and slowly stood straight up. "Well, if you really must know, I need to use the restroom; is that okay with you?" Doris asked her sarcastically.

Sheila watched the old woman begin her walk down the hallway. "I swear, you get more and more like Debbie everyday," Sheila said, watching Doris shake her head in disgust.

"Oh my goodness, Sheila, leave that poor girl alone," Doris told her. "If you don't like her, then just leave her alone," Doris intoned, making her way into the bathroom.

"Well, you should both be VERY afraid," Sheila began with her daily lecture. "Neither one of you are going to be going to heaven, I'm afraid," Sheila added, shaking her head sadly.

Continuing right on, Doris had really hoped to drown the whiny voice out, by shutting the door behind her, but, as luck would have it, Sheila merely came down the hallway, apparently standing in front of the bathroom door, while she delivered today's sermon.

"The way the two of you talk, you both have those loud, boisterous voices; neither one of you talk as a lady should. And the language; I'm afraid you both could make a sailor blush," Sheila continued.

"Well, at least you can hear us when we speak. We don't put a show on for the world; we're content to just be ourselves, and people don't have to keep asking, "what did you say" whenever we're talking to someone," Doris told her, making her way back down the hallway now.

"Well, I speak like a lady. I talk softly, the way a lady is supposed to talk. It's just too bad that the both of you have to use such horrible language all the time," Sheila said, picking her coat up and getting ready to leave.

"When are you going to get me some groceries, Sheila?" Doris asked. "All I have to eat in this house is yogurt, bread, and a quart of milk," she added.

"Well, I just don't have time to mess around with you right now," Sheila told her mother. "I'll try to get to the store either tomorrow or the next day," she said, walking through the rest of the house, and looking at all her mother's belongings.

"And why is that old teapot not where it usually is?" Sheila asked. "You're not supposed to be moving things around," Sheila explained, talking to her mother as though she were a complete imbecile.

"I was USING it," Doris admonished. "What business is it of yours, anyways? These are all my things, and a lot of them are things I have had since before you came along," Doris said, rubbing her painful hands.

Sighing once more, Sheila stood now in front of Doris, hands on hips. "Really? Why in the world were you using that; you're as blind as a bat; you can't see a thing. You shouldn't be using the stove or anything else," Sheila explained, ignoring the irritated looks that her mother was giving her.

"How am I supposed to feed myself, then? Would you have me wait until you decide to show up? It's not like you ever offer to help me or do anything for me," Doris told her. "I'd starve to death, sitting here waiting for you to come over and fix me a meal," Doris added.

"Yes, well, there's just one more reason right there why you'll never make it to heaven; you're just too nasty and too bad of a person who's made too many mistakes," Sheila informed her, picking up her purse and walking over to the door.

Launching into her daily tirade with Doris, Sheila said," Your precious Debbie was conceived in sin, with a married man. No, I'm afraid you've made way too many mistakes, mother dear," Sheila taunted, pretending to be sympathetic and concerned.

"I'll see you later, mother," Sheila called out to Doris, who sat in her rocking chair, wishing she could just rock her troubles away.

Thanks for the warning, Doris muttered to the darkness, as she began to feel her way to the kitchen to make some tea.

Now Sheila was blowing kisses at Monty as he looked over her way, and Sheila suddenly felt angry eyes glaring at her.

A tall, blond woman who was clearly wearing too much makeup, Sheila thought to herself, was giving her some really dirty looks. At first, Sheila had turned around to see if perhaps, the person behind her was the object of disgust, but no, there was no one sitting behind her.

Sheila tried to smile at the woman, but there was no smile coming her way. Sheila shrugged, and slumped down a bit in her chair. She looked over again at Monty, feeling pity for him.

Now, Monty stood up to talk, and he began to tell everyone why he had ending up at Vesting County minimum security prison. Sheila felt so much sympathy for Monty, as he proceeded to tell everyone that he made a terrible mistake that day; one that he certainly had regretted everyday of his life. He also offered an explanation of why he was just so sure that there was no way it could ever happen again.

Sheila looked over at the blond woman now, who's features were contorted in an almost painful shape.

The blond woman was now speaking in hushed tones to the tall Neanderthal of a man sitting next to her. They spoke in hushed tones, one or the other of them nodding their heads on occasion. At one point during their conversation, the Neanderthal jerked his head up and looked straight at Sheila, his expression full of sorrow and bewilderment.

Not understanding in the least why two perfect strangers would treat her this way, Sheila busied herself by pretending to rummage through her purse, as Monty continued to talk.

He spoke to everyone about the rage that used to course through him on occasion, and how alcohol worsened that to an almost maniacal state.

At this point, someone on the board interrupted Monty, and asked him why there was never any mention of alcohol in his bloodstream on the night of the murder.

Looking chastened and a bit chagrined, as this part of the story called for, Monty hung his head and said that he'd not been the least bit drunk that night, but he HAD been drinking. He talked about the depression that had begun to take over his entire life, painting a sad tale for anyone who would take the least bit of interest in it.

The man who had questioned Monty about the alcohol didn't appear completely satisfied with Monty's tale of woe, but after staring at him for a few seconds, wrote something down in the notepad he kept, and said nothing.

The blond stood up now, and pointed out that her sister's murder had gone down on record as one of the most brutal and heinous murders in the state. She told the board that her sister's death had devastated her, but it was mostly the WAY she'd been killed. Sheila's eyes had grown wide as the blond talked about her sister having been stabbed twice in the heart and then thrown in a field, left to die. As tears ran helplessly down her face, she talked about her sister's two children who had had to adjust to a life without their mother, when they'd needed her so much as teenagers back then. She told the board that there was no way she'd ever believe that this violent man had changed, and no guarantee that he wouldn't do this again to someone else.

She reminded the board of how close Monty had come to being sentenced to death for what he'd done to her sister, and how he'd only now served 10 years of the 40 that he'd been sentenced. Finally, she begged the board to think of her sister; to remember the kind, beautiful person that she'd always been. The girl who had a smile for everyone, and never hesitated to help someone in need. A beautiful girl that was well loved by everyone that knew her; a girl that had never had an enemy in her life, until she'd had the misfortune of meeting up with Lamont Hallmen. She talked of how this horrific crime had ripped a family apart, starting with her sister's husband

who now drank much more heavily than he'd ever done in the past. How his father had passed away last year from the stress and pain of losing his daughter-in-law, and how her mother had had two strokes now, since her daughter's murder. Dabbing her eyes yet again, she thanked everyone for their time, and sat down.

Sheila felt badly for Monty; he'd just sat there in his seat with his head down low, the whole time that woman had been talking. Sheila could understand that it had been terrible for her and her family, but my gosh, Sheila thought to herself, it had been a long time ago. Staring at her again, Sheila shook her head and wondered about people like that woman who couldn't just forgive and forget, especially after all this time. Sheila had also watched the eyes and faces of all the officials on the board, and saw that they were listening intently, and with very sympathetic faces. Out of the five people sitting there, three of them were women, and they just didn't look like they were feeling any sympathy at all for Monty. Indeed, when he'd stood up and talked to them, there almost seemed to be a sardonic air about them, like they didn't for one second believe that he'd changed or that he ever would change.

Sheila found herself getting angry, and once again, thought about her sister Debbie. Angrily, she told herself that this was Debbie's kind of crowd, right here. These people all sitting here all smug, judging poor Monty, when, as far as Sheila was concerned, he'd already paid for his crime. She really just wanted these people to see that; she felt very confident that he would never do anything at all like this, and it sickened and upset her that no one else seemed to see it.

The prison psychiatrist was talking now, and he was explaining to everyone what he felt had happened to Monty on the night of the murder. He explained in detail, how he felt that the horrible depression that Monty had been suffering from for months, had finally triggered the unfortunate events. He explained to everyone, that aside from the depression that Monty still took medicine for everyday, he'd also been diagnosed with ODD, or Oppositional Defiant Disorder.

Giving everyone a couple examples of the meaning of ODD, the psychiatrist quickly brought his report to a conclusion. When asked if he felt like Monty was better, and how certain he was that Monty would never ever do something like that again, the psychiatrist informed everyone that he believed that Monty was much better now. When pressed further about whether

Monty was capable of committing any more brutalities against the human race, the psychiatrist shrugged his shoulders. He really didn't think so, but he emphasized the fact that he didn't have a crystal ball, either. Sheila snickered, forgetting for a moment where she was, and the blond woman turned and gave her a look.

Suddenly, it was all over. The board informed everyone that it could take a month for them to decide about Monty's parole and that they also had a couple other statements to read that had been sent in to them in a petition.

Monty stood up then, and allowed himself to be led out of the room. He never even looked at Sheila again, but she didn't think it had anything at all to do with her. She felt so bad again for Monty; he must be so embarrassed, she thought to herself.

As Sheila was walking out of the building, she felt the blond woman's stare on her back. Scurrying to the parking lot, Sheila was never so relieved to slip inside her car and start the engine. Slipping her seatbelt on, she began to back out, and almost jumped out of her skin when the blond woman rapped on her window.

Staring at her, Sheila put the car in park and rolled the window down. "Yes?" she asked timidly. There was something about this woman, Sheila thought to herself. She tried to smile at the woman, but the woman was not there to make a new friend.

In a firm voice, she uttered only one small sentence to Sheila, then turned on her heel and caught up with the Neanderthal.

Sheila repeated the comment out loud, feeling a chill come over her, even though it was a fairly warm day today.

If you value your life, you need to get away from this man, now, before it's too late.

Putting her car back in gear, Sheila never even noticed how bad her hands were shaking, as she mulled over this and headed for home.

1979

"Hello, 911, what is your emergency, please?" came the crisp, all business voice.

"Oh my God, you gotta get a ambulance out here real quick," 14 year old Davis Clark yelled into the pay phone right outside of the gas station.

"Okay, sir, you are going to have to calm down for me now," Rachel Gibson informed the caller.

"Okay, now I need for you to tell me exactly what happened, sir," Rachel continued, trying to take down some information.

"Um, okay, well, there's a car down here in the ravine, and it looks like someone is trapped inside of it," the nervous kid continued.

"Okay, son, can you tell me your name? And, how old are you?" Rachel continued to question him. Angrily, Davis yelled," I'm tryin' to get help, lady; this person is gonna die out here while you ask me stupid questions," he barked into the phone.

Sighing, before she could cut him off, Davis said," Okay, I am 14, and my name is Davis. Davis Clark. I was out riding my bike, and I saw this car slide as it came off of the bridge, and then it just ran off the road, flipped over a few times and rolled down to the end of the ravine," Davis told her, willing himself not to start crying.

"Okay, Davis, thank you so much. Can you please give me an exact location, to the best of your ability, please?" Rachel asked gently.

"Yeah, I am talkin' bout Cougars Crossin'. You know, they got that big bridge there. Well, they been doing some road work too. It looked like there was a big oil spot or something at the end of the hill, and she came down the hill really fast, like she couldn't stop," Davis told her.

"Davis, you've been great. You're a fine and brave young man. I'll get an ambulance out there right now," Rachel told him, hanging up the phone.

Remy had just ordered a chicken salad sandwich, and was chatting it up with Susie Vega, down at the diner, when his phone began to squawk. Apologizing to Susie, Remy cupped a hand over his other ear before he said hello.

Within seconds, Susie could see Remy completely change before her eyes. Gone was the joking, fun-loving Remy; now his face was serious; his appearance looking downright grim.

"Suze, I gotta run, hon," Remy told the spunky waitress, throwing a $5.00 dollar bill on the counter.

"But Remy, that's too much," Susie called out after him, watching him just wave her off and tell her it was just enough.

I wonder what in the world that was all about, Susie thought to herself, dumping Remy's coffee in the sink. Poor man didn't even get to finish his cup of coffee, she told herself, shaking her head.

Meantime, Remy was driving like a bat out of hell. He knew that he was closest to Cougar's Crossing, but he also knew that there was a very real chance that the driver of this crash would not be alive by the time he got out there, either.

Remy hated this part of the job the most. He hated seeing people he knew wind up hurt, and sometimes, dead. He hated having to pull a dead body out of a car crash, only to find out it was a good friend's son, or a friend of his in general. Since he knew just about everyone in the area, sirens coming from an ambulance always caught him off guard, and got his stomach all up in knots. The one thing he was thankful for at least, was that this call had come in before he'd had a chance to eat a nice meal. Then he'd have had to deal with the tossing and churning and godawful indigestion he always felt when he got these calls.

Remy could see the huge hill up ahead. At least the rain wasn't coming down in torrents, like it was earlier, he thought to himself. Starting to climb the hill, Remy had never lost the fascination of this hill along with the beautiful scenery once he got to the top of it. He couldn't help but look around in awe, no matter the fact that he'd been up this hill hundreds of times in his life. Still, at the very top, looking around at the huge panoramic view, one had to appreciate the good Lord's handiwork, Remy thought to himself.

Descending the hill now, he was already riding the brake, since it had already rained so much today. Coming to the bottom, he looked ahead and noticed that there was a huge oil spot at the very bottom of the hill. Remy frowned, as he got to it, slowly driving around it.

Looking over to his right, he immediately saw the car that the dispatcher had called him about. Just looking at the wreckage made the hairs on his arms stand up straight. His deputy, Samuel James, had just arrived, himself, as Remy pulled in right behind him.

Giving him a tired smile, Samuel told Remy that he'd be shocked if anyone had been able to survive that crash. As it was, the car lay upside down, and as the two men got close, they could see a lot of blood, along with a stream of long, blond hair. The driver looked like a young woman, and she didn't move at all. Her face was turned away from him, and Remy couldn't tell who she was, with all the blood on her face. Shards of glass, from where the windshield had finally gave out and busted all over were everywhere. The young girl had a few pieces on her face and neck, but Remy didn't think she'd gotten cut up too badly from that glass, as far as he could tell right now.

Samuel was running over to Remy now, his face grim and pale. "This car is registered to Connie Watkins, Remy; you know Dr. Carter Watkins, and his wife, Cassandra?" Samuel was asking.

"I can't even tell yet if this poor girl Connie is even alive. Haven't been able to get close enough to check for a pulse," Remy said sadly.

The paramedics had just arrived, and Remy noticed them trying to gracefully get down the embankment. He saw one of them talking to a freckled faced teenager with long blond hair and brown eyes. The teen was accompanying the paramedics now as they got closer to Samuel and Remy.

The kid's bike looked like something straight out of the 70's, with its long banana bars and a jet black banana seat to go with it. It was clear that the teen loved the bike, because he could do all kinds of stunts on it.

Normally, he would have been happy to show everyone all the neat things he could do with that bike, but his hands were shaking, as he told Remy and Samuel about how he saw the car *going down the hill, faster and faster. He saw the car skid off the road after it hit that large oily spot, and he told them it was like watching the car just fly off the road, until it started rolling down the embankment.*

"I just couldn't believe my eyes," the kid told Remy. "Are you Davis Clark?" Remy asked him then.

"Oh yeah, I am, I'm the one that called the accident in to you guys," Davis informed them all proudly. "Man, I can't believe I am still shaking. Is that girl okay? Is she alive?" Davis fired off questions to Remy now.

Shaking his head, Remy gently led Davis away from the scene, so that the paramedics could do their job. It'd been awhile since he'd seen that much blood, he thought to himself. Poor kid; he'd heard stories about the Watkins girl, but she'd always been a good kid, otherwise. Remy had just seen Connie at her graduation party, and couldn't believe how beautiful and all grown up she was.

"Come on, Davis, I think you seen enough for one day, son," Remy told the kid gently. "I know I have," he added.

Just then, Remy thought of Dr. Carter and Cassandra Watkins, and asked Samuel if he'd had a chance to get a hold of Connie's folks yet.

"No, not yet; I was about to get their number," Samuel told him.

Remy decided to go ahead and call them himself, so he told Samuel not to worry about it; he'd handle it himself. Samuel sighed gratefully, since that was a part of the job that he just absolutely despised.

As the paramedics pulled Connie out of the wreckage, Remy had told Davis to stay put for a moment, and walked over to look at the car again.

He wasn't looking forward to having to call Dr. and Mrs. Watkins, either, and he decided he would wait until he found out what Connie's prognosis was, first.

The paramedics were working feverishly now, as one of them had just announced that he found a pulse.

"It's really weak, though," he added, as he helped his partner administer CPR, since Connie wasn't breathing.

After a couple minutes that seemed to last forever, Connie began to cough, and the paramedics both sighed with relief.

"Praise the Lord," Remy said out loud. As he looked at Connie, he mentally wondered why there was so much blood that had run down Connie's legs.

He couldn't see an injury with her legs that would cause that kind of blood, but since he wasn't a doctor, he knew he was just guessing.

He agreed to meet the medics at the hospital, but now he needed to call Connie's parents; for now, he was just plain relieved that the poor girl was alive and that he didn't have to tell her parents otherwise.

After calling their home number and not getting anyone there, Remy ended up leaving a message on their machine, telling them only that Connie had been in a car wreck, and that she'd been taken to Cedar Pines Hospital.

Remy knew that Dr. Watkins checked his messages pretty regularly when he was away, and as much as he'd hated to leave anyone that kind of a message, he felt like it was the best thing to do, under the circumstances.

Walking back over now to Davis Clark, he patted the boy on the back, thanking him for his quick thinking in calling for help.

"*You know, you just might have saved that poor girl's life,*" *Remy told him.*

Davis gave Remy a small smile, his hands finally starting to shake a lot less.

"*I'm just glad she's still alive,*" *Davis told Remy.* "*Well, sir, I think I'm going to be heading home now,*" *Davis added, as he began pedaling down the road, giving Remy one last wave.*

1988

Roger opened his eyes, finally, having slept for over ten hours straight. For just a moment, Roger had forgotten where he was, but then, he'd had to cough, and the awful pain in his ribcage reminded him in a hurry.

The nurse came in now to check his vitals. "How you doin' today, hon?" the day shift nurse Andi asked him.

"Doing okay, at least until I had to cough," Roger told her. "Pure torture," he added, trying to laugh a bit.

"You got that right. You ready for some good news now?" Andi asked. "You get to go home this afternoon; how do you like that?" Andi asked Roger, looking genuinely happy for him.

"That's going to be great; I can't hardly wait," Roger told her. "Not like you haven't taken good care of me," he added.

"Oh, I know. It's always nice to get home to your own bed again. Not too mention having your kids and your beautiful wife hanging out with you, as well," Andi added.

Just as Andi was leaving the room, Remy walked in, taking his hat off as he greeted Roger.

"So when are you springing outta this place?" Remy asked Roger, plopping a couple "Outdoor Men" magazines on his table.

"Hey, thanks buddy. Actually, this afternoon," Roger told Remy. "I can't wait; this place is getting old fast," Roger lamented with a short laugh.

"Ugh, I don't know why I can't remember not to laugh or cough or sneeze," Roger informed Remy. "Can't wait till these ol' ribs are all healed up," Roger added. "So hey, Cathy and I were just talking about you; we were wondering how it went with Hallmen when you went out there and talked to him," Roger asked.

Remy smiled at Roger and said," Well, now, here's the thing; he says he did go out but that he was back home around midnight. He told me that he was out with Jack Higgins, till about midnight, and then he went home because he had to get an early start the next day. Of course, I already got hold of Jack, and he totally corroborated the whole story," Remy told Roger. "Of course, Monty's parents can't corroborate anything, because they were in bed sleeping the whole time, at least according to Monty," Remy added.
"I checked with Joey, who was the bartender down at Eddie's that night, and he told me that Jack and Monty got there around 9:30 or so that night, and left a little before midnight," Remy finished.

"Okay," Roger said. "Well, I guess that's a dead end then," Roger told Remy.

"Well, I do want to go back over to the Hallmen place and talk to Monty's folks myself just to be completely thorough, you know, see if maybe they heard anything," Remy told Roger.

"I guess, though, if they never heard anything, we'll be back to square one," Remy told Roger sadly, shaking his head.

"It's just that for the life of me, though, I can't think of anyone off hand that would have done any of this," Remy added.

"Okay, well, I'll get out of your hair now; let you get back to your resting," Remy said, patting Roger's knee on the way out.

"Oh hey, I hear you're goin' home this afternoon; I bet you can't wait," Remy laughed.

"You're right about that, Remy," Roger told him. "Keep us posted if anything new happens," he added, waving Remy goodbye.

"I surely will, young man," Remy said. "I surely will."

1979

Connie Watkins opened her eyes slowly, as though the shooting pains she was having in her head could possibly be caused by having her eyes opened. Still, the pain was so intense, and Connie was very confused. She'd had a terrifying dream right before she awakened just now, and very slowly, she was starting to remember what had happened.

She'd been dreaming about driving off of the road, and rolling over and over again in her car. With frightening clarity, Connie was beginning to wonder now if maybe this wasn't a dream; was this what really happened?

Her mother was half sitting, half laying in the chair that was directly across from Connie's bed. Her makeup looked stained, and her mascara had ran, earlier, from the looks of things, Connie had thought to herself. She tried to remember if she had ever seen her mother look like anything less than perfect before, and couldn't think of a single time. Black streaks were smudged across her eyes, as well as over her cheeks, and Connie noted that her mother must have been crying when she'd gotten here.

Feeling closer to her mother in this moment, Connie wanted to stretch her arm out and grab hold of her mom's hand, but for some reason, her arm just didn't seem to want to cooperate.

Fighting hysterics, Connie now noticed that her legs didn't move either, not her toes or her feet at all. Nothing seemed to move at all from the waist down, she discovered, panic beginning to take over.

Connie tried desperately to remember if the dream she'd just had was real. She thought that it must be; why else would she be dreaming about it and then wake up to find herself in a hospital, Connie wondered. She tried to remember what had happened before the crash, if indeed there was one. Where had she been driving? Was she going home?

Suddenly, it all started coming back now, with frightening clarity. Connie remembered that she had left Mrs. Gordon's house after giving it a very thorough cleaning.

A storm had been coming in, and had just began when Connie got into her car and began the drive home. She vaguely remembered sliding off the road, but why hadn't she been able to stop, Connie wondered to herself. She'd hit plenty of oil spots before, and nothing like this had ever happened. Try as she might, though, she just couldn't seem to remember why she hadn't been able to stop.

Her lower abdomen hurt; it felt like bad cramps when it was that time of the month, but so much worse, Connie thought to herself now. And then it hit her; the baby.

Oh my God, the baby, the baby, she frantically wanted to ask about her poor baby. Her and Monty's baby. Wait a minute....the brakes, oh my God, the BRAKES, that's why I couldn't stop, her brain was frantically screaming.

Connie tried to clear her throat to speak. Her lips felt dry and chapped, and she knew that her voice would be very raspy.

She felt like she could drink a gallon of water, right now, if they'd let her. With tears beginning to roll down her face now, she kept staring at her mother, willing her silently to wake up. Connie tried unsuccessfully to speak, and nothing happened. Maybe I just have laryngitis or something, she told herself. But that nagging thought kept hanging in her brain, I can't speak. I can't move anything on the lower half of my body.

Just before Connie could launch herself into full blown hysteria, Dr. Fong walked in. He looked over at Connie's mother, still sound asleep, then looked over at Connie. He nodded at her, when he realized that she was awake.

"You feeling better now?" Dr. Fong asked her pleasantly, waiting expectedly for an answer.

Connie tried again in vain to speak, and then finally, she just shook her head.

He stared at her for a moment, then walked over and began to ask her questions, as he picked up first her right arm, then her left.

"You feel this?" Dr. Fong asked, picking her right arm up again, and making it go up and down.

Connie shook her head no, and finally, finally, she was able to say a few words.

At least I can talk now, she sighed deeply to herself. "No, I can't feel anything from the waist down at all," she heard herself now telling Dr. Fong.

Suddenly Connie's mother began to stir, and seeing that the doctor was there and that her daughter had finally woke up, she rushed to Connie now, wanting to ask her a million questions.

Dr. Fong however, wanted his own questions answered first. Lifting up Connie's arms, Connie told him that she felt all of that, and could move her upper body quite well. It was just the entire lower half that seemed immovable for now, but Dr. Fong didn't seem too concerned.

"This happen sometimes," he admitted, his English a bit broken. "You in terrible car crash, and you flip, over and over," he explained, his broken English making Connie want to laugh out loud. Trying to listen to the doctor, she was trying to will herself to not laugh at his speech.

"You paralyze right now," Dr. Fong pointed out, in the remote chance that perhaps Connie hadn't noticed that herself. "We need to run more tests to see if it go away or not," he added.

"You know about baby?" Dr. Fong suddenly asked, as though he'd completely forgotten about it.

"Huh? What did you say?" Connie asked, fear suddenly clutching her heart. She could feel her heart beating so fast; the terror she was feeling was evident on her face.

Before Dr. Fong could answer, Cassandra Watkins interjected. "The baby; what baby? What does that mean? IS she pregnant?" Mrs. Watkins asked Connie now, her face just inches away from Connie. "Tell me

Connie; tell me the truth, are you pregnant?" Mrs. Watkins demanded, her face a mask of pain and disbelief.

"Yes," Connie said quietly. "I was, I mean, I am," she corrected.

"No, no more baby," Dr. Fong said sadly, shaking his head gently, and holding Connie's hand.

"I am sorry for that one," Dr. Fong said, looking helplessly at Mrs. Watkins and giving Connie's hand a final squeeze.

"Can you tell us what happened, Dr. Fong?," Cassandra asked gently now, her face looking suddenly haggard and exhausted.

"Yes, I tell you, but then I must go for now," Dr. Fong nodded quickly.

"Baby died from the crash, from car rolling over too much," Dr. Fong tried to explain.

"You lose lots of blood in crash; baby was already gone. You understand?" Dr. Fong asked Connie gently.

"Policeman say that brakes didn't work in your car; you go down that hill very fast, and then you slide and go down embankment," Dr. Fong explained patiently.

As the hot tears coursed down Connie's face, she swiped at them helplessly as she nodded her head at Dr. Fong. Her mother began to speak, and Connie just shook her head and asked her mother if she could be alone now, and after staring at her for a good long time, Cassandra Watkins nodded her head, picked up her purse, and walked out of Connie's room.

"You must rest now; you lose lots of blood in crash," Dr. Fong said, writing notes in a chart. "I come back tomorrow and see you," he added, and with a quick nod, he walked out of the room, as well.

Finally alone, Connie thought about calling Monty and telling him the news. As she picked up the phone and heard the dial tone, she suddenly just put the phone back down on its cradle. She didn't want to see or talk to anyone. It just all felt like too much right now, and Connie never realized how much she had wanted this baby.

As the silent tears turned into loud shudders of all the sorrow she felt inside of her, Connie didn't think she would ever be able to stop crying. Her whole face and nose was plugged up now, and still she cried. Finally, sheer exhaustion took over, and Connie passed out, sleeping the sleep of the dead , until finally 13 hours later, she awoke again.

Samuel, Remy's deputy stood outside of Connie Watkins' hospital room for a few seconds, before he opened the door and went in. He could see Cassandra Watkins seated on the overstuffed chair next to Connie's bed, talking animatedly on the telephone. Connie appeared to be awake, but her eyes were puffy and swollen, and Samuel suspected she'd been crying a lot.

Sighing, Samuel opened the door and let himself into Connie's room. With a cheerful smile that he really didn't feel, he asked Connie how she was feeling. He always hated stuff like this; for one thing, he could just look at the poor girl and see how she was doing. For another, he needed to ask her a few questions about her car; mainly, he wanted to know if it had been worked on lately, and if Connie had experienced any kind of problems with the brakes right before she crashed.

Connie turned her head and looked at Samuel. She really didn't feel like talking to anyone right now; all she cared about was her baby, and her baby was gone now. The pain in her heart was so intense, that sometimes Connie almost couldn't breathe, with the weight of that pain bearing down on her. The only other time in her life she'd felt this bad, was when her Siamese cat, Trixy, had slipped out of the house and gotten ran over by the next door neighbor. Ellen Hunt had been devastated almost as much as Connie, and she knew it had been an accident, so she couldn't be mad at Ellen. Besides, it seemed like nothing she could have said to Ellen would have been any worse than the guilt trip the poor woman was heaping on herself.

"I should have been driving a bit slower; maybe I could have stopped in time," Ellen had cried into the tissue that was balled up in her fist.

Connie had felt like there was a huge hole inside of her now that Trixy was gone. Connie had only been 4 when Trixy was a kitten. She'd carried the cat all over the house, for years, and had loved playing with her stuffed animals and her dolls, but after Trixy came along, it was even more fun to have a living and breathing stuffed animal.

For the most part, Trixy would go along with the tea parties and the fashion shows, when Connie would dress the beautiful white, blue-eyed cat in her doll clothes. At some point, though, after about an hour of all that, Trixy would have enough, and jump off the bed or the table in Connie's room and make a mad dash for the door. Sometimes she ran all over the house in one of the doll's outfits, and Connie would laugh hysterically to see Trixy acting so crazy. All those memories and hours of fun, Connie thought to herself now, and suddenly, in the blink of an eye, it was all over.

Connie tried to concentrate on Samuel's questions, but found that her mind was wandering aimlessly to places that she really didn't want to go. When Samuel asked if anyone had worked on her car recently, Connie told him that she'd just gotten the car back a couple days ago from Monty Hallmen, who was a natural when it came to fixing cars. She told Samuel that the brakes didn't seem to be as touchy as she'd expected them to be. She'd had to pump them quite a bit after she'd left Mrs. Gordon's house, and then when she went down the big hill, she kept pumping her brakes, but no matter what she tried, she couldn't stop.

Samuel was taking notes, and every now and then, he would pause and look up at Connie. He felt genuinely bad for the girl. Remy had told Samuel earlier this morning, that Connie had been with child, and that was probably what accounted for all that blood that they'd seen at the crash site. Samuel remembered that besides the glass that had shattered, that there was lots of blood that had run down Connie's legs, and in the whole seat area of where she was sitting, in general.

"Well, I'm going to be heading out to talk to Monty, here in a little bit," Samuel informed Connie.

"Why is that?" Connie wanted to know. "Well, we DID find that the brake line had a tiny hole in it; it's next to impossible to tell how it came about, though," Samuel said thoughtfully.

"Plus, with a car as old as yours, we don't even know how long it's been there or anything, but that's why your brakes gave out; you were totally out of brake fluid," Samuel told her.

"I see. I still don't know why you have to talk to Monty about it, though," Connie told Samuel, watching his face for any kind of expression changes.

Sighing inaudibly, Samuel tried to explain to Connie as tactfully as he knew how, that they just wanted to make sure that it had really been an accident, and not something that had been deliberately done.

Connie bristled at what Samuel was getting at. "Seriously? What makes you think for one second that he would do something like that on purpose? I could have been killed," Connie added.

Cassandra just gaped at her daughter, and, Samuel mused to himself, it appeared that this would be one of those rare moments when she didn't have anything at all to say.

Samuel was getting mighty uncomfortable now, and he shifted from one foot to the other. He hated to be in the middle of any kind of family problems, and this was personal family stuff that wasn't any of his business, he thought to himself.

Clearing his throat now, Samuel decided he was done here, anyways, at least for now. He'd go over to the Hallmen place and see what was going on out there. He doubted that Monty even knew what had happened to Connie, and he figured he'd better get out there and give him the news and ask him some questions about Connie's car.

"Thanks very much for your help, Connie," Samuel said to her with a gentle smile. "Please accept my deepest sympathies for the loss of your baby, ma'am. Does Monty know about your accident yet?" Samuel asked.

"No, I doubt that he does," Connie said, her voice starting to quiver.

" I sure hope you heal quickly and get out of here soon. These hospitals give me the creeps," Samuel told Connie, with a smile.

"I know what you mean. Thanks, Samuel," Connie told him, sinking down under the covers and feeling suddenly so exhausted.

Her mother was standing there by the window still, apparently lost in thought, but Connie didn't care. She hoped her mother would take the hint that she wanted to be alone and wanted a nap. Either way, it doesn't matter to me, Connie thought to herself, before she dozed off.

Clara Hallmen sat outside on the porch, fanning herself against the heat of the day. With dinner now over, she'd just finished cleaning up the kitchen and doing the dishes.

These days, Clara didn't go into town very often, anymore. The stroke she'd suffered last winter hadn't been too major, but it had done some damage to some of the nerves in her legs. She'd had a couple falls, as well, and because of the extended nerve damage to her legs and to her spine, she was never sure when she would fall, until she was already laying on the ground.

Her friends from church came over once in awhile, but they never stayed long. Their chats centered around the latest gossip going on, both inside and outside of the church.

Clara was always glad to see them, but completely exhausted when they would leave. She'd often thought lately, about how much time she used to spend with all these people, on a regular basis, and how rarely she saw anyone anymore.

Her own sister had passed away just months before Clara's stroke. Her death had shocked many people in their town, but Clara had seen it coming. Since her son Dwight's death, her sister Sally had never been the same. The occasional social drinking that Sally had enjoyed before Dwight's death seemed to have turned into a nonstop binge after he died.

Clara had lost track of how many times she'd begged her sister not to take prescription drugs while she was doing all that drinking, but Sally would just look at Clara as though she were looking right through her. At one point, Clara thought she'd finally convinced Sally to check herself into rehab, but the booze and the pills had taken their toll before Clara had had a chance to get her in there.

Sally's husband, Jim, hadn't been much help to his wife after their son died. Jim had always been a hard worker, but soon he became a workaholic, spending 14 hours or so a day at the office.

Dwight had been an only child that had taken Sally 4 years to conceive. Between the gestational diabetes and other things that had happened during her pregnancy, Sally had been advised to not conceive another child after Dwight had been born.

Dwight had been a bright child; witty, humorous, reckless, but also rather manipulative, even at a very young age. He'd been the typical spoiled rotten only child, and, knowing he'd be the only child she'd ever bear, Sally indulged him constantly.

Jim had tried to step in a few times when Dwight was little, but Sally would argue that, as the child's mother, she knew much better than he what was good for their son, and so, Dwight continued to be indulged.

For the most part, at least to them, Dwight had seemed like a good kid. He made good grades in school, and while they'd heard an occasional rumor of Dwight's bullying tactics, they could never bring themselves to believe that he was actually a bully himself. Dwight seemed to have friends, and he'd been fairly popular with the girls, as well, but the breakups were always beyond ugly, it seemed.

Then one day, he was just gone. When Dwight hadn't come home for dinner that night, Sally and Jim just assumed that he was out with friends. When it was bedtime, and Dwight was still nowhere to be found, Sally was beginning to worry desperately, and when midnight came and went, Jim called the police.

While Sally plied the two police officers that came to their house with coffee and rolls, Jim was out in his Mercedes, driving down every road, calling everyone they knew, and finally, around 3am, there was nowhere else to look.

Sally had thought for sure that Dwight was hanging out with Monty, his cousin, but when no one had ever seen him, she began to know real fear. By the time the police left, Sally was pretty drunk. While Jim drove anywhere and everywhere, and the police officers drank coffee, Sally was downing gin and tonics, like they were water.

She was passed out on the living room sofa when Jim finally came in at 3am. He smelled the alcohol on her, and noticed the empty bottle of gin. After rinsing out her glass and covering her up with an afghan, he made his way upstairs, in the hopes that when he woke up in the morning, Dwight would be home, safe and sound, and all Jim would have to do is fight with Sally on how they were going to punish him.

Jim lay in bed that night, thinking about how long he'd ground Dwight when he got a phone call. Sally was still passed out, so Jim talked to Remy on the phone. He asked Jim if he knew who Mrs. Crason was, and Jim had said, "Sure; my boy goes over there on occasion to give her a hand with some chores that have become too much for her to do herself," and then what followed next seemed to slow everything WAY down to the point where Jim felt like he was watching all this bad shit happen to someone else in slow motion.

"I'm so sorry, Jim," Remy, the sheriff, was saying. Feeling as though his mouth was full of cotton, somehow Jim got another sentence out. "Are you absolutely sure?" he'd whispered into the phone, his mind so resistant on going where it did not want to go.

"Yes, we're absolutely sure, Jim. We had to use old dental records of Dwight's but yes, it's definitely him," Remy had told him.

"Can I see him?" came the faint whisper. After a long hesitation, Remy had told Jim that he didn't want him to see his son that way, but Jim had been adamant. He told Remy that Sally was passed out, and that he could be down there in just a few minutes, but Remy told him he would stop by and pick him up.

"You don't need to be drivin'," Remy had said. "Be there in just a few minutes," he'd added, and Jim had somehow made his way up the stairs to change his clothes, and then he was waiting at the front door for Remy to come. While he waited, he watched his wife sleep, and wished that somehow he could protect her from ever having to know any of this information, but he knew that was impossible. As Remy's headlights loomed closer, Jim grabbed his keys and gently pulled the door shut, waiting to begin his journey to hell and back.

Clara thought about all of that now and then, on evenings like this one, when she was alone and her mind just wandered. She wondered how Jim was doing these days. After her sister's death, Jim had put the huge house on the market and had completely moved out of the area. Once in awhile Clara would hear from him, but only a couple times a year or so. Clara had always gotten the feeling that Jim couldn't wait to get out of this town; he'd told Clara that he felt it was best if he made a new start somewhere else, because he just couldn't stay here anymore.

Clara couldn't say that she really blamed him. Aside from them, Jim didn't really have a lot of reasons to stay here anymore, and when a promotion at his office came up that required him to move half way across the country, Jim didn't hesitate for a second.

Clara knew that it had been especially hard for Jim to look at Monty's older brother, Wendall. The resemblance between Dwight and Wendall had always been uncanny, but after Dwight's death, it became almost impossible for Jim and Sally to look at Wendall.

Clara watched her husband Carl out there in the garage, slaving away still, working on a neighbor's old tractor. Monty was supposed to be helping him, but he'd ended up going to the car dealership to fill in for a salesman that had been out sick the past three days.

Now as the faintest beginnings of a beautiful sunset got underway, Clara saw a police cruiser making its way up their drive. She narrowed her eyes as she continued to watch it get closer, and she slowly got herself up. A light breeze blew through her hair, and Clara felt thankful for it, since it had been almost a hundred degrees today.

Bringing the cruiser to a halt, Samuel stepped out and brushed the crumbs off his pants. As he looked up, he saw Clara Hallmen standing on the porch, watching him. She smiled pleasantly at him, and he politely touched a hand to the brim of his hat in greeting.

"Good evenin', Mrs. Hallmen," Samuel said, climbing the old wooden steps of the porch.

"Now don't be silly, Samuel; you just call me Clara; Mrs. Hallmen is my mother-in-law," she added with a chuckle.

"How about a nice cold glass of iced tea, Samuel?" Clara asked, already moving to the door to go into the kitchen.

"That would be wonderful, if it's not too much of a bother, ma'am," Samuel told her.

"I got some apple pie left over from dinner; you look like you could stand a nice slab of pie," Clara told him.

"Oh, well, I never say no to any of your good cookin', Clara," Samuel told her. "But really, you don't need to go to such trouble," he added.

Before Samuel could protest any further, Clara had him sitting down at the table, and digging into her famous apple pie.

"What are you doing out here on this side of town tonight, Samuel?" Clara asked, when Samuel had finally paused to drink some of his tea.

"Well, Clara, I really came out here to talk to your boy, Monty," Samuel told her, wiping the crumbs from his mouth.

"That sure is some awfully tasty apple pie, by the way," Samuel added.

"Monty is working at the car dealership today; he should be getting home any minute, and then I'll be heating up his dinner for him," Clara explained, looking at the clock, and busying herself getting food out of the refrigerator.

"Okay, well, since he'll be here soon, I'll just wait here, if that's alright with you," Samuel said, draining his glass.

"How about more tea?" Clara asked. "Monty isn't in any kind of trouble, is he?" she added, furrowing up her brow.

"I'll take another glass, sure; no, he's not in trouble, but I needed to ask him about a car that he worked on," Samuel told her.

As Clara poured more tea in Samuel's glass, Monty walked in the door. He nodded to Samuel, looking surprised to see him there.

"Man, I'm hungry, mom," Monty told his mother, kissing her on the cheek. "Did you save me any of that fried chicken you made earlier?," he added, lifting the foil off of the platter.

"Now don't be silly, Lamont; of course I got your dinner right here," Clara told him, moving slowly around kitchen.

"Sit down, ma; you know you ain't supposed to be on your feet so much; you don't wanna be falling again, now do you?" Monty told her, shaking his head at Samuel.

"Samuel came out here to talk to you, Lamont, so don't waste anymore of that good man's time; you just sit down there and drink your tea while I finish heating up your dinner," Clara scolded, deliberately taking the platter from Monty's hands.

"So, Samuel, what can I do for you today?" Monty asked him. "Sure was surprised to see your cruiser in the driveway," he added, drinking some of his iced tea.

"Well, I got some news for you, and it's not very good news, either," Samuel told him. "I always hate to give folks bad news," he added.

"What happened to bring you all the way out here today?" Monty asked him, a serious look on his face now.

"You know Connie Watkins? Well, she was in a really bad car accident yesterday afternoon, heading back home," Samuel told him. "She was going down the hill at Cougar's Crossing, and couldn't slow down or stop at all," he explained. "Apparently, she said she kept pumping on her brakes, but no matter what she did, she just couldn't get the car to even slow down, much less stop," Samuel finished.

"My God," Monty exclaimed. "Is she okay?" he asked, his face a mask of worry.

"She's still in the hospital; she's lost a lot of blood, and she appears to be paralyzed from the waist down. The doctor seems to think that there's a good chance that it's just temporary. They still have more tests to run, before they know for sure whether she will be permanently paralyzed or not," Samuel explained.

"Wow, that's terrible; so you drove all the way out to this side of town to tell me about Connie?" Monty asked Samuel.

"Yes, that's part of it; Connie asked me to let you know about what happened," Samuel said.

"Part of it? I don't understand; what's the other part?" Monty asked, his face settling into a frown.

"Well, when she was finally able to talk to us, we asked her if she'd had her car worked on at all, recently, and she'd mentioned that you'd done some work on it for her, including the brakes," Samuel explained.

"Yeah, I did. I gave her a tune-up, changed the oil, and checked her brakes, replacing one of the brake pads; no big deal," Monty told him.

"Yes, well, you see, the problem is, that we happened to notice that there was a small hole, more like a nick, in the brake line. Connie wasn't able to stop, because there was no brake fluid whatsoever," Samuel said.

"Okay...well, I still don't understand what that has to do with me, though," Monty said slowly.

"Well, I just wanted to check this all out well, and ask you if you'd noticed anything like that at all the other day, when you were working on the brakes," Samuel prodded.

"No, like I said, I only fixed what needed fixin'. Are you trying to ask me if I nicked that brake line?" Monty demanded, irritation beginning to surface.

"No, no, nobody's accusin' you of anything at all, son," Samuel soothed. "It's all part of my job; I gotta check everything out, you know. I told Connie that I would let you know what happened and see if this was anything that you might know about," Samuel told Monty, as he moved his chair back to stand up.

"I see; well, I will probably take a drive out to the hospital tomorrow, since I won't make it out there before visiting hours end tonight," Monty informed Samuel, taking a quick glance at the kitchen clock.

"Samuel, that was so good of you to come out here and tell us about Connie and all. I know Lamont appreciates it as well, don't you son?," Clara asked, pushing the hair out of Monty's eyes. "You have to know, Samuel, that my boy Lamont wouldn't hurt a fly, let alone do something that nasty to someone's brakes," Clara added, grimacing her face as though the mere thought of her son doing something like that was impossible to fathom.

Tipping his hat at Clara, Samuel began to make his way to the door. He thanked her again for the pie and iced tea, and began to walk down the stairs of the porch.

Monty followed him out to his car, and Samuel was making small talk with him, asking him if he would be attending college this fall. Finally, he opened the door of his cruiser, and slid in. Turning over the ignition, he thanked Monty for his time, and began his drive back to the police station.

He shook his head to himself, as he continued to ponder the events of Connie's accident, and the loss of her baby. Wonder who had been the father of that baby, Samuel mused. His mind kept going over all the facts, and he rubbed his forehead in irritation, as the beginnings of a headache was settling in. Finally, he turned on the radio, hoping to lose his thoughts for awhile, especially the nagging thought that kept coming back to him, over and over again. The thought that Connie Watkins' accident was no accident at all.

Clara watched her son Lamont gobble down his dinner. She brooded quietly to herself, her mind unwilling to take a break from all the thoughts tumbling around in it.

Lamont happened to come up for air, halfway through his dinner, and eyed his mother. She seems strange tonight for some reason, he thought to himself. I wonder what her problem is, he

ow, as he got up and poured himself another glass of iced
tea.

Clara snapped out of her reverie finally, an odd look on her
face. "What's the matter, ma?" Monty asked her.

"Oh, nothing, son, I just got a lot of thoughts rolling around
in my head tonight, is all," Clara told him.

"Why? What's going on?" Monty asked, stuffing the rest of
his biscuit in his mouth.

"Oh, it's nothing Lamont; just an old woman thinking about
the past a lot today," Clara told her son.

"Well, tell me what you're thinking about. Anything in
particular?" Monty asked, peering into her face.

"Well, I was thinking about my sister right before Samuel
got here, and it seems like when I think about Sally, then I
always think about Dwight, as well. Then I was wondering how
ol' Jim's been doing these days," Clara said. "Never do seem to
hear from him much, you know," she added.

"I just keep thinking about how poor old Mrs. Crason and
Dwight died in that horrible fire," she continued. "It's just
always gave me the creeps. "You know, they always said that
poor Dwight was murdered, because he had those contusions
on his skull when they done his autopsy," Clara told Monty, her
eyes misting up with tears.

"Ma, why you making yourself sad thinking about all that
stuff? Dwight's been gone over five years now," Monty told his
mother, shaking his head at her.

"I just don't understand any of it; I never have, not from the
time it happened, and I have never stopped giving thanks to the

Lord that you didn't go down to Mrs. Crason's that day. It could have been you that died in that fire," Clara wept.

"And then I think that maybe if you HAD gone over there with Dwight, then maybe none of that stuff would've ever happened, because whoever beat Dwight, set that fire, and left poor Dwight and Mrs. Crason to die in it," Clara finished, her hands shaking as she dabbed at her eyes.

Monty looked over at his mother then, and felt sad for her for a moment. He knew that she'd had a rough couple years, watching her sister drink herself to death while she was popping pills, and then having that stroke. He remembered the days when it seemed that his mother was always rushing off to town to help the church ladies bake or cook or do something for someone.

"Now, ma, I know it's been a rough time for you, but it's all in the past now, you know?" Monty said gently, patting her on the hand.

"You just gotta let this pain go; it's not gonna do you any good at all to spend time dwelling on these things, and you don't want to have any more of those episodes of fainting or falling, and you surely don't want to worry yourself into having another stroke," he added firmly.

"I know, Lamont, I know you are so right," Clara agreed, patting her son on the shoulder. "I am just so glad to have such good boys," she added, smiling at him.

"Oh, I know what I was gonna ask you," Clara suddenly added. "Is Connie Watkins a girl you're interested in?" his mother wanted to know.

Shaking his head firmly, Monty assured his mother that that was most certainly not the case. "No, ma, she ain't the kind of girl I would want to bring home to my mama," he told her.

Clara laughed then, taking Monty's dishes to the sink. "I guess some of that talkin' I did when you boys were younger must have sunk in after all," Clara told Monty.

"I always told you boys that you only bring those special girls that you're thinking you just might marry someday over to meet your mama," Clara agreed, nodding her head emphatically.

"So I take it that she isn't a very nice girl, since you never brought her here to meet me," Clara persisted.

"She's fine, ma; she's just not really my type, you know?" Monty told his mother with a laugh.

"Well, why not?" Clara persisted, and Monty got up from the table, laughing.

"You sure are awful nosy, ma; that's for sure," Monty told her, and kissing her cheek, he thanked her for dinner and told her he'd be out in the garage helping his dad with that tractor.

" I have such good boys," Clara said to herself, and taking her iced tea with her, she walked outside to sit on the porch.

Walking down the drive towards the garage now, Monty was glad this day was almost over. What a long, boring day, he thought to himself. Thinking about Samuel coming by, he wondered if Samuel was really suspicious about Connie's brakes, or if he was just checking out every little thing, because he was on a fishing expedition. Monty found it hard to believe that

Samuel would spend anymore time than he already had trying to figure out why Connie's brakes had failed her.

Sighing loudly, Monty told himself to make sure that he made time to go see Connie in the hospital tomorrow. From Samuel's description, Monty was shocked that Connie made it out of that crash alive.

And what the hell is with my mom and her never ending trips down memory lane, Monty wondered. She seemed to be thinking a lot lately about her sister, which always made her think about poor Dwight. Yeah, Monty muttered to himself, poor Dwight, my ass.

Monty had never spent a day since his cousin's death thinking about him. If anything, Monty had been relieved to finally be rid of Dwight the bully, Dwight the spoiled brat, Dwight the little rich kid, Dwight the sadist. The list just went on and on. Monty snorted out loud now, as he imagined the shock his mother would have if she knew what all "poor Dwight" had been capable of. She'd have another stroke for sure, just thinking about all of that, Monty snickered.

If Monty had felt sorry for anyone on that fateful day, it sure as hell wasn't Dwight. Mrs. Crason hadn't deserved to die that way, Monty mused. She'd always been genuinely nice, although quite eccentric, but Monty knew that lots of old people were that way, and he didn't hold it against them.

Mrs. Crason was a victim, just like I had always been, when it came to Dwight, he told himself.

Suddenly Monty had a thought. He just remembered that Connie had been pregnant. He wondered if she still was, or if she had lost the baby, since the crash was so bad.

He thought about Samuel saying that she was paralyzed and how they had to run more tests to know whether she would be that way permanently or not. The more Monty thought about it, the more he seriously doubted that that baby could have survived all of that, but you never know, Monty told himself.

His dad was banging his tools around, a cigarette butt hanging from his lip.

"Damned tractor was made in the stone ages," Carl told his son. "You'd think with all that money they got, they'd just get out there and buy a new one, instead of always wanting to fix this old jalopy," his dad added, disgust framing his normally pleasant face. "Hell, I just spent half of this here day, callin' around to every place I can think of, trying to find a couple parts that this here thing needs, and hell, they don't even make the damned things anymore," Carl complained, his frustration becoming more and more evident.

Carl's best friend was Frank Denton. The two had been friends since the 4th grade and still remained very close to this day, but Carl never understood how someone that had lots of money, like his friend Frank, could just keep throwing money after a bad piece of machinery, when it was just time to hang it up.

"You mark my words, son; it'll be nothing shy of a miracle if I get this ol' fossil up and runnin' again. Frank needs to open up that wallet of his once in awhile and let those moths out," Carl laughed, obviously pleased with his joke.

"You're right, dad. Well, if anyone can talk Frank into buying a new tractor, it would be you," Monty told his dad, clapping him on the shoulder.

"I just came out here to see if you needed any help," Monty added.

"Well, now, that's nice of you, son, but I'm about to quit for the day, but now that I think of it, you COULD give ol' Thunder some dinner," Carl told him thoughtfully. "I reckon that's probably why he keeps on kicking at his stall," Carl laughed.

"Yep, probably right; I'll take care of it, pop," Monty told his dad. Famous last words, Monty thought to himself, and laughed.

Monty drove around the parking lot of the hospital, trying to find a place to park. He didn't feel like parking a mile away, but it looked like that's what he'd have to do, he thought to himself, irritably.

He really hadn't been looking forward to this part of his day, either. From the time he woke up this morning, having to go to the hospital and see Connie had weighed heavily on his mind.

As Monty turned the corner, he saw someone backing out of their space, and Monty flew around the corner, almost hitting the car that had been waiting, head-on.

Pounding on the steering wheel, Monty uttered a string of profanities that would have given his mother that deadly stroke. Finally, he found another open space, and threw his car into park.

In a foul mood now, Monty stalked up to the hospital entrance, lighting a cigarette.

Sitting down on the bench, Monty still couldn't believe that Connie had survived that crash. When he'd heard that she'd gone down that hill at Cougar's Crossing, he couldn't believe his luck, that that would be the time those brakes would prove useless. The oil slick had sounded like a gift from the gods that had caused Connie to slide off of the road.

He sighed now, putting out his cigarette, and looking at his watch. He had a lot to do today, and not enough hours in the day to do it, so he'd better get up there, he thought to himself.

He also hoped like hell that Connie's parents weren't up there in the room with her, but he knew that was too much to hope for.

He really didn't want to have to deal with that today, too; the main reason Monty was coming up to see Connie was to see if she said anything about the baby.

As the elevator door shut, Monty calmed himself down, so that his performance would be flawless, just like he planned.

Glancing up at the room numbers, he found Connie's room with no problem. A tall, older man with a mustache and goatee was just leaving the room. As he ran a hand through his hair, Monty could see the beautiful Rolex he was wearing, and instantly knew that that must have been Connie's dad. He seemed to have been in a hurry, Monty thought to himself, as he walked into Connie's room.

Connie had bandages on her face from where she got cut from the windshield shattering, and she had a black eye, as well. Monty fought the urge to laugh when he saw the black eye, because even though he wasn't the one that had given it to her, God knows he'd wanted to give that bitch a black eye for a long time. He knew Connie would be beside herself if she could see what she looked like right now, and that gave him a lot of pleasure.

His mother had told him to stop and buy the poor girl some flowers on his way up, and insistently shoved a twenty at Monty until he took it. As soon as she was out of sight, Monty had shook his head and stuffed the money in his pocket, knowing full well that the one thing that Connie Watkins was NOT getting from him, was a bouquet of flowers. He also found it irritating the way his mother was so concerned about Connie's well-being.

Walking up to her bed, he smiled a big smile, and kissed her gently on her cheek. Connie turned her head slowly and looked at Monty, and managed a small smile.

"You got pretty banged up there, kiddo," Monty told her, making sure that he looked absolutely devastated at what he saw.

"Oh, Monty, it was just awful," Connie gushed, and suddenly she was babbling nonstop and Monty wasn't even listening. He stood there pretending to listen and having one hell of a hard time trying to keep his mind focused on Connie's incessant blathering. He sighed to himself and thought, man, some things don't ever change.

Suddenly, without any warning, Connie just stopped talking. Monty looked over at her, and seeing the tears that ran down her face, at least for a moment, gave him pause. The loud sobbing was disconcerting and irritating, all at the same time. Still, he was playing a part, he told himself.

"Connie? What's wrong? Why are you crying?" Monty asked, his face a mask of genuine concern.

"I jjjust keep thinking about our bbbaby," Connie stammered, already starting to hiccup from crying so hard.

"What about him? Or her, I guess," Monty chuckled.

"Noooooooooo," Connie let out a loud sob that sounded like a moan.

"You don't undersssstttaaannnddd," she finally got out, as her breathing kept getting faster and faster, and she kept trying to gulp air to breathe, talk, and cry all at the same time.

"Shhh," Monty soothed, "Now don't you worry; I already told you that we'll be alright; we'll make it work out, somehow," Monty told Connie, as he tried to wipe the tears away from her eyes.

"Noooooo," Connie sobbed again, gulping again, and sounding like someone who had held their breath under water for too long.

Monty sat on the edge of her bed, holding her hand, and waiting to see what it was that had gotten her so upset. He actually found himself feeling just a bit sorry for her, much to his dismay.

He hadn't seen anyone quite this banged up in a long time; although, he mused to himself, he DID remember his brother getting banged up pretty good a few years back when he decided to take a case of beer and two of his friends and go cruisin' on Main Street. He'd been showing off to a couple of cute girls huddled around their cars, and after polishing off his 6th beer, decided to race one of his other friends that had a souped up old mustang.

Instead of turning where he was supposed to, though, he ran into a parking meter, and because he was going so fast at the time, he went right through the windshield. Monty still teased him from time to time about it, because his brother had a long scar on the side of his left cheek, and Monty was always asking him if the girls thought it was sexy.

Another wail out of Connie brought him back to reality in a hurry.

Just as he was getting ready to open his mouth and say something soothing and helpful, suddenly Connie let out a primal cry and informed him that their baby was dead.

"What? Are you serious?" Monty asked, his face looking serious and grim, although inside he was ready to dance and celebrate.

"Yes, it's true," Connie told him, another tear trailing down her face. "I know you probably didn't want this baby," Connie added.

"Maybe not in the very beginning, but I was getting used to the thought of us getting married and starting a family," Monty told her, all the while thinking that he should be on a screen in Hollywood, since his acting abilities were just that good.

"I 'm sorry, Monty," Connie told him in a quiet voice, and at least for now, she had finally stopped bawling.

Abruptly, Monty made a show of looking at his watch, and lamenting on the time.

"Shit, Connie, I really gotta go; I'm sorry I can't stay longer," Monty lied, fighting the urge to run out of the room, then out of the hospital, and then kick up his heels in the parking lot and dance for joy.

"You gotta go to work?" Connie asked. "I wish you could stay longer," she added, her voice sounding small and strange.

"Yeah, baby, I know, I know; I wish I could stay too," Monty told her, once again laying it on as thick as he could get away with.

"Will you come back and see me? I'm so scared, Monty. The doctors aren't sure if my paralysis is permanent or temporary, just yet," Connie explained. "I am going to have some more tests run this afternoon; a cat scan and something else; I forgot what's it called," she added.

"Don't you worry, babe; I'll be back. Think positive; I bet you will start getting feeling back in your legs real soon," Monty told her, beginning to inch his way to the door.

"Did you see my dad on your way in here; he had just left when you were coming in," Connie asked Monty.

"Yeah, I did; I figured that was your dad; saw the fancy Rolex," Monty said, grinning up at her.

"Alright, well, I really do have to go now, or I won't make it to work on time, and then I'll have to listen to my boss give me a bunch of shit for being a couple minutes late," Monty muttered.

"Okay, I understand," Connie looked at him sadly. "You'll be back again, Monty, won't you?" she added.

"Of course; first chance I get, I promise," Monty told her, leaning down now over her and giving her a kiss on the cheek. "You just hurry up and get better so you can get outta here, ok?" he added, as he headed out the door.

With a final wave, Monty was already halfway down the hall, fighting the urge to yell with giddy excitement.

Pushing the elevator button down, he felt complete and utter relief wash over him. Alone in the elevator, he let out a loud sigh of relief. Monty my man, you dodged a major bullet, he said out loud. No baby, he thought to himself; like it was ever mine in the first place, he thought with disgust.

No slutty bitch was going to get in the way of his plans, Monty thought to himself, with a chuckle. Not today, not EVER.

With a derisive laugh, Monty climbed into his car and turned the radio up, singing along to a favorite song.

Glancing back at the hospital, Monty mimicked Connie begging him to come back and see her again real soon. Good luck with THAT, he said to himself, laughing as he drove away.

1998

Sheila Hardesty's nerves had just about had enough. First, there was that wretched hearing that Sheila had had to sit through, and then that blond, who was the sister of the victim, telling Sheila to get away from Monty. Sheila had such mixed feelings on all of that anyways; she had often thought that that gal had gotten just what she'd deserved, the way she'd treated poor Monty. And then there was her damned kid sister, who made it her mission in life to just blab everything to their mother.

She should have known that she couldn't trust her sister Debbie to keep that big trap of hers shut. Sheila paced around her living room, her frustration and anger building to a dangerously high point. Ever since her idiot mother had begged and pleaded with Sheila to do the adoption search for her, her life had become a living hell, Sheila thought to herself.

If it wasn't one thing, then it certainly was another. Why her sister and her mother felt the need to stick their big noses where they didn't belong, was beyond Sheila.

Debbie apparently felt the need to discuss Sheila's choice of men with their mother, Doris, and even though Doris had gone for years without seeing, speaking to, or knowing anything at all about her youngest child, you would have thought that they'd just stumbled upon the Christ child, as far as Doris was concerned. Words couldn't describe how much Sheila was beginning to resent the hell out of Debbie. Every time she turned around, it seemed that Doris had something to say about Debbie. How funny she was, how talented she was, how great her kids were and what they were doing, and the list just went on and on. Sheila felt most days like she could just puke in a bag, once Doris started on her usual daily chatter.

Doris lived alone, and her vision was very poor; she couldn't see much at all these days, but apparently her mouth worked just fine, Sheila thought to herself, gritting her teeth.

She'd gone over to see her mother, and drop off some groceries, and taken her usual walk-through of Doris' apartment, just making sure that the idiot woman didn't have the audacity to give any of her prized possessions away to that nasty Debbie. Doris had made the mistake of commenting to Sheila the other day that she wanted Debbie to have one of the little figurines that she used to collect many years ago, just as a token to have something to remember her by, and Sheila had completely lost it with the stupid old woman.

"Are you out of your stupid mind?" Sheila had yelled at her mother. "I swear, you get more daft in the head, with every day that passes. You are not to give ANYTHING to her, do you understand me, mother?" Sheila had demanded, her normally whisper-soft voice climbing up a decibel or two.

"Sheila, these are all my things, you know," Doris had started out explaining. "I don't understand why on earth it matters to you if I give away one of my belongings. Don't you think your baby sister deserves to have a little memento to remember me by when I leave this world?" Doris asked Sheila, trying to keep the irritation she was feeling out of her voice.

"No, I do not. I am so sorry everyday of my life that we found her. She's loud, boisterous, and says bad words, just like you. Yes, she's definitely your child, that's for sure," Sheila sneered.

"And I couldn't be more happy about that, either," Doris answered her, a smug look coming over her face.

"Just remember, if you think you will give one thing away in this wretched dump you call your home, I WILL notice," Sheila told her mother, her voice taking on a menacing tone. "These things all belong to me; they always have and they always will, so just take that stupid idea of yours and get rid of it," Sheila finished, gathering her purse.

"You've never been happy, have you Sheila?" Doris asked her. "No matter the fact that you had a mother who always put you first and catered to your every whim and need, and bent over backwards to make sure that you

always had plenty of love and everything you needed; it's just never been enough for you," Doris continued sadly.

"Poor Debbie had a terrible childhood, just absolutely awful," Doris lamented. "I cry whenever I think that I gave my baby away, thinking she would have a much better life and a better chance at life, growing up with a mother and a father. I believed everything everyone had told me; at the adoption agency, I was made to believe that these people were the perfect parents for my Debbie, and that she would have every opportunity that perhaps I never had had. A good education, lots of love, a father to love, which I never had, and just lots of love all the way around. My poor, poor, Debbie," Doris lamented, a lone tear coursing down her cheek.

"Poor Debbie, that's all I ever hear. Poor Debbie? There's nothing at all poor about her," Sheila raged. "She lies all the time about everything, and you stupidly believe everything she tells you. Poor Debbie, my foot; she probably just made all that up in that book she wrote; she probably had the nicest mother in the world, and just made it up. No wonder her mother hates her," Sheila spat out, having had just about enough.

"And while we're on the subject, I have studied my bible. Her father was so mean to me while I was growing up; I had to force you to get rid of him because, let's face it, you were living in sin with a married man," Sheila continued, a look of glee on her face as she watched Doris' face fall.

"He was just plain awful; he never liked me at all. It's too bad he's dead and gone; I would have loved to wrap my fingers around his neck and kill him myself," Sheila shouted at Doris.."AND, I'll tell you another thing; you have made so MANY mistakes with your life, that if you had any kind of brains at all in your head, you would be doing everything you could to ensure that you have any kind of chance at all to get into heaven, which I seriously don't see ever happening, not with all the mistakes you've made," Sheila told the old woman, a look of triumph on her face. "Debbie, her father, and you; the three of you will never get to heaven, because you and

her laugh and talk loud and say bad words, and her father was mean to me," Sheila finished.

"Her poor adoptive mother probably had her hands full, having Debbie for a child, and trying to raise that wicked seed to be any kind of a decent Christian girl at all," Sheila said, remembering at the last minute that there was something more she wanted to dig at Doris about. "Having that wretched man as a father, and a foul mouthed adulteress as a mother, hmm, yes, I can see that the poor woman had her hands full, to be sure. She is probably the nicest woman; I'd like to go meet her, actually, and ask her myself what kind of a person Debbie is," Sheila said smugly, watching Doris, who wasn't even looking at Sheila anymore.

"Well, you certainly are quick to judge all of us, aren't you, Sheila?" Doris commented.

"Apparently you keep forgetting that good Christians are not supposed to judge others. AND, in case you've forgotten, when I had petitioned the courts to try to get Debbie back after I gave her up, the judge had been bought off, and had heard nothing but horrible things about me that weren't even true.

He told me that his hands were tied, and that I had been completely misrepresented. He said," I'm sorry young lady, but there's nothing I can do. When I go back out there, you will have lost your child forever." It was all about money; that's why I lost my baby," Doris lamented again.

"And I'll tell you one more thing; I saw her mother in that courtroom, sneering and giving me nasty looks, even after the judge awarded custody to her and her husband. The woman was vile, and also quite lucky that she had a sister who had a lot of money to make things happen, so to speak," Doris finished.

"Let's face it, Sheila. You're just angry at your sister, because you got caught in a web of lies, and now she knows what kind of person you really are. You only like the people that you can lead around by the nose; people that you think are too dumb to know what's going on. The people that will believe all the lies that you tell and never question anything you say. People who will constantly tell you what a sweet, lovely girl you are; those are the only people you have any use for at all," Doris said sadly, a long sigh escaping her.

"To think that I raised you to go into a PRISON to find a man to marry you? A man that killed in cold blood? That's premeditated murder, Sheila, and I just don't begin to understand how you think this is a good choice for a husband. How will you close your eyes at night, when you finally go to sleep, if you are sleeping next to a murderer?" Doris cried.

"Just go, Sheila; I'm in no mood to fight anymore with you; I have a heart condition and an ulcer, and all you do is upset me all the time," Doris told her, turning her back on her oldest daughter.

"You know, I will say one thing that I have spent a lot of time thinking about these last few weeks. I do believe that I gave up the wrong child," Doris mused. "And that's probably the saddest thing of all," the old woman mumbled to herself, as Sheila closed the door behind her.

1988

Roger took one last glance around the room before he sat down in the wheelchair that the nurse, Andi, had provided for his departure from the hospital.

Roger had raised a fuss over it, but Andi would have none it. "Hospital policy, young man," she firmly told him. "Just suck it up and enjoy the ride, okay?" Andi had informed him. Rather than fight a battle that he knew he'd never win anyways, Roger chuckled and sat down gingerly in the wheelchair.

He sure would be glad when those ribs healed up, he thought to himself. He'd never been sick a day in his life, hardly, and had had no idea that something like this could hurt so bad. He wasn't used to reminding himself not to cough, sneeze, or laugh, either, he thought to himself.

Cathy patted Roger's shoulder now, and kissed his cheek as she walked beside him, and everyone stopped to wait for the elevator. Roger smiled at her, feeling strangely happier in his marriage than he had in a long time. Whenever Cathy smiled at him, he saw the girl that he'd fallen head over heels in love with years ago, and that always made him smile.

He'd missed the kids too, he mused. Suddenly, he thought of Duncan, and his mind started going in overdrive with all of that. Duncan would have given him a huge, soggy, welcome had he still been around to do it, Roger thought sadly.

Thanking Andi one last time, Cathy helped Roger climb in the car, and shut the door behind him. As she slid in beside him, Roger looked at her and asked," Cathy, do you want to get another dog? Maybe a puppy?"

Cathy sighed, and turned the car out of the parking lot. "You know, I can't really decide, Roger. A lot of times, I think, yeah, I really do want another dog, but then I will remember seeing Duncan like that..." as her voice trailed off.

"Yeah, I know. I can't imagine how hard that was to come home from work expecting his usual greeting that he had for you everyday, and then finding him bleeding to death like that," Roger said, shaking his head.

"I just don't get any of this. If it was Hallmen, I don't see that Remy is ever gonna make it stick, either. He had told me that there were no witnesses and no proof. The time that he'd gone out to the bars with Jack Higgins was vouched for, and while Jack isn't one of my favorite people, I just don't see him flat out lying about it," Roger finished.

Suddenly Roger looked straight at Cathy, as they sat waiting for the light to change.

"Cathy, sweetheart, please; you gotta promise me, you'll stay away from Hallmen; you really are done with him, aren't you?" Roger asked her intently.

"Yes, Roger, I really am done with him. I didn't lie about anything that happened, or anything that I told you. It just about killed me to have to tell you all of that, but I couldn't not tell you, especially after what happened to you."

"Also, I never told you either, because at the time I was just thinking that I was being foolish, but.....Cathy began and then drifted off, while she watched the traffic up ahead.

"Uh no way, Cath; don't start a story and stop; you know that drives me nuts," Roger admonished.

"Okay, well, it's kinda silly, is all," Cathy told him. "The day after I told Monty that we needed to take a break from each other was a Saturday, and I went for a run around noon, and you were back in the garage, polishing up the snowmobile," Cathy began. "I ran up the hill, and you saw me out running, and I waved at you as I went by," Cathy continued.

"Yeah, I remember that; that was the weekend before this last one, right?" Roger asked.

"Yeah, I think so; anyways, as I came down the hill, and went around that corner away from our house, suddenly this car comes careening out of nowhere, and came so damned close to me, that I ended up jumping into the ravine, just so I wouldn't get hit," Cathy told Roger.

"WHAT???And you didn't think that I needed to know about this?" Roger asked incredulously.

"No, that's not it. You don't understand; I really thought I was just being paranoid after awhile. I couldn't figure out who in the world would do something that crazy. I swore that the person was deliberately trying to hit me....or scare me to death. And I was scared after that for awhile," Cathy admitted.

"Did you get a look at the car; did you recognize it at all?," Roger asked her.

"No, I never really looked at that car, because I was afraid I was going to get hit, so that's when I jumped off from the side of the road, and rolled down the ravine," Cathy explained.

"Did you tell Remy about this?," Roger asked her.

"No, honestly, I had forgotten about it for a few days, until just now when we were talking about all of this," Cathy said.

" I dunno, Cathy; do you think it could've been Hallmen?" he asked her now, his face tense.

"A part of me does, because I don't know who else in this town would ever do such a thing. But why? I don't have any enemies; at least I never thought I did," Cathy admitted sadly.

"But the other part of me just doesn't think he would be capable of doing such a thing. I don't know; maybe I just don't want to believe that anyone could be capable of doing such a thing, especially someone that I had ever been involved with," Cathy said in a quiet voice.

"I'm so sorry, Roger, " Cathy told him now, tears beginning to roll down her face. "I never should've....she began, her voice breaking.

"Alright, well, I am not going to beat a dead horse to death," Roger told her. "I just don't want anything like this to happen again," he added.

"How many people know about this?" he asked her suddenly.

"About what? You getting hurt, or Duncan, or Monty?" she asked him now.

"Well, I guess I was asking how many people know that you, you know, were having an affair with Hallmen," Roger said, sounding embarrassed.

"I mean, does the whole town know, except for me? Was I the last to know, as the story goes?" he asked.

"No, Roger, I was always very discreet. I never wanted you to find out, and I never wanted to hurt you. Despite the problems we've had, I have always loved you, and never wanted to see you get hurt," Cathy told him now, looking him straight in the eye, as they sat waiting for the train to pass.

"Okay, well, I appreciate that. I've always loved you too, and I guess part of all this is my fault, because I never wanted to fix our problems when you'd come to me years ago and talked to me about it. I have never been a big fan of counseling, I guess," he added, sheepishly.

Cathy grinned at Roger then, and leaned across the seat and kissed him gently on the mouth.

Roger felt all the old feelings, the old sensations of how incredibly attracted he'd always been to Cathy, since back when they were kids, and all those old feelings came rushing back to him now. He wished they were back home in their bedroom, so he could show her how much he still loved her.

As the caboose went by, Cathy watched the gates go up, and put the car back into drive. They rode in silence for a few minutes, and then Roger told Cathy again to be very careful of Hallmen.

There was just something about all of this, he thought to himself, that just made him so nervous. He didn't know exactly what it was, since he really didn't know Hallmen anyways, but between what had happened to Duncan, and with the beating he'd taken, Roger didn't want any of them taking any chances.

Now as they pulled up the drive, he found himself missing Duncan's greeting and a shiver of fear that he couldn't quite explain crept through his bones. Roger shivered, in spite of the warm day, and was glad to see that Cathy hadn't noticed. With a confidence he didn't feel, he climbed out of the car and went in to greet his kids.

1979

Connie was really sick of being in the hospital. If her legs weren't going to move here, then she could be at home watching them not move just as easily, she thought to herself.

Connie had had a huge argument with her mother a bit earlier today, when Cassandra had launched into a long lecture on teen pregnancy. She wasn't getting any of her questions answered, though, much to her chagrin, and she was running out of patience. Why Connie wanted or needed to keep secrets from her was mind-boggling, Cassandra thought to herself. The few questions she'd asked about the pregnancy and the baby's father never got answered, as Connie had told her mother that since she wasn't pregnant anymore, none of it mattered.

Connie had just gotten the news early this morning, that her spinal cord had apparently suffered some damage during the accident. There'd been so much pressure on it during and after the crash, which Dr. Fong seemed to think was why she had so much nerve damage.

No one could say for sure yet whether or not she would regain full use of her legs. She'd thought often of calling Monty, but Monty had told her he'd call HER, because he didn't want his sick mother disturbed by phone calls. Connie had understood at the time, but now she was beginning to feel ignored, and she didn't much like it. So irregardless of whether he liked it or not,

Connie called over by Monty's house three days later, after he'd been to see her at the hospital.

"Connie, what's up? Why are you calling me here; don't you remember that I asked you not to call here because I didn't want my mother disturbed?" Monty demanded, slight irritation creeping into his voice.

Later that day, Monty had finally made his cameo appearance, as Connie called it, and thankfully, her parents were nowhere to be found. He let out a sigh of relief, and looked at the clock on the wall, noting the time.

Monty asked Connie how she was feeling, and tried to strike up some type of conversation with her, but she only seemed to answer in one syllable monotones. After a few minutes, Monty had had enough.

"Well, I can see that you really don't feel like having company, so I'll just go on ahead and get going," he told Connie, pretending to be hurt by her attitude.

"Seriously, Monty? Do you even care at all about what I'm going through here, day after day? You know, maybe I was wrong to protect you like I have been doing so far," Connie snapped at him, turning her head away.

"Protect me? From what? What the hell are you talking about, Connie?" Monty growled, his voice taking on a menacing quality.

"You don't scare me, Monty Hallmen, so you can just drop the injured party act. I never told my parents who the baby's father was, and I never told them either that you had worked on my car. And, of course I never told them that you had RAPED me, either," Connie spat out.

"Oh my God," Monty yelled, "I can't believe we're back to this shit again.

"What else, Connie? You might as well just get all this shit off your chest right now," Monty challenged.

"You must've fucked almost all the guys in our class, Connie, and you had the audacity to just assume that that baby was mine, anyways? Really? How fucking stupid do you really think I am?" Monty asked her now, his face dangerously close to hers.

"I even gave you the benefit of the doubt when you told me that there'd been no one after me, but tell me honestly, Connie, do you really expect me to believe this mountain of shit you've told me?" Monty asked.

Connie just stared at him with her mouth open for a few seconds, then closed it. Suddenly she put her hands up over her eyes and began to cry, softly at first, but then her tears became heartbreaking sobs.

Monty shook his head now, his anger beginning to lose some of its momentum. He stood there, staring coldly at Connie, his face no longer any kind of a mask of sympathy.

Connie had glanced in his direction as she reached for a tissue, and seeing his face hardened, his jaw set, she suddenly felt overwhelmed with love for him, yet again. She hated herself for how much she wanted him, but Monty was like a drug that she'd happened upon, and now she wanted him all the time. Looking into his eyes now, though, she couldn't say that he felt the same. In fact, he looked at her with an almost murderous gaze of contempt.

Seeing that look on his face, that apparently was for her alone, broke Connie again, and the tears began to spill. The last thing she wanted to do was give Monty the satisfaction that she was in love with him, and that his opinions of her really hurt, but she just couldn't seem to stop crying. Her voice quivering now, she reached for Monty's hand. He let her hold it, but his gaze didn't soften.

"Monty, I'm sorry I yelled at you," Connie began, her voice barely above a whisper.

"You said you would marry me," she added, looking into his eyes again.

With a contemptuous snort, Monty pulled his hand away from hers, and shook his head in disbelief.

"Why on earth do you think we would get married now, Connie? There's no baby now, so we can all just move on with our lives. School's going to be starting in another month or so, and I got plans to get out of this big shit hole one of these days," he told her, a sneer forming on his face.

"And let's get one more thing straight right now, Connie," he added, leaning in closer for effect. "NO ONE threatens me. There is no reason to run your mouth, talking about your version of the story that I raped you. We all know that's not true. No one will ever take that story of yours seriously, Connie, not after you've had sex with half of the guys in this town," he explained, a small smile working at the corner of his mouth.

"I didn't do anything to your brakes, either; I replaced a fucking brake pad, changed the oil in your car for you, and gave your car a tuneup; and then I didn't even charge you hardly any labor at all, and you have the nerve to throw out all these ridiculous accusations?" Monty asked incredulously.

Connie reached for him desperately, and Monty made a show of not being sure that he even wanted to touch her, but after making her sweat it out for several seconds, he allowed her to take his hand. He came over to her then, a silent truce between them, and kissed her on the cheek, but Connie moved his face so that their lips touched, and kissed him hard.

"I want you, Monty; I think I've been in love with you forever; that's why I always gave you such a hard time, baby. Please don't be mad at me. I'm so scared, Monty, of being paralyzed like this forever; of not being able to move these legs. What if I can't walk or run or do all the normal things I have always been able to do? What if I can't wrap my legs around you when you make love to me?" Connie half whispered, half cried these questions in his ear.

His face was softening now, mainly because he knew he had her eating out of his hand. Monty made a show of caressing her cheek, and brushed the tears away from her face.

"It's okay, baby girl; it'll all work out, I promise," Monty told her. "Then someday, after we've gotten our degrees, we'll be able to get out of this dump, and go live somewhere warm and beautiful," he added, tenderly touching her cheek.

"Hey, I'm dying of thirst," Monty suddenly told Connie. "What do you say I go downstairs to the soda machine and sneak us in a Coke?" he teased, in a conspiratorial voice.

"That would be awesome, baby; I have been dying for a nice cold coke, probably since I got here," Connie complained.

Standing up to leave, Connie grabbed his hand and he moved over to her. Bending over her, Monty kissed her cheek. Connie was loath to let go of this moment, even as Monty took his hand from hers.

"Be right back, beautiful," Monty winked at her, as he left the room.

Alone again in the elevator, Monty let out a long, disgusted sigh. How fucking long am I going to have to keep playing these games, he asked himself. The whole point of coming up here today, was to keep her from making anymore phone calls to his house. Plus, he thought to himself, he wanted to make sure that nothing else was going on that he needed to be aware of, as far as the police investigation of Connie's accident and the nick in the brake line of her car were concerned.

He didn't want her calling the house, because chances were extremely good that his mother would answer the phone, and Lord knows what kind of gabfest would take place after that, Monty thought with disgust.

He couldn't keep up this charade for much longer, he knew. With every day that passed, chances got smaller that no one would find out about the car, the baby, or the rape. He couldn't afford that information getting out there, and he didn't trust Connie to keep her mouth shut. He knew he had definite power over her, but yet, he would feel so much better if the problem just flat out didn't exist anymore, period. As the elevator door opened, Monty had made his decision. A slow smile began to spread over his face, just for a moment, as his resolve grew stronger.

Frowning now, his mind began to formulate a plan of action. Stepping off the elevator, he headed over to the vending machines. Knowing Connie the way he did, he would bet that she would guzzle the first coke in no time at all. He also reasoned that although she was technically paralyzed right now from the waist down, she was having excruciating pain throughout both of her legs, which made the doctors think that there was a real chance of her regaining full use of them, at least down the line. For now, though, they were keeping her pumped full of morphine, at least until they decided to let her go home. How convenient, Monty thought to himself with a smirk.

Pushing the elevator button again, Monty's biggest fear was that Connie would be asleep by the time he got back up there. He had one coke in his large pocket of his carpenter jeans that he always wore, and the other coke had the fast-acting tranquilizer laced in it, which was now lost inside the big bottle of coke.

He couldn't believe his luck that no one was on the elevators with him on either trip. That was good, he smiled to himself. That was REAL good. Now he had to hope that no one was in the room with her now, either, and that her stupid parents wouldn't suddenly decide to come pay their little girl a visit.

Moving purposely back into the hallway of Connie's floor, he hesitated only for a few seconds before going into Connie's room. He'd heard no noises coming from inside her room, and the nurse's station had only one nurse there, typing feverishly on the computer, her back to him.

Perfect, he thought to himself.

Walking back into the room now, Monty was ecstatic to see that Connie had not fallen asleep during his absence.

"Hi baby; I got you a little something I know you've been missing," he told her cheerfully, bending down to kiss her cheek.

Smiling up at Monty, Connie was beginning to feel better all the way around, at least where her and Monty were concerned. *He really does care about me*, she'd told herself while he was gone.

Unscrewing the cap for her now, he put a straw in the bottle for her. After she'd taken a couple big swigs, she offered the bottle to Monty, but he shook his head.

"No, sweetheart, this one's all for you," he told her, beaming at her.

"You just enjoy; you've been through hell these past few days, and you deserve a little something. I'm just sorry that I can't offer you more than that," Monty said sadly, his face now looking appropriately disheartened.

"Oh, Monty, you are such a good man," Connie gushed, in between swigs. As Monty had earlier predicted, it was taking her no time at all to drink that 20oz. bottle of coke. Peering over at it, he was happy to see that it was almost gone.

As she was chugging the last of the coke, the bottle suddenly slipped from her hand, and fell to the floor. Her face contorted with panic and fear, as she suddenly had trouble breathing.

Eyes wild, she began clawing at her throat, and trying to grab Monty, her eyes never leaving his, as the desperation in her last moments became obvious. Seconds later, she'd sagged down against her pillow, trying in vain to get air.

Gasping like a fish out of water, her eyes bulged wildly, and finally, mercifully, she was gone.

Looking around the room, and checking the hallway, no one was heading over here anytime soon.

Connie Watkins had passed away with the wild fear of what she was experiencing in those final seconds, mapped all over her face. Monty bowed to Connie now, pretending to pay homage to her, and seeing the box of latex gloves on the cart next to her bed, he slipped one on, and closed her eyes. Smiling to himself now, he pulled the glove off his hand and stuffed it into his pocket. Picking up the empty coke bottle, he glanced over at Connie one last time.

"Rest in peace, my beautiful little slut," he told her, and then he turned his back on her, leaving her behind forever.

Feeling lighter than he'd felt in days, Monty almost skipped out of the hospital. As he got to his car, he slid the key in the lock, and opened the door. Sliding into his seat, he picked up the empty plastic grocery sack that lay on the floor of the passenger's side. He threw the empty coke bottle in there and also the glove. Buckling his seat belt, he gave a tall, lithe redhead an admiring smile, as he got ready to back out.

After he'd driven a mile or so, Monty realized that he needed to throw the bag away. He had purposely not thrown it out at the hospital, but he certainly didn't want to take it home with him, either. Rummaging through an almost empty cigarette pack, he pulled out a cigarette and lit it, enjoying the ride and feeling happy that his little problem was over.

Pulling into a convenience store, Monty grabbed the plastic bag and threw it into the big trash bin right outside the door.

He went inside now, nodding to the elderly lady, Betty, who had worked there forever.

He grabbed a candy bar, and went up to the counter. Betty was beaming at him, and asked if he needed anything else. "Yeah, give me two packs of Caringtons, please," he told her, smiling brightly at her.

"I swear, Lamont, you get more handsome everyday," Betty gushed. "Why, if I was 40 years younger..." she told Monty, giggling like a school girl.

If you were 40 years younger, you'd still be an old bat, Monty thought to himself. Aloud, he gave Betty his sexiest smile and handing her the exact amount, he said," Now don't you worry, Betty; you'll always be my girl."

Thanking Betty, he wished her a great day, and hummed to himself, as he walked out of the store. As he was opening up the new pack of smokes, a car pulled up next to his. Looking up, he saw Samuel looking over at him, and he gave him a wave.

"What's happenin', Monty?" Samuel asked, after he walked over and stuck his face in Monty's window.

"Not too much, Samuel," Monty smiled. Making conversation about the near record breaking heat, Samuel asked if he'd been by the hospital at all to see Connie.

"I was up there a few days ago," Monty told him. "Have you seen her?" he asked Samuel now, looking the part of concern.

"I was up there yesterday," Samuel told him. "Poor girl still can't move her legs," he added, looking sad.

"Oh wow, I had hoped that was very temporary," Monty lamented.

"I better get out there and see her then," Monty added. "I'm sure she'd love to see you and enjoy having some company," Samuel told him, and gently thumping the hood of Monty's car, he waved and walked into the store,

Smiling broadly, Monty backed out of the parking lot, cranked up the stereo in his car, and headed home.

With a loud resigned sigh, Dr. Carter Watkins bid his employees a good night, and stepped out into the scorching heat. Having spent all day in the confines of his air conditioned office, Carter felt the heat just about take his breath away, now.

Walking quickly to the parking lot, he rolled up his sleeves and unlocked his car. With mild irritation, he heard his pager go off, and climbing into the Lincoln, Carter turned on the engine and opened the windows.

Frowning, he noticed that the phone number looked like it came from Cedar Pines, where Connie was at. He'd been planning on going over there right after work anyways, so he'd see what the problem was when he got there.

As he neared the town square, he heard the beeper go off again, and as he sat waiting for the light to change, he checked his pager, noticing that it was the same number again.

Mumbling an oath, he sped down the highway, and pulled into the reserved spot at the hospital that had his name on it. As his pager went off again, Carter felt a cold, clammy sensation of fear, that he was quite unaccustomed to, go through his body. Tapping impatiently at the elevator button, he was about to just take the stairs when the car opened. Stepping inside, he fought a rising sense of irritation when two elderly women, walking very slowly, asked him to hold the elevator until they got there.

Finally the doors closed, and Carter noticed a fourth page, again from the same number. Rushing out of the elevator, he was about to charge the nurses' station, when the head nurse for the second shift stopped him.

"Dr. Watkins, we've been trying to reach you," the haggard fifty something nurse told him.

"Yes, yes, well, I'm here now; what is it?" Carter was asking her, not disguising the impatience he was feeling very well.

"Dr. Watkins, it's about your daughter, Connie, I'm afraid," the head nurse, whose name tag read "Angelique" told him.

Dr. Watkins was about to just run over the woman, who was clearly standing in his way. Instead, he took a deep breath, and asked what was wrong.

Hanging her head a bit, Angelique informed him that his daughter had passed away, a few minutes ago.

Feeling more shock than he'd ever felt in his life before, Carter was speechless for a few seconds, and then, gathering his wits, he stammered, "What did you just say?"

"I'm so sorry, Doctor; she's gone," Angelique told him, touching him on the shoulder as she turned and walked away.

Carter felt as though he were living in some kind of twilight zone. Everything felt surreal, and time had suddenly seemed to almost stop. Walking numbly to the room that Connie had occupied, his mind took on the task of making sure that he'd heard the nurse right. He fought the impulse to slap himself awake, so obvious was it to him that he was suffering from a terrible nightmare of sorts.

Entering his daughter's room now, his feet felt like dead weight, as he tried to walk over to her bedside. She lay very still, and Carter thought that she looked like a beautiful porcelain doll that his mother had had years ago as a child. Checking her pulse, he felt nothing at all. No breath on his face. He was about to start CPR, when Dr. Damien Sanders walked in, his face looking grave.

"Carter, my friend, it's no use," Dr. Sanders told him, laying a hand on his shoulder. "She's gone. Her nurse came in to check on her and ask her if she'd like a snack before dinner, and found her this way. We tried to bring her back, Carter, but we just couldn't," he explained.

"I'm terribly sorry, Carter. We're not sure at all what happened, except it looks like she suffocated," he added. "Please don't hesitate to let me know if you need anything, old friend," Dr. Sanders told him, walking sadly out of the room.

Carter stood numbly, staring down at his daughter's body. Her hands were still warm, so Carter knew she hadn't been gone very long at all.

He began to mentally berate himself now, thinking back to what had been so damned important at the office anyways, that he couldn't have left earlier, like he had originally planned.

He continued to gaze at his daughter's face now, and remembered the day she'd been born. She'd been an absolutely beautiful baby, slightly jaundiced, and almost three weeks overdue, with a shock of thick white hair on the top of her head. Cassandra had held her for the longest time.

Oh my God, Carter thought to himself now. Cassandra. He turned on his heel and ran over to the nurse's station, asking now if he could use the phone to call his wife.

"Of course, Dr. Watkins," a tiny little cherubic aide told him. "Just dial a "9" first.

His hands shaking now, he dialed the number to his wife's office and got her voice mail. Forgetting for a moment where he was, he cursed savagely, and dialed her pager number, leaving a number for her to call. After a few moments had gone by, Carter told the aide that if his wife called, to come down to the room and get him. She nodded, and went back to her files.

As he neared Connie's room again, he saw Cassandra coming around the corner, and he felt relief, and then anxiety.

Rushing up to her, before she could go into the room, Carter grabbed her hands. "Wait, Cass. Don't go in just yet," he told her, and he tried to be brave as he told her about Connie, but his voice cracked anyways, and then as his wife's mouth gaped open, he pulled her into the room with him, and together, holding hands, they walked up to their daughter's bedside.

As Cassandra began to weep uncontrollably, Carter felt anger well up inside of him. There were so many questions he had. None of this made any sense at all, he thought to himself. Why had she suffocated? She was on a very controlled dosage of morphine, Carter reasoned. That dose by itself should have never caused her to die, Carter thought, hanging on to his wife's hand, even as his whole body began to shudder from sobs as it never had before in his life.

Hearing someone enter the room now, Dr. Watkins looked up, holding his glasses in one hand, and dabbing his eyes with the other.

He recognized Dr. Fong immediately, and as he came over to offer his condolences, Dr. Carter Watkins hoped to get some of his questions answered.

"Doctor, I cannot tell you how sorry I am," Dr. Fong began. "I go over her chart and I have no understanding how this happen," he continued, his eyes looking pained. "Her dosage of morphine has been gradually decreasing in the past 24 hours as well, because we wanted to start weaning her off of it altogether, before she went home," he added, his voice faltering when he had talked about her going home.

He gently hugged Dr. and Mrs. Watkins now, and offered to help them in any way he possibly could.

"I know right now you can't think like this maybe, but I would like to request an autopsy to be done on her," Dr. Fong gently told them. "You take time to decide what you want to do," he added.

Dr. Watkins looked at his wife, and she nodded her head in assent. He cleared his throat and began to talk, his voice shaky but clear. "We were going to request an autopsy ourselves," he explained to Dr. Fong. "I am glad that you agree with us that it needs to be done," he added. "There are too many questions and no answers right now."

Dr. Fong nodded in agreement and assured them that he would order the autopsy himself.

He looked at Connie's face one last time, and he felt overwhelming emotion build up inside of him, that he knew was taking away from his objectivity, but nevertheless, he couldn't help it. Never had he lost a patient like this, he agonized, as he left Connie's bedside and went to check on the rest of his patients.

Even as he was finishing his rounds, had made some calls, and put the order in for an autopsy to be performed, Dr. Fong couldn't shake the feeling that this wasn't an accident.

He began to think about the car crash that had brought Connie into his care, and thought about all her injuries. He mentally clicked off the treatment that was used in the ER, which included running a full CBC, ultrasounds, and x-rays.

He suddenly remembered that Connie had been pregnant, and they'd done a D&C, as well, when they'd discovered that she'd miscarried. Connie had seemed devastated that she lost that baby, Dr. Fong mused. Many young people, about to embark on college life, would be angry and resentful to have to give all that up to have a baby, but Connie must have wanted that baby. She wanted that baby a lot, he thought to himself, and remembered

how utterly depressed she'd been for the first couple days after she found out that she'd lost it in the accident. Whenever he'd seen her, her eyes were beyond puffy, and her nose was constantly plugged and congested from all the crying.

He wondered now if Connie's parents knew who the father had been. Maybe Connie had been in love with the baby's father, and that's why she'd been so devastated that she'd lost the baby.

Then there was the crash, and he'd heard that the brakes had gone out in her car, and that's why it had slid off the road, going down the ravine. Aside from the severe pain in her legs, she'd seemed to be improving steadily, everyday, and Dr. Fong had still held out hope that she'd regain full use of her legs again. Her dosage of morphine had already decreased, and it seemed utterly ridiculous to him that the poor girl would suffocate from it. The dosage was controlled and monitored, for the express purpose of eliminating the possibility of overdosing, which Dr. Fong liked to do with patients that had lots of pain. No, he thought to himself, there is definitely something wrong here. He was glad that Dr. and Mrs. Watkins wanted an autopsy; many parents of teenagers and young adults hate the thought of an autopsy being performed on their child. In this case, though, nothing seemed to make any sense, and he fervently hoped that the autopsy would answer some of the questions that he and her parents had.

1998

Monty Hallmen was pacing in his cell, like a tiger that had been caged up for far too long. He could feel the onset of a migraine coming on, but for now, that was the least of his problems.

Finding out today that his parole had been turned down had stirred in him the anger and resentment that had driven him to murder in the first place. He felt that there was no need for him to continue to be stuck in this shit hole; he'd done ten years now, and had a stellar record in here from day one.

Deep down, he knew that Cathy's sister's letters and testimony is what probably did him in. Why that dumb bitch insisted on being at his hearing, was beyond him. He despised people who couldn't keep their noses out of other people's business. Cathy's husband and children had been there as well, and the kids were all grown up now, and Roger looked like he already had one foot in the grave. He'd heard rumors that the man had basically turned into a drunk overnight, and Monty didn't doubt that, at least from the looks of him.

He was expecting that ridiculous old cow today. At times, he got really tired of playing this never ending game of charades that his life had been for far too long. For years it seemed, it just had always worked out that way. The things that he'd had to deal with in his life, had made him a fine actor, indeed, he thought to himself. He should be in Hollywood, instead of some shit hole like this, all because of that slutty whore, Cathy Grenaldi.

The warden stopped by his cell now, to tell him that he had a visitor. Time for more fine acting, Monty thought to himself. He had to keep this up now, for as long as he was stuck in here, because he knew he had Sheila eating out of his hand, and he needed to keep it that way. Thinking ahead to whenever the hell he DID get outta here, he would need a place to stay, and he could spot a needy woman a mile away.

He didn't think that he'd ever run across someone quite as needy as Sheila Hardesty. There had been so many times in the past, that he'd had to quell the hysterical laughter that threatened to escape him, when he was playing his part, and laying it all on quite thick.

Sheila was sitting on a chair now, her shoulders slumped, and her whole persona seemed to just reek with melancholy. Once again, Monty had to quell the laughter that was already coursing through his veins, and he willed himself to stay the course and play the game.

"Sheila, honey," Monty greeted her warmly. "So good to see you."

Sheila smiled at him then, and in that moment, it seemed that her face had lit up like a Christmas tree. Monty was once again reminded of how incredibly easy this was with Sheila.

"How are you, Monty? Have you heard anything about your parole yet?" Sheila asked him, her eyes filled with hope.

"Sadly, yes; I got turned down, honey," Monty explained to her, his face patient and kind. "I was really hoping that I would get released, but it's highly unusual, in a case like this, to get parole on the first try," he added, his face a mask of indifference and knowledge.

"When will you be able to have another hearing, you know, to try again?" Sheila asked him.

"Well, I don't look for it to be for awhile. Probably at least a couple more years or so," Monty said flatly, looking downright depressed about the whole matter.

"I'm so sorry, Monty; this must be the most terrible news," Sheila told him, reaching a hand across to him.

"Now don't you worry yourself, beautiful; let's talk about something else now, shall we?" Monty asked, changing the subject, and brightening up his face appropriately, as he readied himself for the next big move.

"What do you mean? What do you want to talk about?" Sheila asked him, her gaze meeting his.

"Well, I think that we need to talk about when we want to have our wedding," Monty told her. "You DO still want to marry me, don't you, Sheila?" he asked her, his eyes looking at her with pure adoration.

Damn I'm good, Monty thought to himself, as he sat there watching Sheila.

"Our wedding? Well, yes, of course I still want to marry you, Monty," Sheila told him. "More than anything in this world," she added.

"But I just don't see how we're going to do that, if you're still stuck in here, and all," she added.

"Well, we just need to get the chaplain here at the prison to perform the ceremony; and you'll need to pick out our rings, too," he added, enjoying the effect that this all was having on Sheila.

"Oh. Well, sure, we could do that," Sheila stammered. "Are you sure that that's what you want to do, then?" she asked him.

"Oh, I'm sure. But what about you, Sheila? Somehow I get the feeling that you are having doubts? You know, you don't have to do this, if you don't want to," Monty told her, his face now looking appropriately sad.

"I mean, I really thought that this was what you wanted, but you don't seem all that excited about it, now that the time has come to actually discuss all of this," he told her, looking dejected and pained.

"No, no, Monty, I'm sorry, I really am. I really want us to get married. It's just my stupid mother and sister," Sheila confided, deciding to just tell him what all she had been dealing with.

"What do you mean? Did you tell them about me, Sheila? You were supposed to keep us a secret for now," Monty told her.

"Yes, yes, I know, but I was so excited, Monty, when you asked me to marry you that I HAD to tell someone, you know," she explained, her face starting to light up and look animated again.

"Now, honey, I DO understand, and normally you would be able to do that. Anyways, go ahead and tell me what you were going to tell me," he said, looking at her gently, and making sure to keep the anger out of his voice.

"Well, it's my sister Debbie," Sheila began. "I was talking to her a few weeks ago, and well, I told her the story about how we met, when I was coming here with Sister Katrina to do prison ministry," she explained. "I told her that I'd fallen head over heels in love with someone, and told her a bit about your past, because, of course, she'd wanted to know what you were in here for," Sheila continued. "I really wasn't expecting that she would just go off on me for almost an hour about how incredibly stupid I was for wanting to marry a man in prison convicted of murder," Sheila said quietly. She hated having to tell Monty about all of this; she was afraid that he was going to get really angry at her, and now she was filled with dread having to tell him the story.

"Hmmm," Monty said, stroking his chin. "So she doesn't think it's a good idea for you to be with me; does that about sum it up, Sheila?" he asked her now, searching her face.

"Well, uh, yeah, that's about right, I guess," Sheila stammered, her face getting hot with embarrassment. She no longer looked at Monty, for fear of what he was thinking about her now. Instead, she kept looking down at her shoes, as though she expected them to suddenly come to life and take care of this inconvenience for her.

"Hmm, well, I guess that's too bad, Sheila, on so many levels," Monty said thoughtfully, an edge to his voice that made Sheila want to fall down on her knees and beg him for his forgiveness. "See, if you would just listen to me when I tell you things," Monty added, shaking his head sadly. "You could have avoided this whole mess coming down on you now, if you would have just kept all this to yourself, like I had asked you to do," he finished, giving his head a final shake now.

"So disappointing," he muttered purposely, seeing Sheila on the verge of tears, out of the corner of his eye.

"Oh Monty, I am so sorry; can you ever forgive me?" Sheila asked, her voice sounding like the petulant whine of a 5 year old.

"Well, I suppose so, Sheila; it's so sad that you have so little trust in what I tell you; that's all I'm saying," Monty told her, laying the guilt just a little bit thicker.

"You know that I love you, Sheila," Monty continued. "But if you can't keep things to yourself, and you can't stop yourself from blabbing all the time, how am I supposed to know that I can trust you?" Monty asked her, searching her eyes now.

Sheila was crying now, trying so hard to keep the tears from rolling down her face, and not succeeding at all. She couldn't hardly meet Monty's eyes for fear of what she would find there. Now she hastily wiped her eyes and cleared her throat, trying to get the quiver out of her voice.

"Monty, I promise you, that I will never, ever do that again," Sheila began. "I just beg you to give me another chance, please," Sheila begged. "I can't face the thought of life without you," Sheila finished, her voice faltering at the end.

"Well, I guess anyone can make a mistake, right? I mean, that's why I'm in here, let's face it," Monty agreed, chuckling a bit to help Sheila relax now.

"Don't forget about that money in my account now, either," Monty reminded her. "Once we get married, you can get us a house to live in, somewhere private, where there's not lots of people nosing around in our business," he added.

"Yes, I totally agree," Sheila babbled. "Thank you so much for giving me another chance, Monty; I promise I will never let you down again," she told him, her eyes misting over with happiness now.

"And you will not tell your sister anymore stories about us, right?" Monty asked, wanting to make certain that Sheila understood his instructions. "You don't want to cause problems for us," he added, looking Sheila in the eye, and letting her hear the edge in his voice.

"No, absolutely not, Monty; I haven't been talking to her much at all, and I can tell her whatever you want me to tell her," Sheila added.

"Well, now, all you need to tell her, should she ask anymore questions, is that your soon to be husband is a born again Christian and this was a one time thing. It will never happen again, so she doesn't need to worry," Monty instructed, fighting hysterical laughter once again, as Sheila sat there bobbing her head.

"Oh yes, Monty, that's good. I won't say anything at all unless she flat out asks me and that's what I'll say. Besides, she needs to understand that you were intoxicated and also had drugs in your system when that happened; you couldn't really help yourself at the time, because it was an accident, really," Sheila added.

"Yes. Now that's my girl; I knew I could count on you, Sheila. When I get out of here, I promise I will make it up to you 200% for everything you have had to deal with, my love," Monty soothed.

"Oh, I would do anything at all for you, Monty," Sheila told him. "Anything at all; you can count on me," she added with a big smile.

Monty's perfectly straight, white teeth smiled back at her. When he looked at her like this, Sheila felt like she could just melt at his feet. How she wished he was getting out now, she thought to herself. But that was okay; she was going to get that money, so she could pay some bills and get a house, she thought to herself. She'd have everything completely ready for when Monty came home, she mused to herself.

The guard came by then, and told them they had 5 more minutes. Monty looked into Sheila's eyes and promised her nothing but love and tenderness for the rest of their lives. He asked her to pray with him then, that God would bless them and keep them safe and Monty also asked God's blessing on their upcoming marriage.

"You leave the chaplain to me, Sheila," Monty told her. "I'll talk to him and see what we can do; just keep your calendar opened, so that we can do this on the first available day he's got. I just can't wait to marry you, Sheila," Monty told her now, holding her gaze. "I have never been in love like this, not ever. That's why it's so important to keep our love affair a secret; we can't take any chances that someone might try to interfere. Besides, people would get jealous to see how in love we are with each other," Monty finished, having laid it on nice and thick, as usual.

"Oh, Monty," Sheila crooned. "You have no idea how happy you've made me," she added. "And don't worry; I won't breathe a word of this to anyone," she told him, getting up to leave.

"I'm the happy man, Sheila," Monty informed her. "I never thought I could find the perfect woman. And then to find her in HERE," Monty added, slapping his knee for emphasis.

"You come back and see me real soon, Sheila. I will give you a call and let you know when our wedding day will be, too," he promised.

"I have to get a hold of my older brother and get that whole mess with the money straightened out, too," he told her.

Gaping at him, Sheila said," I never knew you had a brother, Monty. There's still so much about you that I don't know," she lamented.

"Now don't you worry about that," Monty informed her, "we got the rest of our lives to get to know each other."

Satisfied with that answer, Sheila blew him a kiss goodbye, and walked to the door. Monty was waving goodbye and blew her a kiss as well.

As she left the building, Sheila's heart felt incredibly light and happy. She wondered if she'd ever been this happy in her whole life. No, she thought to herself, I don't think so. Nothing will stop us or get in our way, she thought to herself. Nothing and NO ONE.

With a satisfied smile., Sheila turned over the ignition and drove back to her apartment, dreaming of the day she would become Mrs. Lamont Hallmen.

1979

Dr. Sanders grabbed a couple of antacids out of the pack and popped them into his mouth. He had a nasty feeling that his ulcer was going to get worse before it got better.

Sitting at his desk, he put his reading glasses back on, and with a resigned sigh, read over the autopsy report once more.

"Connie Watkins, 18, died from apparent suffocation, from a lethal overdose of Xanax and morphine. It is believed that a large quantity of Xanax in powder form was ingested shortly before she expired, causing her to stop breathing. Her death is ruled as an accidental overdose".

Taking his glasses back off, Dr. Sanders sighed again heavily. As if anything could be worse than the autopsy report he had just reread, he now had the distasteful job of calling up Dr. and Mrs. Watkins, and having them come in, so that he could share this information with them.

He couldn't understand how on earth this had happened; the patient was not taking any drugs except for the morphine. How the hell had the Xanax gotten into her system? The only logical answer he kept coming up with would indicate foul play. Someone had to have slipped into her room and given it to her, probably in the form of a drink. Everyone had done a complete sweep of her room, not once, but three times, actually, and no one had come up with anything at all.

Frustrated beyond belief, Dr. Sanders never heard Dr. Fong tap on his door, until he appeared before him.

"Drew? I knocked on the door," Dr. Fong began. "Geez, I'm sorry, Li," Dr. Sanders told him, shaking his head sadly. "Did you happen to see this autopsy report on Connie Watkins, our young patient that expired yesterday?" he asked.

"Ah, that would explain your face," Dr. Li Fong told him, picking up the report and settling in the chair in front of Dr. Sanders, as he began to read.

"What do you think?" Dr. Sanders asked. "I don't know what to think," Dr. Fong admitted, "except to say that it DOES make perfect sense how she died so suddenly," he added.

"Yeah, I know," Dr. Sanders said,"but quite honestly, I keep coming back to the same thing."

"Someone come in and give her the Xanax," Dr. Fong guessed correctly.

"You got it," Dr. Sanders said, popping another antacid in his mouth. "I have gone over her hospital charts at least ten times, and there is absolutely no record of her ever being given any Xanax. Not in the ER, and not since then, either. So there's logically only one explanation, and that's got to be that someone came in her room and slipped the stuff in a drink and gave it to her to drink," Dr. Sanders finished.

Now it was Dr. Fong's turn to sigh. "You call parents yet?" he asked. "No, I really wanted to talk to you first before I did, and make sure that you were in agreement with these thoughts of mine. How the hell am I supposed to tell her parents that it wasn't bad enough that their poor daughter died, but hey folks, guess what, we think she was murdered," Dr. Sanders replied, the bitterness he was feeling becoming quite apparent.

"Yes, I know. So hard to do. Never get any easier," Dr. Fong agreed.

"Do you want to call them and have them come in so that we can talk to them together, or would you rather I called them?" Dr. Sanders asked him now.

"Maybe you call; your English much better I think," Dr. Fong told him,"but I make sure to be here with you if you can schedule the time towards the end of the day," he added, getting up from the chair.

"Okay, that sounds good. Five o'clock this afternoon work for you?" he asked.

"I'll be here," Dr. Fong told him as his pager went off.

"Gotta run; see you later," Dr. Fong said as he quickly walked out the door.

1988

Cathy Grenaldi Hammond was putting the finishing touches on dinner, when she heard Roger's old truck clamor up the long, gravel driveway. She was talking on the phone to her best friend, Shana Hawks, when Roger walked in.

Kissing her on the cheek, he sniffed appreciatively at all the great smells coming from the kitchen. Lifting lids up now, he was stirring and messing around, and generally getting in the way.

"I'll see you at Cal's at 8 then," Cathy said. "Okay, see you then," she added, hanging up the phone.

"Roger Hammond, you nosy devil," she teased, as Roger took off the last lid to inspect the contents in that pan.

"What?" Roger asked innocently. "It's just that everything in here smells so good, and I'm starving," he grinned at her now. "So are you going out tonight?" he asked her, a slight frown coming over his face now.

"Yes, with Shana and her kid sister Lisa, who is in town for the weekend," Cathy explained. "Lisa always wants to celebrate her birthday with us, so we do this every year," she reminded her husband, who nodded his head.

"Yeah, I remember. You just be really careful out there. I still worry," Roger said, cutting his sentence short when he saw the kids coming into the kitchen.

"Don't worry; we'll be fine, and I shouldn't be very late, either," she told Roger.

She couldn't blame Roger for being paranoid about her going out. He was just getting totally healed from all his injuries now, but the thoughts of that night and the whole aftermath of it all still haunted him, it seemed. No charges had ever been filed against anyone; no one had ever come forward with any information at all, so no arrests could be made. Deep down, Cathy knew that Roger still thought that it was Monty, but no one could prove it. This would be the first time that Cathy had gone out since Roger had gotten beaten up, as well.

Cathy hadn't told Roger that Monty had tried to call and talk to her a few times, either, though, because she didn't want him to worry anymore than he already had been. Sometimes, Cathy would get heavy breathing calls, or she would answer, and someone would be on the line, but not say anything at all, and then hang up. She tried to chalk it up to kids playing around on the phone, but she didn't always believe that herself.

After dinner was over, Cathy cleared the table and loaded the dishwasher. The kids were begging to be dropped off at friends' houses on her way out, and she agreed to take them. As she finished cleaning up the kitchen, the phone rang, and since Roger was outside, she answered it.

When she said hello, though, no one said anything at all. In an exasperated tone, she told the caller on the other end that she had a whistle, and that she would be happy to blow it in his ear the next time he called.

Slamming the phone down, Cathy went to change clothes. She decided to wear the new jeans tonight that she'd bought a couple weeks ago. As she checked her makeup, she looked at the time, and realized it was later than she thought.

Calling the kids, she picked up her keys and purse, and headed out to the car. The kids came running and Cathy went to the garage to say goodbye to Roger, but she couldn't find him. Shrugging her shoulders, she walked back to the car, and they all took off.

An hour later, Cathy was getting a stomachache from laughing so hard at the jokes Shana was telling her. Pulling a twenty out of her pocket, she told the girls to get another round while she went to the bathroom.

Coming out of the bathroom, she came face to face with Monty, almost crashing right into him. His slow, easy smile was still charming as hell, Cathy noticed. His white, straight teeth seemed to show off the cute dimples he had at the sides of his mouth.

"Well hello, beautiful," Monty told her, smiling broadly. "Where's the fire?" he teased.

"Oh, hi Monty," Cathy smiled back at him. "No fire, just heading back to my table," she told him.

"Oh yeah? I've been here for a little while, and I hadn't noticed you were here," he told her, smiling still.

"No? I'm with my friend Shana and her kid sister. We're celebrating her birthday," Cathy explained, more to be polite than anything else.

"Ah, a celebration. That's cool. How have you been, Cathy?" Monty asked, his voice turning husky.

"Doing okay. Well, I really need to get going," Cathy told him. "Nice to see you," she added, trying to be nice.

"Same here, girlie. Come back and talk to me when you got time," Monty told her, his smile slowly beginning to fade.

As Cathy was slowly trying to move past Monty, he reached out and grabbed her arm gently. "Cathy," Monty breathed, "I miss you so much, baby. Please sit down and talk to me. Tell me what all you've been up to; tell me how much you miss me, baby," he whispered in her ear, taking her free hand and resting it below his belt buckle.

"Monty," Cathy practically spat out," just don't, okay?" she snapped at him, yanking her hand away as though it were on fire.

She began to move away from him again, noticing now that a few people had turned around and were watching the whole scene around them unfold. Sighing with disgust and exasperation, she had just walked past Monty, when he grabbed her arm again.

"Cathy, we need to talk. NOW," Monty intoned, his whole demeanor seeming to change before her very eyes.

"Damn it, Monty, I told you; I'm here with friends, and they are sitting over there waiting for me. I don't have time for this shit. We're done, okay? We've been done for a couple months now, so just let me get back to my friends, and you can go back to whatever it is you were doing," she explained, trying to keep the anger out of her voice.

Before Monty could say another word to her, Cathy had turned on her heel and stalked off, presumably back to her table. People stared at Monty for a moment, and then the normal Friday night chatter of the bar resumed.

Monty moved over to the bar, now, his faced flushed with anger. He couldn't believe that she would treat him like he was yesterday's garbage, he thought to himself.

As he mulled over all of this, his anger slowly beginning to subside now, he turned around and looked over at where Cathy was sitting with Shana and Lisa. They were all laughing hard, and he saw Cathy wipe tears from her eyes while she was laughing. The waitress stopped over at the table now, bringing a tray of Lisa's favorites; a basket of bar shrimp, and a plate of steak fries. There was also a shot sitting in front of Lisa as well, Monty noticed.

Suddenly, Cathy happened to look right at Monty, and she could tell that he was sitting there watching them. She quickly turned away, and began to talk once again to Shana. After a couple minutes, Shana turned around and looked over at him, and then with their heads bowed low, Shana was talking to Cathy, now. Lifting her head up again, and turning around once more to look at him, Shana shot him a look of contempt, and started to laugh, abruptly.

Monty felt the heat flood his whole face, now, and rage was beginning to consume his whole body. How dare those bitches sit there talking shit about me like that, he raged. He just knew they were all laughing at him as well, and he found the whole scene to be inexcusable.

One thing that Lamont Hallmen never did tolerate well, was being the butt of someone's jokes, he thought to himself. He remembered being in the second grade, and pushing the homely, big-mouthed kid right off of the slide, so that he fell quite a distance to the ground. The whiny, little brat ended up with a broken arm, and Monty ended up in the principal's office. His parents had had to come to school as well, and while his dad had been pretty understanding for the most part, his mom just about flipped out of her mind.

Finding out that her son that was usually so placid and well-behaved had done something so vicious to another child had been a very bitter pill for Clara Hallmen to have to swallow, Monty thought to himself now, smirking. While his dad admonished him to never do a thing like that again, he had told his wife then, that that's what happens to people who feel the need to run their mouths all the time. Monty remembered listening to their conversation while he was alone in his room, playing. Clara had clucked her tongue, and shaken her head sadly, and had ultimately had to call the boy's parents and convey her most deepest sympathies, Monty remembered now, practically laughing out loud as he pictured his holy roller mother having to perform an ass-kissing ceremony that she probably has never forgotten.

Snapping out of the past now, though, he pretended to be interested in the redhead that had just sat down next to him. He introduced himself and told her that he just knew this night was about to get so much better now that a beautiful woman was sitting next to him. The redhead tittered nervously, apparently not used to being given such a wonderful compliment. Soon though, she was chatting with Monty as though she'd known him her entire life. Monty averted his eyes over to Cathy's table now, and her eyes were on him. He thought he saw a look of sadness in those eyes, as she probably hadn't counted on Monty moving on with his life so quickly, he mused to himself. Oh well, that's what happens, he snickered to himself.

Out of the corner of his eye, he saw Cathy get up to go use the restroom again. He looked around the bar, and everyone was busy doing their own thing. The redhead next to him, was boring him with a tiresome litany of what she planned to do this weekend, but Monty was barely listening to her at all. He looked over at Cathy's table and saw that Shana and Lisa were talking to each other, and not even remotely paying any attention to him at all, which he was thankful for.

Seeing his chance, he excused himself to the redhead, who seemed surprised that he'd sat there next to her for as long as he had. Glancing behind him now, he scanned Cathy's table, and her friends were still laughing raucously. Indeed, it seemed like the whole bar was either laughing or talking, with no one paying any particular attention to him at all.

That's a good thing, Monty thought to himself. Just as he was nearing the bathrooms, he saw Cathy heading out the door to her car.

This just keeps getting better, he told himself. With a quick glance at her table, her friends were still occupied, so he followed her out the door. He knew that Cathy hadn't seen him at all, which was exactly what he wanted.

Nothing quite like the element of surprise, he thought to himself with a chuckle.

Walking carefully on the graveled drive, he soon spied Cathy over at her car. She had the backseat door opened, with the light on in the car, and she was crouched down, apparently looking for something.

Coming up to her now, she never heard him approach, until he had his hand down the back of her jeans. He squeezed hard and she let out a howl of fright.

Monty looked at her now in the moonlight, and felt more alive and excited than he'd felt in a long time. With his other hand, he held a huge wad of her hair. He brought his other hand back up now, and had the remaining hair of hers tightly wound in it.

He was literally standing on top of her; the tops of his feet stood on the tops of hers. Cruelly now, he bent her way back at the waist, so that she could feel his hardness, and he began to unzip her pants. His breathing was becoming more ragged now, and Cathy's cries were too muffled to be heard by anyone. Finally, he stopped for a moment, when she begged him repeatedly to not do this to her in the parking lot. She was too embarrassed at the thought of anyone coming out and interrupting them, she told Monty.

Now he stared at her for a second, looking around quickly to make sure they didn't have an audience. He knew that people sometimes came out here to smoke dope or have a quickie, but he DID have to admit that she had a point. The last thing he needed, was for anyone to come out here and see what was going on.

And there was definitely going to be something going on. Cathy Grenaldi was going to have sex tonight like she'd never had it before, he thought to himself with a laugh.

"Here's the deal; no tricks. We're gonna just drive to the back of the old lot across the way," Monty told her. She nodded her head slowly, then suddenly began to babble, as she begged and pleaded for him not to do this to her.

"Please, Monty, please," she begged,"don't do this; don't ruin my memories of us this way."

"Not gonna ruin anything, my beautiful blond whore," he told her, a definite edge to his voice. "Get in the car, and remember, don't try anything cute."

Cathy got in the car, and she was shaking terribly. Monty turned the heat on for her; he figured it was a bit chilly out tonight, and it was the least he could do, he laughed.

Seconds later, they were in the lot, and Monty ripped a belt loop off of Cathy's new jeans trying to get them off. Cathy began to cry now, and Monty began to get angry. He ripped the rest of her clothes off now, and began to devour her, as though he were a starving animal.

Deciding that he wanted more room, he got out of the car, and then grabbed the now naked Cathy and laid her on the grass.

"This is SO much better," he muttered in her ear, as Cathy's tears continued to trail down her face. Aside from her constant shaking, she said absolutely nothing, and Monty liked it that way. At least she was being a very willing participant, he thought to himself, as he began to kiss her deeply.

Cathy was actually kissing him back, which Monty found arousing but strange. He expected her to fight him all the way, but instead, it was almost like she was fine with it, as she wrapped her legs around him and continued to kiss him deeply.

They went at it for what seemed like a long time, but finally, Monty was completely spent. He had himself wrapped around Cathy, and she wasn't crying or shaking anymore. That's good, Monty thought to himself.

Finally, they began to get dressed, and at first, Monty thought everything was fine.

"Don't you have to go in to work, tonight?" Cathy asked him, after checking the time on her watch.

"What time is it?' Monty asked her, sliding his jeans back on.

"It's almost 10:30," Cathy told him, her face looking sullen and stony.

"You sonofabitch," she suddenly began screaming at him, and now her hands were flailing at him, smacking him, and a couple times she nailed him good with her wedding ring.

Caught off guard completely, she almost succeeded in knocking Monty down. At the last second, he caught his balance, and grabbed her by the hair again.

"What the fuck are you doing?" he yelled at her, and pushed her down hard on her backside.

"You raped me, you sonofabitch," she yelled at him again, trying to punch him in the face. Instead, Monty grabbed her arms and threw her down on the ground. He was sitting on top of her now, and her arms were now useless as well. He began to slap her, first one hand, then the other.

Getting bored with that very quickly though, Monty pulled her back up to her feet.

"Raped you my ass, you fucking whore," Monty leered at Cathy now, watching her stumble towards him. " You loved every fucking minute of it."

"Get in the damned car. NOW," Monty screamed at her, and Cathy did what he wanted. There was something very scary about him now, she thought to herself.

Monty drove in silence for the first couple of miles. Cathy didn't think she'd ever known terror before this. She silently had cursed herself numerous times already tonight, for going out to her car alone

She hoped that Shana would wonder where the hell she went, and come looking for her. She'd only had a small chance to tell Shana and Lisa about Monty, and what she did tell them, wasn't anything very significant, Cathy thought to herself now, sadly.

Still....maybe Shana would notice that Monty was gone as well, and put two and two together, Cathy hoped fervently.

They were driving further away from town now, and Cathy was scared out of her mind. Monty seemed possessed by a rage the likes of which Cathy had never seen before in her life.

"Let's talk, Cathy," Monty said now, his voice suddenly more gentle. "Will you talk to me, baby?" he asked.

Cathy didn't say anything at all, at first. She was too overwhelmed with fear to say anything at all, it seemed. In the darkness, she began to pray, repeating the Lord's prayer that she'd known since she was a little girl. She just had a bad feeling, and she couldn't shake it at all. She thought about her children now, and Roger too, and suddenly she really did think that Monty was capable of gutting a dog and beating the hell out of a defenseless person. She shuddered to herself, and Monty turned the heat up more, thinking she was just cold.

"I'm so sorry, Cathy; you should have told me you were cold, baby girl," he told her gently.

Then, "Here we are," he practically sang out. Guiding her by the elbow, Cathy had never seen this place before. Before she could say anything, Monty looked at her and said," What do you think?'

"About what?" Cathy asked him now, not sure of what she was supposed to say to him.

"What do you think of this place? This is it; this is the family farm," he told her, and as he watched her face, she nodded slowly.

"Do ya like it?" he asked her now. "Um, yes, from what I can see of it, yes. It's very big; at least what I can see of it in the dark," she stammered, totally unsure of what she should be saying now.

"It IS big," Monty agreed. "So let's talk now, shall we?" he asked, and once again, Cathy heard that edge in his voice.

"Oookay, what do you want to tttalk about?" Cathy stammered, shaking violently from nerves and feeling like she was freezing to death.

"Oh, now Cathy, you gonna play the coy one with me, are ya?" Monty asked, drawing closer to her.

"C'mon, Cathy, talk to me. Tell me why you don't love me no more. Tell me why you decided it's over," he continued, stepping closer to her yet.

"I'm jjjust trying to save my marriage," Cathy stammered again, her whole body now shuddering violently.

"Hmm, I see. Well, now, that's very noble of you, Cathy, very noble indeed. BUT....not very fucking believable," he snarled at her now, his face literally right in hers.

"I know you Cathy.....You'll only be able to stay home and work on that marriage to that boring ol' Roger for so long. It's a shame, really...He fights like a girl," Monty laughed now.

Cathy was not able to do anything now, besides continue to shake violently, as she had been for the last several minutes. So there it is, she thought to herself. And why is he telling me this now, she worried. Why?

There was really only one reason, and as Monty pulled the knife out now, the horror and shock that she was feeling made her legs rubbery. She felt like she wanted to just let herself fall to the ground.

Monty was using the point of the knife now, to slowly, almost sensuously, trail from her neck, to her throat, then down to her heart. When he got to her heart, he slowly encircled it with the very edge of the knife. Cathy tried to look around for anything at all she could use to defend herself with at this point, but there was nothing. She was facing the road, and she prayed for headlights to appear; please, God, something, she silently prayed. Her legs shook so badly and Cathy wasn't sure if she could walk on them now if her life had depended on it. They were so wobbly, and she felt like her whole body now was in shock. She eyed the highway again, but there was nothing, no one. She looked in Monty's eyes one last time, and then she closed her eyes, as he suddenly took the knife and plunged it into her heart. Pulling it out , he plunged it in her again, once more.

"Goodbye, my beautiful whore," Monty told Cathy, as he laid her on the ground, watching the blood surge out of her. "Guess now you will see what a broken heart really feels like....first hand," he added, his breathing getting ragged with exertion.

Cathy lay there now, and she lifted a hand to her chest, feeling the sticky blood, seeing it everywhere. She saw Monty staring down at her, heard his words, and now she was struggling to breathe, gasping for air.

There were no deep breaths to take, Cathy quickly realized. She closed her eyes now, and asked God to watch over Roger and the kids, Kellie and Dylan. Asking him to forgive her, she gave one final gasp, and then she was gone.

"Rest in peace," Monty told her, and then he picked her up, threw her in the trunk of his car, and drove out to the cornfields. He smiled at the brilliancy of his plan, as he turned off the motor and unlocked the trunk. He didn't have to worry whether lil' Miss Cathy debated the issue of whether or not she'd been raped; actually, Monty chuckled to himself now, he no longer had to listen to anything that tiny little blond whore had to say, ever again.

As he picked her up out of the trunk, even with all the blood that was all over the front of her blouse, he looked at her beautiful face. "Just like a pretty little porcelain doll, ain'tcha, " Monty said to her now.

"What was that? Thanks for one last awesome roll in the hay? Oh sure, honey, no problem at all. Happy to oblige, happy to oblige,"Monty was saying to the corpse. Holding Cathy was like holding nothing, since she may have weighed 110 pounds soaking wet, Monty thought to himself.

Now he'd thrown her over his shoulder," yes, just like a cotton' pickin' soldier," Monty sang along to the childhood song, and then," yes, little princess Cathy, don't you worry, ol' Monty's taking you home now, to your castle, baby girl", Monty chatted away, gazing into her eyes every now and then.

Now he threw her down on the ground, almost dead center in the middle of the corn field, and in a mocking gesture, he bowed, as if paying homage to royalty.

"Yes, your highness," he told the corpse, "I bow before you," he fnished, with a sarcastic smirk.

Cathy's eyes, beautiful and full of love in life, now looked haunted and filled with terror in death. Monty had looked down at her, gazing into her eyes. He thought about taking her one last time, but he decided against it, since he was running late anyways. What a waste of a hard-on, he thought to himself.

With one final glance at her, feeling something that was perhaps as close to love as Lamont Andrew Hallmen could ever feel for another human being, he bent down to the ground and kissed her lips. Deciding that he didn't like the way her eyes looked, he closed them, and then standing up again, gave a final bow; his last dues to his princess.

Monty sang along now to a song on the radio, as he drove down the highway. He was feeling so good right now, he thought to himself. Turning into the entrance of Jaybel Products, he quickly found a parking spot and threw his car in park. Glancing at his watch, he saw that he had just made it, with a minute to spare. Damn, I'm good, Monty chuckled to himself, as he waltzed through the front door and punched in at 11pm on the dot.

"Wasn't sure you were gonna make it in, tonight," his foreman Scott Dwyer told him. "Besides, you look like you were having too much fun before you got here," he added, clapping Monty on the back.

"You know it," Monty told him with a laugh. "Good times, to be sure," he added softly.

"So pray tell what all did you get into tonight? You must've got laid, at the very least," Scott told him with a laugh. "You look too damned happy and relaxed to NOT have gotten laid," he laughed again to Ben Darius, who had just made it in, too. "Maybe that's Ben's excuse, too," Scott clapped Ben on the back as well.

Ben chuckled, but he didn't have the relaxed look about him that Monty did. "Naw, I didn't get laid; hell, I barely got any sleep," Ben complained with a chuckle. "Didja'll forget I got a 3 month old baby?" he added, shaking his head.

Scott looked up from the clipboard that he was writing on. "So Monty, that just leaves you for that juicy story you were getting ready to tell us," he added.

"Now, now, what's that line? A gentleman never kisses and tells," Monty told Scott, pretending to be serious.

"Always the joker," Scott laughed. "Seriously, we're all dyin' here. We live for these stories of yours, with all your exploits, all the women, all the sex....well, you know what we like," Scott added, as Ben waited to hear the story along with Scott.

"Yeah, it's no time to be shy; and hell, you've never been a gentleman; no point starting now," Ben added, with Scott's raucous laughter in his ear.

Monty pretended to sigh with exasperation, but he loved this shit. This place and these people were like his home away from home. Hell, he liked it here more than he ever liked it at that damned farm, Monty had thought to himself on many occasions.

He enjoyed the camaraderie here that he'd really never experienced before. With his devil may care attitude and the stories of all the chicks he'd nailed, Monty enjoyed regaling his stories to the guys, and what he enjoyed the most, was being the popular guy that everyone wanted to be friends with.

Taking a deep breath now, he said,"okay, I guess you guys have had to wait long enough for the latest and greatest. I DID get laid about an hour ago, and it was definitely one of the hottest lays of my life," he chuckled, watching Scott's eyes grow wide, and hearing Ben urge him on with his story.

"You're killin' me, man," Scott laughed. "One of these days you gotta tell us all your secrets," he added.

Monty now pretended to be modest, and shrugged his shoulders with a smile. "No secrets, just a way of making things happen," he laughed. "And that's only the half of it," he added, a smug look coming over his face now.

"What the hell, man?" Scott laughed again. "You better not be holding out on us now."

"Well, if ya'll, REALLY must know...," Monty started, trailing off for a few seconds.

"Oh, no you don't," Ben protested. "You can't just start something and then not finish the story; you just can't do that to us, you know. We live for this shit, man. With me, a married man, with two little kids, and Scott, here, who's just basically all washed up...." Ben added.

"Hey, now wait a minute," Scott laughed, pretending to have his feelings hurt. "I might be over 40, but I'm certainly not washed up now," he advised Ben and Monty, who were both laughing heartily

"Okay, Monty, as your foreman, I am ordering you to finish your story now," Scott told Monty, pretending to throw his weight around.

Monty sighed dramatically, as if he were mulling this over in his mind. Then, with a twinkle in his eye, he winked at Ben and then told them,"Well, okay, then, if you insist, but you know this story just ain't for the faint-hearted now," Monty pretended to admonish his friends.

Their laughter had drawn the rest of the small midnight crew over, and now Jim Basile and Don Wickes walked over. After filling them in on Monty's evening up to the point where he stopped, everyone was waiting for Monty to finish his story.

Monty smiled to himself; this was the kind of shit he lived for, he thought to himself. This is like the family I never had, he chuckled to himself.

"Well, alright, I guess I've made you guys wait long enough," he pretended to lament to them, " so I'll tell you what happened next. First I took that little whore and had my way with her in every conceivable way known to man," Monty laughed again, as his foreman Scott clapped him on his back.

"THEN....and this is the good part," Monty paused for a second, to really add to the suspense of his story," then that little whore had the audacity to scream at me and tell me I raped her," he continued.

"She was screaming at me and then she decided to try to slap me and hit me. So I threw her on the ground, held her arms down, and slapped HER a few times," Monty exclaimed, pausing long enough to let out another roar of laughter.

"Then...." Monty began, but his good buddy Scott stopped him, and said,"Are you serious, man?" he asked Monty incredulously.

"Well, hell yes," Monty told him, and now the others were all laughing, and Scott was telling Monty that he really did show that girl who was boss and all, yes sirreeee....

"So anyways, is that the rest of the story?" Ben asked Monty now, and Monty laughed again, shaking his head and making sure his audience was rapt with attention.

"No, there's actually a bit more to this story," Monty said carefully, teasing the others a little, wanting to see how bad they really want to hear how all of this played out, "yes, there's definitely more...one might almost say I haven't gotten to the best part yet," Monty teased, and Ben and Scott both stared at Monty, unbelieving that ANYTHING could possibly top all of this.

"Alright, enough already, finish this story up so we can get some work done tonight and go home," Scott told Monty, clapping him on the back again in his usual friendly manner.

"True." Monty agreed. "Okay, so anyways, I stop the whore from slapping me, and instead, I pick her up and throw her back in my car, and we take ourselves a bit of a drive," Monty said thoughtfully, enjoying the attention he was still receiving.

"We get to our final destination, and the whore isn't laughing anymore," Monty said to his friends, thoughtfully.

"No, suddenly she is quite afraid, to the point where she is just shaking like a leaf," he continued. "So there we are, literally in the middle of nowhere pretty much, and suddenly I take out my hunting knife I always carry with me, and after I toy with her for a bit, I stab her right in the heart. You never seen so much blood," Monty admitted, not seeming to notice now, that no one was laughing. His friend Ben looked downright nauseous, as though he was literally fighting with himself over whether he would hurl all over the place or not.

"I pulled it out of her, and her eyes were HUGE, man, like she just couldn't believe it. So just to help her make sure she didn't dream any of this, I stabbed her again in the same place," Monty continued, his eyes taking on an almost dreamy look.

"That's it, man. Oh, I did tell her, I said, well, now you know what a broken heart feels like...literally," Monty smiled, obviously quite pleased with himself.

It was so quiet in the plant now, that it was downright eerie, Monty thought to himself. His friends, who had all been laughing hysterically right along with him, were now just staring at him, unable to speak, move, or anything.

Finally, Monty broke the silence. "Wow, I don't recall ever seeing any of you so damned quiet all at the same time, too," he said thoughtfully, stroking the stubbles on his chin.

After a few more seconds, his boss, Scott, started to laugh, and putting an arm around Monty, he said,"Okay, okay, I get it; this is kinda like seeing who is actually gonna buy this bullshit story, right? I gotta tell you, Monty, you ARE good; I mean, hell, I almost fell for it," Scott marveled, shaking his head, and laughing once again.

Monty smiled back at Scott, and Ben just stood there looking at Monty, seemingly in a bit of a stupor.

"Oh, okay, so that was just all bullshit?" Ben asked, a look of pure relief flooding over his face.

Jim and Don nodded too, looking almost relieved when they thought that Monty's story was all bullshit.

Before the guys could waste anymore time, Scott told everyone their assignments and areas for the night, and then, hearing the telephone clanging loudly in the background, he scurried off to answer it.

"Jaybel Products, Scott Dwyer speaking, can I help you?" Scott spoke into the phone, putting a hand over his other ear to try to block out some of the noise.

A woman's voice, sounding somewhat hysterical, practically shouted into the phone, and Scott could hear lots of music blasting, as though the woman was calling him from a bar. He almost hung up the phone right away, thinking that someone was just being silly and pranking him, until the woman told him who she was.

"I am sorry to bother you; who's in charge over there, please?" she asked.

She doesn't sound drunk, Scott thought to himself. "I'm the foreman here on third shift, actually," he told her. "How can I help you?" he asked her again, a gentle kindness in his voice.

"Please, sir, I know this will sound weird, but please bear with me and hear me out," Shana told Scott. "My name is Shana Hawkes. I need to know just a few things. I know that Monty Hallmen works thirds over there, and I need to know if he came in to work tonight," she asked, her voice shaking slightly.

"Yes, he's here; did you need to speak with him?" Scott asked her, getting ready to send for Monty.

"No...at least not yet. Look, I apologize for all of this, sir, but here's the story. My kid sister and I were out with our friend tonight, and now suddenly she's missing. Her car is still in the parking lot here at Cal's, with the backseat door wide open and all. The last I saw of her, she'd told me that she wanted to get a roll of quarters that she'd left out here in her car, and well, she never came back. Monty Hallmen was here, too, and they'd gotten into a scuffle. They'd been seeing each other for awhile, but Cathy had broken up with him well over a month ago, and it didn't sound like he was taking it very well at all," Shana told Scott.

"I honestly never saw Hallmen leave; I just noticed after a time when Cathy never came back at all, that Hallmen was gone, as well. Cathy would never have just left her car door wide open like this, either, and well, none of this is making any sense, and I can't shake this horrible feeling I have," Shana finished, her voice faltering a bit.

Suddenly Scott was hearing Monty's voice in his head, talking and laughing it up when he first got here about his evening and all. Scott had chills running up his spine now; Monty never did tell them that he had just made that story up, did he, Scott thought to himself.

"Look; maybe if you talk to Monty, he can put your mind at ease, and tell you what happened," Scott told Shana. Deep down though, he doubted seriously that that would happen. "Do you want me to get him for you?" Scott asked Shana now.

But Shana was crying now. "I don't know why I am so scared, but I can't get rid of this horrible feeling," she told Scott.

Probing gently, Scott asked," What feeling is that, Shana? If you're scared, there's probably a good reason for it, right?" he added.

Now, Shana just put it all out there. "I'm scared," she began slowly, "because I can't shake the feeling that he did something to her. She's been my best friend forever, and I am so scared that something bad has happened to her," Shana finished, her voice almost a hushed whisper.

Suddenly, Scott had made a decision. "Look, Shana, I don't know if I should be telling you this," Scott began, feeling uncomfortable and disloyal, all at the same time, but still he plodded ahead. "When Monty got here tonight, he spoke of.... well, he spoke of the evening he'd had before he got here," Scott stammered, suddenly not sure of how to even get into this with a stranger on the other end of the phone.

"Please, Scott. Whatever you may have been told, or whatever you have heard, you gotta tell me. No one has seen Cathy for at least two hours now, and I have talked to everyone at Cal's. I called her house and spoke to her husband, who is worried sick as well," Shana told him, "but like I said, this is scary, because Cathy is a very dependable person. She wouldn't just take off like this," Shana explained.

"Okay, well, here's the thing. He told us a story of, well, of getting laid. He never told us the girl's name. And then, he.... well, Oh God, I don't know how to say this," Scott said, "so I'll just come out and say it; he told us that he took this girl somewhere and, um, and, stabbed her in the heart," Scott said, his voice almost inaudible now.

"What? Oh my God; and you didn't call the police?" Shana demanded, now. "Do you think he was for real?," Shana asked him, her voice almost a whisper.

"God, I don't know now," Scott admitted. "When he told the story, especially that part, he looked so damned serious. And then I told him to quit kidding around and told everyone to get to work," Scott told her.

"But you know...." Scott became thoughtful now. "You know, he never did come out and tell us that he was just fooling around, or that he really didn't stab her, or that he was just making up the story," he said now. "I hate to say this....I mean, he's my friend, as well as my employee, but....I dunno, Shana, I guess I am trying to tell you that maybe you should call the police," Scott told her now, suddenly turning around in his office and looking out into the plant. Monty was working, as always, Scott noticed. He'd always seemed to be a decent worker, Scott mused to himself now. Suddenly, as he was talking to Shana, Monty looked right at Scott, and his eyes almost bore a hole right into Scott's.

An uneasy feeling passed, and Scott made a decision. If Monty could joke around about killing someone, about stabbing her twice in the heart, I mean, let's face it, Scott thought to himself, that really isn't funny. Monty WAS a braggart though, Scott mused, and seemed to say anything to get all the guys' attention.

"Shana, call the police. Maybe they can send someone over here to talk to Monty," he told her. "If you need anything else, don't hesitate to call me," he added.

Hanging up the phone now, Ben poked his head in the doorway. He gaped at Scott, and thought that he'd never seen that look on Scott's face before today. Instinctively, he felt like there was something very wrong. Monty was watching both of them now, his eyes taking on a hooded, guarded look.

"Scott? Boss...you okay?" Ben asked. "I don't know, Ben. I just had a very disturbing conversation with a gal I don't even know," Scott was telling Ben.

"Well, tell me about it; I mean, you look like you've seen a ghost or something, I dunno," Ben told his boss, concern furrowing his brow.

"Maybe I have, Ben," Scott told him, looking straight at Monty now. "Maybe I have."

1979

Dr. and Cassandra Watkins sat nervously in Dr. Sanders office, now, waiting for Dr. Fong to arrive. Cassandra looked over at her husband now, and he saw the utter pain and heartache he felt, mirrored in her eyes. Her eyes were beyond puffy at this point, and he knew he didn't look much better.

He'd taken the rest of the week off, and told his secretary to cancel all of his appointments for the next week. In a quiet voice, he told her that his daughter had passed away, and the shock of it all came through Cara Lindsey's voice, as she gave him her heartfelt condolences. The whole feeling in their office now, seemed to be one of sadness intermingled with unbelievable shock. As Cara had watched Dr. Watkins walk away, she thought she'd never seen such a sad, dejected sight in her whole life.

Dr. Sanders had just come in his office right before they'd arrived a couple minutes ago, and aside from greeting them warmly and asking them if he could get them anything to drink, he'd been silent. He didn't seem to dare to want to ask them how they were doing, because, in his mind's eye, it seemed like an incredibly stupid question to ask. Besides, Dr. Sanders thought to himself, the pain and sorrow on their faces pretty much said it all. He thought that they'd both aged ten years at least, overnight. Dr. Sanders thought of his own wife and children. He had two sons and one daughter, who was still living at home with them. His sons were both away at college, and his daughter seemed to thrive at home with them in the evenings, having her mom and dad all to herself, for once.

Dr. Fong was walking in Dr. Sanders office now, wearing a very troubled and serious face. He apologized to everyone for keeping them waiting, but the Watkins just waved it off, knowing full well how difficult it was for doctors to keep a schedule.

Sitting down next to Cassandra, Dr. Fong cleared his throat. He wondered if he was supposed to start talking first, but then Dr. Sanders began to speak.

"As you know from our earlier telephone conversation, I wanted to go over the autopsy report with you. I also took the liberty of making sure that you had your own personal copy," he added, passing a sheet of paper to Dr. Watkins.

Looking over at Dr. Fong now, Dr. Sanders nodded at him, and Dr. Fong cleared his throat again and began speaking.

"I am horrified," he admitted. "This report clearly tells us that your daughter Connie died from a drug overdose. The coroner found large traces of Xanax in her bloodstream, which, when combined with the morphine that she was still hooked up to, basically slowed down and suppressed her breathing, until she just stopped breathing altogether," Dr. Fong added, his voice having dropped to just above a whisper. He'd been dreading this since this morning, even though he knew that it must be done. How the hell does one convey this information to a broken hearted parent, though, he'd asked himself off and on all day.

Although he was much younger, Dr. Fong had come from a larger family than most, and he was very close to the four sisters and one brother that he had. He couldn't begin to fathom what it would be like to lose one of them, he'd thought to himself. Having just gotten engaged to Mia Lee earlier in the year, he not only looked forward to their life together, but of starting a family one day soon. He couldn't imagine going through something so unbelievably awful. His heart went out to Dr. and Mrs. Watkins, and he wished to God that they had more answers, but they didn't.

Dr. Watkins was looking at Dr. Fong now, a mixture of shock and anger contorting his features. Cassandra Watkins just looked shocked; twice, she'd opened her mouth as though to say something, and then, just shut it again.

"How the hell could that be?" Dr. Watkins thundered at them. Normally a very placid, easy going man, Dr. Watkins was now demanding some type of action, some type of recourse, or something that made some kind of sense, for heaven's sake.

Cassandra touched her husband's arm gently, and he tenderly took her hand into his own. Still, he pressed on. "She never took Xanax a day in her life, as far as I know," Dr. Watkins claimed. "She was never one to even take a damned aspirin, unless she had such a bad migraine that she couldn't stand it anymore, and then she would take the aspirin and go to bed. She always claimed that sleep made the migraine go away," he prattled on.

Almost as an afterthought, he looked again at Cassandra and asked her if he'd left anything out, as far as their daughter's prescriptions went. Cassandra thought for a second, and then mentioned the birth control pills that she had taken for the past several years to help control her extreme menstrual cramps.

* * *

Nodding his head, Dr. Fong scratched at the new stubble growth on his chin thoughtfully. "I know, Dr. Watkins," he added. "That's what makes this so damned frustrating," he said. "None of this makes any sense at all; Dr. Sanders and I both have gone over everything many times. There was never any Xanax prescribed to her; as far as we know, she didn't seem to be anxious or anything, and she didn't have any trouble sleeping, either. She DID seem very depressed when she lost the baby, of course. I got the feeling that she really did want that baby; maybe she was in love with the baby's father," Dr. Fong mused, closing his folder shut.

While Dr. Fong set his report down on the desk, Dr. Sanders picked up the rest of the conversation.

"The fact is, no one knows anything. No one knows how the hell the Xanax got into her bloodstream, or why, and not one single person on this whole damned floor saw anything or anyone," Dr. Sanders told them, frustration in his voice.

"You know, it just completely blows my mind how someone could have snuck into her room and gave it to her. They had to have put it in a drink; but there were no cups, glasses, bottles, nothing. And let's face it; people are constantly complaining how they never get any rest when they are in the hospital, because someone is always coming in the room to see how you're breathing, take your temperature, and so it goes," finished Dr. Fong, standing up to leave now.

"We did not want to tell you all these things on the phone," Dr. Fong said gently.

Dr. and Cassandra Watkins stood up now, as well. "Where would you like us to release her body to?" Dr. Sanders asked.

Cassandra spoke up then, saying," I called Simmons earlier this afternoon; they will be handling it all." Holding out her hand to first, Dr. Fong, and then Dr. Sanders, Cassandra thanked them both for their time and for their courtesy. Dr. Watkins also thanked them, and added a big thank you for all that they did for Connie when she was brought into the hospital after the accident.

"You know...I know it's not my business," Dr. Fong suddenly said. "I have always wondered about that accident. You know she lost all her brake fluid in that car, which is why she could not stop," Dr. Fong mused out loud. "I remember deputy saying brake line was nicked. Maybe you go talk to the guy that work on her car, see what he says," Dr. Fong added, and wishing them the best, he excused himself and left the room.

Dr. Watkins looked a bit confused for a moment, and looking at his wife, she said aloud," Well, Dr. Fong DOES have a good point; maybe I need to talk to that Hallmen kid that worked on her car." "Good idea," Dr. Sanders agreed, waving goodbye as they left.

1988

Shana Hawkes barely heard the last sentence or two that Scott Dwyer had told her. She was completely blown away by hearing that Monty had stabbed Cathy twice in the heart, and then went to work and laughed and joked about his evening.

A combination of rage and grief were playing on her emotions now. Begging to use the phone again, Shana called Remy. She didn't care what time it was now; the sooner someone went out looking for Cathy, the sooner we will find her, Shana told herself, not wanting to believe for a second that her best friend since school days might have been murdered.

At home, Remy was stirred awake by an annoying noise of some kind. As he finally woke up enough out of the deep sleep he was in, it finally dawned on him that it was the telephone.

Turning on his lamp, he put his glasses on and looked at the clock. It was damn near 2am, Remy thought; nothing good usually comes out of phone calls at this hour, either, he said to himself, as he hurried to grab the phone.

"Yeah, hello," Remy told the caller. "Remy, Sheriff, thank God," Shana babbled. "Thank God you're home," she said to him again.

"Yeah, Shana, I'm here; what's wrong? Has something happened?" he asked her, and then suddenly recalled that Shana was Cathy Grenaldi Hammond's best friend. A chill went through Remy, even though it was probably 80 degrees in his bedroom.

His gut was telling him something, Remy thought to himself. "Shana, tell me what's wrong, hon," Remy repeated to her patiently, since she didn't sound quite right tonight.

"Sheriff, Cathy Grenaldi is missing," she breathed into the phone. "We were celebrating my kid sister's birthday at Cal's, and Monty Hallmen was there, and him and Cathy got into it, cuz he was trying to talk to her and Cathy got mad and told him to leave her alone. Then she got up a bit later to go out to her car and get a roll of quarters that she thought that she had left out there, and she never came back. After she didn't come back and didn't come back, it occurred to me that Monty Hallmen was gone as well," Shana told Remy, wanting to make sure that he had all the facts.

"Then, just a minute or so ago, I called Jaybel Products; that's where Monty works; the only reason I knew that, was Cathy had told me that tonight when we were talking about him. He was sitting at the bar looking at us sometimes, but then he started talkin' to a redhead that sat down next to him, and we figured he was cool, cuz he didn't seem to really be paying attention to us anymore," Shana continued.

"Anyways, this guy named Scott answered the phone at Jaybel, and said he was the foreman for 3rd shift, and I asked him if Monty came to work tonight and he said yes, did I want to talk to him, and I told him, "No, not right now," and then I proceeded to tell him about Cathy disappearing at the bar and how Monty had been there as well, and then all of a sudden this guy is telling me how Monty went to work talking about his evening, and saying that he stabbed her twice in the heart. These guys thought he was just kidding around, at least till I called, and so this Scott guy told me I should just call the police," she finished, taking a deep breath afterwards.

For as out of it as Remy had been when the ringing phone had roused him from his bed, he sure as hell was awake now, he thought to himself.

"Is Cathy's car still over there at Cal's?" he was asking Shana now.

"Yeah, it's still here; her husband Roger wanted to come out and pick it up and drive it home, but I told him the police would want to look at it first," Shana told Remy.

"Well, that's certainly true, Shana; good thinking," Remy said.

"Thanks for calling me and letting me know what's going on, too," he told Shana. "We'll take care of everything from here," he added.

Hanging up the phone now, Remy quickly got dressed and called his deputy Samuel. "Sam, we got a problem," he greeted him with, and then filled him in on his conversation with Shana.

"This ain't sounding good," Samuel said. "No, not at all; I got me a bad feeling about all of this, " Remy told him. "So get dressed and make us a thermos of coffee, Sam; I'll be there to pick you up in ten minutes or so," he added, looking at his watch now.

"Won't that be out of your way, though?" Sam asked, feeling a bit confused.

"Normally, yes, but you and I are gonna pay Mr. Hallmen a visit," Remy replied, an edge to his voice that Sam knew was pure anger because Cathy was missing and no one knew where she was.

"Okay, see you soon," Samuel told Remy, hanging up the phone.

Samuel felt sick inside. He wanted desperately for Cathy to be alive and well, but he kept getting the nagging feeling that when they found Cathy, they would find a corpse.

Chiding himself now, he had been going to have a quick bite to eat, since he'd had such an early dinner last night, but he found now that he had no appetite at all. He'd known Cathy since they were kids, even though he'd had a crush on her sister Kellie, all through high school. Cathy was genuinely sweet, and such a beauty, Sam thought, picking up his service revolver now.

Oh dear God, Samuel thought to himself now. He wondered if Roger, Cathy's husband, had called Kellie and told her that Cathy was missing.

Flipping on the kitchen light, he started a pot of coffee and his buddy Roscoe, a rescued police dog that had belonged to a friend who had gotten killed in the line of duty, came up to him now, wagging his tail.

"C'mon, boy, let's go outside, ok? I gotta go to work," he told the dog now, and while they walked to the backyard, he told Roscoe that he was very worried this time.

The dog always seems to have this capacity to look like he is listening to every word I say, Sam chuckled to himself. Still, he was so grateful that he had Roscoe, and for someone who had never really been much of a dog person, Roscoe certainly had changed all of that.

Roscoe quickly did his business, and Samuel brought him back in the house, pouring some food in his bowl. He sighed to himself, and scratching his ears, he told the dog that it could be a long day, today. Roscoe looked at him, seeming to understand, and licked Samuel appreciatively.

Pouring the coffee into his thermos, Sam looked out the kitchen window, and seeing Remy's headlights in his driveway, said goodbye to Roscoe and locked up the house.

Remy looked like hell, but it struck Sam that it was more about the fear that seemed to have permeated both of the mens' very core. As he settled into the cruiser, he poured Remy a cup of coffee, and the older man sighed.

"Good coffee, son," Remy told him. "God, Sam, I can't shake this feeling that this is gonna be bad," he told the younger man, and pouring himself a cup of coffee, Sam agreed.

"Let's do this," Sam said, and nodding firmly, Remy backed out of the driveway and headed out to Jaybel Products.

Roger Hammond was shaking; Kellie, Cathy's sister, had just walked in their house, and after she laid Dylan back down, she made a pot of coffee.

Sitting across the table from him, Kellie thought that her brother-in-law looked like a mess. His right arm still spasmed and shook, frequently, apparently an aftermath of the night he'd gotten beaten up. His eyes were wet, Kellie noticed, and she knew that he'd been crying.

She extended a hand to Roger now, from across the kitchen table, and he gratefully took it.

"Let's pray, Roger. Would you pray with me?" she asked him earnestly, and Roger nodded.

"Dear God," Kellie began, and suddenly her voice began to break. Roger picked up the prayer for her now, and squeezed her hand. "Dear God, we are so scared," he began. "Please, please, let Cathy be safe; please bring her safely home to us; we all need her so much," and now Roger's voice broke, and the unshed tears that had filled his eyes, began to trail down his cheeks.

Kellie nodded, and squeezed Roger's hand again. She let Roger do whatever he needed to do; sometimes he cried, and sometimes he sat in silence, as though completely lost in thought.

Now, it seemed like Roger needed to talk, so filling up their cups with coffee, Kellie sat back down with him and listened.

"You know, I kept watching the clock and waiting for Cathy to pull up in the driveway. She'd promised she wouldn't be late," Roger continued, staring morosely into space.

" She was so good about always letting me know where she was going, and what time she would be home," he added now.

"That's why none of this makes any sense," he told Kellie. " Tonight, when midnight came and went, and she still wasn't here, I called over by Cal's, and then a few moments later, Shana got on the phone".

"I was floored when she told me that Hallmen had been there earlier, and had given Cathy a hard time. Cathy walks out to her car to get a roll of quarters and never comes back," Roger said, shakily. "Then she says that after more time goes by, and

Cathy still never came back, she notices Hallmen is gone too. She asked the bartender how long Hallmen had been gone, and he thinks a good ten, fifteen minutes, at least," Roger tells Kellie, his voice filled with exhaustion and fright.

"But her car is still there, right?" Kellie asked him now. "Yeah, her car is still there, and Shana says the police want to check it out before I come get it," he told Kellie.

"None of this is making any sense," Roger continued. "I know for a fact that Cathy really had ended things with Hallmen when she'd said that she did. "Things had been going so well between us, Kellie; it was like we had fallen in love with each other all over again," he practically whispered now, his voice cracking again, and the tears slid down his face.

"Roger, don't," Kellie told him gently. "Now, we don't know yet for sure what has happened, so let's just keep praying for her, and let's try to keep an open mind until we DO know," Kellie added, surprising herself on how well she could say these things that, deep down, she just didn't feel.

Roger nodded his head now, and Kellie got up to check on Dylan, who was sleeping in Cathy and Roger's bed. She bent over and kissed his soft little cheek, gently pushing the curly blond hair out of his face. Pulling the cover up on him, she noticed he had his thumb in his mouth. He hadn't done that in a really long time, Kellie mused, wondering if even poor Dylan was picking up the nervous vibes of his uncle and his mom.

"So what's happening now?" Kellie asked. "Did you say that Remy and Samuel were going out to where Hallmen works? "Yeah, that's what Remy had told me," Roger explained. "He said that he would keep us posted, too," he added, standing up now and dumping the rest of the coffee in the sink.

The phone rang now, and both Kellie and Roger almost jumped out of their skin. Roger grabbed the cordless, hoping for some news.

"Hello," he answered, hearing Remy talking to Samuel in the background. "Hey, Roger, listen, I'm just calling to tell you that Sam and I are heading over to Jaybel's now; we're going to take Hallmen in for questioning, so I'll keep you posted on anything we find out," Remy added, saying goodbye and clicking the phone off.

"Remy and Sam are heading over to Jaybel, where Hallmen works," Roger told Kellie. "He says they are going to bring him in for questioning and he'll keep us posted," he added.

"Okay, well that's good. I am glad that they're going to question him thoroughly this time," Kellie told Roger.

"This time?" Roger asked. "Well, you know, I just mean that after Duncan got killed and you got beat up, I really thought that Remy would be breathing down Hallmen's neck pretty hard, but he didn't seem to do much about it," Kellie shrugged now.

"Yeah, I know what you mean; I understand where Remy was coming from though, especially when Hallmen seemed to have airtight alibis for his whereabouts. Nowadays especially, things can get ugly when there's no proof," he admitted.

"Why don't you try to lay down with Dylan for a little while?" Roger asked Kellie now. "I am too wired to ever go to sleep, so I will be right here to answer the phone," he added.

"I don't think I can sleep, either," Kellie admitted, "but I think I will lay down with Dylan for a little bit and see if I can't doze for a few minutes," she added, patting Roger's back on her way out of the kitchen.

Roger took the cordless phone with him to the living room and sat down on the overstuffed chair that Cathy had surprised him with, two summers ago for their anniversary. The chair was a huge recliner, and sometimes, Roger had often thought, much more comfortable than a bed.

The TV sat across from the chair, but Roger didn't turn it on. It was very quiet in the house now, and Roger found it to be soothing to his frayed nerves.

Closing his eyes, he fell asleep almost immediately. He dreamed of Cathy now, in their younger days together, and he dreamed of their wedding day.

But the dreams, although they'd started out so sweet and wonderful, turned into a nightmare that woke Roger up with a start; his body shaking in fear. Seconds before he awoke, he saw Cathy, bleeding, crawling towards him, begging him to help her. He saw her gasp, fall to the ground, and then she was no more.

1979

Mindy's hands had begun shaking since that horrible phone call, a little over an hour ago. She felt like she was in a state of shock like she'd never been, in her whole life.

When she'd gotten off of work late this afternoon, she'd had absolutely no idea that a person's day could fall apart this quickly.

She was bone tired now, and the big dinner she'd planned on cooking for everyone tonight would have to wait until tomorrow, perhaps, she'd mused to herself. There were 4 nurses out with the flu, right now, so everyone that had managed to stay healthy so far was trying to fill in wherever they might be needed.

Within minutes of walking in the door, the phone began its loud, shrill ringing.

She could hear her sister say something, but something seemed very wrong, what with the little bit she could hear. For a moment, Mindy had thought that she had gotten a prank call, because she really couldn't hear much of anything on the other line.

"Hello? Hello? "Oh, Cassie, it's you. I can barely hear you, honey; we must have a bad connection or something," Mindy told her sister. A moment later, she heard Cassie say something very weird, her voice sounding as though she was calling from a continent away. The small, broken voice sounded so unlike her sister's usual manner of speaking, and now Mindy shivered against the chill that had risen up her spine, in spite of the blistering heat she'd just come in from.

"Cass? Cassie, are you okay? Is something wrong, honey?" Mindy asked.

"Oh, Mindy," the crumpled voice said on the other line. "She's gone, Mindy," the voice kept saying, over and over again.

"Cassie, what are you talking about? Who's gone? What are you trying to tell me, honey?" Mindy asked her sister now, her arms having broken out with goosebumps.

After what seemed like forever, the small voice said," It's Connie, Mindy. She's gone," Cassandra told her sister.

"Well, what do you mean? Where did she go?" Mindy asked, trying to be patient with her sister, but feeling irritation beginning to creep up into her voice.

"No, Mindy...you don't understand; Connie didn't go anywhere.....she's dead, Mindy....my baby is dead," Cassandra told her sister, and then the tears muffled out anything else coherent that perhaps Cassandra might have been able to say.

Just as Mindy thought she would go mad, suddenly Carter got on the phone. "Mindy?" he asked into the phone. "Yes, Carter, I'm here; what the hell is going on? Connie.....what happened? Is she really gone?" Mindy asked, her voice catching now, her mind mentally asking just how long had it been since Connie had been here for a visit; a couple weeks? My GOD, Mindy thought to herself, as she wiped away the tears that had begun streaming down her face.

"Yes, Mindy, it's all true. Connie is gone. She passed away yesterday afternoon, actually," Dr. Watkins explained to his sister-in-law.

For the next few minutes, Dr. Watkins brought Mindy up to speed with a condensed version of what all had transpired in the past week, with the car crash and everything else. He didn't tell Mindy that Connie had been pregnant, as well, and had lost the baby in the crash.

Mindy cried with him now, even as her mind started methodically making arrangements to get out to her sister's house. She decided that if she couldn't get a quick flight, then perhaps she would just drive.

Hanging up the phone now, she looked around in shock, and found that she was in her kitchen, although she didn't seem to even remember walking in here. With shaky legs, she walked into the living room and collapsed on the couch. She felt physically and now emotionally drained as well. Hearing a car, she looked out the window to see Stanley and the kids pulling into the driveway, and now Mindy faced the horror of having to tell her family that Connie was gone.

Knowing how much the kids loved Connie, she dreaded having to relay this news. She thought of her daughter Lorna, who had been overjoyed to have Connie staying with them. Lorna had always been especially close to Connie; God, she will be devastated, Mindy wept.

Stanley came in the house first, holding a couple pizza boxes, grinning broadly, until he saw his wife's face. He set the boxes down now, and grabbed Mindy, who looked as though she just might collapse.

"My God, Mindy, what's wrong, honey? Are you okay? Are you not feeling well? You're not getting that darned flu, are you?" he fired away all the questions at her, and she just kept shaking her head. The tears rolled down her face, and Stanley sat down on the couch next to her, pulling her close to him.

Just as she was about to tell Stanley the news, the kids all walked in, and one look at their mom told them instantly that something was terribly wrong.

Trey and Linc had been having a good-natured debate when they'd walked in the house, and Lorna had been refereeing the whole mess, until she'd glanced over at her parents. Her dad had a weird look on his face, and her mom looked like she'd been bawling for awhile now. Rushing over to the couch, she sat down on the other side of her mom now, even while her dad was holding her mom's hand.

With a voice even shakier than her hands were, Mindy set out to tell the kids about Connie, but before she could even get two words out, her voice cracked terribly, and as the tears flowed again, she looked at her husband and shook her head.

Composing herself now, she decided she had to get this over with, while everyone was together. She knew she didn't want to have to go through all of this again, so after she blew her nose, she began to tell everyone about Connie.

Trey looked as though he'd just seen a ghost; Mindy couldn't remember the last time he looked that way. Linc was fighting back tears, while shaking his head in disbelief, and Lorna was leaning into her mother now, tears coursing freely down her face.

"She was just here," Trey broke the silence, his voice sounding incredibly small.

"Yeah, I know," Stanley admitted, his eyes welling up with tears as well. He couldn't begin to imagine the pain and suffering that Carter and Cassandra were going through right now, having just lost a child. Their only child, too, Stanley mused to himself now. My God, he thought to himself.

Clearing his throat, he asked Mindy how it happened. When Mindy had mentioned an accidental overdose, Trey's eyes got wide. "How the hell did that happen?" he demanded to know now. "Connie didn't DO drugs; hell, she wouldn't even take aspirin for a damned headache," he complained now, shaking his head with total disbelief.

Trying to keep her voice steady, Mindy looked over at Trey now; she had always heard, for a couple years now, off and on, that Trey sometimes sold drugs. Now, she hated having to ask him this, but a thought HAD occurred to her, and she had to ask.

"Trey....you, um...you didn't give Connie anything when she was here, did you?" she asked, and Trey could see she almost looked apologetic, but he stood there now gaping at his mother.

"Absolutely not, mom. Like I said, the Connie I've known my whole life doesn't do drugs...the only thing I can see that she's addicted to, is Coca-Cola," he added, now.

Lorna blew her nose loudly, and gave a half-hearted laugh to Trey's last comment, about the coke. "Yes, that's very true," she smiled through her tears. "She only needed one bottle a day, but boy oh boy, she sure would seem to go through withdrawals when she couldn't have a coke," Lorna laughed now.

"This is unreal," Linc told everyone. "My cousin....Gone? How do we even process this?' he asked, finally letting the tears escape his eyes.

"I know, guys," Stanley told everyone. "I was just imagining to myself the complete and utter sorrow that her parents are having to live through. What a nightmare," he added.

The hot pizza grew cold, as it lay uneaten in the boxes. The huge appetite that everyone had had seemed to vanish, as a dark foreboding cloud hung over all of them.

Mindy told Stanley that she needed to get over to her sister's as soon as possible. Stanley murmured his agreement, and asked now if she wanted to fly or if she thought she could handle the long drive.

"You know, Mindy, I would really feel a lot better if either we all went together, so that I could drive you, or if you flew, especially if you want to get over there as quickly as possible," Stanley told his wife.

"Yes, I can understand that, honey...I really don't know that I am up for that long drive all by myself, to be honest," she told her husband. "What about work for you; I am going to call the hospital and talk to my supervisor," Mindy told him now, getting up from the couch, and crossing the living room.

"I can probably get the time off," Stanley told her. "I'll call my partner and see what's going on, but I don't think there is anything especially pressing right now," he added.

Trey and Linc sat on the floor looking at each other now, and Lorna plopped down on the floor next to them.

"You guys okay?" she asked. "As okay as I'm gonna be for awhile," Linc told her, while Trey just miserably nodded his head.

"Yeah, I know. None of this makes any sense at all," Lorna said now, looking at Linc to see what he thought.

"You probably spent more time with her than the rest of us, though," Linc pointed out to her. "Did she say anything at all when she was here, about anything?" he prodded.

"Linc, do you realize how crazy that sentence sounds? Of course she said things when she was here," Lorna giggled, in spite of herself. Suddenly the smiles faded from her face, and she wore a pensive expression now.

"What?" Linc asked. "You thought of something; don't deny it, I can see it on your face," he told her.

"Well, she DID tell me some private stuff, that's for sure," Lorna said thoughtfully.

"Well? Is that all you're going to say?" Trey asked her, a look of disgust crossing his face.

Sighing loudly at him, Lorna snorted," You know, Trey, sometimes in life, private stuff needs to stay private," she retorted, giving him a dirty look, just as their parents both walked back into the living room.

"What's going on, guys?" Mindy asked now, a look of concern passing over her features. She noticed that Lorna looked angry and Trey was rolling his eyes at her. Linc just looked confused.

"We were talking about whether or not Connie had confided anything to Lorna when she was here, and it became obvious that she had, but now Lorna is saying that some things that are private need to stay private. But what if someone deliberately gave her the drugs and she didn't know it?" Linc pointed out to everyone now.

"It DOES sound like someone came in and gave Connie the drugs in a drink; that's what her dad seems to think happened," Mindy mused aloud. "The morphine that she was on, plus the Xanax that had been deliberately given to her, caused her to basically stop breathing altogether," Mindy explained.

"But maybe it was someone that Connie had mentioned in passing, when she was here; I know she would have confided in Lorna," Linc added.

"You mean like a guy? Well, that IS a thought, I guess," Stanley said thoughtfully now.

Linc was on the phone, now, to his employer, telling him that he wouldn't be in for the rest of the week, and Trey finally got up and made a move to the pizza boxes.

"Is anyone gonna get mad if I eat some pizza?" he asked, almost forlornly, and Lorna almost laughed out loud.

"Yes, Trey, we are gonna be really mad, especially Dad, because he bought all that pizza so we would all just look at it," she joked.

At that, Linc had to chuckle, then Trey; soon everyone laughed at Lorna and Trey's exchange, and they all went into the kitchen.

"Seriously, though, I would think that it would be so easy to mix the drugs in a cold bottle of coke," Lorna suddenly piped up, out of the blue.

Getting up to answer the phone, Stanley nodded his agreement. Everyone sat quietly for a couple minutes or so, seemingly lost in their own thoughts.

Stanley was back now, and told everyone that everything was all squared away for him, as far as work was concerned.

"Henry said to take as much time as we need; he can cover everything for the next week or so," he added.

"What a great guy," Mindy said, pouring herself a glass of merlot. "Definitely," Stanley agreed, then,"hey, pour me a glass of that too, will you, honey?"

Helping themselves to another slice of pizza, the boys asked Lorna if she knew anyone that Connie had mentioned that might have deliberately wanted to kill her. Chewing thoughtfully, the next comment out of Lorna's mouth practically blew everyone away.

"Actually, I have been thinking about that a lot, and yes, I do think that there may be someone that Connie mentioned that might have been happy the way things ended up turning out," she mused out loud.

"What? Seriously?" Linc asked, the shock quite evident in his voice.

"Yes, Linc....I am dead serious....actually, I don't think I'll be using that expression for awhile," she added. "There IS something that I had only found out about the night before Connie had gone home," Lorna told everyone.

"I mean, I'm sure you guys could tell that Connie was unbelievably quiet this time when she was here, right? I mean, she was the same ol' sweet Connie, but she didn't talk anywhere near as much as she normally does," Lorna explained to everyone.

"So....we went for a walk around the neighborhood, because you know how much Connie loves these fountains here at night," she continued. "I just flat out asked her what was going on," she added. "It was becoming more and more obvious to me as time went on that she wasn't going to talk about whatever was bothering her, and THAT wasn't like her not to confide in me, so I knew it was something really big.....and possibly bad," Lorna sighed now, taking a deep breath before she continued.

"Anyways, she finally confided in me, and told me that she was pregnant...

"PREGNANT?" Linc and Trey asked in unison, and if the whole thing wasn't so awful, having to tell everyone poor Connie's secrets, Lorna probably would've started laughing.

"Yes....you all heard right. She was pregnant, roughly around a couple months along. She hadn't told her parents, yet," Lorna added.

"She mentioned the guy a couple times....the baby's father....I think she was in love with him, maybe, but then she referred to him as Satan's child, too" Lorna admitted.

"The baby, or the baby's father?" Trey asked, who sometimes had trouble keeping up with conversations.

Linc burst out laughing now, in spite of everything. "I'm pretty sure she was talking about the baby's father," Linc explained to his older brother. "C'mon, Trey, keep up with us now," Linc laughed again.

Mindy waved an impatient hand now, signaling Lorna to continue with the story.

"Okay, so anyways, there's not much more than that, really... oh yeah, she DID say that she dreaded taking her car over to his place to get work done on it, and that when she did, she was going to have to tell him about the baby," Lorna added.

"This guy worked on her car?" Mindy asked incredulously. "Yeah, that's what Connie had said; she was going to get over there a week or so after she'd gotten back home," Lorna recalled now, thinking over their conversation. "Why, mom? You said that like it almost meant something, somehow," Lorna asked her mother now.

"Uncle Carter had told me that all this started from a car crash. Apparently, she was going down that one really big hill, I forget what it's called.."

"Cougar's Crossing?" Stanley offered. "Yes, that's the one," Mindy said, nodding her head.

"Anyways, she was coming down this hill and she had no brakes at all, so the car just kept going faster and faster, and then there was construction going on soon after that, so before she could do anything, she hit an oil slick on the road, lost control, and the car went flying off the road and into an embankment, where it rolled three times before it stopped," Mindy told everyone, looking as though she might start crying again at any time.

"Oh my God," Lorna exclaimed. "Okay, so now I get it... so that's why she was in the hospital," Lorna said, thinking aloud.

"Yes, that's what happened," Mindy said. "Neither Carter or Cassie had mentioned that Connie had been pregnant, though," she added thoughtfully.

"Maybe they didn't know yet," Lorna guessed. "Maybe she hadn't told them yet, and then she'd had that accident and maybe she lost the baby then; it seems logical, with the car rolling and everything," Lorna added.

"Yes, it does; oh yes, I remember the other thing Carter had said; he was saying that after the accident, the police had examined the car and said that the brake line had a small hole in it, almost like it had been nicked, instead of cut," Mindy remembered now.

"But....wait a minute," Mindy thought out loud now, furrowing her brow deeply. "Carter never mentioned anything about the fact that Connie had had her car worked on," she exclaimed

"If that's the case, we'll have to tell him," Stanley decided. "Well, I don't know about the rest of you, but I'm going to start packing my suitcase," he told them. "If we are planning an early start, we should all probably get busy doing that as well," he added.

Clearing the table, everyone now shuffled off to their own bedrooms, looking through closets, and starting to pack.

Lorna pulled out a blouse from her closet now, and holding it close to her, she remembered Connie wearing it while she was here. "It still smells like her cologne," Lorna said out loud to the empty room. And then the tears began to flow like a river, and still clutching the blouse to her chest, Lorna lay down on her bed now, feeling suddenly very alone.

1988

Monty Hallmen was sauntering up to the water fountain now, eyeing the clock on the wall, as he waited for the buzzer to go off.

He had seen his foreman Scott huddled in the corner of his office, talking in earnest to Ben. Their voices had seemed to be hushed, because try though he might, Monty couldn't hear a thing. Scott's face looked very serious, though, and at one point, Ben looked kinda freaked out. THAT was something, Monty thought to himself. His heightened senses were on high alert tonight, and his adrenaline was just now starting to slow down some.

Walking nonchalantly into Scott's office, his head jerked up at Monty as he heard him walk in.

"Damn, boss, you sure seem awful jumpy tonight," Monty said with a laugh, and he noticed that Scott had a weird look on his face.

With a chuckle he certainly didn't feel, Scott replied," Am I? Guess I drank way too much coffee before I got here tonight," he chuckled again, trying to just blow the whole business off.

"So...it looked like you and Ben were discussing something serious in here a little bit ago...we're not having layoffs again, are we?" Monty asked him now, knowing full well that Scott was not allowed to discuss that information with him, anyways.

"Now, Monty, " he began, and Monty cut him off. "Yeah, yeah, I know, you're not allowed to talk about it, right? Well, Ben looked like he'd just seen a ghost or something, so I was just curious," Monty told him, playing his part of the indifferent employee quite well.

"Really? Huh, I hadn't noticed," Scott told Monty, studying his clipboard now.

"C'mon, Scott; you and I have been friends for too long now to play games," Monty told him, a small smirk playing at the corner of his mouth.

"Huh? What are you talking about, Monty? " Scott muttered. "And why are you standing here talking? It's not break time yet," Scott added, his tone a bit put out.

"Yeah, I know it's not break time, Scott; listen....I know you want to know if what I told you was just a story or not," Monty began, willing Scott to quit looking at his clipboard and look at him.

"The girl you had sex with tonight?" Scott asked innocently, now writing new projections on the clipboard.

"Yeah; well, of course I had sex with her; we've already established that; but I'm thinking that you would really like to know if I actually did stab her in the heart, or if I made that shit up?" Monty continued, looking at Scott's face intently.

After he finished writing, Scott now looked up at Monty. "Well, I know you have a weird sense of humor, Monty; you WERE making that up, right?" Scott teased, turning around in his chair to throw some trash away.

Monty hunkered down a bit in front of Scott's desk now, so that his boss was almost eye level with him. Scott was getting more nervous now, because he really had no idea where the hell this shit was going, and he was getting more uncomfortable by the minute. He wished to God that the cops would get here; the sooner, the better. Monty just seemed too over the top, and too weird in general, tonight, and this whole entire conversation was making Scott feel weird.

"Weird humor or not, boss; it's the real fuckin' deal, man," Monty bragged now, looking like a man who seriously thought he was getting a medal for a job well done.

Scott slowly looked up again, this time looking Monty right in the eyes. He had a sick sensation in his stomach, and now all the coffee he had drank in the last few hours was churning up into an acidic inferno. He took a deep breath, and with a sigh, he threw his pencil down now on the desk.

"So....you're telling me that that story about stabbing that girl twice in the heart really happened?" Scott was asking now, suddenly noticing how insanely warm his head and his ears felt. Looking out of the corner of his eye, he saw Ben outside of his office window, staring intently, with a frightened look on his face.

"Yep, that's EXACTLY what I'm telling you. I tried to tell you before, but everyone just assumed I was kidding around, and then you made us get to work," Monty explained in a matter-of-fact voice.

"Yeah, sure, I remember that," Scott said slowly, not sure at all now what the hell he was supposed to be saying to Monty. Did this freak really think that he was going to high five him or something? Scott was getting the impression that that is exactly what Monty was waiting for.

"I seen you talking on the phone too, before you and Ben were in here huddled up," Monty observed, talking about all of this as nonchalantly as if he were discussing a grocery list.

"Yeah, I answered a phone call. So? That's part of my job; I AM the foreman," Scott told Monty now, the sick feeling inside beginning to turn into complete irritation. Damn, this fucker had some nerve, Scott thought to himself now. And where the hell were the damned cops, he asked himself again for the third time since Monty had walked in here.

Before Scott could say anything else, Monty asked," So did you call the cops on me?".

"No, I didn't; but I bet someone else did," Scott said now, rising slowly out of his chair. "You're going to be stuck inside for a long time, Monty. I hope this chick was worth it," he told Monty, shaking his head.

"They'll never be able to make it stick," Monty told Scott then. "There were no witnesses; and SHE ain't talkin'," Monty added, a sick, raucous laugh emanating from him, now.

"And if they do take me in, they better just lock my ass up and throw away the key," Monty continued.

"If I get out on bail, I will run so far that no one will ever see me again," he told his boss now.

Scott had had just about enough of this whole conversation. He really just wanted to go somewhere and have a drink. Or a dozen. Just as his nerves were on the verge of completely snapping, Scott could hear a small commotion taking place out in the lobby area.

Suddenly, Samuel and Remy loomed in, and Monty turned his head to look just in time to see the barrel of a gun pointed at his head. A detective whose name was Pete Krisp, and two other officers, swarmed around Scott's office now. The detective was 53 years old and had seen more shit in the 30 years that he'd been a cop than any human being should ever have to see. He'd spent over ten years in LA, and had just come out here last year from New York City, when his marriage broke up. He knew his parents' health was failing; his mother had been diagnosed with Alzheimer's last year, and his father had been battling prostate cancer off and on for a few years now. He had two sisters that lived somewhat close, but they never seemed to be able do much of anything to help out.

In fact, he'd had a pretty shitty day today, what with only getting three hours of sleep and getting into a bad fight with his kid sister, because he'd had the audacity to tell her that one mother managed to take care of three kids quite nicely, but now it seemed that only one kid wanted to be bothered to take care of their mother, and he'd lost his temper and told his sister that she was a selfish bitch.

Looking at this slimeball, Hallmen, Pete almost wished this guy would do something stupid, so he'd have a reason to shoot him. Pete was definitely up for that, today. Now he cocked his gun, aiming for Monty's head.

He didn't bother with niceties; there was really no point, Pete reasoned. He and Remy had gone way back together, and he knew how upset his friend was over this poor girl missing.

"Alright, asshole; this whole place is swarmin' with cops, just to pick your dumb ass up; can you believe it? Put your hands up where I can see them," Pete added, a snarl forming across his face.

Monty looked with almost contained amusement at Remy and this detective that had his gun aimed for his head.

"Let's talk about how many laws you're breakin' right about now," Monty asked, stupidly taunting the detective now.

"This ain't "Let's Make A Deal", Hallman; we ain't fuckin' around with you," Remy retorted, and Samuel nodded in agreement.

"Okay, okay, I got my hands up. What the hell is this all about?" Monty asked, and all Scott could seem to do was gape stupidly at Monty. He just couldn't believe this shit was happening here, tonight, in his office.

"You're coming' with us, boy," Remy added, putting cuffs on Monty. Pete was still standing there with the gun pointed.

"Are you sure you don't wanna do anything stupid tonight, Hallmen?" he asked. "Cuz I had me a really shitty day today, and somehow, if I could pull the trigger, I just know I would feel better," Pete chatted away.

Remy and Samuel were now leading Monty out of the plant and the rest of the guys just stood there and stared. Monty seemed totally unconcerned, though, and even told his boss that he'd be back tomorrow.

"The hell you will," Samuel said, under his breath. "The hell you will."

Two officers stayed behind at Jaybel's to interview Scott and Ben, mostly, but they also talked a bit to the others, as well.

Basically, everyone all had the same stuff to say, so after they got Scott's statement, they moved on to Ben, who still had a frightened, almost wild look in his eyes. He just couldn't believe all that had happened. How could he have been friends with someone who could be capable of such a vicious crime, he'd asked himself a few times already tonight.

The officers were sympathetic with Ben; they'd seen firsthand how devious killers often times were. There certainly wasn't anything Ben could have done differently, they assured him now.

Jim Basile and Don Wickes were sitting now in the break room, eating their dinner. Every now and then they would talk, but mostly, it seemed that they were still too blown away by the evening's events to talk much.

Scott walked over to them now, and sat down for a second. He snapped his fingers now, and quickly got back up and said," Damn, I forgot something; be right back," as he quickly walked off.

Ben walked over to the break room too, now, and set his heavy lunch pail down on the table, with a clang. He made the motions of opening it and setting everything out before him, but afterwards, he seemed almost oblivious to the food sitting in front of him.

Scott was back now, and he had a bottle of tequila, that he'd kept in his office for the past few months. One of their customers had vacationed in Mexico and given it to Scott. Opening the bottle, he sat down now with the other three, and after taking a big slug from the bottle, passed it around to everyone.

Seeing the look of surprise on their faces, he told them that after lunch, he was closing the place for the evening. He'd already checked in with his supervisor, and everyone looked at Scott with relief.

Now, suddenly Ben began to talk. "I just can't wrap my brain around this," he admitted to everyone. " I mean, Monty was supposed to be my friend. If I have a friend that can do something like that, what's that say about me?" Ben asked everyone, his features looking intense and frightened.

Scott looked at Ben now, and shook his head firmly. "No, Ben, you can't go there," he told him with a frown. "We all considered Monty a friend, but obviously, we only knew what he wanted us to know about him," Scott continued, taking another swig from the bottle.

"You'd have to say that about all of us; that we're all incapable of good judgment, because we never saw this coming. But we didn't kill that girl; HE did," Scott adamantly told everyone. "And seriously, who the hell wants to ever think ANYONE they know is capable of something like that?" he asked.

Ben sighed now, and had a drink from the bottle. He got up to go now, and thanked Scott for the drink. "I have two little girls," he said in a hushed voice. "I picture how devastated this poor girl's parents are going to be; I think about that now that I'm a parent, and I think if someone ever did that to my girls, I'd have to kill him myself," Ben said decidedly now.

The others agreed wholeheartedly, and wished Ben a good night. Scott walked with him to the door, then closed and locked it up behind him. The others would be leaving very soon as well, and as weird as this whole night had been, he didn't want to take any chances on anything else happening to anyone.

Jim and Don cleaned up their mess now, and stood up as well, preparing to go. It was obvious that no one was really going to get any work done tonight anyways, Scott had mused to himself. He was glad the place was closed for the rest of the night.

Grabbing his stuff now, Scott walked out with the others and locked up behind them. Wishing them a good weekend, he watched them drive away, and with a sigh, he headed out for the weekend.

Back at the station, Remy was fighting an ugly war inside of himself. He'd always known that part of being a cop, was that you had to be objective; you couldn't run around half-cocked, and throw someone's ass in jail, just because they were a smartass, or because they sat there and smirked at you when you tried to question them. You also couldn't just start punching the shit outta them, either, just because you'd only gotten three hours or so of sleep, and, more importantly, they may have just murdered someone you loved.

All of that and more, though, was what Remy was having to contend with now. Hallmen thought he could just sit there and act like he was being wronged, somehow. Usually though, Hallmen liked to brag about himself, and talk a lot of shit, especially when it came to the ladies.

He'd sat there now for almost an hour, thinking that somehow he deserved better than all of this. First, he wanted to eat, and have something to drink. Then, he made the mistake of calling Remy and Samuel, "The Keystone Cops", and laughed and guffawed hysterically, as though that was the funniest thing he'd ever said.

Just when Remy was about to throw Hallmen against the wall and punch the smirks right off of his face, Samuel came and got him.

There'd been a big break, and apparently, Hallmen was totally unaware of what the "keystone cops" could and couldn't do. Remy had immediately called and gotten a search warrant issued, and while there were absolutely no clues at all for them in Cathy's car, Monty's car was a totally different story.

Now Samuel was talking in hushed tones to Remy, and as Remy kept one eye on Hallmen, he noticed that the smirk seemed to have slid from his face, at least for the moment.

Hallmen sat in his chair, as if trying to stare them down, but now they were ignoring him, and it was beginning to frustrate the shit out of him. How dare they haul my ass in here, treat me like garbage, and then just ignore me, he thought to himself now, his anger starting to surge.

Watching Remy's facial expressions now, he was suddenly struck with a bad, ominous feeling. He could tell by the deep-set scowl on Remy's face that something big had happened; he just didn't know what it was, yet.

Without any warning, Remy came flying into the holding room now; the fury he was feeling was undeniable; his disgust, without disguise.

Hurling the chair across from where Monty was sitting now, Monty felt the beginnings of fear. Banging a huge, beefy hand on the table, the plastic cup of water fell over, and Monty jumped. Remy reminded Monty of a raging bull, and he half expected to see smoke coming out of his ears and nose.

"Alright, boy, I'm done screwing around with you. Your car was impounded, and there was blood in the trunk, along with a hunting knife that has blood all over it as well, and I'm just willing to bet that blood belongs to Cathy Grenaldi Hammond. So.....here's the deal. IF you tell me now, and I'm mean RIGHT now, where that little girl's body is, I MIGHT be inclined to tell the prosecutor that you cooperated, and then, maybe, just maybe, you can avoid a death sentence. You got ten seconds, boy," Remy barked at Monty.

He sat there now, staring at Remy, then looked over at Samuel, who was standing in the doorway, with his arms crossed, looking almost as pissed off as Remy.

"Maybe I just gutted an animal; a little blood in the trunk and a little blood on a hunting knife don't prove nothin'," Monty began now, and Samuel stalked over to Monty in about 4 seconds flat.

"Listen, you piece of shit," Samuel began, as he picked Monty halfway out of his chair with one arm,"what part of "we're not screwing around with your ass" did you NOT understand?" Samuel told Monty now, looking at him as though he wanted to throw a few punches at him.

"Damn, okay, okay," Monty muttered, making a show of straightening out his shirt that Samuel had just grabbed hold of. "Hell, it's probably easier if I just show you," he added, his voice taking on a monotone quality that Remy found interesting.

"What the fuck do you exactly plan on showing us, Monty?" Remy asked him, now, towering in front of Monty in a very intimidating fashion.

Monty said nothing, at first, and just sat there, staring morosely at his shoes. Finally, after what seemed like forever, he spoke up. "Well, I guess you boys are chompin' at the bit to find a body, am I right?" he asked them now, a sneer coming over his face.

Before he could even get a laugh out, though, Remy packed one hell of a powerful punch at Monty, and damned near knocked him off of the chair he was sitting on. Monty's sneer had quickly left his face, and he now had quite the bloody nose to contend with, but neither Remy or Samuel seemed to be the least bit concerned.

"Don't you waste my time, boy," Remy told him, his voice menacing and shaking with anger. "Don't you dare do it, or so help me God, I'll make it my life's mission to make sure you FRY," he shouted at him now. His beefy fists looked like they were itching to go for another round with Monty, and with a resigned sigh, Monty nodded his head.

"And while we're at it, I wanna know right now; are we going to find a girl, or are we finding a body? Should I bring EMT's along, or just have the coroner follow us out there?" Remy questioned, his face inches from Monty's now.

A shiver of fear ran down Monty's spine, and with a resigned sigh, he knew that the game was over now. There would be no more games or anything else, he thought to himself.

Looking at Remy and Samuel, he knew now that they were waiting for his answer. He also knew that they would not like the answer he had to give them, either. With a small sigh, Monty opened his mouth to speak. In a hushed voice, he told them to just call the coroner and be done with it.

Remy was fighting the bile that was desperately trying to make its way out, and his insides felt as though they just might explode at any moment. He felt tears springing at the corners of his eyes, and as he turned away from Monty, he calmed himself, took a deep breath, and told Samuel to call the coroner; they were going for a ride.

As Samuel had practically lifted Monty Hallmen out of the chair that he'd been sitting in, Remy walked out of the room. He went down the hallway, and opened the door to the men's room, and in the privacy of the stall, began retching.

He knew this was going to happen, the moment Hallmen told them to just call the coroner. His insides were shaking, and the tears that had sprung to his eyes, were now given their dues, as Remy finally finished his bout of dry heaves, and walked over to the sink. He let the tears fall freely down his face now, as he washed his hands, then splashed cold water on his face, trying to get it together.

Breathing deeply now, trying to steady his frazzled nerves, Remy silently prayed to God for strength today; not only strength to face however they found Cathy, but also, and this practically made Remy begin retching again, the fact that he would need lots of strength to have to face Roger, and also Kellie, Cathy's sister, not to mention Cathy's children.

He quickly dried his face and his hands now, and let out another deep breath. Next to losing his beloved Janene, Remy had a horrible feeling that this was quite easily, going to be one of the worst days of his life.

He walked out the door now, feeling a bit more in control, and more refreshed. He opened his desk drawer and pulled out some gum to try to take away the sickening taste in his mouth.

With a shiver, he slammed the drawer shut now, and went outside to meet Samuel and the coroner. He couldn't avoid it any longer, he told himself now. If Cathy was really out there, he needed to find her; the sooner, the better.

Hallmen sat in the backseat of the cruiser with his head bowed now, apparently out of jokes.

Remy climbed in the front seat, and turned around facing Hallmen. "Alright, cowboy, where are we going?" he asked, his voice calm and steady, but seemingly having a dangerous edge to it. That edge was not lost on Monty, who was realizing in a hurry, that the sheriff would sooner beat the shit out of him for sport, than take anymore bullshit from him.

Nodding slightly, Monty cleared his throat now. "You'll want to head out on Highway 9; actually, just head over to our farm," Monty told him, his voice very matter-of-fact.

Samuel and Remy had just exchanged a look; was Hallmen serious? Could he really be that cold and heartless to murder someone on his parents' farm, and then leave the body there? Remy just shook his head, for the moment not trusting anything at all that he might say.

Instead, though, Samuel started the cruiser up, then turned around and glared at Hallmen.

"Are you seriously trying to tell us that you killed Cathy on your parents' property?" he barked out at Monty, who unconsciously shrank back in his seat.

"Yeah, I guess so. That's where we're going if you wanna find a body," Monty told Samuel. "Last time I checked, I wasn't one to stutter," he commented, apparently not smart enough not to piss off Samuel and Remy further.

His jaw clenched now, Samuel shot a look at Remy, and Remy just shook his head. With a tired but gentle voice now, he said," It's okay, Sammy, just take us on over there now, son," and then Samuel nodded, feeling so many different emotions. He patted Remy's shoulder for just a second, and the older man gave him a small, wan smile in response.

Samuel couldn't even begin to imagine how terribly difficult this must be for Remy. He knew that he'd known Cathy her whole life, and he felt genuine sorrow for what he suspected they were soon to find.

As they drove along now, the sun was just beginning to come up, and it looked to be a beautiful summer day ahead, but the three drove along in silence; each of them, lost in thought.

Finally, they pulled off the highway onto the Hallmen farm, and suddenly, Samuel threw on the brakes. He didn't need to explain himself to Remy, though, who had also saw the blood-soaked grass. Getting out of the car, Samuel and Remy looked down at the area now, noticing how fresh the blood looked. Staring straight ahead now, they got back in the cruiser and were getting ready to ask Hallmen where they were heading next, when they saw Carl Hallman beginning to walk over to them.

"Aw, geeez, you're not gonna let my old man see me like this, are you?" Monty had the audacity to ask them now, as Remy balled up his fists and fought the urge to turn around in the cruiser and slap Monty.

"Shut the fuck up," Samuel growled at Monty. "If you're ashamed of all of this, maybe there's hope for you yet. You should have thought about all the heartache your folks are gonna be in for when you were stabbing an innocent girl in the heart," he added.

"Well, now, if you all had known Cathy the way I knew her, you'd know that there was nothing innocent about her at all," Monty informed them now, a wicked little chuckle coming out of him. Before he knew what hit him, literally, Remy had turned around and punched him hard, this time splitting his lip open. Fresh blood oozed gently out now, and Monty wasn't smart enough to leave well enough alone.

"Jesus, I think you assholes knocked one of my teeth out," he commented now, anger surging in his voice. "My pop's family's got some serious cash, so you sons of bitches better watch yourselves," he added, a snarl on his face now.

Remy sighed deeply now, and Samuel just shook his head. Carl Hallmen was almost up to the car now, so Samuel opened the window.

"Good mornin', Carl," Samuel nodded to the older man, a somber look on his face.

"Mornin'," Carl muttered. "What in the hell are you people doing on my property at this hour?" Carl added, looking more bewildered than angry.
Suddenly, he saw Monty in the backseat of the cruiser. "And what the hell's my boy doin' back there?" he demanded, now sounding genuinely pissed off.

Remy sighed again, and motioned to Carl to come to other side of the vehicle. "Look, Carl, " he spoke gently, "your son was brought in for questioning for the disappearance and murder of

Cathy Grenaldi Hammond," Remy explained, his voice gentle but weary.

"What?" Carl asked, his face looking suddenly very pale against his summer tan. "There must be some mistake, Remy; that just can't be," the old man stammered now, his voice starting to crack a bit.

"Now you known us for years, Remy, YEARS. You know Clara and I didn't raise no bad kids," the old man continued, with a small quiver in his voice.

"Tell them, son, don't just sit there and say nothing; tell them you didn't do this," the old man pleaded with his son now, a tear falling from his eyes.

Monty sighed now, and bowed his head down a bit. "I'm sorry, pop," he said quietly now, not wanting to meet his father's eyes.

"You're sorry? You can't be sayin' you really done this awful thing; no son, I can't, no I WON'T believe it," the old man told his son now, as tears fell down his face. "You're gonna kill your ma," he added, shaking his head sadly now.

As bad as Remy felt for Carl, they had work to do . "Carl, we're getting ready to search your property out here. Monty tells us that this is where we will find Cathy," he told Carl, his heart breaking for him. "We have to continue our search now," he added gently.

Looking beyond grief-stricken, Carl nodded his head, and stepped back from the cruiser now, his slight but sturdy body starting to tremble.

"You'll need to back up a few feet," Monty told them now. Samuel nodded, and putting the car in reverse, he allowed them to be led to Cathy.

A couple minutes later, they were parked into the entrance of the corn field. Remy looked around for a minute, never aware, until now, of how far off the main road the farm sat. He shivered suddenly, waiting for Hallmen to tell them where Cathy was.

"I can show you; I think I remember where she is," Hallmen told them, as Sam helped Monty out of the backseat. Still cuffed, they led Monty into the field, and moving over four rows, they began to walk. A couple minutes later, they all saw her.

Samuel had been ahead of Remy, and he crouched down now, looking at her beautiful face. He checked for a pulse, even though he already knew he wouldn't find one. Looking down at her now, her shirt was soaked in blood, and Samuel was horrified. He couldn't begin to imagine what kind of rage and anger it would take to stab someone in the heart. It was obvious that that is what had happened, Sam thought to himself.

Sam turned his head away and saw Remy coming up fast now. Hallmen had said nothing at all, as he stood there and watched Samuel check for a pulse and now Remy's face was threatening to crumple at any moment, and Sam caught his gaze and shook his head sadly. Standing in front of Hallmen now, and pulling him away, he gave Remy the space he knew he needed right now.

Sam walked Monty back to the cruiser now, and stood outside the car waiting. A moment later, the medical examiner showed up; a wisp of a guy around 50 with glasses that took up most of the space on his face, and a heavy mane of copper colored hair made David Hazel easy to spot. David was both well known and well liked here in town, and now he wore an uneasy expression on his face.

"Pretty gruesome?" he asked Samuel now, who nodded his head and told him," Hope you didn't just eat breakfast."

Remy had just finished up with everything he needed to do. There were some snapshots he'd just taken too, and his queasy stomach was threatening to let loose again, Remy noted to himself. He dabbed at his eyes now, with his handkerchief he'd kept crammed into his pocket, and as he stuffed it back into his pocket now, his face shook with fury at the sight of Hallmen, sitting in the cruiser.

He greeted Dr. Hazel warmly, and shook his head sadly. "I just can't believe any of this," he admitted to Hazel. "I keep askin' myself, how can this be?" he added.

Dr. Hazel nodded, sympathetically. Suddenly he said to Remy," Hey, didn't Hallmen's mom have a stroke several years ago?" he asked him. "Yep, she sure did; if this whole mess doesn't give her another one, it'll be a miracle," Remy added, walking back to the cruiser now.

"Let's drop this trash off at the station and officially book his ass," Remy told Sam now, as he started the car and they drove off. "Throw his ass in there and forget about it," he mused out loud. Looking at Sam now, Remy sighed. "God, I don't even want to go out to the Hammond place," he said with a shiver. "This whole mess is gonna get worse before he gets better; mark my words," Remy said sadly, settling back in his seat now, as they got back on the highway.

Samuel nodded his assent now, and, turning on the siren, he laid his foot on the gas, as they raced back to town.

1979

Trey, Linc, and Lorna sat in the sunken living room, watching a chick flick that they had all seen at least three times already. They gazed at the gigantic screen without really seeing anything. It had been this way now for over three hours, since they'd arrived at Connie's house, Lorna thought to herself with a deep sigh.

She got up now, sick of the movie, not really knowing what she wanted to do, but just knowing that this wasn't it. She stretched and yawned, then ambled away from everyone, deciding to go up to Connie's room, on an impulse.

Connie had been the ultimate girlie-girl, as Lorna used to call her. Without any warning, hot tears once again began to course down Lorna's face, and she wandered over to Connie's antique bed and sat down.

Connie had absolutely loved stuffed animals, Lorna mused to herself. Her collection took up three quarters of her bedroom, but Connie never complained.

Lorna remembered one time a couple years ago, hiding some of the stuffed animals, just to prove a point to Connie, that she had so many of them, that she'd never miss some of them at all. Connie had proved Lorna wrong though, because when she'd gotten back, she'd immediately noticed four of them right away that were missing, and then began to question her cousin, knowing that Lorna was probably involved. They'd laughed about that for quite awhile, she thought to herself sadly.

She rummaged through some of the dresser drawers now, wondering if she could find anything at all that would give them some clues as to the last couple weeks of Connie's life, before the accident.

Connie's birth control pills lay on top of her nightstand, and her yearbook from school lay on the floor.

Picking it up now, Lorna wanted to get a look at this guy that her cousin had been in love with. Lorna let out a sigh of irritation. What the hell was his name, she thought to herself.

Finally, she just plopped back down on Connie's bed, and began to look at all the seniors, telling herself that she would know the name when she saw it.

A couple pages in, there he was. As Lorna had predicted, she immediately remembered his name when she saw it. Hmmm, she said aloud, he's really nice-looking. Actually, he's really hot, Lorna observed, then chided herself, remembering that Connie had referred to him once as "Satan's Child".

Now though, she suddenly remembered Connie telling her about that night in the shack , alone with him, when she swore that he drugged her. How, when she woke up, she had no idea where she even was, and had no memory at all of any of the events that had taken place. Yet she'd known what had to have taken place, as she quickly got dressed. Was Connie being for real, or was she just being a drama queen, Lorna mused.

Suddenly, Linc was in Connie's room as well, with Trey on his heels. "So this is where you disappeared to," Trey commented. He sat down next to Lorna now, and looked at the pictures.

"Did you find that guy that she liked?" Linc was asking Lorna now.

"Yeah, actually, I did. I knew that as soon as I saw his name, I would remember what it was," she laughed out loud now.

"So is this the same guy that got her pregnant?" Trey asked, his loud voice booming across the room.

Before Lorna could admonish him for being so loud, or give him any kind of answer at all, Dr. Watkins was in the doorway of Connie's bedroom now.

The look on his face almost gave Lorna the creeps, and she felt so sorry for him. His brow was creased now, in an almost permanent furrow all the way across his forehead.

"What did you say, Trey?" Dr. Watkins asked him now. Trey seemed embarrassed now, and before he could respond, Dr. Watkins asked all three of them if they'd known already that Connie had been pregnant.

Looking at Lorna now, Dr. Watkins' eyes were filled with tears. "Please tell me the truth, Lorna," he begged now.

Looking him squarely in the eyes now, Lorna said," Yes, she told me about it when she came out to visit."

"Did she tell you who the father was?" Dr. Watkins asked. "Yes, she told me who she THOUGHT the father was, " Lorna told him gently trying to emphasize the word thought. She was pretty sure that her aunt and uncle were pretty clueless when it came to Connie's sexual prowess, and while she felt terrible for them, she wouldn't be the one to fill them in now, either.

Now Dr. Watkins looked positively ill at the apparent thought that his daughter had been pregnant AND may have been unsure of who the father was. His wife came in now, followed by Mindy and Stanley.

"So this is where the party is, huh?" Stanley joked with his kids, who gave him a wan smile in response.

Not sure what he had just walked in on, Stanley looked at his wife, an apology on his face, and Cassandra smiled at him.

Cassandra came over to Lorna now, who was still sitting on Connie's bed, and sat down next to her. She put an arm around her and hugged her close, telling her that Connie had told her she'd had the best time with her cousins.

Cassandra also told Lorna that if Connie had any jewelry pieces she liked, to please feel free to take whatever she wanted. "I know Connie would be happy for you to have them," Cassandra told Lorna, her bottom lip quivering a little.

Thanking her, Lorna hugged Cassandra, and then Linc and Trey hugged their aunt as well. They shared stories with their aunt and uncle about their last night with Connie when they all went to the pizzeria.

The adults were all leaving them alone now, saying it was late and they were tired. Trey figured his own parents were tired from the drive, and his aunt and uncle were exhausted from their grief.

"I just can't believe all this is happening," he told his sister and brother now, in the quiet of the room.

"Yeah, I know," Linc told him. "We should go to our room down the hall and let Lorna get to bed. Tomorrow will be a long day for everyone," he added, looking sad.

"Hey, guys?" Lorna asked, looking at her brothers tentatively. "Um, well, it's okay if you say no.....but....I was just wondering..."

she told them, her sentence dying midway through, as she looked down at her feet, feeling embarrassed.

"You want us to sleep in here with you tonight?" Linc asked her now. Smiling at him sheepishly, Lorna nodded her head. "Yeah, that would be great...unless you guys really don't want to...I guess I really just don't want to be alone tonight," she added.

"I don't blame you. I feel like I would definitely like company tonight, myself," Trey told her.

With a grin, the boys went down the hall and fetched their pillows and blankets from the other room.

Plopping everything down on the ground now, someone was going to have to sleep on the floor, they reasoned. There was the twin sized bed, and then there was also the futon. The boys made a decision to play rock, paper, scissors, but as usual, midway through, someone was supposedly cheating.

Tonight, though, Lorna went to sleep happily listening to her brothers and their silly squabbles. Closing her eyes, she fell asleep quickly.

At some point in the middle of the night, Lorna had had the most horrible nightmare imaginable. In her dream, she was watching Connie suffocate to death in the hospital, and she saw Monty Hallmen's face looming over Connie's. A few seconds later, however, Connie's face slowly turned into Lorna's, and at that moment, Lorna woke up screaming.

Her brothers both woke up with a start; Trey almost screamed, himself. The blood curdling scream that had awakened them, seemed to jump-start their hearts for a few seconds.

Connie shared the dream with them now, after the adults, who'd also been scared out of their beds, went back to their rooms.

She told her brothers about the hospital room, about seeing Connie's face, and about her suffocating and trying to breathe, but just gasping, instead. She remembered to tell them about Monty Hallmen being in the dream as well, as he sat there next to Connie, just watching her. And then she told them that at some point, Connie's face became her own.

"Ugh, that's a terrible dream," Trey complained. "How am I supposed to get back to sleep now?" he complained.

"Yeah, I agree with Trey; that IS terrible, sis," Linc told her. "Do you think it means anything? Maybe Connie is sending you a message or something?" he asked Lorna earnestly now.

"I guess that's a possibility," Lorna admitted. She told her brothers to go back to sleep now, and for the next hour, she tossed and turned in the bed. Finally, much to her relief, she fell asleep again, until her mother woke her in the morning.

Lorna felt like she was trying to awaken from a heavy fog. Her thoughts were muddled, and for a few seconds, she couldn't remember where she was. As she lay there in bed, it all started to come back to her now, though.

She wanted to bury herself under the covers and go back to sleep; maybe, this was all just a terrible dream, she told herself. Deep down, though, she knew that her cousin Connie's death was now her reality, and the pain of losing one of her best friends in the world made Lorna catch her breath, with a gasp.

If someone had asked her what she was feeling, she would have told them that it was like a terrible, constant pressure laying on top of her chest; a feeling of intense pain and suffocation. She really couldn't seem to describe it any other way, but it never went away. It was the last thing she felt before she finally drifted off to sleep at night, and the first thing she would awaken to in the morning.

Her uncle, Dr. Carter, as her and her brothers called him when they were little, looked like he'd gotten little, if any, sleep at all. The bags under his eyes seemed to grow heavier everyday, and he seemed to get through his days on autopilot.

Aunt Cassie hadn't looked like the perfectly coifed, made-up doll that she'd always appeared to be, since they got there. Her normally perfectly manicured nails looked ragged, and the nail polish on her nails that was left had certainly seen better days. Her hair, always so polished and perfectly groomed, now appeared to have broken out of its prison and took on a whole new life of its own. She'd finally managed to wash her face last night, Lorna had noticed, and had finished washing all the old mascara and eyeliner off.

Meantime, her own parents looked smaller and more helpless to her, but in watching them now, she realized that she'd never loved them more, either. The depth of their very souls, along with the gentle love they constantly bestowed on Dr. Carter and Aunt Cassie made Lorna see her parents in a way that she'd never really seen them before, at least not to this extent, she thought to herself now.

Trey was thoughtful but also very quiet again today. Lorna knew that Connie's death had really been quite a blow for him, and she also knew that Trey was re-examining his life now; thinking more about what else he should be doing with it, instead of getting lots of cash for selling drugs, here and there. Because he only had ever dealt with prescription drugs, to boot, knowing that his cousin passed away because of a drug overdose on one of the very things that he'd peddled often in the past, had forced him to step back and take stock of it all. While he knew there had been nothing he could have done to help Connie, maybe, he thought to himself, he should be making sure that that sort of thing never happens to someone else because of what he was selling.

Linc often looked out into space, as though he basically just felt a little lost. Lorna could definitely identify with that as well, since she now felt very lost, too.

Everyone moved about this morning, almost in a robotic trance, Lorna mused to herself. Adults nodded their heads when spoken to, but otherwise, drank coffee and ate bites of danish quietly.

Lorna's dad, Stanley, had volunteered to run out and get fresh croissants and danish at the local bakery, and the kids all rode out there with him. It wasn't until they were pulling up in the driveway, that Lorna realized that no one had even cracked a joke about Stanley's bald head, shining in the sunlight, the way they always normally did.

After breakfast, everyone cleaned up and got dressed. Mindy ended up helping her sister with her eye makeup, because her hands shook too much.

Dr. Carter seemed to pace the entire house for hours, like a caged lion that desperately needed to get out. When everyone was ready to head out to the funeral home, he seemed almost relieved to have something to actually do, besides pace.

As they walked in, the director greeted them, and sat down for a few moments to talk to Dr. Carter and Cassandra. The rest of them waited in the vestibule area, almost loathe to walk into the room where Connie lay. Lorna felt physically ill now, and hoped and prayed that she'd be able to keep the croissant down that she'd eaten. The thought of getting sick in public didn't appeal to her at all, even though at some point, she mused, it would provide entertainment for her brothers.

Now everyone was together again, and Cassandra's legs seemed to be made of lead, when it was time to walk into that room where her only child, her beloved Connie, lay. Just thinking about having to see her that way, made Cassandra's legs collapse from under her, and as her legs gave way, Stanley and Carter had managed to grab hold of her on her way down.

People were beginning to congregate in the lobby now, already. Every now and then, as she looked around and studied all the different faces around them, Lorna caught her brothers watching her. It dawned on her finally, that they wanted to know if she saw Monty come in or not.

Feeling a bit overwhelmed and nauseated, Lorna decided to step outside. Turning the corner, she almost ran right into Monty Hallmen. She'd recognized his face right away; that handsome face, those dimples, and those eyes. God, he WAS handsome, Lorna found herself thinking.

As if he could read her mind, Monty bestowed a big smile on Lorna now, his dimples deepening in their crease, and his straight, beautiful, white teeth smiling up at her, as though seeing her made him deliriously happy.

Looking at his face now, Lorna understood exactly why her cousin had been in love with this man. But Lorna would not be swept away by this man's charm and good looks; not today, not ever. Excusing herself and mumbling an apology, she'd began walking away, when he turned around and said," Hey, are you Lorna?" Nodding her head dumbly at him, she'd been too shocked to do anything else. Nodding at her, he introduced himself to her. He offered his condolences, and told her that Connie had always just adored her.

Lorna felt a chill go through her body now. Unsure of what to say or do at this point, she mumbled yet another excuse, and took off, rounding the next corner quickly, until she came to the huge oak trees that sat at the back of the property. She felt grateful for the nice breeze that came up suddenly. Now, sitting here alone, she tried to dissect what had just happened. She still couldn't believe that he'd been standing right there in front of her. Chiding herself now, she realized that she'd just stood there and stared, like a bumbling fool.

Meantime, Monty was still chuckling to himself as he walked in the door. Show time, he thought to himself, putting on his most forlorn and sorrowful face.

He shook hands with Dr. Carter Watkins and Cassandra; he introduced himself to them, and told them that Connie was a good friend of his. Because of the shock they were in, though, they never made the connection at all, until that evening, when they were all at home, and suddenly Dr. Carter asked Lorna the name of the guy that had worked on the car.

When Lorna told him that it was Monty Hallmen, he nodded his head slowly.

"Yes, that is the young man that I asked the police about, after they'd examined her car twice. They still maintained that there was a small hole in the brake line; when I asked them if they had thought it was deliberately cut, or if it had always been there, they said they honestly didn't know," he commented now, shaking his head sadly.

"You can't arrest someone on a maybe or a what if, " he added. "Besides, he seemed to be such a pleasant young man; I just couldn't see that he could have actually done that to her car on purpose," Dr. Carter said to Lorna now, while Trey and Linc looked on, a numb look on their faces.

Lorna nodded to her uncle. She understood where he was coming from, but a part of her would always wonder what kind of a person Monty Hallman really was.

Her uncle was right, though. No one could prove anything at all. Connie's car had had plenty of scratches, little nicks, and holes all over it, and no one honestly knew if something new had been added after Monty Hallmen had worked on it or not. Whoever had given her the drugs at the hospital had been very smart and very fast, since no one had seen anyone coming or going. So they were all back to square one, and now Lorna felt as though Connie's killer was out there running around; perhaps free to commit murder again, should the need arise.

Lorna stayed up late that night thinking of all the various ways that someone would have to kill someone in Connie's situation. The more she thought about it, the easier it seemed. Finally, her brain had taken in more than it could possibly absorb in a day, and she fell into a fitful sleep. She dreamed that she was searching everywhere for her cousin, but she could never find her. Upon waking up in the middle of the night from that dream, Connie didn't scream this time. After reminding herself that Connie was gone, she held Connie's favorite stuffed animal in her arms; the smell of her giving Lorna comfort, until at long last, she fell asleep again.

Walking out of St. Paul's, Lorna was struck by how incredibly gloomy of a day it was. It was as though the heavens themselves, felt as gray and dismal as all of the mourners here today.

The crowd of teens seemed to move slowly, as if in a trance. Their eyes were puffy and sorrowful as they shuffled out of the church.

Lorna waited outside for the processional to continue. Her mother hung onto her sister now, as if worried that perhaps she could slip away at any moment. Dr. Watkins tucked his arm through Cassandra's, keeping a close watch on his wife.

Last night, he'd had to give her a strong sedative so that she would finally get some rest. He'd had to fight her tooth and nail about it, but she'd finally taken the medicine, if for no other reason, than she just didn't want to fight anymore.

When he woke her up today, she'd seemed fine for the first few minutes, until she'd realized that today was the day her daughter was to be buried. The doctor didn't think Cassandra had stopped shaking since she'd first heard that Connie had died.

Stanley, Linc, and Trey had all offered to be pallbearers, along with Carter's two brothers who had just came in yesterday from California. A teacher that Connie had always liked, Mr. Brandt, had offered as well. Everyone now stood outside in the oppressively, humid heat, almost grateful that it was so overcast; it would have been insufferable had the sun been out, as well.

Now the procession was making it's way out of the church. As everyone gathered close by, the doors of the hearse were opened, and the casket was lifted inside. Cassandra let out an almost primal howl, as Mindy and Carter struggled to hang onto her.

Lorna stood close by them too, just in case she was needed. After the minister said a few words, he invited everyone to follow the procession for the graveside service at Alden Cemetery.

Piling into their SUV now, Lorna turned to her mother and slid her hand into hers. Mindy took Lorna into her arms and they held each other for a few minutes.

Now the procession began its painfully slow trip and Lorna suddenly felt so lonely for Connie. Was all this really happening? Somehow Lorna had kept hoping that this was all just part of a really bad dream, and that she'd be waking up from it, laughing about how incredibly stupid it all was. If Connie were here, she'd be teasing me so much, Lorna mused. But now, instead of having Connie here teasing her, having pillow fights, listening to all her bawdy talk, and staying up all night talking and laughing, we're taking her to her final resting place, Lorna thought bitterly.

She'd tried to think if she'd seen Hallmen today at the church, but she didn't think he'd shown up. A part of her had hoped that he would, and the other part of her was glad he didn't. A shudder went through her again as she wondered for the hundredth time if Hallmen really had cut that hole in Connie's brake line. I guess we'll never know, though, Lorna thought to herself sadly.

Suddenly, they were at the cemetery, and Lorna didn't even remember the car ride out there. She slowly stepped out onto the dewy grass and watched now, as the pallbearers lifted the casket and marched it over to the tent where the short memorial service would be starting soon.

As the minister began speaking, Lorna could feel a pair of eyes boring into her, as if trying to read her mind, or look into her soul. Lifting her head up now, she happened to turn her head to the left of her, and saw Monty Hallmen standing there. His eyes never left hers, and Lorna felt a shiver run through her. As she looked his way again, he was still staring at her, until Lorna finally looked away.

What the hell is he doing here, she wondered. If he really had caused Connie's terrible accident, it took a lot of nerve to show up here. What if he really DID cause the accident? And what if, by chance, he gave Connie the xanax in a bottle of coke, knowing that combined with the morphine, it would easily kill her? What if he had hoped to kill her the first time around, by putting that small hole in the brake line, but although the baby died, Connie had survived? But what if, upon visiting Connie, Monty worried that Connie would begin to tell everyone who had worked on her car, and who the baby's father was? Or told people that she had thought he'd raped her in the shack that night?

Suddenly Lorna's mind just kept racing through, at full speed. As if he could read her mind, she suddenly looked back over at Hallmen, to find that his eyes had narrowed, as though he were trying to study her, and see what was going on inside of her mind. Now, his eyes narrowed a little more, and he almost looked as though he was scowling at her. Lorna gave him a shaky smile, but his eyes were still boring into hers, his expression, unchanged.

The minister was bestowing the blessings now, and suddenly, the service was already over. Lorna felt ashamed that she'd missed most of it Standing up now with the others, her legs felt a bit rubbery, and she took a tentative step. She fervently hoped that Hallmen would just leave before she had to walk by him, but no, he was still standing there; his eyes were still watching her.

He's really starting to creep me out, Lorna thought to herself, suddenly getting angry. How dare he come out here to MY cousin's funeral and just stand there staring at me, as though I did something wrong, she was asking herself now.

As people began to slowly shuffle away from the casket, after offering their prayers and condolences to the family, Lorna came face to face with Monty.

Still meeting her eyes dead on, he gave her a beatific smile, his dimples accentuating his beautiful straight, white teeth. Taking Lorna completely off guard now, he reached over and kissed her on the cheek, telling her that his thoughts would be with her.

As more people dissipated through the crowds, Lorna couldn't even count how far back the line of cars went. It seemed like the whole town had come out today for the funeral, to pay their respects. Lorna saw the sheriff standing off to the side now, chatting with his deputy, and now her uncle was approaching them, and they all hugged and shook hands.

Looking around the crowd, Lorna couldn't spot Hallmen anywhere, now. She wondered if he'd really left, or if he was, perhaps, lurking in the shadows somewhere. Almost laughing to herself, she found herself thinking about how stupid that really was. She told herself that she was being insanely ridiculous about the whole business. Shaking her head, she almost laughed out loud, as she thought about how she'd contemplated Monty trying to kill off Connie. God, this whole mess has really gotten me rattled, she mused, as if I am creating a whole soap opera here in my head. As she was walking back to their vehicle, she decided to just wait there for her parents. Her legs still felt rubbery and useless and she decided it would just be easier to sit down and wait.

As she opened the door, and sat down in the leather seat, she'd kept the door wide open, so that her parents could see where she was. Her brothers were standing to the far right with their dad and the minister, and they all appeared to be having a friendly chat.

Uncle Carter and Aunt Cassie were chatting with some old friends of theirs, along with Uncle Carter's brothers, who were also chatting with Mindy and the sheriff.

Letting out a sigh, Lorna closed her eyes for a few seconds. Hearing a sound, she opened them and almost cried out loud when she saw Monty Hallmen staring at her.

He was crouched half inside and half outside of the SUV. An involuntary shiver rose out of Lorna and she stared helplessly at

Monty, unsure of what to say, or why he was even there at her side now.

Before she could say anything, though, he gave her a kindly, gentle smile. "Hey, I'm sorry if I startled you just now. I just came over here to wish you and your family the best. I know how much Connie meant to all of you," he told Lorna now, his eyes showing her nothing but kindness.

"Oh, well, thank you very much. I was surprised to see you here," she stammered, not knowing why she seemed to have so much trouble talking to Monty.

He studied her intently now, and asked," Really? Why is that?"

Feeling insanely stupid now, Lorna sighed and said,"Ugh, forgive me; I can't seem to talk right or make much sense at all today," she began. "If I ask you something, would you tell me the truth?" she asked Monty now, peering into his face with a desperate plea in her eyes.

"Well, sure, I can do that; what is it that you want to know?" he asked her now, crouching down in front of her, his body now dangerously close to hers.

"Well, please don't get mad; I mean, I'm just trying to get some answers here; trying to make sense of everything," she stammered again, feeling a furious blush coming over her entire face.

Monty was just gazing intently at her now; shocking her further, he picked up one of her hands, and held it inside his own.

"Just ask away; oh, has anyone ever told you how much you look like Connie?" he was asking her now. "I bet you get that all the time, though, don't you?" he laughed gently.

"Well, yes, mostly when we are both together. Our moms are sisters, and they look a lot alike, almost to the point of looking like twins," Lorna was explaining now, as Monty nodded his head in agreement.

"Yes, I've noticed that," he agreed. "So now tell me, what is it that you would like to know, and if I know the answer, I'll be happy to tell you," Monty breathed, his warm breath dangerously close to her cheek.

Lorna was feeling almost dizzy with Monty being this close to her. The fear that she'd felt earlier with him seemed to have dissipated, and now she was feeling something else.

Then, she began to chide herself. My God, this was her cousin's funeral, for crying out loud.

"Look Monty, I know this is going to sound funny, but I really need to know....did you know that Connie was pregnant?" she asked, looking into his eyes and watching his body language.

"Yeah, I knew that," Monty told her in a matter of fact voice. "Why do you want to know?" he prodded gently.

"Well, she had mentioned that when she'd been out to visit; actually, I had to practically pry it out of her on the last night she was at our house," Lorna admitted. "She mentioned that you were the baby's father, and that she was totally in love with you," Lorna told him now, her face looking sad and reminiscent.

"Did she? Yes, she had just told me a couple weeks ago about the baby. I was pretty surprised, at first, but the more I thought about it, I got used to the idea. I'd even asked her to marry me," Monty told Lorna now, a sad look coming through his eyes.

The sadness on his face was not lost on Lorna, whose heartstrings tugged at his pain, now.

"I couldn't believe she'd gotten in such a bad wreck; for a long time, I felt responsible somehow, even though I'd checked everything over well, but I must have missed something important, that's for sure," he told her slowly, watching her eyes, and yet sparing none of the theatrics.

"And when she lost our baby, she was absolutely devastated. She cried almost constantly the first couple days after she woke up in the hospital," Monty continued. "Nothing I could say or do would bring that baby back, but I was glad that at least she'd made it and pulled through. She was just too sad at first to care," he added now, a thoughtful look coming over his face.

"Was there anything else that you wanted to know?" he asked her now.

"When was the last time you saw her?" Lorna asked him now.

"Well, let's see...must've been the day before she died. I went up there to check on her and see how she was doing. She seemed in better spirits that day, although she was still worried about whether she'd get the use back in her legs or not. She was still paralyzed from the waist down," he added.

"Yeah, that's what my uncle had said, too," Lorna admitted. "Did you have any other questions for me?" Monty asked her now, making a show of looking at his watch. "I'm going to have to get going so I can get to work on time," he added.

"Oh, okay. No, really that was all I wanted to know about," Lorna told him, her mind drawing a total blank now. "Thanks for coming out," she added now, shaking his hand, as though they'd closed a business deal.

Monty took the hand she'd offered now, and touched it to his lips, brushing her hand gently with them. He gave her a hand a tender squeeze, then gingerly lay it back in her lap.

Monty grinned now, and told her that it was great to have met her. He wished her well, and then just as suddenly as he'd swooped in on her, he was gone.

1988

Samuel popped open the bottle of aspirin and helped himself to three of the caplets. Chasing them down with a gulp of coffee, he rubbed his temples and gave Remy a sideways glance.

The older man seemed to have aged ten years overnight, Samuel thought to himself. The nervous tic that Remy had on occasion at the corner of his right eye, seemed to be working overtime, and now as they drove along in silence, Remy worked his jaw.

This was going to be one of the hardest things they'd ever had to do, Samuel thought to himself. How exactly do you knock on a friend's door and inform him that, not only is his wife dead, but she'd been brutally murdered? What was he supposed to say to Roger and the kids, or Cathy's sister Kellie, that could possibly be of any help whatsoever, Samuel thought. No, there wasn't going to be anything simple about any of this at all, he thought, looking over at Remy again.

He knew that Remy had known Cathy since she was a baby; he'd always been fond of the girl, and seeing her laying in that cornfield had been the absolute worst for the poor man. Anger seethed through Samuel's veins, as he thought of that horrible mental picture he had now of Cathy; her pretty pink blouse soaked in blood.

Samuel also couldn't understand how a person could even begin to do something that horrible to another human being. What the hell went on in Hallmen's mind, anyways?

Samuel fervently wished that somehow he could just flip a switch and turn his brain off for awhile. His adrenaline seemed to be on overdrive, and his head still pounded dully from the hellacious headache he'd had ever since he saw Cathy Grenaldi Hammond's bloody body.

He really wished he'd never gotten Remy's phone call; how nice it would be to still be at home, curled up in bed.

Remy was too quiet, Samuel thought to himself. He could see his jaw working still, and a vein at the side of his head continued to pulse, as though to keep up with the jaw. This was a side of Remy that Samuel had never seen before; but then, this was usually a peaceable, happy town, with the usual crimes of occasional shoplifting and drunken, disorderly conduct. Occasionally, a bar fight or two, and on rare occasions, someone went to the hospital, afterwards.

The sheer brutality of Cathy's murder would rock this town to its very core, Samuel thought to himself now.

Samuel was almost shocked to be pulling into the Hammond's long, graveled driveway. Goes to show how hard it's been to focus, he thought to himself sadly.

Remy let out a long, hard sigh. He looked over at Samuel now, and shook his head sadly. As if he knew exactly what was in the older man's heart now, Samuel gently patted Remy's shoulder in understanding. Without a word, the two men climbed out of the cruiser, each one lost in his thoughts.

Before Samuel could actually ring the doorbell, the door flew open, and Remy and Samuel looked into the eyes of Jason and Jessie Hammond. Remy looked beyond pained now, and for a moment, all Samuel could think of was, Oh, no, dear God, not these kids.

Wide-eyed and full of questions, Jason held the door open for them, and Jessie ran to get her dad. Kellie, Cathy's sister, came in with Jessie now, as well, and with one look at Samuel and Remy, it was like she already knew. Her hand flew up to her mouth, stifling the cry that she would surely make.

Remy and Samuel stood there now, hating this, and hating Monty Hallmen even more. Remy could feel anger building up inside of him, anger like he'd never felt before, not even when he'd found out that his beloved Janene would be dying soon. No, Remy thought to himself now, not even close.

Roger's face looked pale and drawn, as though the very life blood had been sucked right out of him. He looked as though he hadn't slept in a week, and now Kellie clutched onto Roger's arm, her bottom lip starting to quiver.

Roger must have sent the kids to their rooms or something, Samuel observed, because they hadn't come back out here now. Thank the Lord for small miracles, he thought to himself now, taking in a deep breath and willing his nerves to settle down long enough for him to tell these good people the horrendous news he had come to tell them.

Clearing his throat now, Remy had appeared ready to speak, but then his voice shook, then faltered. Samuel looked at Remy then, and gave the older man a gentle nod. Remy was eternally grateful at that moment that Samuel was willing to step up and tell Roger and his family what happened. His voice was not trustworthy at this point, he realized sadly to himself. He wasn't sure if he'd cry, yell, or what the hell he would do, and in all these years on the job, Remy had never had to stop and wonder what he would do. Until today.

"Roger...Kellie...we found Cathy. There's no easy way to tell you this....we found Cathy on the Hallmen property, in the cornfields," Samuel said quietly.

"Is she...she's okay, right? Is she okay? My God, Sam, is she alive? Is she...", and now Roger's voice had completely trailed off, fear and sorrow making it impossible now for him to speak. As he trailed off, his eyes looked up at Remy's, pleading, questioning; wanting to know, but yet, not wanting to know, either.

And now, Remy was looking into Roger's eyes, and Roger wanted to howl with pain, because he knew what Remy's eyes were telling him. He had never seen Remy cry, except when his wife died.

Remy was as tough as they got, but not today. Roger's disbelief and pain seemed almost mirrored in Remy's eyes, and the big, older man cried now, with no shame as he took Roger in his arms. Samuel was already holding Kellie in an embrace, her legs barely supporting her weight at all now, as she clung to Samuel like a limp rag doll.

Later, they sat down together, and Kellie and Roger listened in horror at what Samuel and Remy had found. At some point, before Roger could go to them and tell them, his children had already heard, and Roger found them both huddled together in Jason's room. He cried with them and held them for a long time. When he went back to check on them a bit later, he found them huddled on the floor next to each other, their faces streaked from all their tears, and their breathing soft and even. Jessie had little Dylan cuddled next to her on the floor, and they were all asleep.

Roger walked back out to Kellie and told her that the kids were all asleep. He walked over now to the liquor cabinet, and selected a bottle of whiskey. Pouring himself and Kellie a shot, they sat there for the next couple hours, until the sun had completely set, until they were beginning to feel numb from the alcohol. Roger drank most of the bottle himself now, and it was his hope that maybe, just maybe, he was too drunk to think. Maybe he could wake up tomorrow and this would all be a terrible nightmare. He would tell Cathy all about it, and they would laugh at Roger's wild imagination.

But as he lay in the darkness, his eyes wide opened, and his brain still moving, he knew that that was just wishful thinking now. He would never lay in this bed with Cathy next to him again; he would never hear her laugh ever again. His children would not have their mother at their graduation, and their children would never know what a beautiful person their grandmother was.

Finally, as the sun was getting ready to rise, Roger dozed off for awhile, sleeping fitfully, as he dreamed of his wife calling his name, begging him to help her, as she tried to stand up, but couldn't, because she was bleeding profusely.

When he opened his eyes a couple hours later, he realized that he had a hangover from all the whiskey he'd drank. And the painful realization hit, that even with all the alcohol he'd consumed, there'd never be a way to numb himself from the pain and sorrow that consumed him now.

☼

Cathy Grenaldi Hammond's memorial service was probably the largest that Remy Dodsen had ever seen. He'd gotten to St. John's a bit later than he'd wanted to, and ended up having to park across the street, since the parking lot was already filled up.

There was a visitation for four hours before the memorial service started, and a steady stream of people kept filtering in and out. Remy stood up front with Roger's family for awhile, and now he was looking at the dozens of floral arrangements that surrounded the area where Cathy lay.
He found an arrangement of flowers from the Hallmen's, and they'd also given a very large check to Roger for the children. Carl and Clara Hallmen couldn't bring themselves to come into town for Cathy's funeral; Clara especially, had been unwell ever since Monty got locked up, and many people from their church worried that the extreme grief and pain she felt would surely be the end of her. Carl kept busy in the fields, but his mechanical work seemed to have reached a standstill.

Clara had written Roger and the children a heartfelt letter, apologizing for her son's actions. She knew that nothing she could say or do could ever bring Cathy back to them, but she wouldn't ever be able to rest if she didn't at least apologize to the family for her son's actions. The ladies from the church that Clara had gone to for so many years, didn't seem to even want to talk to Clara; it felt like since they didn't know what to say, they wanted to avoid her at all costs, Clara had thought. She walked out of her church home that day feeling more alone than she'd ever felt in her life, and Carl watched the dejected figure walk out to the car, when he'd come to pick her up. Not knowing what to even tell her, he just patted her hand as he took the wheel and began the drive back home.

The brutality of Cathy's murder made national news, and if Clara Hallmen had felt embarrassed and sick at heart before, it was now so much worse, on so many levels.

One morning, Carl, who always rose before his wife, got dressed and padded quietly down the stairs to make a pot of coffee. As he flipped on a switch in the kitchen, he almost dropped the coffee pot in fright, as he saw all the camera crews right outside his front door. Turning the light back off after he'd gotten the coffee going, Carl sat in the darkness, feeling like a prisoner in his own home now. He poured a big mug of coffee and went into the living room to sit down. He could hear a couple more cars now, heading up the long, gravel driveway. He listened to see if he could hear Clara yet, and thankfully, she was still asleep. As he sat in the darkness sipping his coffee, Carl thought back to when the boys were little. He'd lived in this town his whole life, as did Clara. Now, he could hardly muster up the effort to leave his farm. Everywhere he went, people stared. Some people tried to pretend that nothing had happened, but their eyes usually gave them away. Carl gave a long sigh, wondering how the hell this could have happened. How could I have raised a boy like this, he asked himself again for the hundredth time? How the hell could my life have turned into this media circus, he asked himself now. Setting his coffee cup down, Carl gave himself up to the sobs that had started somewhere deep inside his soul. An hour later, when his wife came downstairs, she found her husband still sobbing, and his coffee, stone cold.

Roger Hammond sat stiffly in the courtroom, fighting off the waves of nausea that kept threatening to overcome him. The air felt heavy and smelled like a mixture of body odor, sweat, and cheap perfume.

Roger had drank himself to sleep again, as was becoming more of a habit than he cared to admit. Still, he managed to get to work everyday, and functioned at home as best as he could, even if his conversations with his children seemed robotic and monotonic.

Waiting for this sentencing had been brutal, and the police had to keep Hallmen closely under wraps upon entering and exiting the courtroom, since several threats had been made on his life. Roger couldn't have cared less if Hallmen would have happened to eat a few bullets, even though, deep down, he thought that was too easy for him, compared to what his poor wife had had to go through on her last night on earth. Roger found himself fantasizing about getting Hallmen alone, and finishing him off himself. He wasn't sure how he would do it; he only knew that the more pain involved with Hallmen suffering a slow, painful, tortured death, the better he liked it. He knew deep down that this type of thinking was wrong; he'd been raised in the church and had always been taught that God alone should exact vengeance. Unfortunately, that kind of thinking was easy to contend with when it didn't involve someone you'd desperately loved, Roger mused to himself.

He'd actually had a couple of his friends volunteer to take Hallmen out themselves, using their hunting rifles, but Roger had begged for them to just let the justice system do its job. There'd already been enough pain and suffering without adding more, Roger had told his friends.

He took a cursory glance around the room now, noting that Monty's parents, and his older brother sat close to the very back of the room. In his heart, he felt terrible for the Hallmens, knowing how devastated they were.

He couldn't imagine how they were feeling, knowing what their "golden boy", as he'd been described by his Sunday School teachers, and others as well, had been capable of doing.

Mrs. Hallmen looked like death warmed over. Roger knew that she'd had a stroke several years before, and thought that she looked like she could easily have another one, at this rate. Mr. Hallmen didn't look much better; he'd always been a tall, wiry, fellow with a slight, but muscular build. Now, however, he just looked painfully thin. His shoulders drooped, and he sat looking at his shoes most of the time, as if it were too painful to have to meet anyone's gaze.

At Monty's trial, Mr and Mrs. Hallmen had met Roger's gaze at one point, and Mrs. Hallmen began to sob. Mr. Hallmen held her protectively against his chest, while mouthing the words, "I'm so sorry" to Roger, who'd nodded his head, then turned away.

Cathy's sister Kellie had written a brief, but kind note to the Hallmens, thanking them for their monetary gift and for their support. At first, Roger didn't want to take their money, but Kellie had argued and insisted to Roger that it was the right thing to do for the children. She was convinced that Cathy would want it that way, as well. Finally, Roger just got tired of arguing with Kellie, and agreed to put the money into a trust for the kids to be used when they began college.

Now Roger squirmed in his seat, trying to get comfortable. He knew he had to stop drinking so much, but every night was turning into the one before it. He passed out every night, and woke up everyday hung over. His boss had taken notice of it, and while he was a kind and patient man, Roger knew he wouldn't put up with it forever.

Roger had gotten some satisfaction in the fact that the prosecutor had tried like hell to get the death penalty for Hallmen, because of the sheer brutality of the crime. Roger was pretty sure that Monty wouldn't get the death penalty though, but he still wanted to hear for himself what Hallmen's sentence would be.

Having to relive Cathy's last hours of her life had been painful, almost to the point of having it happen all over again, Roger had thought to himself. He had really hoped he would be immune to all those old emotions, but apparently, having to look at pictures of Cathy at the scene that the coroner had taken had just managed to reopen those painful wounds all over again. Roger had been glad that the kids decided at the last minute to skip the trial; he'd practically bribed them to stay home, but initially, they'd balked, telling Roger that they had every right to be there. With a sigh of relief, he'd said a silent prayer of thanks, when, the morning that the trial was to begin, Jason and Jessie had told their dad they'd changed their minds.

Glancing at his watch now, it was exactly 10am, and, as if on cue, Hallmen was brought in. There were two deputies with him, and they looked around as though they were in the middle of a battlefield, expecting gunshots to be fired in their direction at any moment. Hallmen looked almost contrite, at least for the moment, Roger noticed, and he'd gotten a shave and a haircut, as well.

Judge Harris walked in then, and everyone stood for a moment. The judge was known amongst his peers for being a general hard ass, and from the grim look on his face, it appeared that today would be no different. He looked over at Hallmen with an air of disgust, as he sat down and got out his eyeglasses.

Roger's heart was beating a mile a minute; suddenly he thought of poor Duncan, too, and his mind cruelly revisited those horrible pictures of Cathy's bloody body.

He tried to close his eyes for a moment, willing all those bad images and thoughts to go away; he tried to pray, too, but if he were honest, he would say that he had no idea what exactly he was praying for.

Finally, the judge cleared his throat and began to speak. The moment everyone had been waiting for was here. Roger glanced back over at Hallmen's parents now, and Clara appeared to have gone completely white, while poor Carl visibly shook.

Forty years, Roger mentally repeated to himself now, after Judge Harris made his announcement. He tried to focus on what else he was saying, but only seemed to get bits and pieces out of the speech that Judge Harris had made. Now Judge Harris continued his rant.

"I cannot, in good conscience, think of a more despicable, brutal violation of another human being, and as such, I just cannot allow you out into society anytime soon, young man," the judge was saying now. "I don't give a damn about all those reports about what a great kid and a fine young man you were. Somewhere along the line, something happened, and you became an animal. That young lady was almost a foot shorter than you, and almost 80 pounds lighter than you. Not only did you bully and terrorize her, you violated her, and then, you brutalized her to the point of causing her death. You took the life of a wife, a mother, a daughter, a friend. And then you just went on to work, as though this all was a common, everyday, occurrence. The only reason you haven't been given the damned death penalty, is because you'd had a clean record, up to this point. You can bet your ass that if it had been up to me alone, I'd stick the damned needle in you myself," Judge Harris spat out, standing up now, as though he couldn't stand to be in the same room as Monty Hallmen for one more minute.

Monty's eyes followed Judge Harris, as he walked into his chambers, but there didn't seem to be even a flicker of emotion in them, Roger noted.

Clara Hallmen had let out a loud sob as Judge Harris gave his sentence, and Carl continued to hold his wife close to him, even as his body shook like a leaf.

Cathy's parents had decided to skip the sentencing; her father had just recently had a mild heart attack, and the stress was just too much for him. He knew that Roger and Kellie would fill them in later, anyways, and the trial itself had been almost too much for them to handle.

Roger and Kellie had talked about it one night soon after Cathy's funeral.

"As bad as I feel, I can't begin to imagine how painful this is for your parents," Roger had told Kellie. "I mean, it would be so damned hard to lose a child from an accident or an illness. But this? How do you cope with losing your child when they died from someone else's hands?" Roger added.

Kellie had agreed wholeheartedly with Roger and told him that she didn't know how her parents were going to ever get over this.

"I'm not sure anyone ever DOES get over something like this, either," Kellie had admitted then.

Now Hallmen and the deputies were leaving as well, and Roger and Kellie stood up to leave. Their backs to him, they never saw Monty Hallmen's eyes boring into them.

Monty let himself be led away, and for just a brief moment, he saw his parents. He felt sorry for them just because this town was all they'd ever known, and now he had to hope that someday people would just forget all of this. Deep down, though, he knew better.

Later that afternoon, Monty sat in his cell, sketching on his pad of paper. His mind wandered back to that night with Cathy, and when he closed his eyes, he could still see her face, feel the touch of her hair, and smell her perfume.

He personally thought he got a raw deal with his sentence, but his dumb assed lawyer seemed to think that he should be grateful that he didn't get the death penalty. He supposed he was glad for his parent's sake that things turned out the way they did, but really, what did it all matter?

Monty tore the sketch off of the pad of paper, and threw the pad against the wall. He was getting more angry by the minute, when he thought of his trial and all of the things that had been said. He thought of his foreman, Scott, who he had thought was his friend, but no, the sonofabitch sat up there on the stand and helped nail his ass to this fucking cell wall, Monty fumed.

One thing that helped Monty, though, was that his stupid attorney was pretty sure that, if Monty totally behaved himself, he could easily get several years cut off of his sentence for good behavior. Monty focused on that for awhile, and felt the rage that had been building up inside of him, begin to subside.

I won't be in this shit hole forever, Monty told himself. And when I get out of here, I just might have to right a few wrongs, he chuckled to himself, as he settled into his cot for a nap. Closing his eyes, he fell asleep with a smile on his face, thinking about the day when he would get out of here and then it would be business as usual.